AN OTHER

TALE OF TWO CITIES

In the Dragon's Lair

Book I
+
Book II

A Tale by

RAVI KRISH

In Ever Loving Memory of
My Mother & Father

Balambal
Krishnaswamy

Dedicated to

Laishram Sarita Devi,
the Indian woman boxer, who
refused to accept the bronze medal
at the Podium ceremony
at the Incheon Asian Games – 2014
and was banned for One Year,
and the likes of her

Disclaimer: This is an original work of fiction written by Ravi Krish. Names, characters, businesses, places, events and incidents are purely products of the author's imagination and have been used in fictitious manner. Any resemblance to actual persons, living or dead, or actual events is purely coincidental.

Life, it's not right.
We enter it without asking.
We leave it without knowing,
where we are going.
And stay without knowing,
what, here, are we doing!

Dr. Swati Munot

Prologue

Huajin wore a wicked smile! She had been giving finishing touches to the dream she had been working on for the last week or so. No ordinary dream this; to become Queen of China! The more she thought about it, the more she was 'drunk' with excitement!

She had always achieved, whatever she wished; thanks to Weimin.

'This wish would be no different', she knew! 'I would be Queen, when, not if, Weimin is crowned Emperor'.

A small correction; this being Modern China, and not the Middle Kingdom, she actually, wouldn't be Queen. But well, close enough… she could be the First Lady; Mrs President! That is, when Weimin is crowned President!

There was only one person, she believed, to be standing between her and her dream! She hated him.

Weimin had long since decided that he wouldn't be just another Kingmaker after his father. He had decided to be the next President. During the last two years, towards this end, he had been conspiring with vengeance and secretly pushing his agenda and increased his sphere of influence in the Communist Party of China that appoints the Politburo, with the knowledge that with a majority of the Politburo members on his side, he could force a consensus in his favour. If Weimin, who already had a third of the Politburo behind him, could take his influence one notch higher, his powers would be limitless. He would be the next President of China.

It was then, that day, as casually as one would ask, 'I want mei for lunch', she demanded, 'I want 'his' head at my feet…'

'I want to be Empress Wu Zetian and now'!

Weimin shivered first, before a tingle of realization passed through his body, head to toe! It would take a coup, but it was very much in the realm of possibility!

Weimin quickly re-oriented his mission and objective to

comply with Huajin's demand - to place the head of the current President at her feet! And to grab the opportunity to impeach the lame duck President and make himself President.

Huajin would be First Lady, when, Weimin would be crowned President, after all! It was a foregone conclusion.

The entire country was about to tremble at the consequence of Huajin's dream!

Book I

Part 1 : The Table

—

1 The Misfit

The one-on-one battles were about to begin. There were seven of them. Some among them were flexing their muscles, getting ready for long arduous battles. A few others nervously pacing around in small circles and still others smiling and laughing out loud pretending to be valiant... While, one was still missing!

The tension was palpable.

Kula, the eighth contender entered the 'Gladiator' zone. If he was anxious, he did not show any sign of it. He moved easily without a burden, waving at one, patting someone else, smiling at another and affectionately punching one in the stomach...

There was an announcement; 'There would be a total of seven battles today; four Quarterfinals, two Semi-finals and the Finals. Eight will fight the Quarter-finals – they are – Niranjan, Pari, Sai, Kula, Rajiv, Easwar, Govinda and Rajesh. Let us see, who makes it to the Finals and then, who among is the chosen one, The Ultimate, The Victor'!

Kula's making it to the semi-finals of the Table Tennis tournament at his school, the previous year had taken everyone by surprise, though he had lost.

'Fluke'; one of the boys had said then and others agreed. Even the most fair among them had said, 'He didn't deserve to reach the Semis'. And had conceded after a pause, 'though he showed some flashes of brilliance and played a crude, gutsy game'.

One could surmise from the talk around that it was difficult for most to digest Kula's place in the Semis last year; especially for a guy who could not afford the fee to practice at the school table. It was a fact that his father found it difficult to pay his even regular school fees in time, every month.

The school's physical training master who doubled as the Table Tennis coach, Mahadevan, was the only one who believed that Kula's last year's run was due to his brilliant game, when Kula had surprised himself by reaching the semi-final level. That was last year.

This year it was considered a much tougher draw and all the contenders had improved by leaps and bounds since then. The game was played at a much higher level of proficiency due to constant practice and the competitive spirit between the boys. Hence the surprise, when Kula made it to the Quarter-finals; and all the more because he wasn't even seen hanging around the school Table in the last few months, as he usually did.

Kula weighed on everyone's mind like a dark cloud looming in the skies, during an India-Pakistan One Day Cricket match. He wasn't even considered a dark horse... May be a spoil sport?

Kula will reach the final', asserted Mahadevan. They found it difficult to believe him, so they either ignored him or simply smiled at him pathetically.

As Kula moved around the hall, Pari with his usual harsh tongue made a comment to his pals, 'Kula is a misfit in the elite company of the quarter-finalists,' and his pals laughed out loud.

Yes, Kula stood in stark contrast beside the meticulously-outfitted Rajiv. He was wearing a faded set of school uniform and his white shirt that had yellowed from overuse and could have been ironed. His black formal leather shoes, which were a part of his uniform had not seen polish in recent months.

It was evident to the entire crowd that he couldn't afford sport shoes. But for him, it didn't seem to matter. The only weapon that he was carrying around was his treasured, though, worn out TT racquet that he was presented by Mahadevan in recognition of his reaching the Semis the previous year.

One of Pari's pals whispered to him with a wink, 'Did you notice that Kula's TT racquet has worn out, though he rarely plays?'

Pari jeered in reply, wondering deliberately loud enough; for Kula to hear, 'I think his mother uses it to prepare dough for chappathis'.

Kula just laughed with them, just as he always did. He had never been offended and always laughed along with Pari and his ilk. He relied on his friends to let him play a game or two a week, at school. These were his blessed moments and his reward for hanging on near the table every day, watching every stroke, studying every movement, offering unsolicited tips to his friends on their game;

'Didn't you see the ball? Didn't you see the ball swing? Didn't you notice the ball sizzling with a side spin and move to the left, and you moved to the right?'

The referee whistled to bring order to the hall followed by an announcement;

The first Quarterfinals match to be played will be… after a studied pause, 'Niranjan vs. Kula'. As the crowd roared, the players' fears were suddenly drowned in the hooting, merriment and booing!

Kula was in a tough draw. Niranjan, the last year winner was expected to demolish Kula, en route his potential meeting with Sai in the Finals. Sai was the new kid in the school; he joined only six months earlier and so his game was not ranked last year. But the daily matches were always won by Sai and his opponents were lost against him and had no clue on how to play him. Kula never had an opportunity to play Sai; but he had studied his game and had a very healthy respect for Sai's style of play.

He used to plead with others to let him play at least one game against Sai. 'I will try my best to win. But even losing to Sai could actually do me good'. But he never got to play.

Everyone expected the match between Kula and Niranjan to be one sided.

'Hypothetically', someone said, stressing on the word, 'if Kula wins against Niranjan he would meet Pari in the semis.

Kula did just that, to everyone's disbelief and the game was - one sided!

Someone said, 'Niranjan had a bad day' and others nodded. So it was still Niranjan's 'bad day' and not Kula's good game. Pari was relieved the most. He was afraid of Niranjan but did not think much of Kula. No one seemed to think much of Kula.

It was Pari's turn to go next. After the match, Pari beamed, 'I could take a game off Kula, while Niranjan was washed out'.

'So Pari was the better of the two,' they all concurred.

It was as though Kula did not exist. The fight really was about Pari and Niranjan, and Kula was just incidental, like a scale used between them to compare their relative weights. Kula did not seem to mind this snub.

He was heard asking Pari, 'Didn't you see the ball? You should have seen it spin and wobble… when I chopped…'! It was just another evening; just another practice match!

2 The Prophecy

'Drona, the teacher of both the Kaurava and Pandava Princes was giving the boys a lesson on archery. He asked the boys to aim at a bird perched on a tree far away. He asked one by one as they took aim, 'what do you see'. Each one of them saw the beautiful mountains behind the tree, the lush green tree with beautiful red flowers and some fruits. They also saw the bird on the tree; all but one. The lone one said, 'I see the eye of the bird, nothing else'. He was Arjuna, who became the master archer warrior that the world celebrated and feared...'

...Mahabharata, an Indian epic.

The school bought its first Table Tennis Table two years back and prided, 'The First and Only TT Table in the Town, for boys'. There were only two boys' schools. The other TT table was in the 'Girls only' school.

Since then all the students vied for a place at the table. The unfavourable gap in demand and supply was exploited by the school. The limited place was accessible only for a privileged few students, who could pay a steep fee. Sheer inspiration and competence wasn't enough and the table was grossly out of reach for a whole lot of underprivileged students, of whom there were quite a few in the initial days. Kula was one of them and was consigned to be sitting on the benches. For most students in the audience TT was novel entertainment. For some, it was pleasure to watch their friends play and fun time to root or hoot. Slowly the novelty of the table wore off and the audience thinned out.

Kula was different. The TT table became his Bodhi tree.

He discovered himself, while sitting beside and watching the game. He felt the game was playing inside him, just like the flow of blood in his veins and feel of the senses through his nerves. One could see him as if in a trance, mesmerized by the game. He became a talking point for a few; a butt of jokes for most.

As he did not play the game himself, he had the privilege of watching the ball from both the perspectives. He played every game that he watched, in his mind, point by point, shot by shot and frame by frame. He analysed each stroke for its merits. He simulated each stroke in his mind several times and he analysed how best to respond to each of the strokes; the angle, the timing, the speed of the ball the momentum, the spin of the ball, the swing of the ball due to the humidity and it's sway due to the air circulation within the hall. He even surmised that the humidity and the air movement depended on the number of persons in the hall. He visualized all these as a mental picture right from the sound of the tap of the ball being served and he was ready for the ball, well before it reached 'his side of the table'.

Though he was not actually playing, he mentally simulated his movements, the legs gliding without inertia, his body floating and flexing as required effortlessly and his arms positioned accurately and his imaginary racquet either smashed or loop drove with a measured tops-spin and the right momentum, speed, angle, spin and swing that it landed on the other side, exactly at the spot of bother for an unprepared opponent, whose reflexes failed invariably and, who displayed no knowledge of how to handle the complex topspin stroke.

But it was not all over for Kula.

He switched, rather jumped sides, and was ready to meet the ball on the other side of the table, mentally of course. He was there studying the ball on its merit and positioning himself right and effortlessly, with a sleight of arms and wrist, produced a complex stroke combining topspin, sidespin, loop and or a drive, with the right momentum and placement that would have the opponent guessing and on the wrong foot… He continued switching the sides, as he played mentally on both sides of the table every time the ball changed sides and for every stroke and till the point was won or lost.

It was as though someone was mono-acting a Shakespearean drama at racquet speed.

Kula was sometimes overwhelmed by the intensity of his reflexes and physically glided into the play area, ready to take the stroke with his imaginary racquet, only to crash on to the player who was also moving to meet the ball himself. He grinned sheepishly as the players shouted at him, jeered at him, called him a spoilsport, called him a nuisance. But everyone knew it was not intentional, he meant no harm and so everyone forgave him. Everyone, but the vicious Pari loved him and wanted him to be by the table.

'He loves the game of TT', they all declared.

Pari's harsh tongue mocked him, 'His love would never be consummated,' and drew mischievous grins from his loyal pals. Was it intended to be prophecy or a curse? No one could tell.

Most times, Kula saw something the other players did not see about the ball, from the sound of the tap on the racquet, the swing of the ball, or the point and the angle and the speed at which it landed.

He often reprimanded the player in a friendly, yet intense manner, 'Did you not hear the whirr of the ball? It's all right to smash it the way you did when you hear the ball swishshsh, but not when it whirrs'.

The player just blinked and nodded, as he never heard the ball either 'swishshsh' or 'whirr'.

One of Kula's thousand theorems; his favourite, 'the ball could just 'swish', and not 'swishsh' and sometimes could 'swishshsh', just like it could just 'whir' or 'whirr' or 'whirrr'. Sometimes the ball lands on the table with a 'Tink' or ''Tonk, or just 'Tunk', and we are expected to listen to the ball and should prepare accordingly to take the ball'.

Niranjan once just threw his arms up and prayed to heaven, 'God, either he is crazy, or it's me! I am sure one of us is, please let it not be me'. Maybe Kula was crazy, but the game came to him naturally.

One Sunday morning, Mahadevan was watching his favourite serial program Mahabharatha playing on the TV; Drona training his princely students on archery. A young prince, Arjuna claimed he saw the bird's eye and nothing but the bird's eye, before he hit it. The scene became Mahadevan's Eureka moment.

He remembered the voice loud and clear, 'Didn't you see the ball... Didn't you see the ball'?

Mahadevan said to himself, 'Kula sees something more, actually less, than what the others see or hear, including myself. He saw the ball and nothing but the ball. He has enough promise to be a winner'.

Every one of his friends loved such a dedicated audience; a one man cheering brigade. Everyone loved his well-intentioned, unsolicited tips. Mahadevan loved him most. He even considered sponsoring the fee for Kula, but couldn't. So when Kula reached the Semi-finals with a borrowed racquet the previous year and lost, Mahadevan gave him a decent TT racquet and a ball to practice.

3 The Gauntlet

Next, the finals... Sai was silently observing the mayhem caused by Kula. He always wore a disarming smile too that no one could read his mind or the depths of his thoughts. He had a superior game he learnt and carried with him from the city school, where he came from and also had the benefit of his personal coach, Wilson. Wilson had taught him all the tricks from the books as he himself had played for the state several years earlier. All these had given Sai an aura of invincibility. The entire school believed that Sai would stop Kula's freak show and were waiting to watch the eventuality. Kula, personally, believed so too.

The Final Game began.

Sai ran up a huge lead in a few minutes over Kula in the first set. Kula's shots mostly landed out of the table. He was not anticipating as he should be, whenever Sai's strokes landed on the edge. He seemed to have a spatial problem. So, before he could adjust to it, he was trailing badly against his seasoned opponent. The crowd was jeering...

Though no one was hoping for a Kula win... No; not even wishing... some were clearly disappointed at Kula's tame surrender. This wasn't good entertainment...

If there was a sports journalist covering the games, with a passion for the sport and a command over the words, he would have summarized the Finals thus;

'Sai seemed to be giving his lessons with his text book shots and Kula did not seem to have any clue on how to handle most of them. The whole crowd was behind Sai and none showed any sympathy for Kula.

They were rooting for Sai to go for the kill, gladiator style!

Sai obliged , as he showcased the most vicious of the lessons that Wilson taught him in the first few minutes of the match zealously, without saving any for later'.

Sai won the first game, without a whimper from his opponent, 11-4.

'As the players switched sides of the table for the second game of the match, something should have told Kula that he could turn the tables against Sai. While most players would have been demoralized at the barrage of great topspin and smashes from Sai that wrecked the first game for Kula, Kula seems to have used his experience and intelligence to learn. He never lost twice to the same trick. He worked out his response by quick learning, intuition, application, anticipation and great reflexes. He was on top of the ball when the same spin-trick was repeated, however vicious and however complex and had an improvised counter to it. Sai could not use the surprise with his 'off the book' shots, any longer. Kula seems to have just freshly read the same book, courtesy Sai, during the first game'.

'Next, it was Kula's turn to spell bind Sai with his mastery over the game. Kula's innovations were original and he didn't go by any book. He could now anticipate every move of Sai while every mesmerising spin of his own had Sai guessing'.

'The hunter became the hunted! Kula demonstrated several original lessons that neither Sai nor Wilson would ever 'learn' from any text. And it looked like Sai did not have any clue on how to read the new lessons, while on the field. The result was that Kula blanked out Sai in the next four games, 11-3, 11-2, 11-1, 11-0. At the end of the final it was clear it was a war between the champion and the pretenders.

Kula was not affected by all the jubilation around him. This was just another day out'.

The question in every one's mind was, 'how did Kula come to reach the top spot without even a few days of practice'. Even Mahadevan seemed surprised!

The Principal mentioned with a tinge of guilt, 'Kula did not practice at all and learnt the game only by observation'.

The Chief Guest of the day, Jagadeesan was the Secretary of the District Sports Centre. He had watched the match played between Kula and Sai and was impressed by Kula's game.

While receiving the prize, Kula walked up to the mike and spoke, 'Somehow everyone believes that I never practiced. I want to clarify this. I confirm that I had been practicing TT every day in the last four months'.

He paused and to the crowd's giggle and murmur, 'If it was at the girl's School that had the only other TT table in town'!

He confided, 'No. Not at the girl's school, certainly not'.

He explained, 'I practice in my neighbour's home. You may be wondering if my neighbour has a TT table at home'.

'No! We improvised the Home Dining Table by adding a net. It was not the best of tables to play TT. But it was what we could afford. Yesterday, my neighbour won her school tournament. Today, I have won ours. After a devoted practice, though on a lesser table that constrained my game and though I had to overcome a spatial problem, I am now happy with my game'.

'As our principal always says, 'Your best is yet to come', I could have played better. And I will, soon, with more practice'.

Kula continued, 'Thank you Mahadevan Sir. For having faith in me. My thanks to my neighbour, Krishnan Sir, who gave me permission to play in his home with his daughter. It wasn't an easy decision for the family'.

By this time the boys were chanting, 'What's her name...'? 'What's her name...'? What's her name...'?

Kula just blushed, raised his hand, embarrassed by the chant, 'Thank you all'.

The Chief Guest in his speech said, 'I am very impressed and I am happy to be part of this game and the celebration. I carry home lessons and thoughts on how we could encourage youngsters with talent like Kula. I'm happy to announce that I will arrange special training for him at the District Sports Centre. I also assure to get Government scholarship for him for the next 2 years, for his education, TT Training and sponsorship for attending various tournaments starting with the district championship coming up in the next 3 months'.

The Chief Guest threw down a gauntlet to the students of the School, all the while looking at Kula, 'You boys have it in you to rise up to beat the new World Champion and World No. 1, Deng, a Chinese player, at the Shanghai Games, conducted every two years. Best wishes'.

Mahadevan nodded heavily and looked at Kula as if it would be a worthy goal for him; for someone who just became the champion in an upcoming small school in a non-descript small town of India!

Kula chuckled at himself first and the Chief Guest next, who spoke of Deng and him in the same breath. Kula, at best had an ambition to play for the Tamil Nadu State team!

He had little knowledge of China and its people other than the 1962 Indo-China war and Huang Tsueng from his history text books; Bruce Lee, Jackie Chan and some characters with pigtails thanks to the few Chinese martial arts movies.

But somewhere deep down in his mind, without his cognizance, was his entire faculty getting him ready for a long, challenging, arduous and frightful journey to top of the summit; the Games at Shanghai?

4 Rainbow in his Dreams

That evening, after his winning the TT Finals at his school, he returned from school to a special welcome. The news reached his home and the neighbourhood ahead of him. His mother adored him and was beaming from cheek to cheek. His sister ran to the shop to get him a gift and returned with a bar of Dairy Milk. He had become the hero of his entire neighbourhood. Neighbours came in and praised him lavishly. They asked him to help their sons to play as well.

'They are all loafing around like vagabonds'; one of them said.

The boys and girls from the neighbourhood came. Most of them wanted to touch and feel the TT racquet and the ball. Though the racquet was worn out, it excited the children no small amount.

Then the unbelievable happened. Krishnan sir, who lived two streets away in a terraced house, walked in the small one room tiled hut, stooping watchfully at the low door frame.

'Sir', gasped Kula out of huge respect, 'I myself wanted to come later today and take your blessings, Sir'.

Krishnan, still at the doorstep, smiled, 'You have made us all proud'!

Kula's mother, excited by Krishnan's sudden unexpected visit, 'Ayya, please come to our humble home. We should be fortunate that you should visit us. Bless my son, Sir; he will do us all proud'.

He smiled as he stepped in and looked behind him. Mrs Krishnan stepped in.

'Amma'; Kula revered in excitement; 'Welcome, welcome'.

She replied something about how happy she was, but Kula wasn't listening. He was watching the charming Jayanthi, who emerged from behind her mother.

'Hey Jay, what a surprise! Thanks for coaching me'.

She replied smiling, 'Same to you', warmly, returning the complement. Not often do you get a chance to return a nice compliment.

She handed over a small bouquet of roses to him and held her hands towards him shyly, 'Congratulations and thank you'.

He looked around for something to give her; finding none, he felt a jab in his heart. He was then relieved as he gratefully accepted a bar of 'Dairy Milk', meant for him that his thoughtful sister thrust into his hands just in time with a smile and a gesture of the eye to hand it to Jay. He didn't even pause to thank his sister.

'Congratulations and thank you too', he said, accepting her hand as they exchanged the gifts.

A tingle ran up his spine as he touched her hand. He felt guilty and looked at her face, if she knew. She was smiling innocently and as their eyes met, the second tingle ran up and this time he saw fireworks lighting up his otherwise dark sky, bringing the stars closer to them both. For a moment he was lost in the bright fireworks.

He shook his head as if to reprimand himself, 'No, Kula. This is not right'.

But his senses weren't in any mood to listen and betrayed him gleefully. They just teased him and brought up flowerworks this time, flowers showering on both of them, from a large shady tree and he felt as though no one, nothing else existed.

This was fresh new feeling for Kula. He had never felt like this before.

He had touched and held Jay's hands several times while playing at her home in the recent past, without being conscious of the touch or her closeness, but why this today? Why was it different today? And in the public glare of all those he loved and respected so much. What if any of them watched his face? He felt shabby. But the pleasure of just standing near her overwhelmed him and he yearned to hold her hand again.

He shook his head again to dismiss the stray disturbance in his thoughts, scared that others would read his mind and managed to say, though incoherently to Krishnan, 'Without you, we both couldn't have done this, Sir'.

There were just two chairs and too many waiting to be seated. So, Kula's mother rolled out a straw mat for the ladies to sit. Kula was standing near Krishnan with great reverence, even as he was insisting on Kula to sit down on the remaining empty chair. Krishnan wasted no time.

He handed over a new TT racquet and a ball to him as his gift and appreciation. 'I am glad that you have been offered special training at the District Sports HQ. Please come home to practice again with Jay, whenever you wish, even if you get to practice at the District. I would appreciate if she gets some practice too'.

Kula wondered, if he would have extended the invitation if he had read his mind when he was enjoying the fireworks and flowerworks at the touch of his daughter's hand. He felt so unworthy, angry at himself and afraid of visiting Krishnan Sir's home for practice again.

Kula asked Krishnan if he could request the Chief Guest to include Jay in the District Training too. 'After all', Kula said, 'she is as qualified and plays even better than me. She has won her school competition too, just like me. She has outgrown the Home Dining Table too. In fact, Sir, she has more potential than me'.

Krishnan non-committal, said, 'Let us see'.

In a few minutes, the family trooped out, as the hushed, whispering neighbours, who were peeping through the door and window to have a glimpse of the 'important' visitors, stepped respectfully back to give way.

'The girl is beautiful', said someone looking at Jay.

Jay, as she walked into the moon light (or was it the just the streetlight that was giving him a crazy spin?), turned back to glance at him, smile and wave her hand shyly as she walked into the crimson-grey evening behind her parents.

He was most happy. His achievement that evaded his mind, fully sank into him now, thanks to all hullaballoo around that evening, topped by the visit of Jay and her family.

That night was crazy. He slept, but didn't sleep. It started with a TT game in a strange place. 'They call it 'Shanghai'. He plays with a Chinese person, who looks like the guy who came out of the 'Shaolin' movies with a pigtail hanging down a partly shaved head. 'Must be the World Champion, Deng', who played TT as though it were a kind of martial art and as if the result of the game would decide who would live and who shouldn't.

When the champion was about to lose, he doesn't play fair and angrily works up a dirt storm, taking Kula by surprise and shock. Jay somehow gets caught in the melee and surrenders her medal that she just won, at the feet of the Chinese woman opponent.

Jackie Chan 'of the Police Story' drags Kula to jail'. Kula woke up with a start, sweating profusely. He could not recall how he had escaped from the Shanghai Jail, but he now found himself in the safety of his own home. He gulped some water, felt for his hands and face, to know he was really safe, before he hit the bed and slept again.

Then early morning, he had exciting reveries, worthy of the exhilarating day. There were a number of fiery exchanges of the TT ball he had with Sai, Pari and Niranjan. Whenever he got the strokes right, Jay gave him a hi-five, or held out her hands for a handshake, and every time a tingle passed his spine with either fireworks or flowers showering from above.

Every time he touched Jay, he made it a point to withdraw his hands hastily off her, telling himself, 'I'm not doing the right thing' and promising himself that he would behave.

But seconds later, he desperately wanted to hold her hands again.

Next, he had won the Final. The last stroke was delectable, just with a sleight of his wrist and he won. He was being mobbed. He saw Mahadevan Sir. He saw Krishnan Sir. His heart started beating wildly in anticipation. He was looking for Mrs Krishnan following Krishnan Sir, and for Jay following her mother.

Next, he hears the chant and hoot, 'What's her name'? 'What's her name'?? 'What's her name'???

He feels himself blush. 'She is just another friend, like all of you', he yells at the crowd.

'Not any longer, she is special', protests the crowd.

'I like it', hails his inner voice. 'May be', he whispers to himself and the crowd, still confused.

He woke up to the far away rooster, the first rays of sunlight ofthe day and to the fresh fragrance of the moist earth raised by the first drizzle of the season. No wonder, he saw a rainbow in his dreams.

Part 2: Li'll'y

5 Scapegoat

She could not move her aching body much. Her head ached as if it had been hit by stone. She heard rumblings like enormous goods trains were chugging through tunnels inside her head. She couldn't make sense of where she was and why. She felt as though she was buried in a chamber, deep underneath a mountain, with no exit doors.

Slowly she got used to the faint of the dark light around her. Everything around looked either black or in darker shades of grey and she found them distorted as if she looked at them through the bottom of a soda bottle. When she extended her hand to reach them, things seemed to drift away from her.

When the haze in her mind half-cleared, she realized that she was facing incredible questions; questions on her very character – her loyalty to her Nation and her Team.

She wanted to scream, 'China is so dear to me. I would never trade my country for anything else'. She gave up soon, as she realized no one was listening.

She could hear familiar voices repeatedly ringing in her ears, laughing and jeering at her, from just beyond her sight... 'Sleeping with the enemy'... 'Traitor'...

She shuddered to think of the standard punishment for traitors... 'The best case scenario; Lock up in a dungeon for life and the worst case; face the firing squad, branded as a Traitor'. She hastened to purge her fears, for now.

'It should be morning', she surmised from the faint light through her window. 'I should have slept deeply and soundly since last evening in Dan's office'. Dan was the Chief Coach and Manager of the Chinese National Table Tennis Team that she was a part of.

The room wasn't comfortable, smaller than what she was used to, paint peeling off in patches, barely furnished but for her single bed and was too cold.

Next she remembered her meeting with Dan and 'him', the previous evening at Dan's chamber.

'It's a well-known secret that 'he' has been fighting hard to keep 'his' World Number 2 Rank. 'He' would have probably accepted 'his' defeat, ungracefully though, if 'he' had lost to someone within world rank ten; but to lose to an unseeded, 'lowly' player from almost nowhere, hurt 'his' pride and 'he' was reacting'.

'Is it my mistake that the two players happen to be my friends? Should I abandon my innocent, yet talented friends, though friends of just ten days, just to please 'him' and watch 'him' unfairly hound them out of the Games'?

'Is this is Dan's response to the challenge from the two emerging players, who had the potential to upset the established order, like daring bulls in his China shop? Then God save Table Tennis in China!

Is 'he' arm twisting Dan to act against me, to have 'his' sweet revenge on these talented players'?

'Am I asked to carry the cross to reduce 'his' agony? And even for Meiling's poor show'?

'Oh my! I have been made a juicy, suckling, roasted, 'scapegoat' for 'him' and 'his' gang to fine dine on'!

She wanted to meet Dan personally to clear the air, without 'him' being around, when she gets out of this 'run down hospital of some sort'!

Lying in low spirits, she knew she had to cheer herself up, to escape descending into depression.

She thought of her Table Tennis; she found only a dead end!

'Oh My! My TT life has come to an abrupt and humiliating end'! She then pitied herself, 'TT is all the life I ever had…'

She hurriedly switched her mind away from the depressing thought of her now vanished career; thought of her old friends; she wasn't sure anymore who was friend and who wasn't. 'One of them, I don't even know who, had stolen my selfie to fix me. Would the others speak up for me'? It was getting more hopeless!

She thought of her parents. Mom had died, when she was just four. She kept a faded photograph in her apartment, without which she found it hard to recollect her face. Dad passed away a few years ago. She fought her tears. He was the only one who ever cared for her. She realized that she had no one that would grieve for her.

Then she thought of her new friends - Kool and Joy!!!

6 Breaking the Ice

Li Ling stepped into the practice area at the stadium, greeting her friends, who were practicing and warming up. There were more than 30 tables set up for the practice of participants. But all of them were occupied. It was late in the evening and almost time for dinner. She cursed herself for being late once again and was worried that she would have little practice that day. She had to find a space for herself quickly. There were a separate tables set for the players from the host, China. But she preferred to practice against players from other countries, to have a feel of the other styles.

The Games at Shanghai was about to begin in the next few days. The Games are a biennial feature and is the one of the most prestigious competitions for Table Tennis in the world, only next to the Olympics. Li was one of the probable on the Chinese singles team.

She spotted Su Ping, her team mate and he was practicing with a brown, almost black person.

She didn't feel like guessing which country he came from. 'Whichever', she thought.

'Hi Su', she stepped forward to meet him, 'Been playing long'?

Su replied affirmatively and continued, 'I need to run for dinner. Do you want to join me'?

Li, who just found a chance to practice, said gratefully, 'Dinner can wait' and lingered, if she should extend her hand to the stranger friend of Su.

As if reading her mind, Su bent to stare at the ID card that the stranger was wearing and said, 'Meet Kula__(Garble)', he had trouble pronouncing his name.

Kula__ stepped forward and extended his hands shyly, 'Kula'.

Li gave her hand warmly, 'Hi Kool, Li'.

A charming female sprang up from one of the nearby seats, 'Jay' and stuck her hand too, giggling.

Li instantly liked her, 'Joy, I am Li. Do you also play'?

Joy nodded and looked at Kula. 'I am tired, from my long flight.

Kula will play with you. I already had some practice with your friend and Kula;

'Kool', Jay added imitating Li and laughed. They all laughed together. They had broken the ice and were instant friends.

Li was a friendly person and an excellent host. She went out of her way to make them feel at home. She herself had been in different countries with strange names and stranger people. There were times she had felt intimidated by the boisterous presence of the local hosts. She wanted to do her best to let these strangers in her own country feel the hospitality she could afford. In the process, she was about to discover a great friendship that she did not find in her own country, all these years. Kula and Jay, (Kool and Joy as Li called them), reciprocated, rather shyly and they found instant bonhomie with this stranger.

Li did not expect Kool to play much, coming from India, which was ranked low in the world TT fraternity. But she was surprised by the depth of the game he produced and instantly respected and recognized his game as of the same class as of her own men's team mates in the top 8-12 ranking in the world. She herself was in similar ranking on the women's side.

The style of game that Kool played was a mix of several styles she had come across in different continents. She suspected that he did not have a regular personal coach and had been coached by several coaches with different styles. She also suspected that Kool 'should have been self-coaching observing and analysing others games, from around the world'. 'Videos? Youtube? Maybe.

But to have mastered the different styles that he could play and to be able to use the right style against his opponent needed tremendous skill and class.

Still, she felt his game was crude and needed refinement, 'If he could do it, he would break into the top 5 in the world and could reach the podium too. He had potential. Potential was one, but making it was another. Several fell by the wayside, unable to climb the steep, highly competitive, top 10 ranks'.

She herself was working untiringly to reach the Top 5. But it was a hell of a climb.

'But potential is still potential', she argued with herself. Without it, no amount of polishing would help'.

She should introduce Kool to her Team Coach, Dan. If Dan whittled and polished him, he would break into the top 5, for sure.

'She should be of the same age as Jay', Kula thought. That would make her two years younger than him.
'Was it good manners to ask a girl's age? Does this also hold true about trying to guess a girl's age? In any case, I'm not good at guessing age of girls, definitely not that of a Chinese girl'.

7 The Fragrance called Li Ling

The next day, was not their lucky day. Kula and Jay bumped into a selfish crowd of players from other nations, who took over the entire practice tables at the stadium. Kula and Jay were completely spaced out and had nowhere to practice. A few hours of practice for the competitors is like an oasis for a desert traveller. But what Kula and Jay got to see on that day, was just a mirage of tables, they couldn't play on. They moved from table to table watching others possess and practice on. Kula and Jay wanted practice badly and they hunted for a practice table across the stadium and moved to a less crowded corner, where the local host team practiced.

They approached a group of a particularly merry crowd of Chinese players, mostly boys and a few girls, who were poking fun at each other, playing and practicing. Encouraged by the friendly reception they got from Li the previous day, Kula, expected similar warmth, grinned as he held out his hand to introduce himself;

'Kula', he said to the nearest player.

The Chinese player responded with an ugly frown and stuck his middle finger towards Kula and shook his hips in a vulgar gesture. Kula was shocked and stepped back impulsively, to shield Jay from the view.

Thankfully, Jay was too innocent to understand the gesture, though she knew it to be a rude one and was offended nevertheless. As Kula tugged Jay by her arm and tried to walk away from the table, seething in anger and from humiliation, Jay obediently trotted behind him, unable to comprehend, if Kula made any mistake of etiquette, trying to introduce himself. The whole company jeered at them in a disgusting manner.

One of them menacingly stepped in Jay's way, stretching his palms, pointing his index and middle fingers towards her and folding his other fingers and thumb as though he had a gun on hand.

He placed his 'gun' point blank on Jay's 'bindi' decorated forehead as if her 'bindi', the dot, was the target, and crackled a thunderous blast, from the depth of his gut, louder and sharper than a gunshot. Then there was absolute silence... Jay believed for a moment that she had been shot... till the entire crowd exploded in laughter with him. She felt stoned, unable to move her leaden feet and was grateful that Kula was dragging her away by her arm, while she was still trembling. This was the most terrible laughter Jay had ever heard. The Chinese pulled his fingers from her forehead and blew the imaginary smoke from his pointed fingers; cowboy style and shouted obscenities along with a warning;

'No more dots on your forehead, lady. My gun is itching to find its target. Next time it wouldn't be bare fingers'.

They rushed back to Kula's assigned apartment in the Games Village and settled down slowly, with Jay still trembling.

Along the way Kula was trying to pacify a terrified Jay, saying, 'They are 'sledging' us just to break our will before the games'.

The words didn't mean much for Jay, who was still in a state of shock. Then Kula placed two chairs, each against the centres of the long sides of the dining table, asked for Jay's 'Dhuppatta', which she handed over to him, absentmindedly. He folded it into the size of a standard TT net and tied them to the chairs. He did it with quite a flair and deftness and said, 'the TT table is ready', in just a matter of minutes. Jay smiled for the first time, since the scary experience of the morning and was ready for practice in their familiar setting. Kula and Jay enjoyed their game they grew up with, without a concern for tomorrow.

Li stepped in without ringing the doorbell or knocking or any announcement whatsoever.

'What's 'knock'ing, between friends'? she asked herself. They had got that close.

She winced at the apparatus they were playing on.

She reprimanded them both as her right, 'You will spoil your game before tomorrow's friendly', she commanded. Starting the next day, some unofficial friendly matches were planned to give the players some practice before the Games.

Jay spoke first almost in tears, 'What are our options'? She narrated the horror at the stadium earlier that day.

Li apologized profusely, 'Oh my dear Joy, I'm sorry about what happened... and on behalf of her fellow Chinese countrymen'.

Then she asked, 'Kool, would you be able to recognize some of the persons in the hostile group'? as she opened her smartphone.

Li showed them some pictures and found quickly that the perpetrators of the scare were probable members of the Chinese team, from among whom the official team was to be announced before the start of the Games.

'Deng's gang', she called them, for want of a better translation in English. She bit her tongue. Probably, she shouldn't have mentioned this.

She murmured to herself, 'How could they behave so badly? Did they have official sanction? It doesn't look like a chance incident and they definitely appeared motivated. Have I inadvertently triggered a hostile reaction from the Chinese management and team, against these simple Indian friends, when I talked about them to Dan'?

She was not too sure. 'I will have to confront Dan about this later'.

She then a smile and parried Kula's questions on who these were. She diverted the attention from the pictures, praised about their ingenuity in quickly creating a practice TT table.

She also cautioned them, 'This practice in less than standard equipment would spoil your game. Improvisation is good for entertaining yourself, but would let you down in competitive sport'.

Jay explained Li, 'This is how we learnt our first TT lessons'.

Jay narrated Kula's and her own initiation to the game of TT and how they progressed to where they did, Li listened to every word attentively, in total disbelief, as a child would, listening to the adventures of Aladdin and his magic lamp.

'Truly magical', she exclaimed. 'Kool! Joy! Are you saying that you both trained on a table like this and yet you reached the pinnacle that brought you here? And you both trained and at home together, since childhood? Unbelievable! It's a fairy tale to tell the world'.

Jay answered quietly, 'We haven't reached the pinnacle. Moreover, we aren't Kool and Joy... but Kula and Jay'!

Li Ling tried to say, 'Kula... Jay'; ended up with, 'Kool... Joy'! and smiled. It was evident that the names were foreign to her.

Joy came to her rescue, 'Call us Kool and Joy, if you wish so. Sounds cool too! I'm OK'.

Li, still in amazement, did not trust that the dining table was the best apparatus to practice on before an international tournament.

'You both would lose your game before it starts', she argued.

Assuming total command, she ordered them to follow her with their gear, jumped into the car and drove them off to her club, where she practiced regularly. She talked to the manager of the club, who had a characteristic moustache, unusual for a Chinese. He let them use a table, and reserved the table entirely for them till the end of the Games.

'You are welcome any day, any time to practice. Call me if you have any trouble, in or out of the stadium. I can help', he offered his business card. 'Best wishes'.

They thanked him and Li for the help. Li walked away unaffected, promising to come back to pick them up for dinner. She was just doing her bit for her friends. She had to talk to Dan and immediately before further damage is done.

Li came back to take them out for Dinner, in the evening. Kula was suddenly uncomfortable. Should he ask her now or not yet?

He ventured at last, 'What did you say is your name, come again. I must apologize, I forget names', Kula asked.

'Especially with girls' names'! interrupted Jay merrily, 'he had taken nearly a week to be able to recall my name without being prompted'.

'Kool, I'm Li Ling', answered Li again mispronouncing his name and extending her hand as if by habit, as she introduced herself the second time. Kula accepted her hand and her second introduction.

'Li Ling is the fragrance of jasmine, expressed in words', she volunteered to explain.

He asked her coarsely and casually with a heavy accent, 'Oh, 'Li'll'y' means, 'fragrance of jasmine eh'?

She looked shocked at Kula as though he had outraged her name! She repeated rather sternly like a school teacher,
'No; much more than just a meaning. Li Ling is the feel of the fragrance of jasmine. When you hear 'Li Ling', you would be able to feel the mild fragrance of jasmine'.

Kula understood the importance of uttering 'Li Ling', as he

closed his eyes in meditation and said hoarsely, 'Li'll'y', simultaneously taking a deep breath and imagining the fragrance of jasmine.

'It is tough, but anything for you', he conceded with a grin at which Jay giggled.

Li frowned, 'Its Li Ling, not Li'll'y'. Li mimicked his heavily accented 'Li'll'y' with a huge stress on the 'll'.

She was amused, though claimed in protest, 'Li'll'y - sounds too strong. Am right, Joy'?

'Yes Li'll..ll'y', Jay teased her.

'Li Ling' Li repeated as softly with eyes closed, almost meditating, as gently as a feather that floats down the air.

Kula, who wasn't paying attention to the demonstration of her name, continued to hold her hands as he said, 'Li'll'y, like my Li'll'y teacher at school', remembering his teacher, Ms Lalitha, better known in his school as Li'll'y teacher.

'Must be the boys all loved and flocked around her'?

'And you too had affections for her, didn't you'? asked Li'll'y with a twinkle in her eyes.

'Yes I loved her much. There was no one, who wouldn't love her. She taught me to say 'please' and 'thank you'', he said, pretending not to notice her twinkling eyes.

He did not like a less than reverential conversation about his teacher and thought it would be a great moral violation if he acknowledged her irreverent 'twinkle'.

Li'll'y caught his discomfiture and wondered why, before he continued, 'I wished her last on her 63rd birthday last month', unwittingly, snuffing out Li'll'y's twinkle, and didn't realize that both Li'll'y and Jay filled the room with LOL.

Jay saw that they were holding their hands for too long, quite comfortable with each other. Fuming within her, she hastily stuck her hands at Li'll'y.

'I'm Jay, you Si'll'y Li'll'y', she shrieked, forcibly grabbing her hands from Kula's and shaking them impatiently.

Contented that she could break their 'hand-holding ceremony' she laughed heartily at her own concocted rhyme and repeated 'You Si'll'y Li'll'y'.

Kula, who had not been sure of Jay's feelings for him, now didn't have any more doubts. He was witnessing first hand, 'Love at first sign of rivalry'.

Li'll'y was cool and read Jay's love for Kula from her sudden, heavy and jealous hand-grab. But she didn't care. Why should she? But she could see that Jay was strongly possessive about Kula. May be that's being Indian. 'Hope Jay and I could deal with Kula without being possessive about him, someday soon. After all, Jay would be in possession of Kula all her life back in India. How much of Kula would she lose', she argued in her mind. What's between friends'?

She went back to Kula to hold his left hand, just to tease Jay. If this act was misunderstood and brought tears in Jay's eyes, even though she knew Li'll'y was just teasing her, Jay graciously wiped them off without attracting attention. Kula knew Jay's heart and knew her eyes had clouded, without having to see them, courteously freed his hands from Li'll'y and walked up to Jay in an effort to reassure her.

Li'll'y, broke the tension, 'Si'll'y Li'll'y', imitating Jay and all of them laughed. It was as though they had known each other for years.

Thus Kula and Jay, came to be called KOOL and JOY between themselves as pet names, as they clung to their respective Li'll'y given names, both in and out of the company of Li'll'y. just as the name, 'LI'LL'Y', in Kool's heavy South Indian accent, with stress on the second syllable, stuck to Li Ling as well.

Joy thanked her Gods for her friendship in this strange intimidating country. She was jealous; yes... jealous of Li'll'y, who swiftly grabbed Kool's attention along with his hands. Something that Joy herself couldn't be assured of after several years of friendship and togetherness with Kool. But in spite of her jealousy, she liked Li'll'y that she was looking forward to her company, with the faith that Kool was destined to be hers and that he would not let her down or offend her, whatever and whoever came by.

Yet, Joy knew, to keep Kool's attention, she has to express her own affection for him at the first opportunity that presented to her. She made up her mind to create such opportunities, if nothing came by naturally.

8 The Night Shadows

Joy had a disturbed sleep that night. She suddenly felt cold metal pressed on to her forehead. She was too scared to open her eyes and feared that someone broke into the apartment with a gun and she tried to recollect whether she had closed and bolted the door properly. She remembered the face of the Chinese boy at the stadium and sweat formed on her forehead, around the 'bindi', the dot. Was he there with a real gun this time as he had warned her?

Then she heard a reverberating 'BANG' that tore through both her ears and exploding right at the centre of her forehead. She sprang up from her bed, terrified, trembling and sweating all over. She felt for her forehead and found it intact. There was no sign of anyone else in her room; no gun, no shot. It took a while for her to realize it was a nightmare; not until another thunder tore through the apartment, following a particularly strong flash of lightening. It was enough to defeat her spirits and drain her strength.

Joy pondered if she should call Kool for help. She decided to, at the next thunder that crackled through the heavily curtained window and cracked her spirit. Kool, who stayed in the neighbouring 'male' block, rushed to see her, wet all over by rain. Her voice was too distressed and urgent that he could not waste time searching for an umbrella. It was a very cold, rainy autumn night in Shanghai, and being wet from head to toe made him shiver.

Kool cursed himself that he didn't pack enough warm or dry clothing with him for the trip. He rushed to comfort a trembling Joy, and here he was, himself shivering. He had to remove his wet shirt to avoid freezing and stop his shivering.

She offered him her towel and he dried himself while his pants were still wet and cold, but he had no option but to stay in it.

Joy was sitting leaning her back on her bed. Kool sat on the bed beside her and comforted her. She leaned on his strong bare shoulders, clutching his arms with both her hands. He was so cold and she was warm. She seemed too distraught as she dozed off to sleep, in the comfort of his closeness.

A very loud thunder should have reminded Joy of the

nightmarish gunshot that she jolted herself still closer to him and clung to his arm with both her hands in her sleep.

Kool realized for the first time that she belonged to him and that no one could take them apart from then on. He thought of the trust her father had in him and if he was betraying his trust. No! On the contrary he would have betrayed her father's trust only if he had left her high and dry on her own during the nightmarish experiences that she was going through. He felt worthy of his Joy.

He picked up her towel lying nearby and was overwhelmed by her fragrance; the only fragrance that he would let permeate through his breath and the only one that could fulfil his life.

He leaned a little and kissed her hair on top of the head and whispered to himself, 'I love you, Joy'.

She softly whispered back, deep in her sleep, 'I love you, Kool'.

Love flowed naturally and beautifully between them.

Early next morning, Li'll'y stepped into Joy's apartment. It was not bolted from inside and she did not knock as usual; 'What's between friends'? Kool had obviously forgotten to bolt the door from inside as he charged into the room answering Joy's distress call the previous night.

To her surprise, she found them both deep asleep together, Kool shirtless, strong, chest up and Joy sleeping like a baby on it. Li'll'y wondered, if she made a mistake entering her apartment unannounced and if she should slip back the way she came in.

'What's between friends', she moved in further, adventurously with a mischievous twinkle in her eyes. At least they were decently clothed and she was not embarrassed. So she caught them red handed and she smiled to herself. She sat on a couch nearby and picked up an Indian language magazine that lay nearby, waiting for them to wake up.

Then, Li'll'y the naughty, slipped beside Kool on the other side of the bed from Joy and rested her face on the right side of Kool's chest and waited for Joy's reaction. She couldn't resist the temptation and so extended her hand upwards to take a selfie with her Samsung, while she pretended to be asleep on Kool's chest too.

She looked at the selfie with half closed eye and found it to be picture perfect, with Joy and her clinging in their sleep to each side of Kool's bare chest.

Just then, Joy stirred out of her sleep. Li'll'y expected her to wake up, business as usual between Kool and herself and only react in rage to Li'll'y too lying beside him. But Joy hardly noticed Li'll'y.

Joy was startled, nevertheless.She was indeed shocked at the impropriety of herself lying on Kool's shoulders the whole night. She was slowly composing herself as the memory of her nightmare flooded back to her mind and all that followed in the night.

She was confused, and condemned herself for having done something very immoral and wrong.

'What would people think and say? How could Kool do this to me? Should I blame Kool'?

She sat on the edge of the couch covering her face in disbelief about herself. She had no explanation whatsoever and she had to blame herself for her disgraceful conduct.

Unable to either decipher or relate the turmoil in Joy's mind, which is very unique to the Indian culture, Li'll'y whispered mischievously to Joy, 'Had a long night of fun'? still clinging to Kool's chest.

It was then that Joy was shocked at the presence of the third person in the room and that she too had been hugging Kool, as she herself had done all night. How and when did Li'll'y come in? Did she come in with Kool late the previous night and did she stay all night? Joy didn't understand the situation. She stared at her in shock, disbelief and rage.

Then she observed that Li'll'y was washed and dressed at her best and inferred she should have come in just then and had not spent the night with Kool and herself. That was some relief.

Next, she saw the twinkle in Li'll'y's eyes, the same twinkle that she was used to seeing in her sister's eyes, when she used to tease her, hugging her dad and claim, 'This is my dad, go away, go away to your mom'.

She realized that Li'll'y was just teasing her with her prank that she had come to enjoy, in a way. She also realized that Kool, deep asleep, wasn't party to her prank.

Between the times she could scream, 'Li'll'y, you Si'll'y', the tone of her voice changed from shock to anger and into confusion and changed again into a silly laugh. The quick metamorphosis of her feelings reflected in the tone of her voice that changed so quickly and if one were to colour the different syllables of the words

'Li'll'y, you Si'll'y' to represent her feelings, it would have pronounced a rainbow of emotions. She picked up a pillow and beat Li'll'y with false anger, as Li'll'y giggled and hugged Kool closer still for the moment.

When Li'll'y realized Kool too had been stirred out of his sleep due to this commotion, she tried to spring out of his bed, suddenly shy, lest he mistakes her.

But, she found to her own surprise and pleasure that she could not bring herself to prise away from Kool's bare chest and wished to linger as long as decency permitted. After lingering for that silly moment, still half-willing to let go the luxury of Kool's closeness, she had to tear herself away wondering if Joy had detected her unfriendly greed and let Joy chase her all around the bed, both of them giggling.

Kool was startled at the amusement both the ladies were having at his expense. It didn't take much time to understand that he was lying on Joy's bed and felt a pang of guilt, for permitting himself to use Joy's distress the previous night and lying on her bed with her, without her expressed consent, while she dozed off. Consent or not, did he not take advantage of Joy's vulnerability?

No, he said to himself, ''advantage' is just not the word; should be 'malicious exploitation''!

He decided to defer pondering over the right word to describe his own impropriety, for later. He had to apologize to Joy and console her first.

But the mirthful burst of joy as she was chasing Li'll'y around and over the bed confused him. And where did Li'll'y come from'?

Li'll'y's presence and her pranks had softened the guilt both of Kool and Joy and they independently decided to deal with it later. The atmosphere was lighter because of the arrival of Li'll'y and Joy didn't fail to take note of it. Joy loved Li'll'y for it and had never enjoyed as happy a day as this, since the days with her sister Vaijay, now no more. Though Li'll'y overdid her pranks about Kool, she genuinely liked Joy as a friend and so Joy trusted her more than ever as a good friend and was not afraid of her as a boyfriend grabbing fiend.

9 Weird Claim

After Li'll'y left Kool and Joy with the club manager the previous day, she had dumped her training schedule with her team and went straight to meet Dan. She had hoped that the hostile reception to her Indian friends had nothing to do with Dan. Earlier, Li had inadvertently alerted Dan about the immense talent of her friends from India - the same evening she first met Kool and Joy at the stadium. Dan did not seem so concerned at this alert, yet he gave instructions to his team to watch out for the special talent and to prepare themselves for the same. She was sure that his instructions were innocuous and that he definitely had not given any orders to shove up the opponents. He wouldn't do anything so mean; probably the team overdid the brief and bullied her unfortunate Indian friends.

She found Dan at the centre court with his team. She didn't have to confront him to know if the team was responsible for the ill-mannered insults thrown at the Indians. The mood in the centre court said it all. The team was having fun at her expense for taking an interest in some dumb Indian mixed doubles players. 'What chance do they have against our formidable team? And they are already scared stiff', one of them laughed.

The team, armed with Dan's instructions, did not have to look for Kula and Jay as they did them favours by walking straight into their midst, while they were just discussing how they would 'watch out' for and 'prepare' the 'talented' team from India.

Each one was explaining his or her pet strategy that included 'neuter'ing them in public and others that would be shameful to describe in any forum including this book. Their strategy would have remained just jest and talk, if the duo had not landed right in the middle of their boasts, as if to challenge them to walk the talk. The Chinese team members were forced to act their hostile words or eat their humble pride. Thus, two of them had given the Indians a scare that they expected to put the duo's ambitions at rest. Egged on by their success that morning in scaring and driving them out of the stadium, they had decided to hound them whenever they had a chance and to break their confidence further. Li'll'y knew she had been right. The hostility was motivated... The hostility would continue...

Li managed to meet Dan in private and talk to him. Dan agreed with her politely that the team had overdone their brief and would advise them to back off. But he did not seem to bother, as the friendly game between China and India showed the next day.

Dan had the previous day called for the video of the Indians practice sessions they played between themselves, against Su and then against Li. It was Dan's idea to have the entire practice sessions and friendlies recorded to identify potential threats to the Chinese monopoly of the game.

Dan had personally watched the videos of the Indian duo playing. He did not like what he saw, meaning that he was impressed by the game of the two players and saw them as potential challengers to the Chinese dominance. They played like champions!

As a strategy, he made some important changes in the schedule of the next friendlies. He changed the second Chinese friendly to be played against Australia to one against India. India was supposed to have played its second friendly against South Africa.

The press went to town about the changes. That was considered an acknowledgement of an unofficial higher rating for the Indian team, while Dan commented it's much about nothing.

Dan wanted to pitch in not his best, but just the B team against the Indian team, without having to expose his top team. He just wanted to gauge the depth of their talent, analyse their style and to prepare the A team, in case the Indian team measures up to the expectations.

In the first friendly, Jay and Kula displayed their tremendous talent and beat Germany, which was considered one of the traditionally strong teams. Dan took notice and huddled with his team with strategy and advice. Dan raised the threat level from the Indian team to 'Orange', just below red. He was seriously concerned about the game he watched. The Indians were formidable, though clumsy; just that they played an unconventional style that the world was not used to playing or watching.

He cautioned the team enough. Do everything possible to win.

We can't just lose. The B Team felt it was much ado about nothing. He watched them walk away from him and continued to stare behind them long after they went beyond his sight. Should he have front lined the A Team? A lot was at stake and the entire nation's pride and expectations were on the shoulders of his B team, which was considered to be between the eight to fifteen world ranks. He would do everything to see the Bs win; everything!

The friendly with China started. Kula won his singles match against Yuang, without ruffling a feather. The ease with which he, a 'lowly' Indian, overran the 12th ranked player in the world, alarmed Dan. It was the first time the world took notice of India and spoke of India and TT in the same breath. Kool was in the world news, of every Newspaper, every magazine and every TV news channel. In normal times, the Indian tricolour would have been submerged in the sea of red flag. Today, the red flag and the Chinese ship floundered as the Indian stole the wind away from its sail.

Dan's pride was dented; not only his, but the whole of Chinese pride. The next day it was to be a match between Meiling and Jay. He will make sure that Meiling does not lose her match, and was ready to do whatever to ensure her win. He called Meiling into his office and discussed with her briefly. 'I will not go the way of Yuang', said Meiling determined to stop Jay and save the Chinese pride.

Next day at the friendly, Meiling walked away with the first and the second game. There was jubilation all around the stadium. During the third game, while Meiling took an early lead, Kool signalled Joy to concentrate; to meditate. Joy took a few seconds between points to meditate; closing her eyes and drawing a deep breathe during the only few seconds she could afford during the progression of the mach. It helped her a bit. She equalized and then edged past Meiling to win the third game in a see saw struggle. Before each of the fourth, fifth and the sixth games, Joy took seconds off to strike a padmasana pose to meditate, to concentrate, whispering 'Sri Rama Namaha', a chant to invoke the blessings of Lord Sri Rama and to give her the inner strength. She took all the three games.

Meiling didn't do anything right in the seventh game. The fact was that she could not do anything right. With every point that she lost, she lost her patience and her anger rose exponentially. She lost her cool and lost her mind.

She walked up to the referee with a complaint that stunned everyone including the referee. 'Jay is hypnotising me with the 'dot on her forehead'; the bindi. She practices sorcery and is trying to win this game by trying to control my mind. She is not playing fair'.

The complaint was the most outlandish the referee had ever heard. He was about to overrule the complaint. Something told him that he should not meddle in this decision.

There was a game being played outside of the court and that he better play along.

He referred to the Match referee and got the decision; To disqualify Jay for the rest of the Games for using 'mind control and manipulating techniques' and to declare Meiling the winner of the current match.

The Match referee did something better than what Meiling had demanded. He didn't seem to lose sight of the 'sacred' white ash that Kula had smeared on his forehead during the match and determined that Kool was assisting Joy in the control of Meiling's mind. Kool was banned from coming near the tables on any match during the rest of the Games that he was not playing. He was also forbidden to wear the 'sacred' white ash on his forehead during his matches.

Joy protested. Kool protested. The Indian team protested. The whole world was watching an audacious game being played off court by the Chinese Team Management using the referees. There was pressure on the Games officialdom to relent on this case, lest the credibility of the Games be lost even before the Games began.

10 The 'Slow' Command

That evening, Dan seemed to be wholly disconnected with the refereeing decisions that rocked the Games the previous evening. Or was he playing innocent? He seemed to be more concerned at the challenge to the Chinese order from the Indian team. He could not ignore this any longer. That Meiling barely scraped past the Indian in a wholly unconvincing manner aided only by a dubious complaint and an equally or more questionable refereeing decision, added neither to the Chinese prestige nor its confidence.

Obviously, everyone who was relevant to the match's outcome seemed to have been overwhelmed by the weight of expectations on the Chinese team and had chosen to play along with Meiling and had supported her claim.

He thought about Meiling's claim all evening and yet could not concur with her that Kula and Jay were practicing sorcery and he scorned at the idea that they controlled her mind, through something like black magic. He could proudly stand being profiled as xenophobic as he had been all his life and career. But supporting Meiling's claim would brand him as 'irrational', something he could not take. He had questioned Meilling sufficiently to conclude that she had no basis for the 'sorcery' allegation, except that she had been distracted by the red dot on Jay's forehead and that she had been disturbed by Jay's meditation.

Dan noted that while these dots and acts could distract and irritate an opponent player slightly, they are not illegal. He was certain that Meiling was only trying to do 'everything to win', as he had authorized her just the day before.

But even he was not prepared for the outlandish story that she had concocted to escape from the jaws of certain defeat, losing her mind in desperation. He had to be careful and not let his name be dragged into this mudslinging. Meiling was expendable, he thought. He was sure that at the end, such implausible allegations would not stick on the Indians or even on Meiling, but would stick on him, damaging his reputation and career.

He had been more or less sure, until the evening, of the stand he would take before the appeals jury, the next day. But, late evening, after he intently studied the strength and weaknesses of the Indian team from the videos of the friendlies, he wasn't sure any more.

The China-India friendly was a planned event, meriting Dan to order the recording of the matches from every angle and every perspective. He could capture not only the speed, trajectory and angle of the ball along with the position of each player, but also the spin, its axis, the speed of the swirl and the wobble, using powerful HD cameras. Just when he thought that he had found answers for every move of the Indians and had clearly laid out an excellent strategy, one particular exchange between Meiling and Jay bothered him. He viewed this exchange from several angles and he still could not comprehend what happened.

That pertained to the long frenzied rally of the ball back and forth, for the point that Jay scored just before Meiling had made that sorcery allegation. 'Meiling at one moment acrobatically digs out from close to the ground, a well-placed return from Jay and expertly sends it crashing towards Jay's side 'like a bullet'. Dan let a gasp of relief and appreciation for her and noticed that the crowd had gasped and been relieved too. The ball sped exactly like a bullet, till its flight towards the net, still on Meiling's side of the table.

Then the unbelievable happened. Kula jumps up from his seat on the side-lines and shouts, 'SLOW', as if to command the ball with a wave of his arm and the ball actually slows down to his command. Dan instantly thought of Meiling's sorcery allegation and then immediately followed up thinking it was irrational and plain stupid of him. His 'Party' trained mind could not reconcile to this bizarre claim.

But, it did look like Kula had commanded the ball to slow and it did slow in favour of Jay. It was true that Jay, who did not anticipate the beautiful return from Meiling and was a shade late in responding to the speeding ball had the benefit of not only a slower ball but also an alert just in time for her to adjust her footwork and smash it on Meiling's side to win the point.

But was this evidence in support of Meiling and her sorcery claim that looked absurd at first? He replayed the video several times. The two events happened almost at the same instant. One,

Kula jumps out of his seat and waves his arm as though to command the ball to slow, clearly shouting 'SLOW'. Two, the ball 'slows' on the trajectory. But it could be interpreted as Kula's waving and shouting happened a split second later than the slowing of the ball. However many times and whichever perspective that Dan watched the action from, he could neither say for sure if they were related at all. Nothing in his long coaching career had he watched anything that baffled him as much!

Meiling, who lost the point, in desperation had sought the referee's intervention against the 'dot', Jay's bindi, and invoked a sorcery claim. Dan knew that he had enough evidence to build a case against the Indian team, in support of Meiling's sorcery claim. But would he want to do that?

Dan had to present his official position within the next one hour on Indian appeal against Jay's ban. He had a rational mind and he did not want to stake his reputation on this irresponsible story that Meiling seemed to have made up.

On the other hand, the video could be an irrefutable evidence to prove that Kula did command the ball to 'SLOW', and the ball 'slowed'. He could convince the jury; at least, he could confuse them. He could exact his revenge on the Indians on behalf of Meiling. This video, he chided himself would cover him as much as a proverbial fig leaf would. Whatever position he would take would be the official Chinese position! He had an onerous responsibility and he was nervous. He could not decide until he stood up to present his case with the jury.

Having presented his case, he stepped out still dazed. He wasn't sure if the position he had taken was the right one and if it was the best to protect him and his team. He hoped he not only took the right position, but also worded it right.

Next, he let his entire team watch the video several times and come out with their solution to the puzzle. Each one came with a different version, mostly unprofessional and nothing convinced him. But he did not miss the point that all of them bordered on the sorcery claim, confusing him even more.

Li'll'y herself was perplexed by the mystery of the slowing ball to Kool's command, when she retired for the day.

11 Biting the Bullet

But then again, wouldn't it be fantastic if your favourite team's striker (in a soccer world championship) could see the movements of the ball in slow motion! Unfortunately, this advantage only belongs to flies.
Nature Neuroscience July 11, 2010

Why is it difficult to swat flies?
The answer is that, compared with you and me, flies essentially see the world in slow motion…
To illustrate this, have a look at a clock with a ticking hand. As a human, you see the clock ticking at a particular speed. But for a turtle it would appear to be ticking at twice that speed. For most fly species, each tick would drag by about four times more slowly… This happens because animals… piece together images sent from the eyes to the brain in distinct flashes a set number of times per second. Humans average 60 flashes per second, turtles 15, and flies 250… For Killer Flies it is 400…
The speed at which those images are processed by the brain is called the "flicker fusion rate"…
https://www.bbc.com/news/science-environment-41284065
Also watch:
https://www.bbc.com/news/av/embed/p05g6v23/41284065

Li'll'y coughed a bit, as she entered, to announce herself as she didn't want to overhear any confidential talk.

Kool turned around and smiled at her, waved and said, 'Listen, I was explaining one of the rare events that happens; TT ball slowing on its flight. Looks like Joy didn't see it slowing. She almost gave up on the ball that was speeding one moment and the next, slowed significantly. I had to alert Joy 'SLOW' for her to react in time for her to position well and smash a winner.

He complained to Li'll'y, 'How would she fare in the Games at this level, if she is not alert enough even to such changes'?

Joy asked Li'll'y, 'Do you observe slowing balls every time'?

Before she could compose herself to answer, Joy continued, 'Yeah, Kool had been training me to observe the balls carefully, but in spite of my best effort, I tend to miss some aspects of the balls in flight'.

Li'll'y discovered that this extraordinary talent to spot the ball's in-flight behaviour came naturally to Kool and that Joy had been trained on it. She was amazed at the incredible faculty they both possessed and trained themselves on. Li'll'y herself would give up her lifetime earnings and possessions to acquire such a skill.

Joy interrupted her thoughts and asked an important question. 'How did Meiling manage to slow the speeding ball mid-flight and why did she do it, when it wasn't to her advantage'? This thought never occurred to Li'll'y. So, if Kool had just observed the ball slow down, he didn't cause the ball to slow. At least there was no sorcery.

'So how did the ball slow'? She asked!

Kool came up with an equally implausible explanation, 'I don't think Meiling did anything to slow the ball. But consider this... The rally for the point had several highs and lows and when everyone almost thought she lost the point, Meiling succeeded to scoop the ball from a particularly difficult position and send it crashing onto the Joy side of the table. She had displayed tremendous acrobatic skills to retrieve the ball and as well smash it across to Joy's side, setting off a collective sigh and claps from almost tens of thousands of relieved flag waving Chinese supporters, which in turn could have triggered a strong enough air wave against the direction of the ball's flight causing the ball to slow considerably. Remember the TT ball has so little weight and the slightest air movement can alter its speed either way and could even make it sway.

Though he conceded it as 'just probable', it was Li'lly's turn to take a deep sigh at the dubiousness of the story. Either Kool was a genius or crazy. But it was the most probable explanation in the absence of any other plausible theory to explain the event. She had been fed up with the sh*t of a sorcery theory and this story sounded better in spite of it being stamped 'dubious' all around the ball that slowed. Li'll'y looked at him in incredulous amazement and Joy noticed it.

Joy prompted Li'll'y, 'Please ask him to explain his story of how acquired a keen eye for the in-flight behaviour of the balls', with the tone that said, 'that would be another story'.

Kool answered Joy's question without Li'll'y having to repeat it, 'I wouldn't say I acquired it. But rather I chance discovered it. I realized that it was innate in me and I believe it is native, inside everyone else too'.

He continued, 'While I was young, say, just fourteen or early fifteen, the bus I was travelling in met with a severe accident at high speed. I happened to be and I consider myself lucky, in spite of the great risk it posed on that day, to have been in the front seat as the bus that crashed on to a truck coming in the opposite direction. It was dark and probably I was the only one in the bus that was awake and most people in the bus were asleep, including, as was evident, the driver of the bus'.

'Though the bus travelling at great speed, as it crashed onto the oncoming truck, I remember clearly the bus seemingly moving in slow motion as it crashed and the glass splinters from the truck sprayed into the bus and onto my face that I had to impulsively lift my hands to cover, particularly my eyes. Though my response should have been instinctive and quick, I could see my fingers move into position in slow motion and trying to close the still wide gaps between them and to form a protective shield to my eyes and face.

I could see shreds of broken glass float and glide towards me in slow motion, backlit by the head lamp of the truck that we had just struck. It was a beautiful sight to watch dazzling diamonds of glass lazily floating towards me amid pitch darkness of the empty air. The air was empty even of its dust particles, courtesy the shower of rain that ended just a few minutes earlier that had washed them, the dust, down, leaving behind a spectacular darkness; only to be highlighted by the magnificent stars of glass in suspended animation'.

'Some of the glass splinters passed through the still wide gap between my fingers, and impinged hard on my face. The whole sequence of events was watched by me with my own wide open eyes and are still strongly frozen in my memory in slow motion, as though captured by camera. In truth, my face was bruised badly by the flying glass splinters. I was fortunate again; none of the shreds of glass hit my eyes that were open wide enough to afford me the grand view. But that's beside the point. All that is relevant was my discovery that I could freeze the high speed movement in my brain and mentally view the same in slow motion, while under huge stress, like when your life is at risk'.

'I still believe this happens to everyone and that I don't consider myself as special. I tried to ask several other persons who had such front row view of a similar crashing experience; someone who watched the whole crash sequence and still stayed alive to tell me what they saw. I never had a chance to meet any one qualified as above that could confirm my view. The few I met, said they were so scared that they instinctively turned their heads away from the scene or closed their eyes or both. Should I be proud that I could face the threat to my life without instinctively moving my head away or even closing my eyelids? I should have been cold blooded and with icy cold eyes', he shuddered at the memory.

'Should have been your 'bite the bullet moment'', an awestruck Li'll'y exclaimed.

'Talking about 'bite the bullet' moment', Joy interrupted, 'ask him about his 'bite the bullet' training methods', at which Kool frowned at her in annoyance.

Joy hid herself behind Li'll'y pretending to be scared and explained, "Biting the bullet' comment always embarrasses Kool, especially his crawl back at the end and he prefers not to talk about it. At least I am not supposed to remind him in the presence of strangers. But Li'll'y, is not a stranger? Is she'? She reprimanded Kool, as though it would be scandalous to consider Li'll'y, 'a stranger'. Kool smiled.

'Let me tell you, physics and physiology combined can explain this phenomenon. Normal vision does not see a contiguous flow of motion the way we perceive, but the images are presented by our eyes to the brain as sixteen to sixty four frames per second, strung together in sequence. The brain perceives the images served as a fast stream as a continuous moving picture. The basis of movies is similar. Movie actions are captured as continuous frames of individual images captured at the rate of twenty four images per second. When the movie projector runs them continuously and at the same speed, our eye presents the frames in one continuum, the brain perceives the images served as a stream, as an action movie'.

'So, if you wanted to capture a high speed train from close, you could capture at say, either at 24 frames per second or at 200 frames per second. If you re-run the 24 frames per second film on the projector at 24 frames per second, you would see exactly what our eye sees them physically, the train streaking past without capturing any finer detail.

Similarly, if you run the 200 frames per second film at 200 frames per second, you would still see the same; the train streaking past without seeing any finer detail. But if you could run the 200 frames per second film at 24 frames per second, you could see the train moving in slow motion with much more detail of each compartment and even the people moving inside the train'.

'Similarly, if you wanted to capture and show a bullet in motion, capture the motion of the bullet, say at 2000 frames per second and then run them at a normal 24 frames per second projector. You could see the bullet move in slow motion; at least you could see the bullet zip past you'.

'Assume that one is about to be hit in a life threatening accident and that the person's brain perceives that the threat to life is due to the speed of the object about to hit him, then his brain realizes that if it could track the object and present its movement in slow motion and with more clarity, it could help the person respond to the speeding object better and possibly the person could save himself'.

'In such a case, the brain gets so focused on the object or objects that are about to hit the person and most, if not all the power of the brain is utilized in acquiring, processing, visualizing better and instinctively reacting to save himself from the object and thus, the threat to life'.

'Yes, I had learnt in my science class that a housefly uses up to 60% of its brain power for its sight so that it could respond to dangers better; that's why it is difficult to swat a housefly'! Li'll'y observed.

'Exactly! Kool responded... 'I'm glad that you picked up the first time, what I consider a complex idea for most'.

Kool summarised, 'Thus with almost the entire processing power of the brain at its disposal, the accident response system enables the eyes to capture more frames per second than at normal times, say two hundred or more per second, to capture the object in more detail, say down to every inch on its path, against a norm of say, every foot. Not only that, it also activates the brain to visualize the same images captured at 200 frames per second by the eye at a very slow pace, say 24 frames per second or lesser.

It means you perceive more detail in slow motion and at a higher resolution. Instead of just a blurred image that streaks past in your view, you see the object move frame by frame in your vision, about ten times slower. All this happens instinctively and in real time'.

He continued, 'If I could see the details of the fast moving objects during life threatening times, I was sure I could do it under less stressful, less than life threatening situations, if I trained to focus enough.

At that level of detail and resolution, you should be able to see the ball much larger; the size of a cricket ball. You could also see it move, slow down, speed up, swing, spin, sway, roll, whirl, and wobble. Applying the same to the sound, instead of sight, the system should let you hear the ball 'swish', 'swishsh', or 'swishshsh' and sometimes just 'whirh' and at other times 'whirhrh''.

'If we could develop our senses to that level of alertness and attentiveness, agitate our brain and fool it, we could simulate a life threatening situation for the brain to respond to. We could successfully stir our brain to allocate more of its power towards the moving ball or whatever and to look at it at a detail that we wish to. It needs a tremendous amount of discipline, effort and focus to develop such skill. That's what I did'.

'I trained myself consciously to build that slow motion vision even in less than life threatening situations, though stressful; say, a TT ball in-flight. I think I am nature's most fortunate child'.

'I had an uncle who taught me yoga and meditation at a very early age. I didn't just learn them, but also worked hard to apply them. Today, my mind and body are so synchronized and under my control that I see what others could as well, but don't. I can also instinctively, speed up my physical response and flex my body reactively to the physical impulse, say, to a speeding ball; may be a bullet, if it was my lucky day'.

'Yes, I control my mind and what I see and hear; I do control my own mind. But not of others; I have never even tried. I don't even think it's feasible to control others'.

Li'll'y wondered if he had read her mind that was fed with a lot of gibberish about Kool and Joy controlling not just Meiling's mind, but also inanimate objects as a TT ball.

Kool continued, 'During Joy's game against Meiling, I saw the ball speed like a bullet from Meiling's racquet, a great shot from such difficult position, but before it crossed the net, slowed and wobbled as if it was hit by a gentle breeze moving against it. I can still see it spin and wobble lazily in slow motion, frozen in my memory'.

"All my early TT years I was trying to get Rajiv, Pari, Suresh, Sai, Ram, Niranjan and of course Joy to understand, see the ball and hone their skill. But only Joy picked it up from me and she now can see the ball as well as me and sometimes better. It's only very few times that she misses. I would say due to her lack of concentration sometimes. But I don't blame her; she is after all a child and is very inquisitive and her attention sometimes, though rare, deserts her".

'He talks like an ascetic', Li'll'y thought.

She reminded cautiously as if she didn't want to annoy Kool, 'I didn't hear any 'bite the bullet training methods'. Or did I miss something'?

Kool suppressed his annoyance with a quick smile, said, 'It's a long story' and started. 'While in college, I joined the photography course and was interested in high speed photography. I could shoot the breaking of soap bubbles, frog swishing its tongue to capture an insect and many other such fast action physical events on camera. I trained myself on visually capturing the same moments by focusing on the moving objects with just my naked eyes and without a camera.

I found success, largely due to my meditation and yoga. I had acquired or honed my natural, inborn abilities to see speeding objects in slow motion and at a higher resolution'.

"I wanted to test the limits of my newly developed High Speed sight, and track a bullet. But I didn't have access to a gun. For that reason, I joined the National Cadet Corps, NCC; a kind of citizen army, meant for students in India. I was eagerly waiting for our training on the use of guns. We were trained on a .303 rifle and we practiced shooting at the firing range, at painted circular targets 100-150 metres away'.

'After a few weeks of training, when we were confident of shooting at the target with reasonable accuracy, I ventured with my plan to my closest friend. I would stand beside the target, while he takes a shot at it. I would like to watch the bullets in slow motion, just as I did with the other speeding objects. He called me crazy and was against the idea. As it happens with young friends, he agreed at last, with some persuasion'.

'My friend was assigned the duty of cleaning the firing range on one of the mornings. We landed earlier than usual at the firing range well before others arrived. Gathering courage, I moved to the far end of the range and stood among the painted targets boards, quite close to one of them. My friend waved at me, probably pleading with me to abort the idea and come back. But I stood the ground resolutely. He realized that the only way to get me back before others arrived and discovered our plot was to aim and shoot. He did exactly that'.

'With an intense gaze, I could see the bullet whizz past me, though fast and hazy, tearing through the air and I could see the paraboloid laminar wave that trailed backwards from the bullet head. It was a wonderful sight, believe me; enough for a lifetime'.

'I had to instinctively move my head a couple of inches away to avoid being hit.

I had been ready to give my life for this scene, figuratively. It was later that I realized that I almost gave my life for it, literally'.

'The bullet had missed the target board by a foot, while missing my head by a fraction of an inch and hit a rock just behind me'.

'Great shot that was'! Kula took the chance to taunt his friend, who wasn't with them.

Li'll'y trembled as she heard the story. Joy trembled too, though she heard it the umpteenth time, just as she did every time.

'Truly, nerves of steel'! Li'll'y exclaimed, her voice quivering as she still didn't get over her shivers.

Joy giggled at this suggestion, 'Hear him fully'.

Kool continued, 'It was then I realized, I almost paid for the view of my life with my life, when I saw the rock just behind me blown to smithereens. Before it blew up it should have been the size my head! It had been so close and I believe that the instinctive, quick move I made away from the line of the bullet had saved me'.

'This memory still gives me creeps. I realized my nerves of steel had given way to nerves of jelly. I had difficulty walking back to the other side of the firing range and almost crawled the last fifty metres or so, only to find my friend slumped like a grounded jelly fish on the floor with his .303 beside him. He was normally the best shot in our group and seldom missed the centre of the target'.

'On that day, he missed it by a proverbial mile and almost

made a hole through my head. I shuddered to think, what if I hadn't instinctively moved my head few inches to the left'?

'We always don't need answers for our every question. I am still alive and here. That's what counts'.

'Bite the bullet'? Li'll'y trembled.

'Rather, sight the bullet'! Kool, deep in thought as a shiver ran through him too.

They were still all nervous as they all walked for dinner. Joy and Li'll'y were walking close on each side of Kool protectively and for security at the same time, each holding one of his arms tight, as they walked, without any of them realizing the incongruity and unsustainability of their relationships.

12 Saving Face

The Appeals Jury, who huddled together, eventually decided to let Jay play at the Games, though upheld her disqualification for the 'friendly' that she already played and lost. However, she was forbidden to wear the 'Dot' on her forehead as it could be used to 'mind control' the opponents. Kool was permitted to stay near the court when the Indian team played, but was forbidden from using the mesmerising 'sacred' white ash he normally could be seen sporting on his forehead. The members of the Indian team were forbidden from using any form of 'mind control techniques' including 'Meditation and Yoga'.

The ruling was face saving for the Games Management. The whole world had taken notice when they had chosen to suppress the most potential and growing challenge to the Chinese team before the Games in the most impudent manner and the credibility of the Games had taken a beating. The Appeals Jury showed real courage and a lot of sense in quickly and substantially overturning the earlier decision of the match referee and saved the Games from further disrepute. Dan was glad that the Appeals Jury did the right thing; neither here nor there. And he was even gladder that he had taken the right stand and his reputation was intact.

The Indian team was heard murmuring about the partial lifting of the disqualification and were definitely not happy with the loss of Joy's Friendly against Meiling. But there were voices within that said, 'But this is only a friendly, let it go'. Finally it was decided by the Indian Team Management to focus on the real Games and forget this loss at the Friendly as a bad dream and focus on their practice.

13 Spot-on against Deng

The Games had progressed for a week. Kool had booked a berth for a Quarter final show down against Deng. During the week, he had understood from some indirect observations of Li'll'y that Deng could have been behind the problems that Joy faced, including the 'hand-gun shot' scare that Joy was subjected to and the Meiling matter. He believed that Deng had instigated some of his team mates loyal to him, the 'Deng's Gang', to rattle the Indian talent and snuff them out, inside and outside the court.

Kool was looking forward to this match to settle scores. Kool, normally a cool self, never had been as bitter as on that day. It was not just rivalry any more, but chivalry as Deng had offended Joy not just once, but twice. He wanted to beat Deng in the Quarter Finals with vengeance and beat him badly too. This was the first time that Kool had ever got into a match angry with the opponent and with a mind full of vengeance. It showed in his game.

Kool was trailing and trailing badly in the first game 2-8. Nothing was working for him. He was hitting his shots all over, missing the table. He was over reacting to each stroke and making unforced errors. The anger and the vengeance in his mind were working adversely on him. He somehow forgot that raw anger doesn't help him overwhelm a challenge, while he should have been channelizing his anger and raising up to the challenge that Deng was. Deng was no ordinary player and even Kula at his best would have to struggle big against him. But in his anger, Kool exposed a fair amount of the chinks in his armour and was paying the penalty.

By the time Kool realized that his anger was actually counterproductive, the first game was over 11-5 in Deng's favour and that he was trailing the second game at 1-9, that he was almost half way on the path to losing his match.

Kool needed time to compose himself and reorient his energies. He can't afford to let Deng take any further lead. It would be disastrous. Kool knew that he had to act quickly and tactically, or else this game and the match would slip off his hands. He knew that during the last two games that he trailed Deng, his concentration had gone awry. Anger is such an enemy; worse than the actual enemy; the object of the anger itself. He needed to first flush out his anger.

Unfortunately, he was forbidden by the Games Appeals Jury from using yoga and meditation during the game. Meditation was his preferred mode of cooling his mind. He had to do something and quick. He focused hard on the ball. That was always his strongest points. But in this circumstance it was not enough.

Next, he wanted to try bringing up the object of his affections in his mind, between points, to neutralize his anger against Deng. He wasn't sure if it will work as he never tried this. But in the absence of any other proven quick relief from anger, he would try this. He forced himself to think of his mother. But his thoughts always wandered off to his Joy. It was the thoughts of kissing fabric dolls first, then her first handshakes that electrified him and then Joy lying on his bare shoulders deep asleep while he was running his fingers on her hair, and whispered, 'I Love you, Jay'. She smiling, still deep in her sleep, whispering back, 'I love you too, Kula', from her dreams.

When he was through with these thoughts, he had recovered to a healthy 9-10, though still trailing, in the second game. He had not only purged his anger, but also recomposed himself and had been instinctively fighting hard and wining points.

The Game went to the wire. Kool was serving 12-13 against a fighting Deng at his best. Just then, it happened. Kool's reverie was broken by 'Tongk', where a 'Tuck' was expected, as the ball landed on his side of the table from a stroke from Deng. The ball had hit an 'odd spot', behaved odd and scattered from the path, much different from a spin, kept low and unexpectedly quicker. Kool was caught on the wrong foot and wasn't at all ready for the bizarre ball. He lost the point and hence the second game to it. Deng, his coach and the crowd believed that it was his bewildering, killer hook executed as top-side spin or tilted topside spin that did Kula in and were celebrating.

Kool was disappointed, but recovered quickly. He had learnt something and had something positive to work on. He immediately memorized the spot, where the ball had landed, looked around and made sure that Deng was still revelling on wrapping up of the first and second game in his favour and was talking to his coach, Dan. Kool silently walked up to the table near the 'Tongk' spot and dropped the ball inches from above it a few times, around the spot where the ball behaved odd. He smiled when he consistently heard 'Tongk'.

In the third game, in spite of Deng showing his characteristic aggression, Kool was just ahead of Deng, who was hot on his heels. Then Kool did something that had Deng bewildered. He trained his strokes on the 'spot of Tongk' several times, with such accuracy that he found the exact spot on two occasions during the game, and the ball behaved as erratically just as it did earlier, but now to Kool's advantage. The ball actually bounced crazily off both these times, much faster and keeping much lower and randomly darting away from Deng, catching him on the wrong foot each time.

Kool and Joy had trained themselves hard to maintain remarkable accuracy landing the ball at precise spots of imperfection on the table. They had found ample opportunities to train themselves during their early days at Joy's home back in India as the improvised dining table had a few clear visible blemishes.

It took them great amount of focused training together with mental and physical control through Meditation and Yoga, to achieve that kind of mastery and accuracy to be able to exploit the little visible and unseen blemishes, during a fast paced game. They had often challenged each other to score a 'spot-on', meaning hitting the imperfect spots that scattered the ball unpredictably. Joy who was watching the match from the side-lines of the Deng match did not miss the 'spot-ons' and winked at Kool in celebration, when he afforded to meet her eyes after each of the point was won and she displayed the 'spot-on' count with her fingers, lest he lost count.

Deng was bewildered by the ball's behaviour both times and ended up losing the point. With these strokes, Kool mesmerised Deng, the World No.2 and the home crowd.

The fourth, Kool displayed tremendous form and character. Deng who started flying high with overconfidence slowly came back to earth, while Kool did not display any trace of his long lost anger or any of his impatience that he showed just a dozen minutes ago. Deng shook his head in disbelief as he was trailing right through. Kool wrapped up the game 11-8 in his favour. Kool was happy as he was seeing the ball as he should.

Another two 'spot-ons' that nobody else observed, except Joy, widened Kool's lead in the next game that he won too with 11-4 and surged into a lead. The four 'spot-on' strokes from the three games had bewildered Deng as he never had a clue as to what hit him. The bewitched crowd slipped into silent mode. Another day and another opponent, the spectators would have relished the wizardry that Kool displayed. But not today; their hero was being mauled and humiliated right in front of their eyes, by a 'non-person'.

In the last and the deciding game, Kool's characteristic, complex, powerful topspin-sidespin shots that sent Deng, already dented on confidence, scurrying all around the table without a chance.

Kool's mastery over the game found Deng wanting in every department of the game and Deng became nervous. Game and Match Kool!

Deng could not but evoke memories of Meiling's complaint that Joy and Kool used some form of witchcraft to hypnotize the opponents to either immobilize them or set them on the wrong foot. Strangely, the entire Chinese team that watched the action also thought of 'sorcery' during the second half of the match, belying their usually overconfident self and their rational national culture.

The truth was Kool had focused much on the ball and saw the ball better and in more detail, his core competence, to beat Deng. But more damage to Deng's confidence was done by the 'spot-on balls'. Deng had lost the mind-game and his will was defeated long before it showed on the score-line. Those who analysed Kool's game carefully did not miss the point that Kool had not made a single unforced error during the last four consecutive games he won in the match.

The bookies moved him up to the top in their list of favourites and betted on him to win the Men's Gold at the Games, if he continued to demonstrate a similar form throughout the rest of the Games. Connoisseurs and commentators of the game acknowledged the rise and the rise of the Indian duo and their unconventional game that baffled the Chinese team as well as the pundits alike.

14 Time-out

The entire Chinese team went into a huddle to understand the challenge from the Indian team. Dan felt the heat, but did not show it. He held a business as usual attitude. He asked the players to analyse the style of game that the Indians' played and methods to counter the same. The more they analysed using the best technologies at their disposal, the more they were disorientated. There was no style in the book that one could confine the game that Kula and Jay demonstrated and hence there were no ready reckoners to help decipher and help counter their game. They chose to improvise and innovate against each ball that they met instinctively and made an impulsive return that was unpredictable at best and bewildering at worst, for the opponent.

Li'll'y was part of the analysis of the game. She had insights of some extraordinary talent to sight the ball in slow motion and yet did not have answers to beat them, just like the rest of the team and the team management.

As a true Chinese patriot, she shared whatever she knew and learnt from her discussions with Kula and Jay with her puzzled team members. 'Kula and Jay have trained themselves through meditation to sight the speeding ball at a far slower pace and in more detail than others could see them and so responded better to it. They also play by their instinct and each ball was dealt with differently on its merit'.

She did not keep anything to herself as neither Kula nor Jay told her anything in confidence. Her team mates initially teased her when she explained this, 'So you mean Kula has HD camera fitted for his eyes that sees the ball and presents to him in slow motion'?

When she persisted, they first scoffed at her and later she was even accused of misguiding them for the benefit of her Indian friends. She knew it was time to stop then.

The team looked to Dan to provide them guidance and strategy. Dan was reluctant to acknowledge the new force in the game 'as a new force'.

He bravely stated, 'The Indian duo is not actually any threat to the Chinese dominance. They are having a lucky run in the games and that their luck is destined to run out soon'. He, with intent to soften the impact of the decimation of Deng at the hands of Kula and to dispel the gloomy mood that had set in, said, 'Deng is considered the best at the Game of TT ever and is still number 2. Deng just had a bad day. If there were to be a rematch tomorrow, he would win hands down'.

Deng, who was silent with the heaviness of anger, reluctantly agreed with Dan and spoke positively, for the benefit of his team. 'Yes Dan, I will have to wait for my revenge, though'.

But he later murmured something as Dan waved at him to stop before he spoke out his concerns and do any further damage.

Dan spoke aloud, 'The depth of the Chinese talent is so great that the 'lucky' Indians will find themselves against a hard and impenetrable Great Wall of Chinese talent and will be packed off in the next round. By playing meticulously as per the intensive coaching the Chinese team received in preparation for the Games, the Chinese dominance will be established'.

The meeting concluded with grimness that one associate with the military strike force ahead of a suicide mission.

'Status Quo; play as per guideline', was the preferred strategy.

Li'll'y saw nothing short of disaster in the making and that mere bravado was not the best of strategies.

The Chinese players were all whispers, after the analysis, about the black magic the Indians brought to the table. In a society where nothing but the official line can be voiced and heard, the whispers were suppressed, though did not die. The lack of debate stifled any rational explanation to the ascendency of the Indians and the tame submission of the Chinese frontline, while the suppressed whispers gained onto everyone's nerves and spirits. The Chinese team slumped into a negative, defeatist mode long before the start of the next match against the Indians, in spite of the bravado.

The next match happened to be the Semi-Final game between Jay and her Chinese opponent Zhen Zhen.

15 Sleeping with the Enemy

'Li', someone called out, as she reached the stairs on her way out. Li'll'y had an appointment with Kool and Joy to meet them that evening for dinner. She was already late due to the team meetings. So she turned back sulking, but concealing her annoyance with a smile.

'Dan wants to see you', someone yelled from the crowd.

She shrugged, wondering what he had to say, so late after he had already discussed so much. While on the way, she heard the words 'Traitor', 'sleeping with the enemy' distinctly from the conversation her colleagues were having. She thought nothing about them; may be they were some Hollywood movie titles. But as usual, she was ready to help Dan, if she could; if he asked her to run an errand or to train one of the players.

She stepped into Dan's office and he was not alone. Deng was with him. It should be very important if Deng was with him for a discussion. She stepped forward, half curious, half cautious.

Dan spoke first, 'Your Indian friends seem to be having a great run'? as he offered her some black tea. She just smiled cautiously as she had a premonition; saying something now could be used against her.

Deng intruded menacingly, 'This Indian guy, he seemed to know my strength, strategy and training and seemed to have well prepared to counter my style of game. Any guess how he prepared so well'? Deng's blatant hostility was showing.

Li'll'y sipped her tea slowly to avoid replying immediately, was considering her reply.

Then realizing both Dan and Deng were waiting for her reply, she asked, 'Are you sure that Kool had played a counter game to yours? My opinion was that Kool doesn't play counter games. He in fact is known to play counter for every ball, irrespective of the players and styles'.

Deng spoke again accusingly, 'You aren't answering my question. How did he get inside information on my strategy, strengths, weaknesses and training that he exploited my weaknesses quite well? I am reminding you about his selection of shots that caught me on the wrong foot several times. How could he zero in exactly on these shot selections, without inside information on my weaknesses'?

Deng's direct accusation shocked her into silence. She looked at Dan and expected him to support her as he knew her personal integrity. But as Dan shied away from meeting her eyes, she knew that the situation was more serious than she had first imagined.

Deng challenged her directly, 'Did you share our team strategy with strangers'? She was desolate and she did not know what to say. 'What else did you inform them? Strategies? Tactics? About our diet? Our fitness programs? Do you understand that you have caused us great harm'? She was shaken by the direct allegation and was outraged. She realized that anything she said would not help her as Deng and Dan seemed to have made up their minds already.

Definitely an angry response would destroy any chance for her; she composed herself as she started, 'I have not shared any information with my friends. We used to go out to dinner and I played host to them as they were new to China. Nothing more'.

Deng wasn't finished with her yet and asked her coldly once again, 'What kind of black magic do they perform? Earlier, with Meiling and again in today's game'?

'Is Deng joking, or was he testing her'? She suppressed her giggle, replied as earnestly as she could, 'I have not heard of black magic and don't believe in it'.

Dan, trying to be conciliatory, said, 'We will talk again tomorrow evening'. It is better for you to come clean. Don't defend yourself, if you have done something wrong, as you know the punishment would be bigger, if you did not admit your role, and yet was proved by proper evidence. Let me tell you, there is evidence'.

Was he threatening her or advising her? She had no way to learn from his face, as he remained impassive. She had been standing all the while, as she had wanted to go as soon as possible. But now when Dan asked her to leave, she wondered if she should leave too soon without explaining herself properly.

She gathered courage to tell him, 'Dan, I have done no mistake. I have never betrayed my country and never will. Kool and Joy are just friends of just ten days. Though I like them, my friendship with them is insignificant compared to my love for my country'.

At this, Deng stared and nodded at Dan as if to prompt, rather remind him of his responsibility and Dan mumbled something that was not audible to her.

Deng, impatient with Dan intervened and asked her with a cold face, with Dan still shying away from facing her, 'How often do you sleep with this Indian'?

She stood still totally dumbstruck, shaking her head in disbelief, and burst into tears. She did not expect this even from Deng. She expected Dan to protest at this question and protect her; Dan, whom she considered as a father figure, ever since she landed from her home province to train on TT. But, there were no place for sentiments and emotions in China. No support can be expected towards persons accused of betraying the country. Fathers, brothers, sisters, husbands, wives, friends, children; everyone would desert them. She knew that her coffin was being nailed and she was as good as dead.

Dan seemed to soften a bit, before his face hardened again and placed a bombshell, a photograph, in front of Li'll'y.

The printed photograph, her own selfie, showed her lying on one side of Kool's bare chest, while the other side of his chest was occupied by Joy, all of them, including her, possibly sleeping.

Somehow she had managed to capture all of them including her with eyes closed and didn't look like a selfie at all. Whoever saw the photograph did not see the whole picture and would not be able to see it too, even if she explained it now. The question was, how did her selfie get into Dan's hands? Looking at the photograph Li'll'y realized that she was in deep trouble and her fate was sealed for life. Her head was spinning. The last she remembered was her trying to grope for the chair as she slumped to the floor, the tea cup and the chair crashing on top of her. She had a delusion that someone shouted far away 'sleeping with the enemy', before she passed out.

16 Detention

When her mind had run through the wonderful time she had in the last two weeks with her new friends Kool and Joy, she felt better, though still on the cold bed in the 'run down hospital of some sort', lonely as hell!

She decided to talk to Dan and immediately. She looked for her mobile again, but couldn't find it. The nurse who attended her wasn't helpful and answered her just with a purse of her lips. When she asked second time, she just shrugged and walked off without a word. So, she slowly walked up to the door and then to the passage leading to the nurse's cabin.

The nurse was annoyed seeing her. 'Go back to your bed. You are not allowed to move out'.

Li'll'y was irritated at the behaviour of the nurse and said sternly 'I just want my mobile phone. I could not find it in the room'.

She was plain rude, 'No mobile phones, get back to your...'

'Can you tell me, what happened? Why I am here? Which hospital is this? I want to speak to Dan. He should have visited me, when I was asleep. I see some flowers. He must have brought it'.

The nurse got her chance, 'This is not a hospital, if that would please you. You are not allowed to stroll around here. I don't know the answer to your questions. Even if I know, I am not authorized to talk with you. No one here is'.

'What's the time'?

'6:30' the nurse grunted and with a tinge of sadistic pleasure, 'Wednesday, evening'.

Li'll'y was alarmed that she had slept for almost about two days; this was evening and not morning.

The nurse continued proudly having demonstrated her enormous power over her, 'If you do not return to your cell now, I will have to restrain you and report to them'.

Li'll'y felt like she was hit by a bolt, 'Cell? I'm held in detention already'? Her worst fears had come true. She felt dizzy, but managed to hold on to the chair.

She slowly walked back to her cell.

'And there could be more punishments on top of this. Would I be thrown in a dungeon as a traitor and worse forgotten forever. Or, would I have to face a firing squad'? she trembled at the possibility.

'I would want to die rather than carry such a tag. But would they let me die by myself'?

Next she remembered her Indian friends. Had they been incarcerated too? She shuddered.

She wished, 'Let 'his bitterness cool off by harassing me. But with vengeance written all over on his actions, nothing was improbable'.

'Deng had a photograph, a selfie with all three of us together; something that would seal their fate too; the fate of all of us'. She recalled the selfie that Dan had shown her.

'Someone with a vulgar mind had stolen my selfie of a simple, friendly and jestful incident; no, not even an incident, it was a gesture, and concocted a crass story and had used it against me'.

'Why me? I have never consciously offended any one. I have always endeavoured to be the friendliest creature on earth and the most pleasant. I believed that I had no enemies, ever in my life'!

Political relationship between India and China has been low always, ever since the Sino Indian war of 1962 where India was handed a humiliating defeat. India has ranked very low in Chinese public opinion, ever since.

While China has been ascendant in every sphere ever since, India has remained deep in the morass created by their chaotic, crazy, lazy democracy showing only an occasional will to rise, followed by long periods of slumber. Chinese confidence and respect also has surged and the nation has been collectively challenging the world order in economy and geo-politics, while India has been relegated as a sleeping giant, and drawn derision within the developed world, not just in China.

Indian sport has always struggled to gain a few medals in international sports, while China has zoomed to Number 1 position in just a few decades. In Table Tennis, Chinese domination of the game has been complete and TT has been identified with the Chinese nation than any other sport. To be challenged in this domain by the Indians who have never had a single player in the top 50 ranks and to beat world number 2 at the prestigious Games to cap on other successes, was taken as an affront to the Chinese nation. So the key links in the chain of Chinese team management, prodded by a bitter loser, Deng, unwisely chose to make it difficult for the Indians to reach the top and further, to mete out exemplary punishment to Li'll'y, the known friend, sympathiser and possible collaborator of the Indian players.

The second reason could be Li'll'y herself. She has been a face of truth and integrity within the Chinese TT establishment, sometimes to the chagrin of the other team members. By her truth and integrity, she may have stepped on a few toes at different times in her career. While she had been rewarded with enormous goodwill, she had also collected doses of such bad will, albeit small, from her daily interaction with others. Let us say both goodwill and the bad will collects in the pot of the person. The goodwill that's lighter and floats for others to see and the bad will that they have gained being heavier, even if too small, collects at the bottom, as deeper malice.

Soon as the good will is larger quantity, fills the pot and overflows; hence never increases beyond a maximum limit. The bad will that flows in smaller proportion into the pot along with the larger goodwill, gains in size at the bottom unseen every day, displacing the good above it. Thus someday there is more bad will than good in the pot.

Soon without anyone realizing it, the bad will pushes out the last drop of the floating good from the pot and starts showing. Then it is too late for the person to purge the bad will, before it causes significant damage. That's how Li'll'y went from good to bad over the years. All the good she gained has flowed over and would not help her now. Her woes, 'bad will' filled her pot and will never recede from now, and any goodwill that is poured in next will just flow over without being retained.

'Yes, I was too good for my own good'!

She strongly suspected, 'I could have been sedated rather heavily or drugged'.

She remembered the tea served by Dan, 'That was unusual. Why did he make an exception on that day? May be he spiked it to make it soft and easy for me to reconcile with my detention. Else I may have been walked out of Dan's office at the stadium in handcuffs'. She shuddered to think of that possibility. But again drugging could be standard procedure on criminals to break the person's Defenses and help interrogators extract information from them while they stayed subconscious and in delirium'.

She shocked herself by thinking of herself and criminals in the same breath.

'I believe that the entire situation is out Dan's hands now. It would be Deng all the way'.

She searched her memory, 'Did I ever rub Deng on the wrong, any time'?

She couldn't remember; except that Deng had shown an interest in her more than a year ago.

Deng was known to have a voracious appetite for young girls of class. The girls didn't mind and they obliged. It would do them good to have a relationship with the then World Number 1 and China's favourite hero. They fell on him like fleas against a bright street lamp, standing tall. They gave him what he wanted, but got nothing in return; no relationship and eventually perished - 'like fleas'. He didn't even remember them next time. Li'll'y was one of the very few of the girls who ignored Deng. Deng never asked twice.

'May be he felt snubbed and wanted to show me, my place. Or maybe I offended one of his several mistresses, unintentionally though. I may never get to know'.

While she had slept for two days, probably sedated, her world had turned topsy-turvy. She fell on her little hard bed and sobbed, till she lost herself into sleep again.

17 Recalled to Life

Large numbers of Chinese citizens have been held incommunicado for days or months in secret, unlawful detention facilities. These facilities, known informally as "black jails" (黑监狱) or "black houses" (黑房屋), are created and used primarily by local and provincial officials to detain petitioners who come to Beijing and provincial capitals seeking redress for complaints that are not resolved at lower levels of government. Public security officials in Beijing and other cities have... in at least some instances, have directly assisted black jail operators... Detainees are often physically and psychologically abused. Many are deprived of food, sleep, and medical care, and they are subject to theft and extortion by their guards. They have no access to family members or to legal counsel or to courts... The Chinese government denies the existence of black jails.

Human Rights Watch (HRW) is a non-profit, nongovernmental human rights organization

Li'll'y was later moved to a different cell and was under intense interrogation, using coercive, brutal and sometimes inhuman methods for over a month.

After the dreadful month, she lay crumpled on her bed; half-dead, physique and psyche; resigned to wait for further horror to unfold on her.

At last they gave up and concluded, 'She is innocent; neither intention nor action that betrayed the Nation and her team'. The interrogators surprised her, though pleasantly. They did not produce her 'selfie' as evidence of her nexus with the Indians.

Just when she believed that her fate was sealed for life and nothing but a miracle can save her, the miracle was happening.

'How come they did not use the most formidable evidence at their disposal against me? Or are they playing a cat and mouse game and toying with me, before the final formalities? They should be sick in their mind to be playing games at this stage'.

Li'll'y waited in suspended animation for the eventuality, but it never happened. They decided to let her off the hook without any reference to the 'selfie'.

There seemed to have been protests from the Chinese TT Federation and the Chinese Team Management for letting Li Ling off so easily. The Chinese Federation pushed hard by the 'powers that be', accused the interrogators of buckling to certain power centres and wanted justice for Deng and Meiling. They tried hard to justify her detention and the humiliation that they wrecked on Li'll'y and they knew that if Li'll'y was let off they would have to face her with their faces blackened. They hung on to their cooked up theory about her misdeeds and claimed that the interrogators did not use strong enough methods to extract the 'truth' from her.

The chief interrogator just shrugged and said, 'This is our finding. But if you still suspect her, she is still with you and you could do what you want with her'.

At last the authorities and the interrogators appeared to have worked out a compromise. Li'll'y will not be let of just like that, but will be sent to reformation 'Home' to undergo 'soft' labour for six months. There was nothing soft about the labour and neither was it 'Home'. The work, in fact, was back breaking and could be called torture.

'Home', also infamously known as the 'Black Jails' or 'Black Houses' was euphemism for Hell or a torture chamber, where extra judiciary authorities decided to punish a person for the 'crimes' they didn't commit or when they consider any one as a nuisance to the Government, like petitioners against unpopular Government actions or those adversely affected by court judgements.

Li'll'y observed, 'This particular 'Home' had the reputation of subjecting the inmate to undergo the entire miseries that the inmate sentenced for life would be expected to undergo during his life term and serve them compounded and compressed in a short term of 6 months. Most detainees sent to this 'Home' can't stand the pain of the hard labour and humiliation and chose to violently confront the authorities, and were charged of violence against the state and were sent to dungeons. Many of them went mad from the experience, while some are known to have committed suicide. Quite a few died of torture. Either way it was called death due to natural causes of heart, renal or liver failure. Once they were dead, it made no difference, did it? A few, but very few, who were still sane at the end of the 'home' experience, escaped to live a low profile, sedate life. It was the extremely lucky few who could at least redeem a part of their original life'.

Li'll'y was one of the 'extremely lucky' very few'. She indeed considered herself privileged to be 'recalled to life'.

18 Picking up pieces

Six months later, when Li'll'y was released from 'Home', she tried to find what happened to Joy and Kool. She learnt that the next day after Kool had demolished Deng, while she was still under detention and in sedation, Joy had lost her Semi Final game against Zhen Zhen, her Chinese opponent due to dubious refereeing. She was afraid to talk to her colleagues, who could have first-hand knowledge of what happened on that day. So, all she knew was hearsay. She however, corroborated most of the hear stories watching TV snippets, videos from her friends' mobiles and some of the videos of the Games coverage.

Joy had a tough match against her Chinese opponent, Zhen Zhen and the game was on the decider. She had earlier faced the match point against her at 10-6, from which she had rallied and managed to gain a one point lead over her opponent and was serving for the match at 11-10. The referee had given a wrong call against illegal serve – as the ball was struck inside the playing surface for the serve. It was evident during later replays that the ball was struck well outside the playing surface and the serve was quite legal. The spectators, largely host Chinese, who had expected an easy Chinese win, first gasped and then booed Joy and bayed for her blood. Li'll'y first thought that it was just a bad umpiring call by a smart alec referee, who habitually taught a few rules to champion players, though he himself may not have got a single serve right in his lifetime.

Next, the Chinese girl had found the side of the table, at the edge, rather than the top, which the referee ignored and awarded the point to her. There cannot be two wrong umpiring decisions in succession. It somehow seemed sinister.

'Was the referee playing for the Chin54ese team'? mused Li'll'y.

Li'll'y didn't fail to notice that none, except the small Indian delegation, bated an eyelid at this wrong decision and a visibly enraged referee disallowed the appeal from the Indian girl. Distrustful and helpless, Joy had to serve the match point against herself.

It was a great intense topspin serve that had kept just above the net and on touching the other side of the table, had hurriedly dipped past the table barely an inch above it's edge, that a bewildered Zhen Zhen, responded by lofting the ball sky high. But all of Joy's gallant effort was in vain as the referee intervened to declare a re-serve, saving Zhen Zhen some embarrassment.

'Nets', he had said.

Li'll'y watched Joy at her wits end, as she could only stare in disbelief at the referee, arms open as if in appeal; the Indian team manager had also thrown up his hands as if in appeal, but had been disregarded. The re-serve had ended dismally, as the referee again called Joy for a foul. He contended that Joy had touched the playing area of the table with her non-playing left hand, while Joy was quite conscious and sure she didn't. As she threw her hands in appeal, she instantly knew from the look of the umpire that it would be dismissed, and burst into sobs. The Match was lost for Joy. Zhen Zhen had coasted to the finals to make it an all Chinese Final encounter at the Games.

It was evident to Li'll'y that Joy had been served with at least three consecutive wrong umpiring decisions in the end game, if not four, even giving Zhen Zhen the benefit of all doubt. That sealed Joy's fate. She should have won the game and match, but she had lost both. She was declared a losing semi-finalist assured, of a Bronze medal for joint third place.

Next, Li'll'y heard of the shockwaves that had shaken the Games and the entire TT world, set off by Joy during the Prize Ceremony the next day evening. Joy had broken down during the Prize Ceremony and declined to accept her Bronze medal at the podium. She had left the Bronze medal at the feet of Zhen Zhen and topped it saying, 'You deserve it'. Her bold voice was heard on TV news all over the world. The shocker from Joy was covered live across the world and had the entire Games Management up in arms against Joy. She probably thought that her action would bring the attention of the whole world towards the injustice meted out to her and probably believed that with a kick in the back, the system would be spurred to correct the injustice. But the system that she had faith in proved to be paranoid and myopic and saw ominous threats to itself from the actions of distressed players like Joy.

The Games organizers were not kind to her and had recommended to ITTF to ban Joy for life.

But the ITTF that had stripped her of her Bronze, banned her for just three years, probably convinced that three years were enough to kill the spirit and the game of a young player. By her immature actions, Joy had precipitated her own doom.

The Indian team management had initially had supported Joy and made a protest and were determined to bring justice to Joy. However, the next morning the Indian team management had withdrawn their protest to the rude shock of Li'll'y. Instead the team management had backed the ITTF ban on Joy and announced that there would be a detailed enquiry back home on Joy's conduct and suitable action would be taken in the 'spirit' of the game. However much Li'll'y tried, she couldn't find what transpired during that intervening night. Thus the Indian official justice for Joy ended rather miserably. 'The Indians will have to be defeated, somehow', Dan had commanded. Li'll'y reflected long afterwards that Joy was defeated exactly as he had said; 'somehow'! All that Li'll'y could was to shed silent tears for her unfortunate friend from India.

Li'll'y did not know what had happened to Kool, except that that he did not play his Semi-finals against Jiang. Unfortunately, there was no information except that the website listed the match was conceded to Jiang, as Kool had reported sick. She did not believe the official version on the website. There should have been something more sinister than that.

She was afraid that Kool and Joy could have been arrested too. Anything could have happened, being China, especially, when powerful, yet insecure people like Deng felt rubbed on the wrong side. She considered her options to find out about them. One of the ways she could have found out about them was to contact them in India. But she had an uneasy feeling her phones, emails, even her Air Mails were being monitored. She had avoided discussing this topic with her team mates for the fear of being reported and retribution that could follow.

After going through what she went, she neither knew who her real friends were nor whom to trust. Most of the friends she counted on avoided her and she had lost confidence in them. She scanned all the Chinese news sites and the 'Games' news for reference to Kool and Joy. But she did not get a single news story about them both. It looked like the news about them was censored. Finally, she took courage to scan all Indian newspapers online, to check for any players who were missing in China during the Games, assuming that there would have been a furore in India, in case of either Kool or Joy or both being arrested. She found none.

Just when she was about to bury Kool and Joy in the depths of her mind, an Air Mail brought her a wisp of fresh air and kindled pleasant memories that were a torment only days earlier.

Who wants to send an old fashioned Airmail in these days of email and social media? The Airmail didn't carry any name or address of the sender. But by the handwriting she recognized it was from Kool. She had learnt to be careful. She did not open the Airmail immediately. She looked for tamper marks and if the letter had been subject to scrutiny, as casually as she could. She would only be surprised if an Airmail, wasn't being scrutinized, given her past troubles with the authorities.

'There aren't significant marks that were visible; or it is just not evident'? Li'll'y thought, 'Have I become so paranoid in the past year or so that I suspect everything'. In a way being paranoid helped her survive, though not succeed. But it also made life difficult for her as she lived in fear of the authorities' every day. One wrong word or deed could send her spinning back to the Home, or worse, a dungeon for life.

She remembered the only time she had hugged Kool for a selfie, though just for a short couple of minutes, while he was asleep in Joy's apartment. She was aware that every copy of the selfie had to be destroyed long back, but the picture had been frozen in her mind.

She could see from the stamp that the Airmail was sent from within China, not India. That was reason for more excitement.

She did not open the Airmail immediately. She had reasons. First she had to conceal her excitement. She looked around if someone was watching, as she did not want to give herself away to 'watchful' eyes or to the surveillance camera focused on her all day. She considered taking the letter to the washroom, the only safe and private place in any of the buildings in China, without being watched. However, she decided to open Kool's air mail only when she was in the privacy of her car on her way back home later that evening. Consciously, looking disinterested, she tossed the air mail on the corner of the desk that would be glaring to the camera and pretended to work on her laptop.

She smiled again thinking of Kool. Blame it on love? She was all of 21 years and didn't have any boyfriend. It was a scandal in Shanghai for a girl over twelve not to have a boyfriend. But she never thought it important. She had never aspired for a life like her other friends. She had been brought up by her father, who she respected, as her mother had died while she was still a child. Her father brought her up as a beacon of virtue and maturity. After her mother, her father never married again and was content living in the memory of her mother, till he died a few years ago.

She told herself very often, 'I would give myself up when I meet a person who shared my feelings about love, marriage and life'. She hadn't yet found one.

Kool! Just his thoughts made her heart flutter and her mind dance, as she whispered his name to herself.

She wasn't ready to concede to herself that she loved him, as she watched her blemish less face on the front camera of her smartphone in delight and adjusted the strands of hair that fell on her temples as though she was all ready to meet him.

Somehow, Kool had broken the unseen cordon around her by tracing and reaching her from within China. She felt a wondrous joy as though she had been fertilized by one of a million Kula's sperms that succeeded in breaking the cordon around her ovum at last. She blushed and chided herself for such exciting yet unholy thoughts about Kool and herself. After all, she knew he belonged to Joy, her good friend. However, the next moment Li'll'y's spirit sprang up and she with her characteristic twinkle of the eye exclaimed to herself, 'What's between friends'.

She had tasks to do. She decided that she will think of Kool and his letter only while on the car on her way back home and not before.

19 The Bristo Bar

Kool's letter was short. 'I'm in China. I had sent several emails and Airmails that weren't responded to. I hope all's well. I don't think your silence is voluntary.

I had the fortune of finding your current position from a contact in China, where I am currently travelling. I also heard that you used to work as a TT coach in Shanghai till a few months ago and hadn't heard of since. I hope that you still stay in Shanghai'.

He didn't mention his contact and left no contact coordinates of his. He neither mentioned his name anywhere on the letter.

'I would find an opportunity to meet you soon. I hope I could afford the time and space to meet you during his stay. He found a good restaurant and would be glad to host her soon. Please wait to hear from me'.

It looked like he was elaborately plotting to find her and meet her clandestinely. So he has had bitter experiences with the Chinese authorities too, during his last visit. That explains at least partly why Kool and possibly Joy had dropped off their next matches at the last Games. For the moment, it looked as though, he was also playing cat and mouse game with the authorities, as he wasn't ready to expose himself and fall in any trap. If his Airmail had been pried into, the investigator would have no clue where to find Kool, except that he was in China and he would attempt to meet her very soon. Of course, it would be easier for the snooper to follow Li'll'y and aid a trap around her. But Li'll'y hoped that Kool had worked out some smart plan to hoodwink that someone. 'Kool is not dumb', Li'll'y smiled to herself.

She had been averse to risk these days. But, whatever the risks, dropping a chance to meet Kool was not an option for her.

Li'll'y was ready to be surprised. She knew Kool's entry would not be dramatic, but will be exciting. She had to wait for him to make his move as she could not do anything proactively. The next two days she watched every shadow, hoping to find Kool at the end of its feet, but was disappointed. The third day, while she was returning from her Training centre near the Shanghai Indoor Stadium, she went through her normal Line 4 and changed to Line 8 at the South Xisang Road Junction and reached the Huang Xing Park Metro Station, near where she stayed. As she was pushing herself against the crowd to get off the metro at her destination, somebody ahead of her, trying to get off too, stuffed a piece of paper into her hands, walked off quickly, without turning to look at her. She was not the type to pick up all the hand-outs that were pushed into her hands by youngsters promoting shops, products and local events. She didn't bother about the piece of paper that slipped off her hand as she stepped out of the train.

Li'll'y then realized that she has been expecting somebody, somewhere, sometime soon. She looked at the one who pushed the piece of paper into her hands. She found him walking briskly towards the escalator, covered fully from head to toe, protecting against the autumn cold that was not yet so severe for such total coverage. She measured him and weighed him with her eyes and could he be…! Her heart pounded in excitement. She turned and tried to step back into the train to pick up the yellow scrap of paper, with green print. But alas the doors of the train closed before her and she could only watch the sheet of paper gaining speed and vanish from her eyes as the train sped away from the station, carrying the yellow coloured litter that could have carried the directions to him.

She cursed herself for not being alert enough to the possible reunion with Kool.

As she ran out of the Huang Xing Park station, Li'll'y looked for signs of the gentleman, fully covered with winter clothing. He had melted in the crowd without a trace. So she could have lost the most important message of her life. She decided to linger on for a while waiting for a miracle that could bring Kool back. She tried not to look stressed as she was observing all around her. A young boy was filling promotional hand-outs on a newspaper stand, marked 'Please take one'. The brochures were bright yellow ones with green print. She impulsively pounced on to the news stand and pulled out a single copy, upsetting the whole stand. The boy shouted at her in annoyance, but she didn't seem to care, said 'Sorry' and walked away with the prize catch.

The green print on the yellow hand out announced.

Happy Hours for Two
Buy any drink and get one free

At the
The Bristo Bar
Huang Xing Park
Metro station

Li'll'y charged back into the Metro station without giving any option for prying eyes to follow her.

Part 3: Joy

20 Twin Sisters

The twin sisters in their early teens, Jayanthi and Vaijayanthi lived in Mathur, a small town in Tamil Nadu, India. They studied in the same class and the same section. They were known to be chatterboxes of the school as they could chat incessantly on a good day, on a normal day and on a bad day. The Principal who was one of the fans of their incessant chatter was sure that it would do them good rather than bad. They both played TT in school regularly and always played for fun, so never could move up to the top three medal spots. They were never known to leave each other's company. They were so close that other friends never ventured either among or between them.

One Sunday, when Jay and Vaijay were playing in their bedroom, they were jumping on their bed and they were throwing their colourful dhuppattas up and down and they enjoyed the dhuppattas soaring like kites and gliding downwards from the ceiling, within the room. Some of their dhuppattas hung from the wings of the ceiling fan and looked splendid; flowing down like frozen, coloured waterfalls. The ceiling fan wasn't running due to power cut in the area.

Jay's mother called out for one of them to come to help her. They weren't decided who should go and demanded of the other to go. When Mom insisted, Jay left as she was more amenable of the two. Mom had sent Jay on an errand and she ran skipping away with her rope.

After nearly fifteen minutes of silence from the room, their Mom came into the room to check. She had a chuckle in her voice, as she went into the room, 'How could my chatterbox stay so silent'?

She found a ghastly sight. Vaijay was strangled by her own colourful dhuppatta that was hanging from the ceiling fan that was now creaking, unable to run; power having been restored. She tried to revive her, but no use. Her neighbours rushed to her help, but no avail. Her husband rushed from his office with the doctor only to confirm the tragedy.

The entire streets wept. The entire school wept. Jay did not weep. She wasn't reconciled to her dear Vaijay passing away, leaving her alone. She believed that she was having a bad dream and she would eventually wake up to find her sister Vaijay playing beside her full of life.

Jay felt shattered and refused to go to school, without her sister. She grieved all days and all nights, but without tears. She had started avoiding all friends from school and from her own neighbourhood. She avoided all her relatives. She had stopped playing TT as she didn't go to school. She didn't watch TV and was without any entertainment. Her closest cousin, Chandra, came from Lasem a town just less than an hour drive from Mathur. He, just 2 years older than her tried to cheer her up; but without any effect. He invited her to Lasem and she politely ignored with the stare at the ceiling. He tempted her saying that they could play TT, while at Lasem, without having to go to her school; no, she didn't want to.

She got duller by the day, both physically and mentally. All doctors that attended her didn't have a clue to get her back from her pent-up grief. They couldn't find a way to push her into tears. She just refused to recover. For the parents it was a double tragedy. They just lost one of their beloved daughters. Another was going wasted in her memory.

Chandra came every weekend, determined to give company Jay till she recovered. That evening, he went out to meet one of his friends, Kula, who lived a couple of streets off Jay's home.

Kula dropped Chandra at Jay's house on his father's moped and waited for him in the drawing cum dining hall, when he had a flash of an idea. He found Jay's dhuppatta lying nearby. He folded it the size of a TT net and moved the Dining Table a little making some space all around; placed two of the Dining table chairs in the middle of each of the long side of the table and tied the ends of the dhuppatta as a 'net' to each chair. A TT table with a net was ready.

Chandra came out and saw the Table ready and could not resist himself. He asked for the TT racquets from Jay. She handed over the racquets but shook her head as if she didn't want to play. Chandra knew enough by this time not to press her harder. He asked Kula, who was raring to go as he had been starved of an opportunity to play at a table. He didn't have a dining table at home. They ate squatting on the floor.

As Chandra played, Kula gave him a demo of the game he had by and large imagined in his mind. To Chandra's surprise, Kula beat him quite easily, every single game they played. The sound of the tuck and tuck in the comfort of her own home and the excited shouts and shrieks of the two friends, drew Jay to the hall. First she watched them silently. As the games progressed, she got involved and kept the score and volunteered to act as a referee. When Chandra lost his next couple of games too, she smiled at him and naturally walked up to him and grabbed the racquet from him and readied herself to play with her cousin's stranger friend.

'You have lost your right to play and I have earned mine'.

Kula had never played with any girl before and was shy. But Chandra, pleasantly surprised at the change in Jay's mood, patted himself, called, 'Love all'. That's how Kula and Jay got initiated to the Dining Table Tennis.

The next week, Chandra came to Mathur on vacation, to stay with his cousin, for a couple of weeks. Kula, who played the role of Chandra's 'chauffeur' on the Moped borrowed from his father, frequently escorted him home and found himself in the drawing cum dining hall of the Jay's home.

First days, Jay's father, welcomed Kula as Chandra's friend. But as Kula's visits became frequent, her conservative father was not pleased. But Chandra in his enthusiasm kept bringing Kula in.

When Chandra left after his vacation, the TT games stopped and Jay went back into her cocoon. Jay's father invited a number of Jay's school friends and they failed to enthuse her. Every conversation of theirs invariably led them to Vaijay, or to their studies and the teachers or of School gossip mostly about the infatuation stories of her friends, in hushed voices. All these irritated Jay without fail. With no common subjects between them, Jay preferred to be lonely and stepped back into her brooding moods.

One of her friends, who played TT at school, refused to play with her on the Dining Table, as she said, 'It would spoil my game'.

Jay got snubbed and withdrew from her. Slowly, her friends found other pastimes better than in the mournful company of Jay. Their visits turned into a trickle and stopped eventually.

Chandra returned to visit Jay's family every weekend without fail and Jay also looked forward to Chandra's visits for the TT game she could play in the confines of her home. Kula also became a standard fixture every weekend evening at Jay's home, much to the consternation of Jay's father. Her mother was OK, as long as she could see Jay smiling and advised her husband not to make an issue of Kula.

21 A Place at the Table

One of the weekends, Kula expecting to find his friend Chandra at Jay's home, walked in as usual. Jay's father Krishnan, who was sitting in the hall with Jay's mother snorted, 'Chandra isn't coming for a few weeks and I will let you know…' with a triumphant smile, having stopped Kula's entry that day.

Kula said, 'Thank you sir', and walked out of the small gate that could only let one person walk across at a time, disappointed.

Just as he was getting on his moped, he heard someone call his name from behind. He turned around to see Jay juggling two TT balls with a TT racquet in each hand, watching the balls carefully. 'I was waiting for you', she said, without taking her eyes off the balls.

Though she did not realize that this was the first time she had stepped out of the walls of the house and let sunlight fall on her, her parents who had followed her out of the house, realized it instantly and were happy for her.

Kula said, 'But, Chandra isn't here. So we can't play'. She replied again not looking at him, 'Chandra promised, but now has cheated me. But you are not letting me down'.

It was a pleasure to see her talk to Kula, a stranger to the family with so much familiarity and command. Jay's mother was all eyes for Jay and was happy that she was coming out of her self-enforced shell, voluntarily.

Kula wasn't sure, if he should accept her invitation and play with her. He stared at Jay for an answer. 'Come on in', she commanded as she walked back to her table still juggling.

'Dad, give way for us', she ordered her father who was blocking the doorway and he spellbound, obediently stepped aside making room for her to go.

Kula hesitated at the gate waiting for a formal invitation from her father.

Jay's mother broke the stand-off, 'Kula, what will you have; tea or coffee'? as she stepped into the house behind her daughter. Jay was still juggling the ball with her two racquets as she reached the table.

Her father announced, 'I'm going to play with you, Jay'. He didn't mention if Kula was invited to the game.

Jay laughed at the idea. 'This is TT dad; not your old 'Bullworker'!

Krishnan tightened his dhoti, the traditional garment of Tamil Nadu and plucked one of the racquets from Jay's hand, as she whined in protest. Her mother brought steaming hot coffee for Kula and he had no option but to sit and watch with his cup in hand. He wanted Jay and her father play it out and decide, if he would have an opportunity to play at all.

Krishnan could not meet any of the balls that Jay gently tapped to his side, still murmuring. When he picked up a ball to serve, he struck the ball with the force of a hammer that the ball bounced off the table with a squeak and hit the ceiling of the room and scattered away. Jay's mother had to join her to find the ball. They eventually found the ball from an adjoining room, from under the wooden cot. The next few attempts had the ball ricocheting off the walls, the fan, off the glass cupboard and once had to be picked up from the neighbour's garden.

Next, with great alacrity, Krishnan folded his Dhoti halfway around his limbs, above his knees, stood stooping to meet the next ball.

'Dad, this is just a small little ball, not a raging bull', Jay laughed out loud as she served.

Krishnan, was not about to give up yet. He stood his ground again in the fashion of a sumo wrestler, waiting for the bell and the ball. As the ball spun away from him, he leapt to his left, fell all over the side table where his wife keeps fruits for the family and crushed them all into a mixed fruit squash in one fall. When Kula and Jay's mother helped him back on his feet, he was dripping fruit juice from all over him.

Respecting the poignancy of the moment, Kula suppressed his laughter, while Jay and her mother did not hold back theirs.

'Krishnan sir, are you hurt'? Kula asked with genuine concern.

Krishnan smiled at him awkwardly and limped into the wash room.

Jay thrust the other racquet into the hands of Kula, 'Well matador, tame this bull; I mean ball', as she served a pun.

It was as though sun was shining at last within this home for the benefit of Jay, who had been seeing nothing but darkness in the last several months. This was the beginning of Kula playing TT with Jay on his own, without having to escort Chandra. This became a regular feature every weekend and slowly during the week days too. Jay's health both mental and physical gained every day. Though she refused to go to school for a while, she started moving with others, and chatted up with them, especially if the subject was her home TT. To the chagrin of Krishnan, she narrated his first and only experience at the dining table TT repeatedly and enjoyed herself thoroughly. Kula supported Jay as much as he could as he felt his responsibility did not end just giving company to Jay for the home TT, but he did everything for her to get over the loss of her twin sister. He, in fact became the only person, with whom she shared memories of her sister, something she didn't feel comfortable even with her own mother, father or Chandra, or any of her school friends.

Though Kula was at an age to explore friendship with girls, Jay's age and take it to certain romantic levels, he was strict with himself and did not take any advantage with her and did nothing to corrupt her mind or throw in baits to attract her. Jay, who was very vulnerable and malleable at this point and her mind could have been moulded by Kula, the way he intended. But that would have been against his character. Krishnan's watchful eyes didn't fail to notice the healthy discretion that Kula voluntarily maintained with Jay and started trusting him and slowly endeared him as a member of his own family.

Krishnan once commented to his wife, 'I am happy about Jay's friendship with Kula. While she is still too innocent and doesn't know the world, I trust Kula would treat her with respect and dignity and guide her too. Most importantly, Jay would not miss Vaijayanthi'.

Jay did more than recover from the loss of her sister by her friendship with Kula. She gained the gold medal and cup as the winner of her school Table Tennis Championship; as did Kula in his school the very next day!

22 First Steps

Kula and Jay were to be trained at the District Sports Centre three days a week along with similar recruits from other schools from the District. Jay's father had reluctantly agreed to send her for the training after Kula promised to take utmost care of her. Everything was organized in the next two weeks. Formal training was planned on Mondays, Wednesdays and Saturdays; 3 to 4 hours each day. They got special permission from their respective schools to leave the classes by 3:00 PM.

Both of them picked up the game very fast. Initially, it was tough as there were a whole lot of styles of play and were frequently beaten by other players. But whenever beaten, they got more resolved to win and more important, they learnt lessons from the defeat and they did not give up, till they won. They always exchanged notes, tactics and strategies to play against the others.

Kula did not make many friends. He had Jay for company and had to protect her. Most boys nudged close to the charming Jay and many of them didn't have good intentions, when they talked or got closer to her. Innocent Jay seemed not aware of all the scheming around her and that they hung around her to meet her eyes and worse, for a touch of her hands. But she was happy for Kula's company and the security and wanted nothing more.

Jay often played together with Kula as his mixed doubles partner and frequently against each other too. Kula, was very careful not to press win against her; He just couldn't. Jay liked to win. And more, she seemed to like Kula's attention and was happy for it.

There was method in the whole madness. Each month, all the players were set up to play against each other at least once. In three months, they had played against each other at least three times. Each player was identified for one of the six different styles of play and informal groups were formed. Each player was to go through practice with different groups, aka styles on different days. Their basic strengths and weaknesses were profiled and customized coaching was provided to individual player within the period. The individual skills were ranked each month and their progress tracked.

Mahadevan, who accompanied them for most of the training sessions, seemed to have a great mastery of all styles of play. He could play any style and beat any other style. He was an accomplished coach and he gave them good tips to tackle any player, any style. His analysis of the game, the tactics and strategies he came out with were simply stunning against opponents of every class.

Mahadevan introduced both Kula and Jay to a strict regimen of physical exercises for strength; a regimen of Yoga, to keep their limbs flexible and fit to move like a cat; meditation, to concentrate and focus on the ball; lean and healthy diet of natural protein, vitamins and greens. There were boys and girls who possessed equal or slightly, only slightly, better skills and talent than Kula and Jay. But they lost to the quadruple power of physical exercises, Yoga, meditation and a healthy lean diet, in a combination that Mahadevan served them. Under this regimen, Mahadevan moulded two simple players from the dusty streets of the small town, Mathur into champion material.

Kula was careful not to venture his thoughts beyond friendship with Jay and break the trust of several of the most important people in his life, including her.

He knew that she trusted him and that she would do whatever he asked her to, even if he chose to take advantage of her.

Kula was very careful during the days that he travelled with Jay to the District Centre back and forth by bus. He avoided getting too close to Jay as far as possible and consciously avoided her eyes, as he did not trust himself. He never sat close to her in the bus and always found a seat in the next rows, even if a seat was vacant beside her. He felt her touch was not the same as before and his thoughts were not as pure. The occasional contact now and then electrified him from head to toe and he resented himself for that feeling.

He clenched his fists, sat stiff as a Yogi, told himself that he should not be distracted by stray thoughts and he prayed that her presence does not disturb him as it did. One day he looked back at her casually and caught her eye, triggering a very pleasant reaction exciting his nerves. He looked at Jay's eyes once again.

'She's innocent', he concluded. 'She did not yet pass the threshold that I passed through recently. 'She is still a child', he thought 'and should stay that way, for her own and for everyone's good'.

He felt that he was corrupted and that some wrong influence had taken over him. If this was part of growing up, he was afraid of growing up. He grew up with high moral values and was true to himself. This was the first black mark on his pure self. There were times, when the mischievous cupid overcame his Defenses and he enjoyed the happiest moments of his life and entertained pleasant thoughts of Jay.

He consoled himself, 'Small black marks do enhance the value of a person in terms of beauty and pleasantness just like the black marks on the face of the moon', courtesy Mahakavi Kalidasa, a great Sanskrit poet of ancient India.

If there were black moles in his thoughts, he welcomed them on those days, though, he was afraid that his character could end up painted black, dot by dot.

At the end of three months, the ranks were announced. Kula and Jay came out third and second, respectively among the boys and girls training at the District Sports Centre. Kula was happy for Jay and Jay was happy that Kula was pleased.

23 The Kiss that Wasn't...

The next month the District Championship Tournament was announced. The tournament was open for all players in the district and any school could nominate as many as three of their boys and three of girls in their respective sections. The fact was that most schools didn't participate as they didn't have TT players at all since there was no TT table in the school and several schools couldn't find even three keen students willing to play.

Kula breezed past the opposition, till the round of 16. But he encountered new styles of play in the round of 16 and again in the Semi-finals. He had to use all his imagination and innovation to stay alive. The final was easy. It was the style, he had always bested during the three months at the Sports Centre. He romped home with little opposition and became District Champion. Jay came second among the girls in the district. She was a little disappointed. She could have easily won, but for a couple of unforced errors that Kula attributed to the 'devil of the day'.

When they had completed the prize ceremony and were on the way back to Mathur by bus, carrying their respective Trophies, Mahadevan reminded them that they should try to win the Nationals and then go on to win against the Chinese, the World Champions. Kula wasn't in any mood to think about the Chinese. He first wished to achieve his dream of stardom by getting into the State TT team and failed to see the big world beyond his State. He just smiled at Mahadevan. Jay did the same and the coach did not press both for answers, not yet.

One day Jay took some time off to shop a few things for herself, on the way to the District Sports Centre. She found a pair of beautiful fabric stuffed doll pouches that could be used to cover TT racquets. One of them had a face of a boy with protruding lips, nose and eyelashes and the other, a matched pair made like a girl complete with twin pigtails and blushes on the cheeks. She presented the boy-cover to Kula. They used them regularly to keep their racquets in.

A few days later, Kula was at Jay's house for practice. Kula and Jay practiced for about half an hour before he stepped out for some fresh air and returned. Jay was nowhere to be seen. On his return to the table, he found the TT racquets were positioned on the table one over the other, with the boy's lips rightly placed on the girl's as though in a passionate kiss. He suspected that Jay should have deliberately positioned them so, to arouse his interest in her. Or was he was reading too much from the chance position? Kula was concerned if Jay had started expressing her feelings for him. It made him pleasantly giddy at first to know that Jay thought of him with affections too, which soon turned into a scary dizziness.

He wasn't sure how to respond. Some how he felt it wasn't a good thing for either of them and would not reflect the strength of their characters. He had to nip such thoughts in both of them in the bud. He had promises to keep.

'That would damage Jay and me, our friendship and our game beyond repair', Kula knew.

As Jay stepped into the hall, Kula after allowing a short deliberation in his mind, just pulled the figures apart, as though he didn't read anything from their 'silly' position, well before she knew he knew. He wanted to avoid an embarrassment and put off responding to her feeling for him for another day. He looked at her eyes, but however much he explored her face and eyes she did not betray any knowledge of the kissing figures, if she had any. He had no reason to suspect that it was her handiwork.

On the contrary, was she testing his intentions for her own precaution? Or was she just teasing him?

He was ready to give up his entire world and more to know her mind.

24 Aiming High

There was huge buzz in the Sports Centre, when the state tournament was announced. Kula trained intensively and with a great focus. His dream of representing his state could be his reward. Jay was also in the tournament on the girl's side. She also was training equally hard. Unlike Kula, she had not much of an ambition or a dream. She had achieved more than she had ever dreamt. But she wanted to keep Kula, company. She was comfortable when he was by her side. She wanted to train so he could be close to her, so that she could encourage him to win. But she never confided her feelings to Kula about this. Nor did he look to know this from her eyes.

The State tournament was expected to be much tougher and Kula was getting tougher too. The city boys and girls intimidated both of them with their vulgar breed of easy English slang, their disruptive fashions, their freaky hairstyles and the fancy cars they came by. It seemed that they had appropriated all the bragging rights in the stadium on subjects varying from girls, to cars, to para-sailing. They noisily chattered profanities away and if the tournament was about vulgar display of their limited, yet decorated assets, they would have won hands down, any day. Unfortunately, it was a TT tournament and skills mattered. A couple of the city school boys did have the required skills and that's how Vinod happened to progress to the finals. Kula stood taller in TT skills and quick adaptation to any style of play, cat like movements and innovative strokes and placements were his forte; he won the State Championship without conceding a game. Jay won her matches too and stood first in the state. She was surprised by her win. But Kula was not.

Both came back home as State Champions. The winning of State level Championship – both Kula and Jay – was beyond Jay's wildest dreams. Having Kula for company excited her without end.

The Chief Guest, Jagadeesan's novel approach to the sport at the district level that produced two state winners in the same year was rewarded by a promotion as the president of the State Sports Academy at Chennai. He needed a dedicated deputy and picked up Mahadevan.

25 Bombshell at the Podium

The TT game that thus started on the home dining table, drew to a close at the podium of the Games at Shanghai, for Joy.

Joy had taken the manipulated Semi Final loss against Zhen Zhen with a certain amount of deep hurt, but did not show. But the next day, Zhen Zhen, who lost her Finals to Qing Zhao, during the interview, devoted her entire time discussing her Semi-final game against Joy, rather than her Finals against her Chinese opponent.

Her response at the interview was a vitriolic attack against the Indian girl, who she remarked, 'Pretended to be champion and who was already accused of using sorcery and mind games against the highest rated Chinese hosts and tried all tricks to run away with the Semi Final against me. I am happy to have taught such a despicable creature the right lessons and stopped her advance'.

The ITTF administrators were aghast at this open animosity, but did not take action against Zhen Zhen, as the Indian quarters were silent and didn't protest. In any case, the Indian Team Managers decided not to displease the hosts on such 'trivial' outburst.

Zhen Zhen rubbed salt into Joy's unhealed wounds and her memories of the deceit at the Semi-final match that seemed to have been fixed, well before it begun, flooded back in her mind. She was so charged and enraged that evening and needed nothing short of a lightening conductor. Kool was the only one she knew could help her dissipate her anger and from burning herself down, just by holding her hands.

But she remembered Kool, who requested leave of absence for two days, including from Joy's match against Zhen Zhen.

He had told her the previous evening, 'I need to prepare myself for my tough Semi-final against Jiang, the World No1 in two days. I need some rest, yoga and meditation. I have also arranged a practice session with a Japanese friend, Saito, who has promised to help with some tips against the World Champion. Saito is the only non-Chinese who has beaten Jiang this year and has a favourable head to head career lead 4-1. Unfortunately, Saito is available for practice exactly the same time as your match against Zhen Zhen'.

She couldn't find Kool since.

Joy's anger mercury kept rising all night. She had a bad sleep and woke up hazily, lethargically and with a temper. She showed uncharacteristic anger against one of her team managers, who instead of supporting her appeal, threatened her with action against her when they get back to India. Somehow since the day after her loss to Zhen Zhen, the team managers seemed to be hostile to her and were very unhelpful. She had to back out hastily and apologized to the manager. She longed to see Kool, but he was nowhere to be found. His mobile was switched off.

The next day, Wen Qiang, the Gold medallist, Zhen Zhen the silver medallist and Joy along with Ehuang, the other Bronze medallist were waiting for the call to the podium. Zhen Zhen did not hide her contempt for Joy and for that matter all Indians. Joy tried as much as possible to swallow the insults.

When Joy could take it no more, she told Zhen Zhen, 'You won the Silver, because of my own grace and not because of your good game.

Zhen Zhen nastily retorted, 'You have only disgrace left as you and Li are known to be 'bi***ing with your Indian boyfriend'.

She continued angrily, 'Li is now paying her penalty for she had a dishonourable relationship with both of you'.

Joy was shocked by the words that hit her, considered it to be the rudest remark anyone can make against two honourable friends. It was unthinkable for her that any one in decent society could speak such words. She was dumbstruck. It took a while for it to sink in that her dear friend Li'll'y was in trouble, because of friendship with Kool and her. She wasn't conscious of what happened in the next fifteen odd minutes.

When she became self-aware, she realized that she had refused to accept her Bronze medal at the podium and placed it at Zhen Zhen's feet.

She had said, 'You deserve this medal, so keep it. About the silver, just return it to where it belongs'! She later remembered seeing the bewildered face of Zhen Zhen that was shown repeatedly on TV in response to Joy's words, for the next few days.

Joy did enough to kill herself and her beloved game.

The reprisal that followed her 'bombshell at the podium', as one of the News Anchors described it and the rest caught it, that evening was very swift and merciless.

Nobody cared to check with her and to ask her 'Why you did, what you did'?

She became an outcaste with immediate effect. Even the Indian team managers became hostile to her and treated her shabbily, without trying to understand her turmoil, on the face of her being regularly insulted and tormented by the Chinese hosts. She did something very unsavoury, no doubt, but she had been provoked beyond decent limits.

She did not look for unconditional redemption. She only begged for her story to be told and heard. But the hosts were cautious and imposed an unofficial censorship of any positive news related to her. They prevented inquisitive journalists from reaching near her, by cordoning off the Indians for any journalist.

The Chinese Games organizers thought it fit to talk on behalf of the 'vicious' Indian girl, who they claimed, 'though unrepentant, has accepted her responsibility for having spewed venom on the Games and humiliated the Chinese team 'verbally''.

Strangely, the Indian team managers also toed the Chinese line on this incident.

26 Hindi Chini Bhayee Bhayee

Kula stormed into the Indian team quarters breaking his rigour well before the impending, biggest match of his life. Jay had been made an outcaste by the Indian Team Management and was being harassed for having done what she had done. He could not be a mute spectator to the events of the day. He had a heated argument with the entire team management, who were all ready to toe the Chinese line and none of whom were supportive of miserable Jay.

On further inquiry Kool found out that only one of the team managers was strongly pushing in favour of the Chinese line, saying, 'The spirit of the Games was more important than the sentiments and mental turmoil of individual players'.

The vociferous manager carried the other 'dumb' managers with him, who were particular in avoiding a spat with him. The particular Team Manager, who had developed an unexplained cudgel against Jay, insisted on banning her for the rest of the Games and hence was pushing for her ban from the Mixed Doubles in partnership with Kula.

By then the Indian Team Management had received information from the Games Management that they have banned Jay for three years from ITTF tournaments. That made it impossible for her to play in the Mixed Doubles Finals, even if the Indian management let her play. Kula was shocked beyond belief at the turn of events at the Games that they worked so hard for. He begged the Team Management to appeal against the ITTF decision, explaining the harrowing treatment that Jay had to put up with due to Meiling and Zhen Zhen.

The Team Management reluctantly agreed and decided to meet the Games Organizing Committee in this regard. The two management officials (one of them, 'the vociferous', fairer of the two, wore a beard and the other, his pal, was short and stocky), who went to meet the committee returned late night, almost early next morning with bloated hanging over eyes and reeking heavily of alcohol and the perfume of the couple of voluptuous ladies that attended on them. They were accompanied back by two Chinese TT Management officials, who were frequently seen on the side-lines, during Chinese matches and the two ladies that hosted them. They all colluded into one of the rooms in the Indian quarters.

The one with the beard and said, 'We thank you for the gala time we had at the party. It was the best party that I had in my life'.

'Oh no', replied the Chinese host. 'This is a standard party; we didn't have much time. Next time we will have the party in real heaven'!

'And thanks for the Dollars at the gambling table. How nice of you to let us take this back home without any taxes and confidentially too!

The Chinese host graciously said, 'It's your win! Please take them home without guilt'.

The ladies stood up to leave after smooching with the Indian Managers for a while. The Indian officials pulled the ladies back on to themselves spilling the remaining cup of 'joy' that they were sipping, on all of them. One of the Chinese officials signalled to the ladies to stay a little longer. He seemed to be keen to close some business and appreciated the presence of the ladies.

Then they discussed a certain list of lifestyle digital goods that the Chinese hosts had promised to ship to them as a return favour for letting Jay's ban stand.

The Indian official with the beard asked the highly inebriated, short and stocky one, still under influence, 'It's time for us to please the hosts, pointing to the Chinese Federation official. 'Else we will lose their favour'.

When he didn't get the expected response from the short one, he cautioned, after a long pause, 'It's now not even about losing favours; It's all about our as*es being roasted in public in India. Better we fall in the Chinese line'.

The other one managed to raise his eyebrow and 'whispered' loudly into the other's ears that it could be heard very well outside the apartment, 'What makes you think my as* could be roasted'?

He demanded, 'Did you sign any contract committing yourself? Then count me out, I don't want any part of this. I will rather support our team player, Jay. I wouldn't trust the Chinese any way to deliver the goods, once we board the flight back home. I didn't sign any contract; in any case, 'Jai Hind'.'

The bearded fair one annoyed, raised his voice too, 'No I didn't sign any contracts either. But we signed all over their cameras graphically. Think of your as*, if or when the videos play on YouTube and in all the news channels back in India'.

'I would better hail, 'Hindi Chini, Bhayee, Bhayee'. Forget Jay, forget 'Jay Hind'. She not only pushed us this deep into sh*t by refusing the medal', raising his palms until his nose.

He continued, 'She could bring us more trouble back in India, if we supported her now. It looks like the Chinese premier is ready to talk to our Prime Minister in support of the ITTF official stand'.

The shorter official got up, and touched his bottom with one hand, as if to cover his as*, hailed in salute with the other hand, 'Hindi, Chini, Bhayee, Bhayee'.

The senior Chinese official nodded, satisfied, thanked them both and took leave of the gentlemen along with the giggling ladies.

They didn't expect anyone to overhear them, so late in the night. That they still were under heavy influence also was a reason they did not practice discretion. They forgot to lock the door and draw the curtains as they entered. They didn't realize Kula had followed them the whole evening, smart phone camera in hand.

He had managed to follow them on taxi and video record the managers' movements since the previous evening from the organizing committee office to 'Paradis' in the company of the sensuous ladies who entertained them. Visual equivalent of the acquired fragrance of the opulent ladies still lingering on them along with the stench of the infamous Chinese native alcoholic beverage, baijiu that has undertones of paint thinner and reeked of exotic, yet disgusting Chinese 'baby mouse wine' that they 'gānbēi'ed 36 times in all at the party were all on his record.

Kula, was shocked and ashamed as he videographed their titillation with the ladies even as they stepped outside the private confines of room nos. 535 and 536 of 'Paradis', still in 'high spirits'. Then, he had covered their return from 'Paradis' while the car doors were open as they got into the car at 'Paradis with great difficulty' and as they struggled to get off the car at their quarters, still in the arms of their lady escorts. He had also covered their drunken conversation at the quarters as well, including the 'Jai Hind' salute to be quickly followed up by the 'Hindi Chini Bhayee, Bhayee salute' meant to erase the earlier 'Jai Hind'.

Kula was so shocked at the betrayal of the Indian Team Management, that he barged in and grabbed the fair, bearded official by his scruff of the neck, 'You traitors of India, I heard every word of what you spoke. I promise that I would go public tomorrow, exposing your nexus with their Chinese counterparts in compromising Jay's fair position'.

He was unmindful of the consequences as he was armed with the video recording of his managers' misdeeds. Enraged by his scruff-grab-act, they attacked Kula and in the scuffle one of them was bruised.

'You better pursue the protest in favour of Jay and have her reinstated... or else...'. Kula charged out of the quarters.

Back in his own quarters he felt his pocket for his smart phone, determined to call their bluff and the Chinese deceit. But alas, his phone was missing. He remembered to have firmly placed the phone in his pocket before charging at one of the managers. But he had lost his phone in the scuffle. Kula was devastated. All his adventures and the risk he had taken that evening were to come to naught. He had behaved violently with the officials, only on the strength of this video. Now he knew that years of building his game and his life were lost to one minute of madness. Now, he had no evidence against the traitors and it would be a lost case; his word against the most influential, in the team management. On the contrary, he was at the mercy of the same treacherous managers, who could destroy him if they wished to. Was he going to beg for their forgiveness? It was the most miserable stage of his life.

He ventured cautiously to the manager's quarters, where the scuffle took place, to surreptitiously check for his mobile. The mobile was the key, his last hope, for him to defend himself and to redeem Jay at the Games. He found the quarters being fully lit and occupied by a number of strangers. He peeped in clandestinely, to see two officers of the Chinese police.

Kula got alert, 'What are the officers doing inside the Indian quarters at this odd time? Did these two stupid managers complain about the scuffle'?

He hid himself beside the window and listened carefully. The matter of the violence and the bruise did appear in the conversation but it wasn't the primary reason the police officers were there for. They were joined by the same Chinese TT Team Management officials that had left minutes earlier. The officials seemed to be on their mission to understand how much Kula knew of their deal and the extent of damage that Kula could cause.

The senior of the police officials, who was addressed as Mr Lee, mentioned 'Kula had broken certain rules and had violated some laws and done acts that were not consistent with guests of the country'.

Kula wondered, which rules he broke.

The Police Officer continued, 'Two taxi drivers had reported to the police that Kula had followed you two Indians forth and back to 'Paradis', without your consent. If it had been just about the Indians in the car, it could be treated as an internal matter of the Indian team and he would have been let off with a light reprimand, even though it was against law. As 'elite' Chinese nationals were accompanying you both in 'official capacity', it is no longer an internal matter of the Indian team and has to be treated as crime in China, and that Kula should be dealt with under Chinese laws'.

Kula's head was spinning and wanted to run. But he wanted to know the whole story before he would do anything more stupid. In any case, he had nowhere to run to and nowhere to hide. He was certain he would go to a Chinese jail and hoped he could keep Jay out of his story and out of such a misery. He wanted her to fly back to India safely. No more TT for her. No more China. He was willing and ready to die this instant if only he could save Jay from such ignominy. But he quickly corrected himself; he will save himself just for one more day to ensure she was on her safe flight back to India.

'God give me just one more day to live', he prayed silently as he was preparing himself for his destiny; the Chinese Jail.

He thought of Li'll'y, but decided strictly not to involve her as this incident would harm anyone that sided with him and Jay, blissfully unaware that she was already under detention…

The miffed Indian officials repeatedly begged, 'Please Sir, we are offering to hand over Kula to you, Chinese police, whatever the case. Please arrest him today itself, for assaulting us. If that is not sufficient, please arrest him for following on Taxi'.

The Chinese Officials were angry and demanded an explanation from the Indian Managers.

Of course 'He had no evidence', they whispered to their Chinese counterparts.

Just then, the Police officer, who was searching the hall in the quarters for evidence of a scuffle, picked up a mobile phone from underneath the sofa with his gloved hand. All eyes were on it.

'Is this either of yours'? He asked.

Both the Indian officials shook their heads in tandem.

'Whose could it be'? The two drew blank.

He checked the Mobile; 'Kula' he said.

'Most probably, should have fallen off him during his scuffle with us', said one of the Indian officials, relieved.

Lee took the mobile from his assistant and checked the camera folder for the last recording of the camera.

'The camera is warm', Lee announced. 'Two files recorded between 8:00 PM evening and 3:00 AM. The last file was saved just fifteen minutes back. The size of the two files are 1 GB and 2 GB'.

One of the Chinese hosts said to the Indians with concern, 'It means that he has recorded our visit to 'Paradis' and back. Most likely he recorded our conversation back in the quarters in this second file'.

The Indian manager claimed, 'We hit him hard you know that he had to drop it, before leaving. Else the entire Games, Chinese teams and the all of us would be in deep soup'.

The Chinese hosts dismissed his claim glaring at him in anger.

Lee put the mobile in a zip seal bag and as he carried it away said, 'Let me know if this 'Kula' turns up'. Though the Chinese team officials were happy that immediate danger has passed by, they squirmed at the thought of the police officials confiscating the mobile. They knew that from now on they were to be puppets in their own system and have to play along with that 'someone in the power train' that would soon mark them.

Kula followed the police officers covertly till their car. As they reached the car, the officer in charge stopped to open the sealed cover and wanted to play the video files to know the contents.

Two minutes later he cursed, 'Sh*t, encrypted'.

Kula had to beat retreat to his quarters, shattered at the turn of events as it was daybreak already and he was losing the cover of darkness. He had no way to sound an alert to Jay as he had no mobile with him. He only prayed that Jay did not come to see him, when the police officers took him into custody. He did not want her to do something emotional when she sees him in harm's way. He lay down calmly on his bed and waited for the knock at his door.

27 Flight Back

There was no knock on the door as Kula had feared…

However, later in the morning, Kula was served a notice by the Indian Team Management, asking him to explain his physical violent attack on the members of his team management and why appropriate action should not be taken against him for his act.

The 'injustice' was swift. Kula was framed for violent indiscipline and was thrown out of the team with immediate effect by the Team Management along with Jay and they could not play at the Games any longer. Thus, Kula was forced to miss his Singles Semi Finals against Jiang, the world no. 1, the match he was looking fervently forward to.

The Police Officer, Mr Lee was a little considerate of Kula. He understood that there was much more than what met his eyes.

Kula narrated the events of the previous night as truthfully as he could afford. While he accepted that he went by taxi to the 'Paradis', but did not concede that his motive was to follow the Indian Team Officials or their Chinese hosts.

'I went looking for a female escort and a massage parlour. I had beaten the World No.2 and was next to meet the World No. 1 in the next two days. I needed to cool off my nerves', with a wink and hoped that the Police Officer bought the story.

'So you were the guy, who beat Deng! I have great respects for you' said the Lee. 'Did you find an escort? She could be your witness'.

'No, But I did meet a girl at the reception and she may also remember me asking for the way to the massage parlour'.

'Can you identify the girl'?

'Yes sir, I can', a confident answer from Kula.

Lee called the 'Paradis' Hotel and located the girl at the reception matching the description given by Kula.

The girl replied to Lee's enquiry, 'Yes Sir, this young man you just mentioned, asked me for a reservation at the massage parlour. I checked the masseuses and informed him that they are all booked for the day and asked if he would take an appointment for the next day. He replied he can't take an appointment the next day as he said it would be close to his Semi-Final Match. I didn't realize it then, but after he told me, I watched the TV and he was in all the news'.

Kula had actually enquired with the girl at the reception about the massage parlour, as he waited in the lobby of the 'Paradis' for the two Indian Team Officials who disappeared into their rooms with the Chinese escorts, just to provide an alibi for hanging out there.

The girl continued cheerfully, 'I spotted him again after an hour and a half at the lobby and asked him if she could help him. He explained to me that he had asked someone to meet him at the lobby, in the next half hour.

''She, I suppose'? I winked and teased him. I liked him. He was shy and fidgeted for an answer, but didn't reply'.

'What happened next'? intruded an impatient Lee. But the girl had had a brush with a celebrity with whom she actually had a crush on and wasn't ready to pass up an opportunity to describe the event in detail.

'I asked him teasingly, 'An escort, Sir? Let me know if she doesn't turn up. Sometimes they get double booked. I would like to keep company of a handsome young man, who has just beaten the World No. 2 and is all over the TV. I won't charge; only standard expenses'.

'However, I am on duty and can't make it till 12:00 midnight. You can hang around the lobby or the curio till then'', she recalled her words verbatim without an effort and was excited talking about her experience.

'Again sir, He was shy as ever'.

She continued, this time imitating Kula, 'I am sorry, I can't wait that long. Do you mind if I wait here for my party some more time'?

'I replied, 'you are welcome to stay as long as it pleases you, sir''.

'How long did he stay at the lobby'? Asked Lee.

'As I said, he disappeared into the restaurant and appeared after an hour and a half. Then he waited for the next hour at least. I smiled at him from my desk frequently as he was hanging around the lobby, hoping he would change his mind about me…'

Lee thanked her and disconnected, though she kept on talking excitedly. He had heard what he wanted to know.

Lee did not ask him much about the scuffle, which was one of the complaints.

He dismissed it as unimportant, saying, 'It is between you Indians and does not concern me. And nobody was killed, not even hurt...

'I can understand that the Chinese Team Management may want to stop you on your tracks before you could surprise Jiang. But what could the Indian Team Management have against you'? asked the Police Officer.

Kula wanted to confide in Lee and tell him all that happened. But the turn of events in the last 24 hours had shocked him into silence. He did not want to fall into another trap.

'Yes, both the Team Managements are forcing me to register a case and have you arrested, for the assault against your Team Officials and the Chinese Team officials have registered as witnesses'.

'I also have my own case against you for following Chinese citizens on a taxi. I could have you arrested on either or both these charges. But you have reasonably explained your reasons for being on Taxi to 'Paradis' and back. Even if I give you the benefit of doubt, you still have to face the assault charges. But you are a great player and you seem to be harmless. You seem to be under great stress and the devil is against you'.

Finally, evil won the day and a phone call from a senior party official had sealed the fate of Kula. Lee had conceded and registered a case against him.

'I had to register a case as I have been 'advised' by a Chinese party official, I can't but pay heed to. I intend to let you out with a warning. But you have to leave China by end of today. Tomorrow would be another day. With the kind of hunt for your head, I don't think you can save yourself from getting into jail tomorrow'.

And so Kula agreed to be put on a flight back to India along with Jay, without further protest.

The Chinese Team Management rejoiced their lucky stars that removed two of the most unpredictable, yet potent challengers to their domination of their game. It was not until Kula and Jay were ushered into their flights by the Indian Team Management that the Chinese hosts sighed in relief.

On the way back home Kool and Joy didn't talk much as they were dumbstruck by the turn of events. The news of the disgrace of the two players should have reached the shores of India, much ahead of them. When they landed back in Chennai, India, instead of getting heroes' welcome they deserved, they were treated as outcastes. They rode lonely on an autoriksha back to their homes.

The Indian Team Management, armed with the case registered by the Police, had requested ITTF for a ban on Kula, '…For assault on the Indian officials, in sympathy with Jay. Also, they had claimed that an internal enquiry has 'revealed Kula's intentions' to disrupt the match against Jiang and to disgrace the Games further'.

The ITTF, under the silent coercion of the Chinese Team Management, gave in and suspended Kula too for three years from playing in ITTF tournaments. Kula didn't know of his ITTF ban until several weeks later.

28 Once Bitten...

Kool explained to Joy, 'I met Mahadevan Sir two days ago. He has now become an important functionary in the Tamil Nadu State TT Federation. You should also remember Jagadeesan Sir, the Chief Guest who helped us train in the District Centre. He is now a senior functionary at the Indian Federation at New Delhi. They together can pull the right strings to pull us out of the mess and have our bans revoked. But it could take some time'.

Joy, who had undergone one of the most harrowing experiences in China with Kool, just smiled. She had seen enough trouble for one life; maybe she would like to attempt redemption in the next life, if she would have the pleasure of Kool and Li'll'y for company.

'Are you still interested in playing for India'? she quizzed and pitied Kool.

He replied, 'Joy, a country never lets her citizens' down. Only other citizens do. I would never let my country down. I was given an opportunity to hold my head high and lift the National flag at the Games. When we met first time in the company of your cousin at your home, I didn't believe that we both will soar so high. It was the will of God that we came up this high and I can say I was most fortunate and progressed like I could make no mistake'.

'We came close to proving a point. We didn't lose to the TT talent of the Chinese. But we lost to a collective conspiracy that we were least prepared for. The Chinese play their game differently. I am not going back to China in a hurry. But when I do go back to China, I will beat the Chinese, 'At Their Game''.

'I can never forget your loss at the Games to Zhen Zhen and the humiliation that you had to undergo immediately after. It would be for your sake; for our sake. We are no less than the Chinese. Or for that matter any other nation in the world, whatever their game'!

'Mahadevan Sir has promised to hold the protective umbrella with the right official backing and we will not be let down again'.

She took his hands and pleaded, 'I trust you, Kula. But we don't have the strength to take on mighty countries. I don't believe the Indian system would come to our rescue. It didn't last time. I have no reason to believe it would come to our side the next time. Just one person, even with all the goodness of Mahadevan Sir, will not make any difference in this corrupted system. Whereas just one venomous person can poison the entire system'.

Clearly, she was a victim of the official hypocrisy that has doomed this country and wasted many a dreams!

She advised Kool, 'I am not being negative, but you have a family to support. You have your elder sister's wedding to perform. I suggest you to concentrate on your studies and become a worthy Computer Science Engineer in the next few months. May be you can still beat the world with your Software expertise. I trust you will. If you can apply so much of your mind in the game of TT, which none has fathomed and had the mighty Chinese running for cover and taking cowardly sniper shots at you, you could repeat the feat in the area of Software Applications too. I will be a Software Engineer, just two years behind you. We are destined to have a decent life, without all these machinations against us. Let us not take any risks'.

'I sometimes feel that we shouldn't have met Li'll'y at all, both for her sake and mine. For me it is a double tragedy that I lost my 'second sister' in Li'll'y'.

She clutched Kool's arms in a fit of emotion as she continued, 'I don't want to lose you too, Kool. I have a premonition that something terrible will happen to you, if you travel to China again. As she said this Kool felt his body quiver in response to Joy's tremble that passed through his arms and stabbed his heart; that settled his decision, at least for now.

29 Joy-Li'll'y TT Academy

Kool joined a private firm as a Software Engineer and was quite successful at that. Joy still had two years to go for her to complete her Engineering course. Ever since return to India from Shanghai, she had looked quite confused, paranoid and without focus. Kool still had hidden ambitions in TT that he wanted to fulfil, someday, when Joy cooled down.

Meanwhile, Joy and Kool, at the instance of Mahadevan, started a TT coaching centre in the city. They called it Joy-Li'll'y TT Academy. Joy was the chief coach and spent most of her evenings and weekends coaching players and promised to prepare the trainees for the National team. Kool was a visiting coach and faculty, who found time between his busy work and overseas travel, to give inputs to the team. Mahadevan Sir helped them manage the affairs under the overall guidance of Jagadeesan Sir.

The Academy recruited most of the player members from the districts and not just from the city. Joy toured the schools in the neighbouring districts extensively to identify players with a flair for the game of TT. They were made associate members in their Academy and they would become eligible for a TT racquet, 6 balls per year and a net at less than half the retail price, so that they could start playing on their home dining table. The balance costs of racquets, balls and nets were covered by sponsorships as they got the sponsors names printed on them.

Full membership would be offered to such of those who performed well. Joy-Li'll'y TT Academy conducted TT tournaments amongst associate members every three months. The tournaments were called Home TT Open Challenge. Any one registered as Associate members of Joy-Li'll'y TT Academy can enter into the tournaments and show their mettle. The Academy also topped it with an annual tournament at the state level conducted at Chennai.

The reputation of Kool and Joy was the biggest draw and attracted new recruits to the Academy. Kool's reputation of having beaten the current World No. 2 could not be suppressed by the corrupt managers of the then Indian TT team, though they tried.

The Meiling and Zhen Zhen episodes were also kept very much in the public memory. Soon the parents flocked around the Academy for an associate membership, and prayed for full membership for their children.

In less than one year of inception of the Academy and within 14 months of the Shanghai Games, the Academy selected twelve excellent players making a formidable team to represent the Academy at the State championship. The Academy players won laurels at the State championship, winning 9 out of 15 medals on offer; a grand success from any perspective.

30 Whirlpool Monster

When you drive over the curved bridge of the Mathur Reservoir, you could watch a whirlpool formed by the water rushing from the reservoir into the submerged tunnel linking it to the Hydro-Electric Power Station.

Joy had always been scared of the whirlpool.

When Vaijai and she were still children, there had been regular news stories of several people who had got sucked in by the giant whirlpool and lost their lives. There had been stories that even boatloads of people have disappeared into it and without trace. The illiterate neighbours had spun mystery stories around such tragedies and Joy and Vaijai had not only taken to such tales, but added their own livid imagination to the folklore.

In their own imagination and words, 'A multi-armed monster, that resembles a giant octopus living beneath the whirlpool, grabbed and devoured unwitting people who ventured deep into the waters. The seemingly innocuous surface streams that are invisible to the eye, unless one viewed the waters at an angle and unless the light was right, gently dragged the victims deeper and closer to the whirlpool to please the monster. Once they were within its reach, the whirlpool monster with its long and powerful arms grabbed and gobbled them'.

'Sometimes the monster did also let go some persons out of pity. But if they dared to enter the waters again, the monster would not forgive them and the consequences would be as terrible as it was certain'.

Joy used to hug her mother tightly, scared by her own imagination and whenever they passed the bridge close to the whirlpool as did Vaijai, who tightly hugged her father.

As Joy grew older, she had learnt enough about the science of the whirlpools to demystify the physical phenomenon and she could have easily exorcised her irrational fear of this whirlpool. But, Joy was reluctant to unbelieve her favourite myth and willingly chose to be terrified of the whirlpool and the monster that lurked beneath.

Kool had earlier promised Joy that he would not go back to China earlier. But now he had an offer as a software consultant, as fate would call, from a Chinese Sports Equipment manufacturer. The company had asked an Indian software major for the services of a Software expert developer who had knowledge of the TT game, preferably as a player who could understand the nuances of a TT ball in its flight trajectory. As there were not many qualified software developers with profiles meeting this strange requirement, Kool secured this opportunity of his lifetime and commanded a huge fee. But Joy had her concerns about Kool going back to China even for other than competing and confronting the Chinese in TT.

So when Kool wanted to go back to China, Joy fearfully imagined Shanghai to be the whirlpool; the harmless game of TT to be the seemingly innocuous surface stream that took him close by and that the monster that lurked beneath to be the vicious monster, that of course could morph itself and roam around Shanghai in the form of their nemesis; 'You know who! The vengeful Deng'!

She couldn't understand why Kool always hobnobbed with fate and underrated the risks. Would he be the second time lucky and escape the claws of the monster this time?

But he was too excited about his assignment and his trip to China, to heed to her inner fears.

As the departure day approached, she was very nervous. She cautioned Kool a million times to be extra careful, not to get emotional and not to invite trouble like he did last time.

He promised her as many times that he would do nothing stupid during this trip.

At last Joy asked, 'Could you find Li'll'y for me? I miss her. Please find her for my sake'.

And with a teasing twinkle in the eye reminiscent of Li'll'y, joked to ease her own concerns, 'Not for your sake'!

Kool grinned happily and said, 'I will find her. When I find her, I will remember you. Only you'.

He promised to himself to give her a surprise gift, when he came back, a video recording of at least the first conversation he would have with Li'll'y.

Joy waited for Kool's message every day, since he landed in

China. It was now over one week. But she heard nothing from him. She had a mortal fear. What if something happened to him? What if he had bumped into someone from the Chinese TT team at the Games or some one official at Shanghai, who alerted the police of his arrival and had him arrested? Just when she could not bear it any longer, Kool called, very late hours.

Joy asked after the usual courtesies, 'Li'll'y'?

'No clues yet', he replied. 'You will be the first to know'. He hung up.

A few days later around 9:00 PM, she received Kool's email with a link to his Dropbox. She found a video file. She was excited and assumed it to be either a video of his weekend sojourn or possibly the video demo of the TT equipment he promised to talk to her about. The video opened with a view of a semi-lit room, looked like a bar. Then the camera view swept across the hall, still low in light, and settled across a girl, who walked toward the camera.

'Li'll'y'! Joy gasped.

Part 4: Kool

31 Happy hours

The green print on the yellow hand out announced.

Happy Hours for Two
Buy any drink and get one free

At the
The Bristo Bar
Huang Xing Park
Metro station

Li'll'y charged back into the Huang Xing Park station without giving any option for prying eyes to follow her. She found Kool at the corner table at the 'Bristo Bar'. She rushed in to see him and to talk incessantly about the last year that they missed each other. But all she could do was to sit opposite to him and look deeply into his eyes for several minutes, till Kool's heart throbbed.

At last, after she recovered, Kool explained the business of his visit to Shanghai. Jiangsu Sports Equipment Company has developed equipment, TT Server Machine, coarsely called TTSM that helps train TT players with different styles, serves and strokes.

He tried hard to keep his promise to Joy that he would remember her through the entire conversations with Li'll'y. He had earlier switched on his mobile camera as she walked in and now re-focused it on Li'll'y and explained, 'A surprise recording for the benefit of Joy'.

Li'll'y advised him, 'Please delete the file as soon as you send the video out to Joy'. Precaution! She didn't want a repeat of the 'selfie' triggered problems.

Kool talked excitedly about the TTSM, 'There are two parts to the equipment. One, it captures the video of every stroke the players make from different angles and records the ball move, slow, speed up, swing, spin, sway, roll, whirl, twirl and wobble. I was always thinking of designing such equipment for the benefit of Indian players'.

'Oh'! Li'll'y exclaimed. 'It should help one bite the bullet'?

'Exactly', yelled Kool in his enthusiasm, forgetting that he was in a public bar and that people turned to look at him. He had to be reminded by a tap from Li'll'y before he became self-aware.

'The second part is more mechanical. This machine serves the stroke with the same trajectory that it has frozen in its memory using its cameras, precisely with the same flight path, speed, swing, spin, sway, roll, whirl, twirl and wobble and can replicate the stroke any number of times. I have seen other robots for the job, but this is the best machine and it would be a boon for someone to practice, especially to hone his or her response to various strokes. I will show you a live demo sometime'.

'Don't take the trouble', said Li'll'y, 'I have been involved with the design of the same Machine, not as a designer, but as a Subject Matter Expert on TT and how the ball is supposed to behave in flight. I am glad that they found you to support their venture. But you are talking in the third person about the challengers whom the Chinese team will practice against. Didn't you realize that they have a huge library of your action and strokes, Joy's and yours, that are considered the most complex that the Chinese team would want to practice against and beat? And that you are helping the Chinese in their effort to beat you'?

'Oh! I didn't realize', Kool replied. 'I have contracted to help them building this machine. I can't withdraw now'.

She continued, 'I am one of their testing and feedback consultants. You may find my notes that I send frequently as quite a few of my notes have implications on the software design'.

Kool was very glad that both Li'll'y and he were engaged in the same project and that they could learn and work together at some point in time. But he was also aware of the dangers of both of them working on the same project.

When he mentioned to Li'll'y, she assured him, 'I work on one of their prototypes installed in my institute and I never visit Jiangsu'.

But after their dreadful experience during the Games, both agreed to be very careful. She then, got up and sat close to him, clinging on to his arms and adjusted the camera towards them.

Kool asked about Li'll'y, 'Where did you disappear to, midway into the Games? We were worried for you. Joy got to know that you were in trouble with the authorities. But we couldn't ask any one. None of our emails to you were answered. Joy has wept several times, as she believed something bad happened to you, and because of us'.

Li'll'y replied with a sigh, 'I was undone by a 'compromising selfie' that somehow reached Dan and Deng's hands. I will explain sometime later. I was charged as a traitor of my beloved country. I was detained and ruthless interrogation followed'.

'Cheng pulled me out of sure dungeons for life. I owe my life to him' she shuddered.

'You have met Cheng', she remembered.

'Cheng? Who'? asked Kool.

She looked around as a waiter passed by 'shsh... sometime later'.

When the waiter moved away from them, Li'll'y briefly narrated her horrible experience that she faced from her authorities.

She alternated between deep melancholy and pride at having endured the torture.

She continued, 'Shocks from high voltage electric batons were routine. Thrusting the shocking batons into my private parts weren't uncommon, when I painfully wished I died of these shocks, rather than live with the shame and the scalded skins. But I lived through each of them'.

She held him tightly as she narrated her ordeal and had fear and tears in her eyes; she felt the pain all over again.

He fought the anger and the tears that were showing up in his eyes and tightened his arms around her in protection.

He thought he had heard it all, when she continued, 'I was deprived of sleep for an entire week. And was asked to stand without support continuously for a few days at a time... I don't know how, but I had learnt to sleep standing for brief minutes during these days'.

Kool could only shake his head in dismay.

'The most ghastly was of course the 'anchor torture', when both my wrists and one of my ankles were anchored to a metal ring on the floor. The other leg was spread almost 130 degrees behind and the ankle was locked into another ring on the floor. I had to stand on my feet stretched nearly a metre apart, bent down in an inverted U position with my hands touching my forward leg and locked into this position by the metal rings for 3 whole days and nights', she said in a voice drained of all emotion.

He was agitated and wanted to shout, 'I want to kill them all'. All he could do was to let out a gasp.

She felt his body tense, lifted her head to look at his face, seeing it red with anger and pale with fear and soft with pity at the same time, smirked with new found pride and said, 'It's all over… they could break my back, but not my spine'!

Li'll'y continued. 'In spite of these inhuman torture that I had to go through, do you know, I considered myself lucky'.

'What'! a surprised Kool asked!

She narrated the second part of the horror story, 'There were other victims, my co-occupants at the 'Home'… particularly the Falun Gong members, who were persecuted by the Government. Many of them had undergone two years of such torture at a stretch. And a few of them were served several repeats of the two torturous years. One of their leaders, whom I was friendly with, had been forced into the 'anchor torture position' for months together, even before I was interred at the 'Home'.

'I was there, just a week, when he was sent back from the torture chamber. Though he was 5'9" tall, he hardly weighed 86 lbs, less than 40 kg, if you are familiar with Kg. He could hardly feed himself and had to be sustained on liquids. He couldn't stand straight up. He stayed always lying limp on his sides, curved like a boomerang and was so withered that he took almost two months even to be able to crawl', she shuddered in anger and in disgust.

'Yet he had a spirit as tough as steel. He spoke with surprisingly powerful, and a clear voice, motivating all of us, even as he was lying down, unable to even move. By comparison with him, what I had to undergo was just a slap on my wrist'. She cheered up quickly!

By the time she narrated her story, she settled her head on his shoulders, still holding his arms and cuddling close like a lover.

Kool felt so sorry for her, for all the terrible things that she went through and felt it most important to show he cared for her. He, by this time, was resigned to her closeness and put his arms around her and ran his fingers through her soft and silky hair with the hope that she would recover from her trauma faster.

She felt like heaven in his arms. He felt the same too, though he was fighting not to concede to himself.

She had secretly yearned for his affections during his last stay in China during the Games. He had never responded and there were never opportunities for him to show his personal affections other than being truly friendly. Moreover, she knew his heart was with Joy and that he would never do anything sacrilegious. Today was different.

Kool realized that Li'll'y never had an opportunity to narrate the horror she went through to anyone so close; someone whose shoulders she could cry onto.

'What are friends for'? He convinced himself and held her close as he would hold a lover.

Her touch and feel had affected him in spite of his restraint and his thoughts wandered wild. He had a strong urge to kiss her on her lips and had to pull his eyes away from her lips. She was resting so comfortably on his shoulders, as if she owned him; he gave up resisting and hugged her gently and affectionately.

Li'll'y asked, 'But till date, I am unaware of what had happened to both of you at the Games and after it. Why did both of you walk out without playing further at the Games. Deng should have been behind whatever happened to you'!

Then without waiting for an answer, she started explaining her life after detention and confinement of the 'Home' and how she managed to find a job as a TT coach.

'I am partially successful as a coach. In fact, I have a huge flair for the job and am the best coach in Shanghai. Yet, I'm not the most sought after, due to the stigma that I had a brush against the authorities that is difficult to erase in the minds of the public. Players who aspired to have a career in TT are concerned that I may still have powerful enemies in the system and my troubled past may affect their chances of growth as well. This in a way helps me'.

'I have to devote lesser time as a coach and could concentrate on my own training and fitness and am determined to win Gold at the coming Games; the only befitting reply I can to give to Dan and Deng'.

'I'm waiting for Joy and you to come back to China to defeat the Chinese; Meiling, Zhen Zhen, Deng, Jiang and all and claim your righteous Gold at the coming Games. Not just to vindicate yourselves, but as a vengeance! However, on the way to the Gold, Joy would have to beat me, Li'll'y, a rejuvenated player. I have set my eyes at the Gold too and have an aggressive game that Joy will find hard to beat'.

She didn't smile and looked mean and Kool sensed the intensity of the competition that Joy would face.

Kool reassured her, 'Joy and I have given up playing TT and the Gold would be yours without having to fight Joy'.

Li'll'y was disturbed at his assurance, hoped it was a joke. First things first; she asked Kool, 'Whatever happened to Joy and you after you blanked the formidable Deng'?

Kool then, narrated the series of incidents that led to Joy's ouster from the Indian team followed by his. He said, 'Don't feel too guilty my dear; we imploded due to the treachery of two of my own Indian Team officials, in collusion, of course, with the Chinese Team Management'.

When Li'll'y heard of Kool's adventures; chasing the Indian officials to 'Paradis' and back and catching one of them by the scruff of the neck, commented, 'Another bite the bullet event'?

'Yes, but this time, 'the bullet bit me'.

32   Blast from the past

Then the conversation moved on to what Joy and Kool were doing back in India. Li'll'y was impressed by the ability of Joy and Kool to bounce back into the game through the Joy-Li'll'y TT Academy in spite of having a hostile Team Management that virtually ended their careers. She saw stark contrast with her own life that she is struggling to pull herself back upward after her disastrous fallout with the Chinese Team Management. May be, India being a democracy made a difference. The autocratic rule in China meant that she could be buried forever.

Li'll'y mentioned that her career faces an uphill task and that she had less chances to play again for China, unless there was a change in mind of her Team Management. She also added, 'Cheng is working towards getting my unofficial ban revoked and I hope to compete for the Gold'.

Kool explained, 'Though Mahadevan Sir, who occupies some important position in the Sports Secretariat and he is working on our reinstatement in the Indian team, we aren't pursuing it seriously as we have in effect abandoned our playing careers because of Joy's concerns'.

Li'll'y was confused and angry by his answer and hoped she misunderstood him. 'What are your chances to beat the Chinese in the next Games to be conducted in China later this year'? she asked.

Kool fumbled for an answer that would satisfy Li'll'y, 'As I said, we have dropped our ambitions to play TT at the international level. Our Academy has achieved small successes in recruiting good talent and we have made a mark in the State level championships. It worked as we planned'.

'Now, we have set our sights on the nationals for the players and a couple of them are assured of medals in the National Championship,' he said with pride written in his face. And continued, 'The National Champions, whoever they are will take on the mighty Chinese at the next Games. We would have trained them'.

He was satisfied that he got his answer right.

'Kool', sighed Li'll'y, 'Whatever you are doing is kid stuff'! Are you going to be content with this? Don't you want to beat the Chinese? Did I go into detention to see you play with kids with the view to prop them up against the Chinese dragons? Did you save yourself from a sure Chinese Jail and did Joy bravely shock and shake the world at the podium for you to hand hold and spoon feed babies, while you should be fighting for Gold against your formidable opponents'?

Kool could not do much else but to gape at her, unable to comprehend what she was driving at.

Li'll'y continued, 'Do you know why you didn't win last year'? She paused for an answer. Kool was looking askance, not knowing what answer she was expecting from him.

But she wasn't ready to help and she insisted sternly, 'Do you know why you didn't win last year'?

'The Chinese team management played dirty and the Indian team management betrayed us', Kool summarized.

Li'll'y shook her head, 'Sorry, that was not the case. Let me ask you some questions. To help you try and discover yourself'.

She continued probing, 'What was the level of satisfaction when you won over Deng'?

'Quite high' he replied.

What would have been your level of satisfaction, if you had won over Jiang, the World No. 1'?

'Highest satisfaction', he replied.

'How confident were you of beating Jiang in the Semi-Finals'?

'I was expecting the Best man would win'!

'Do you consider yourself the best'?

'No, I intended to find out at the Semi finals'.

'How would you have felt, if you had lost the Semi-Finals against Jiang'?

'I would have been happy that I could reach this far'.

'Wouldn't you feel dirty that you lost the Semi-finals against Jiang'?

'No, why should I'? asked Kool. 'As I told you the best man should have won! I had no expectations when I came. I had no expectations, the day before the match that wasn't played. No expectations, now'.

'If you had lost in the third round, would you consider that you were a great failure'?

'No, I would have been happy that I came this far'.

'Are you looking forward to the next game against Jiang and are you ready to beat him'?

'No. Joy has forbidden me to play, especially against the Chinese and she isn't playing too. She is scared for our lives after the last year events. I would like to watch him play though'.

Li'll'y shook her head slowly in dismay. 'The reason for your not winning any medal, leave alone the Gold was because of Joy and you. Both Chinese and the Indian managements did help you lose. But you were losers already. You would have found another excuse to lose even if both the team managements had played fair and yet you lost. Neither Joy nor you had come to China to win. You had come to see how you fared against the Chinese. Not to win'. She paused again and looked into Kool's eyes probing his mind and his thoughts.

Her words were ringing in his mind, as she continued after the enforced pause, 'You would have gone back home contended with any result and still your whole country would have been rejoicing that you participated in a Chinese event and played and won a few points against the mighty Chinese'.

'The Indian National consensus would be that the best of you were born privileged for an opportunity to handshake with the Chinese winners, rather than win against them. Remember a significant number of you guys were complicit with the British for three hundred years, shaking hands with them and another good number appreciating how strong they were, as they enslaved your country.'

The words hit him hard like only raw truth could. He could not deny that.

Encouraged that she got him thinking, she continued, 'Last year it was the Chinese and the Indian Team Managements that scuttled your ambitions. Now when you don't have any more excuses, you are determined to scuttle your ambitions and opportunities yourselves, fearing threat to life from an imaginary, hypothetical enemy. Don't let Meiling, Zhen Zhen, Deng, Dan and Jiang know about how you chickened out and that you both are now celebrating changing diapers for your adopted kids from various schools in your district. If they get to know, I, not you, will be ridiculed to death. But I will survive. I will not chicken out like you both. You have deserted me and I am having to fight your war; our war. Don't mistake me. I am preparing hard to win the Gold this year'.

'There was a time you had the courage to 'bite the bullet' and I was proud of you both. Now, I am not. There was a time I looked forward to meet you again, so some of your courage will rub on to me. I was waiting to meet the Tiger and the Tigress from India ready to take on the Dragons of China all these many months. Now all I see are two pussy cats fighting over what, a piece of Indian pancake, while you should be slaying Chinese Dragons motivated by the feel of the cold Gold. You disappoint me'.

'I hope that you don't bump into the crowd of Chinese players that pushed you into tears and back to your Dining Table on the very first day at the Games, faking a gunshot. Think of the reception you will receive amidst them. This time, they may be justified doing what they would do to you'. She walked half way to the door, only to walk back to dumbstruck Kool, as if she wasn't finished yet.

'Your elaborate plans to hoodwink the Chinese snoopers, who might have been monitoring your movement was the most ludicrous game you ever played. You amaze me with your own dim sense of self importance. The Chinese may play unfair. But they know tigers from pussy cats. They know winners from wimps. They don't monitor, follow and build Defenses against pussy cats and chicken. Please walk around without any fear of being watched. I promise you that the Chinese won't bother about you. You just don't count'. Kool murmured, 'I planned elaborately, not for my sake, but for yours'.

She looked at him angrily, unwilling to be interrupted. He just shook his head, as if 'nothing'.

'We Chinese are different. We always push to win. We win. We are born to win and live to win. We will die to win'.

'Oh, No! I correct myself. We don't die. On the contrary, we may kill to win. We may have a system that's not fair to all, that's because we have built a tremendous social will to win. Remember 1962. We gave India a smacking. What did your country do? Coloured history text to show you didn't lose. Showcased a few valiant individuals who martyred and claimed glory and covered up your defeat. The very few times that you accepted defeat, you invented a host of reasons for your defeat including that the Chinese played unfair and stabbed at your back while singing your old Prime Minister's favourite rhyme, 'Indee Chinee Bhee Bhee', or something like that. Yes my dear, there's nothing unfair in love and war'.

'As a nation you love your underdog tag and are satisfied at the little sympathies doled out to you, like sissies. No one respects sissies'.

'Now history repeats itself in a miniscule scale with you both abandoning your potential Gold for the safety of your home. How much more will you Indians lose and how much more humiliation will you take before you will fight back? Or will you ever? Are you destined to wallow in defeat and disgrace? I expected tenacity in you to fight for your dreams. But all I can see is your tremendous 'tolerance' to disgrace. Unfortunately, I can't tolerate your tolerance'.

'Please go back to India to find peace along with Joy, singing lullaby for your kindergarten kids', she charged out in frustration.

The hands that held his for security just now, had just given him a knock-out punch. He was the one who felt less secure after her sudden outburst.

By the time he composed himself to say, 'I'm like most Indians, guided by our Bhagwat Gita... 'Do your duty and don't look for the fruit', she had walked out of his audible range.

He was afraid that Joy and he would lose Li'll'y's friendship forever, if they didn't chose to fight at the next Games.

Though he fully agreed with Li'll'y that they should make a match of it against the Chinese this time – to win, he himself wasn't confident of convincing Joy.

He decided, 'Let Li'll'y convince Joy'.

The video file was large. So he uploaded it on his DropBox for Joy with a reminder for her to check his video.

33 With Love from Li'll'y

Li'll'y felt bad all night that she had roughshod Kool. She could have given him the same message in a hundred different ways and intonation. All that she yearned for in her last one year could have been lost due to an hour's madness. She actually didn't mean to be so harsh with him. But whatever happened to her, she had stood in judgement about Kool and Joy's decision. She realized that she had no right to torment both just because she had big hopes on them. Instead of helping them make a decision, she might have actually discouraged them from returning the Games; and to her.

In her anger, she had not taken his contact number. She tried to call him at Jiangsu, without disclosing her identity, the whole of next day. But to her dismay, he did not report for work and none at Jiangsu seemed to know his whereabouts. She was disgusted with herself and was worried for Kool. That day was a particularly bad day for Li'll'y and had innumerable things to do; several things had gone wrong and she had to spend extended time at her office.

Later exhausted from the late hours, as she passed the Metro station she stepped on a piece of yellow litter with the familiar green letters 'Happy Hours...' Something struck her. It was way beyond Happy Hours; almost midnight, when she made a mad rush into the Bristo Bar.

There was Kool, staring like a Sphinx into the dark yonder, unsure if it was time for him to leave the bar.

Li'll'y ran up to him panting from her long sprint, managed to say between her breath, 'I am sorry, I made you wait. I tried to contact you all day. I am sorry'.

She almost fell and frolicked on him like a lost little puppy that found her way back to her master.

Still short of breath, she said, 'I want you both to enjoy your days of peace. Forget what I said yesternight. If you both do really win Gold, I would be happy for you as I would be for myself. But, NO, you both deserve the peace that you both decided to have. I will fight our wars and I will share the honours with you, when I strike Gold'.

Kool assured Li'll'y, 'We appreciate your affections for both of us. We always felt honoured by our friendship and were most pained at heart by the terrible experience you had to go through because of our acquaintance. We understand that we could never ever be able to repay the debt even by our utmost gratitude. We thank you for reposing enormous confidence in us, which we both would be glad to deserve. I apologize on both our behalf that you had been hurt because of our friendship and again we also apologize that you have been hurt by some of our decisions too...'

'Cut it out', she screamed to interrupt. 'I can't stand you being so formal and ceremonial to me. I value your friendship much more than the Gold. I will not push you again. Trust me. Give me back my friendship'! She plucked his hands and shook wildly!

Kool smiled and said, 'It's time to celebrate. Let's drink to our friendship', Kool toasted with a glass of mocktail and Li'll'y picked up her own.

Li'll'y joined in, 'Let's drink to the greatest friendship ever known'.

Kula added, 'Joy sends you her regards' as he showed Joy's email message on his smart phone to Li'll'y.

Li'll'y read aloud, 'I will be gunning for my own Gold at the Games! I caution you Li'll'y, just don't get into my cross-hairs. Don't let any of your Chinese friends either. I will be very mean'.

'So do I' declared Kool, before Joy's message sank into Li'll'y.

She jumped with joy and hugging him closer than ever, kissed him on his cheek. Kool smiled shyly at her first kiss ever, actually the first kiss ever by any girl. He thought that it was not time to be either precautious or serious.

'What's between friends'? he asked himself, Li'll'y style, broke his formal mask and said in jest, 'Jesus says, if you are kissed on one cheek, show her the other too', as he presented his 'other cheek' to her.

She pulled him closer, hugged him and kissed on the right. 'This is for Joy. Please pass it on to her, with love from Li'll'y'.

34   Meeting Cheng

'Our dreams are hostage to our National TT Federations and Team Managements. I liked your brave talk. But stark reality stares at our faces. How are we going to break this jinx'? asked Kool.

Li'll'y thought for a moment and replied in confidence 'I was facing jail for life. I didn't have hope. But I didn't give up. I had truth on my side and I was sure it would show and help. Keep thinking of playing at the Games and you will be provided an opportunity to play. But when this opportunity knocks, you should not fail to recognize. You will have at least one opportunity to break the jinx'. Kool nodded with a smile.

He was convinced and was determined to incessantly look for solutions to the problem and to break the jinx.

Kool was busy at work for the next couple of days; same with Li'll'y. A few days later they met again at the Bristo Bar.

He thoughtfully said, 'The key to our acquittal by the Indian Federation, is the evidence. The evidence is in the recording on the smartphone, confiscated by the Chinese police. I know it's just a very, very, long shot. I don't have a better idea than that'. Li'll'y considered this idea for a while.

'I think we should talk to Cheng. He helped me with a miracle last time. If only he could pull this off too'! She picked up her mobile and spoke to Cheng. 'Cheng, who?' Kool looked askance; Li'll'y said, 'You have met him. Tomorrow, same time, same table'. They broke off for the day.

Li'll'y advised Kool that they should behave like strangers, when they stepped out of the Bar the next evening and so he kept a safe distance from her and was looking at the other side. Kool instantly recognized Cheng, as he stepped into the street, though he looked much different, without his characteristic moustache; he was the Club Manager, who had given a chance for Joy and him to practice after both of them faced an offensive Chinese team. But wasn't so sure, when the person who he identified as Cheng, first passed by him and then by Li'll'y as though they didn't exist. Even Li'll'y looked the other side. Probably he made a mistake about the man. Most Chinese men looked the same to him. Then he saw Li'll'y scanning the floor of the porch of the Bristo Bar and picked up a business card lying in one corner.

Li'll'y waved for a cab and both of them got quickly in.

He asked, 'Was he Cheng'?

She gestured to him not to talk; and looked at the cab driver. Kool knew it was best to keep quiet. The last time he used a cab in Shanghai he was reported to the authorities and he nearly landed in jail the following day. She dismissed the cab in the middle of a very traditional Chinese street with a lot of neat but cheap Mei shops. They dissolved into the crowd instantly before entering one of the mei shops. She sat at one of the tables and he took cue and seated himself at another on the far side. Cheng appeared from nowhere and guided her to the Family room and hung a small Chinese signboard on the door. Probably says, 'Occupied', Kool thought. After a while Kool knocked and was welcome inside.

'Hello Sir, We met before at your club'.

Cheng nodded affably, 'Yes, I remember. How is your girl'? Li'll'y jumped in with a reply,

'Oh yeah, Joy is in great spirits', remembering her swift change of mind to 'gun for Gold at the games'. Li'll'y explained gratefully how Cheng saved her from sure jail.

She explained to Kool, 'Dan had the picture of my lying on your bare chest with Joy lying on the other side while both you and Joy slept'.

Kool, who could not remember such a sacrilegious behaviour between them frowned and declared, 'ludicrous, should have been some graphics'.

Li'll'y, who had not had a chance to explain her behaviour on that day to either Joy or Kool earlier, clarified guiltily, 'The picture wasn't a fake and it was a 'selfie', taken by me as I joined you while you both slept at Joy's apartment one day. It was supposed to be a prank to tease Joy, but turned out to be scandalous and dangerous'.

She continued solemnly, 'I would like to apologize, but, No! What's between friends'! she grinned with a mischievous twinkle in her eyes. 'I loved it, when I hugged you then and I will love it, if get to do it again'.

She bit her tongue in reverence, realizing they were in the company of Cheng, who shook his head to say, 'Some people never learn'. Kool seemed petrified.

Cheng took off from where she left. 'When I heard that Li was detained just for the reason of your friendship, I was in a fit of rage; Oh! No! Not against you', he explained.

'But against the authorities. In China we don't have a system of Godfathers and God daughters. But I am like a Godfather to Li. I have enough contacts in the sports circle and believe me, in the police circles too. I found out about Deng's vicious stance against her, only because he was vindictive. He had lost to you, and he wanted to punish everyone associated with you; that makes it all the three of you. By the way, I appreciate your tremendous talent. Li told me that you can sight a speeding ball in slow motion and as well as a bullet. Is it true? I just can't believe. If true it would be truly amazing' complimented Cheng heartily, without pausing for answers to any of the questions.

'Where did I leave? Oh! Yeah, you were all victims of a vindictive Deng. Dan was OK on his own, but again has no sense of his own'.

Li'll'y nodded with satisfaction. She still would not agree Dan was against her, by himself and Kool wondered, 'Does it made any difference'.

'I understood that the photograph was the only evidence against Li'll'y. I hoped they didn't distribute too many copies. I had to act quickly. I had asked my hacker friends to find and permanent delete all copies in all the servers, laptops at Dan and Deng office and home networks, wherever they were and they successfully hacked into and deleted all the copies that existed within the target hardware in the network'.

'Next we targeted the smart phones of most of her friends among the Chinese team mates including those of Deng and Dan. We suspected one of Li's friends to have passed on a copy of the photograph to either Dan or Deng. We had asked Mia to help and she gathered from the team that Lou could have picked up crucial evidence against Li, without mentioning what the evidence was. Lou might have passed on the picture to either Dan or Deng. It was a perfect photo opportunity of a different kind for Deng and he should have gladly grabbed it. We found a copy each on Lou's Samsung, Deng and Dan's iPhones and their respective clouds'.

'The smartest job was to delete from Dan's pen drive, where suspected Dan would keep a copy. Our Timmen, an alibi for Tiananmen, hacker group is one of the best and had created an intelligent crawler, programmed to seek and destroy the file on the storage devices within milliseconds of their plugging into the known networks and devices of any of the above persons. And the crawler did it in a record few microseconds, from Dan's pen drive, when he plugged it into the laptop. We continuously checked and Deng doesn't seem to have any on his pen drives. We had deleted 8 copies in all'.

'The programs are still looking for other copies outside the known networks. So we have an alert Defense seeking the file whenever it surfaces in any network, known and unknown'.

'Fortunately, none of the fools in the chain had chosen to email or publish on the net, or change the file names, or change the formats. Else, it would have been a wild goose chase'.

'The next job was the print copy of the selfie at Dan's desk. Mia helped again' explained Cheng. 'Mia is a fellow player and happens to be in Cheng's network', interrupted Li'll'y. Cheng continued, without pausing for Li'll'y to finish, 'She just walked into Dan's desk, while he wasn't there, picked up the print kept between his diary pages and walked out. Easy, wasn't it? But, no! We had to temporarily stop the surveillance cameras from recording anything for a five minute period, and she stayed only for two'. He sighed relief.

'Though the surveillance camera wasn't operational, one of the girl's saw Mia stepping out of Dan's office that afternoon. When Dan and Deng couldn't find the copies of the photograph and had hauled up the entire team for questioning, this girl reported seeing Mia stepping out of Dan's office and the time almost coincided with the surveillance camera being stopped from recording. Of course, Mia denied and cried enough asking, 'how would she know the camera's stopped working'? Dan took pity of her and suspected the other girl's motives as due to previous enmity. Of course Mia is still not out of the woods, as Deng wasn't impressed by Mia's tears and continues to harass and threaten her. We have found a suitable alibi for Mia and are trying hard to protect her. But we could save Li from real danger'.

Li'll'y added, 'I wasn't aware of any of these efforts of Cheng as all the while I was in detention during the interrogation and I was preparing myself to go to jail. In fact I was surprised when I was acquitted, though sent to 'Home''.

'All that I heard was some secret whispers that there was no evidence. So what happened to the selfie? Was it not sufficient to nail me? How dumb? I couldn't believe when I heard that Dan and Deng had lost the picture and couldn't hand them over to the investigators. Whatever was happening to the meticulous Chinese machinery? The answer was that Cheng had happened against the entire machinery. Until I was released, I wasn't even aware of what he did and far less aware of his powers and his prowess'.

'You should have a powerful network and are you not taking the might of the Chinese Government'? Kool asked, as his body shuddered, remembering his only brush with the police officers and was genuinely concerned for Cheng and Li'll'y.

Cheng mentioned, 'It is not the Chinese Government that I'm taking on, though I am not a friend of the Government of China, he quickly clarified.

'In this case at least, the Chinese Government wasn't involved; not even the Games Management; none of these would be motivated to scheme up as to who won the Gold at the Games. Though they would be happy if the Chinese won and would celebrate just like in any other country... and couldn't be the Chinese TT Federation. At their level, they do not see a threat to Chinese domination whenever the Chinese team loses a game or even a match. They don't follow the Chinese team fortunes point by point stroke by stroke. So they should have been out of this'.

'Dan is a suspect as he has enough motivation as a Chinese nationalist and a chauvinist. He watches each point and each stroke and judges his challengers and prepares his team. But to be fair to Dan, I know him; we went to University together, he isn't as vicious; he isn't as mean and wouldn't seek revenge'.

'That leaves only Deng as my strong suspect. I know he is nasty enough and has even disrupted several Chinese challengers to his own crown, by the sheer vindictive power that he used brazenly against them. Now that he has lost his No. 1 position and it is obvious that he is struggling to retain his No. 2 position, he was unable to reconcile himself with his last defeat, especially at the hands of this 'minnow' Indian'.

Cheng pointed to Kool. "I had watched your match against Deng. Simply superb. It wasn't a game of 'Minnows' at all. With this form, you have a chance to become a real Champion.

35 The Network

Li'll'y explained, 'Cheng was against certain Chinese Government policies and organized voices and protests against such policies in a very light description of his activities to provide a perspective and glanced at Cheng, as if to ask 'Did I say too much'?

Cheng smiled as if in reply to her concern, 'If he is your friend, I would trust him too.

He explained, 'I was at the Tiananmen Square in 1989. I was still young then, around 30. I was one of the lucky protestors to survive after having been hit by a bullet. I was treated underground. Since then, we have been plotting dissent and protests against the Government and sabotaging some of their policies and decisions that stifled democracy, though on a much local diluted scale. I could move around over ground without arousing suspicion, well covered by the activities of the club. I was one of the key links between the underground and those in the Universities, Administration and the Police, who were our silent backers and provided our backbone and strength. Without these persons, we would not have been able to do what we are doing. I became a suspect after I retired from the club as I had been spotted by the Chinese intelligence cavorting with the Hong Kong student protestors for democracy earlier this year. Ever since, I have moved underground. You saw the elaborate precaution for our meeting today'.

'In the last decades Computer networks have become the backbone of governance and not just the Defense organizations, the scientific communities and the business houses'.

'We have one of the best hacker groups, Timmen, which walks in and out of the most secure servers and files in every country and county. Our reach across the world is impossible to describe and incomprehensible for lesser minds'.

'Some times we feel that we can make or break every Government on earth as every one of them holds such secrets that are indefensible if they inadvertently reach the public domain. You saw what havoc Edward Snowden could cause'.

Kool asked innocently, 'I remember reading that Snowden was in Hong Kong when his files were first published by Guardian. "Was there a connection"?

Cheng just smiled, winked and continued, 'You can come to your own conclusions. All I can say is that the network is broad and deep and has support groups in most countries. Simply put, we could control lesser Governments, if not the largest of them. The larger ones know we are capable of more than pin pricks. But our aim in China is not to replace the Government; pushing an autocratic Chinese Government out only to be replaced by equally hedonistic, rebel, hacker backed, power unaware group that may be incapable of owning responsibility. It can't be so. On the contrary, we are trying our best to educate those in our Government to appreciate democracy'.

'We are very slow in the process as you may see for yourself, over quarter century since Tiananmen. But what you see on the surface is the hard face of the Government. But we are seeing the face soften below the hard face. Before Tiananmen happened, the people were afraid to revolt against the Government. But today, we all know that the Government is afraid of people's revolt, and is trying to pacify every group that is potential trouble to the status quo. I repeat, 'are trying to pacify every Group' and they are shy of confronting them'.

'It is the same that happened in Hong Kong earlier this year. After 79 days of the Yellow Umbrella Movement, we saw the white face of the Government, we chose to back out. It was enough for now. We don't want a confrontation as they would not want either. We are working to convert more in the Government to support democracy, rather than confront and lose the goodwill of everyone, including the Government we are opposed to. When there is change in China it will be more of persuasion than a revolution. It is as it should be'.

'We use all methods to convert talented, strong willed, honest and honourable persons. Li is one of our recent recruits. Our conversions take place voluntarily. Our recruits have imagination, they have faith and they lead. Of course, I didn't help Li for selfish reasons, with an aim to convert her. I had made a promise to her father to take care of her, when she came to the city. When Li was accused, her father was already no longer around, to put his protective hands around her. I had to do it. I didn't even want her to join our group; it's too risky. But she was willing and volunteered. She is now part of the group. She also recruits. But we live in fear of being found; fear, not for our lives, but fear of setback for the movement and the goals that we cherish. I would have asked you to join if you were Chinese. But don't worry; you are not at such risk'.

Kool, impatient, asked Cheng directly, 'Could you help me find the video file that I recorded on my mobile'? even as Li'll'y tapped his thighs indicating him to stop. But Kool had by then finished his question.

Cheng's became uncomfortable and he recovered to say, 'We do what we should to help a Chinese, who the system has been unfair to. I may personally want to help you as you are Li's friend. But my group would not have any incentive to help an Indian against the Chinese Administration'.

'Let me tell you, every one of our group loves our country as much or more than Dan does. Most of our group are Chinese nationalists and many are chauvinists. We are against certain policies of our Government. That doesn't mean we will let our Government down against a foreigner however unfair to him that our system has been'.

Kool's heart sank. He said, 'I am sorry, I was anxious to play at the Games this year. I appreciate'. Then there was an awkward silence.

Li'll'y spoke first, 'Cheng, if you could find a copy of the video, would that help my restoration in the Chinese team'?

Cheng laughed at last, 'Li, you will make a great career as a Diplomat. You have won the argument and my sympathy'.

He knew that her restoration would not be automatic, even if he found the file. No authority would touch the evidence and he cannot find legal redress for her unofficial ban. But the video could help blackmail someone in the conspiracy train and if it was as potent as Kool thought it was, it could help. First he had to find the video file and watch it himself before he will decide if it had enough sting.

He continued, 'Let me see what I can do; anything for you Li'.

Li'll'y got off to her feet. 'Thanks Cheng' and kissed his cheeks to say good bye. 'It's already too late'. A cab was waiting to carry them off to their respective homes. 'It's safe', Cheng said.

'It's a long day. Let's hope. When Cheng is at something, miracles could happen. Could'! was all she spoke during the entire ride.

Kool was bewildered at the depth of what he had stepped into. He wondered again at Li'll'y's guts, who in spite of going through a lot of trouble with the system and yet showing enough courage to fight back against it.

How he thought of her as a frail young girl who needed his shoulders! He realized that all the while he was the jelly. If he was scared, it didn't show in his face, but his silence during the ride did speak of it and aloud.

36 TT Server Machine

After committing to play at the Games, Kool explored all the functions of the 'TT Server Machine' or TTSM that he had hitherto ignored and applied to his game and training methods. He was pleased with what he learnt. He was already thinking of the enhancements that could make the machine more effective for training. Kool met Li'll'y a few evenings later at the Bristo Bar. They spent time exchanging notes about the 'TTSM' as they called it. Kool was extremely excited about it. But Li'll'y had reservations on its effectiveness. She seemed to have some concerns, but could not define it in a way Kool could understand.

One day, Kool told Li'll'y, 'I had asked for buying a similar machine for the Joy-Li'll'y TT Academy at Chennai, as I wanted the powerful machine to train our players. But, the machine isn't on offer, whatever the price. As an intellectual property of China it would not be shared with others'.

Li'll'y added, 'There are only five such prototype machines of this version built and it was placed in some of the best TT coaching centres. It wasn't yet complete and was expected to be completed in about three months and put in for serious practice. However, I'm aware of the first prototype that had a failed motor that we returned to Jiangsu for repair. Jiangsu decided to supply a new prototype in its place rather than repair the faulty one.

Kool was interested, 'Is there any way of finding where it could be? Would that be available for sale, if they are not planning to revive it'?

Li'll'y just pursed her lips; obviously, she didn't know.

The next day while Kool was working on his software, he was going through his notes and some papers that he received form Jiangsu Subject Matter Experts on the design aspects of TTSM. He found a fortune cookie under his papers. He was excited about it.

"A 'broken Tea Server' can be found in the cold and old shops. Work backwards to find it".

Was it a clue to a fortune in a cookie or was it a cryptic clue served to solve his puzzle, crossword style or just an 'un'fortunate plain simple dumb cookie that had no meaning? Shuffling the words backward, crossword style, he found a clue - 'old work.shop'.

He looked around Jiangsu to see if Li'll'y strayed around and served his 'Fortune Cookie' either directly or through her connections. She was the only one who knew his interest in the machine. There was no trace of Li'll'y. In any case, she had told him that she does not visit Jiangsu at all. Was today an exception?

An hour later he discovered an old workshop used for storing scrap at the back yard. Kool walked around the old workshop after lunch. 'For some fresh air', he smiled at his colleagues. He saw the old machine through the closest window. It looked to be in good condition, except may be the motor was faulty. Kool wanted to have this machine direly for including as part of his training routine for his trainees in the Joy-Li'll'y TT Academy. 'I can repair the faulty motor and revive the machine', he thought.

"May be you would not be so excited, if you had more experience with it during your training", commented Li'll'y, when he met her that evening. Kool wouldn't buy the argument. May be she was saying this just trying to wean him off something he wouldn't be able to buy. Answering a direct question, Li'll'y expressed her innocence about the fortune cookie and its clue. But he did not miss the twinkle in her eye.

Two days later he found another fortune cookie served along with his tea, when he returned from another meeting. 'Confused carps Merchant buying goods from the cOLD room'. He shuffled the confused 'carps' merchant and found a 'scrap' merchant. He wasn't sure who was passing these clues. The same day, he happened to know that the Jiangsu management was debating if there was any use for the TTSM that was lying at the old workshop. The management decision was to dismantle the machine and sell off to the scrap dealer, to ensure that no one could identify or use the machine even if they found it at the scrap dealer. So he himself was the beneficiary of this fortune clue, but who was his patron? He had no idea. He decided that he would follow the tips and it would do him good. He didn't want to let slip even a single hint, so he could probably 'win' the TTSM. Hope this wasn't a trap to catch him red handed. He didn't like the idea of stay at a Chinese jail, long term or short term.

However, Kool threw caution to the winds as he visited the scrap dealer's warehouse leaving the Jiangsu premises, within an hour of the scrap sale and found the dismantled machine with all the parts kept together in a box. The dealer claimed them to be parts of a laundry machine, his only efforts at maintaining secrecy. Kool enquired for some used parts for his friend's machine spare parts business and the dealer obliged when Kool was generous and didn't bargain much.

Kool purchased all the parts of the machine that he wanted, one bunch a day for three days and booked them directly by FedEx, DHL and EMS Speed Post, using different services on different days for each bunch of parts purchased on the day and sent them to his friend in Singapore. He also purchased a few other cheap scrap parts from other laundry machines, so as not arouse any suspicion'.

'Only one of the parts, a metal frame that was too unwieldy, remained with him. He purchased a suitcase that would fit the part and hid it under the hotel bed to be carried with him as check in baggage on his flight back.

Next he saved all the documents he came across on the design of the machine. Jiangsu was a small company and wasn't much concerned about the confidentiality of the documents within its walls, as much as they did about the secrecy of the machine itself.

A few days later, as he checked into his flight to Singapore on the way to Chennai and walked past the customs at Shanghai airport, he was asked to identify his checked in baggage that was kept for examination on the table. The customs officer had found an unusual part in his baggage during X-ray. He asked for an explanation and Kool said it was a part of a laundry machine, promptly. The customs officer checked the name plate printed and embossed in Chinese, found that it was made by Jiangsu Sport Equipment Co 'I may not be intelligent, but I know that laundry machines are not sports equipment', the officer commented as he put it aside as if to confiscate. Kool knew that his game was up. Then he pretended to be shocked, 'Oh my God, the scrap dealer cheated me'.

Kool gestured pointing to PA system announcement to the

Officer, 'Last Call for 'Kula', passenger checked in to board Flight No. SQ 833. Please report to Gate no. 126 immediately'. The officer, considered for a minute and said, 'I don't think it is crime to be cheated by a scrap dealer. You may go. Have a nice flight'.

When Kool tried to pick up the part, the officer placed his hands on it and said, 'We have some investigation to do. In any case it will not be useful for your laundry machine'.

Kool almost resigned to leaving the part back with the Officer and turned away.

The young Officer clicked selfie pictures of himself with the part for reporting purposes. He obviously pleased with his picture and his good work, clicked a close picture of the part and even closer picture of the name plate as an afterthought. His magnanimity overflowed when he called Kool who seemed heartbroken and was reluctant to leave.

He handed the part to Kool with a big smile and said, "I have got what I want for the investigation", tapping his mobile phone camera. "In any case this is no missile component. You may take this with you. Now run or the gates will close". Kool thanked him profusely and ran for the security check.

Back in India, Kool and Joy spent the next month plotting their practice in earnest. They hung up portraits of the Chinese all Chinese finalists; Jiang, Deng, Ding Xiang, Zhen Zhen and Qing Zhao, the eventual Gold medallist at the last games at their practice area to give them fighting determination to win against them. Joy added Meiling for the heck of it. Joy downloaded all the videos of the matches that the six played during the last Games and since then from YouTube.

With the help of Mahadevan Sir, Joy and Kool played some of the World Tour Open Championships that technically did not come under the ITTF ban, other than those held in China. As the Chinese players played in all the open tournaments, Joy and Kool had the privilege of playing and practicing against the lower ranked Chinese and won each time. Kool had an opportunity to play and win against Ding Xiang, the World No. 3 after Jiang and Deng, the No.1 and No. 2 respectively.

Kool and Joy were cautiously optimistic of taking a swipe at Gold at the Games later that year.

37 Quake at Kyoto

One of the most important tournaments that Kula played in was the Kyoto Open that had the best players from China pitted against the best of the Japanese. It always used to be fought like a war between the two countries, well almost; especially the last Open, when Saito had defeated Jiang, the then World No. 2 behind Deng, to claim the Championship. Kula had earlier at the last Shanghai Games and practiced briefly with Saito just before Kula's aborted match against the World No. 1, Jiang. Saito had a favourable record against Jiang, but had lost every time to the World No. 2 and World No. 3 ranked players; Deng and Ding Xiang. Jiang, a normally proud and confident Chinese seemed to have a jinx against the Japanese player.

The war in Kyoto started off peacefully. The Chinese mayhem started soon and any one, non-Chinese bit dust. Only two among the world of men stood amidst the wreckage and successfully blunted the Chinese challenge; Saito and Kula.

As the draw would have it, Kula was slated to meet Jiang in the finals, if all went well. Saito was in the opposite side of the draw and if Saito progressed through all the levels just as Jiang was expected to, he would meet Jiang in the Semi's. But Saito the World no. 4 had to meet his nemesis Deng at the Quarters, on the way to his Semi Finals against Jiang. Kula had to get past a couple of Chinese players and finally Ding Xiang in the other Semi Finals. While Kula had the advantage of having won once over each of Deng and Ding Xiang earlier, Saito had yet to overcome Deng against whom he had always lost to. The last time they played just three months earlier, Saito had lost quite badly. The experts expected a Jiang - Deng semi-final and a Jiang - Ding Xiang Final.

Kula and Saito entered into a pact to train each other; for Kula to play against Jiang, if he met him in the finals and for Saito to play against Deng in the Quarterfinals. Kula did not gain much of an insight from Saito. While Kula understood this, he did not hold back anything. He taught and advised Saito all the tricks that he knew on Deng's style of play as also how to overcome him.

Saito had a tough Quarter final match against Deng. He used all the tips given by Kula and at his disposal and managed to scrap through against a fading Deng. The experts opined that co-training with Kula helped Saito win over Deng. He was poised to meet Jiang in the Semi-Final. Kula progressed to the Semi Finals against Ding Xiang.

Ding Xiang, who would be officially replacing Deng as the World official No.2, after Deng's loss to Saito, played with much vigour and was determined to cement the World No.2 position he just acquired. Kula didn't have a place at the ranking system as the ITTF didn't recognize Kula. Ding Xiang looking stressed by the weight of expectations as the new No.2, made some unforced errors that cost him his first game against Kula. But he fought back valiantly winning the next two. Kula got back into the match in the next games as his opponent became listless and hesitant and subsequently romped home as a clear winner in the next three games to win the Semi Finals against Ding Xiang to progress to the finals.

Kula was excited at the prospect of meeting Jiang at the Finals. He was looking forward to the rematch of the abandoned Finals at the Shanghai Games. The last time, Kula was in a mood to test the waters against the formidable Chinese and would have been happy with 'any result''.

'This time around, his mind was besieged by the shameful and bitter experience he and his friends had and was in a fighting mood to extract his sweet revenge on all those who almost ruined the careers of Li'll'y, Joy and his own. Jiang was the motif and the icon that he had to defeat.

But he would have to wait till the Games, as it transpired. Saito, true to expectations had beaten Jiang quite easily. Jiang looked so diffident and insecure against Saito. Kula understood that Jiang, though had a great game, was psychologically vulnerable and if he effectively played a game on his mind, he could pierce this chink in his armour.

For now Kula would focus on Saito. This was his chance for an effective mind game against the now exposed, not so formidable Jiang. So he chose to be brutal with Saito and demolished him at the finals.

News of Saito's capitulation against Kula in the Finals rattled Japan as it happened in Kyoto. But the tremors were known to have shaken Shanghai much worse. Dan was alarmed. Deng, who watched the havoc in person, was also convulsing in fear, hatred, anger and shame, not exactly in that order. A group of five of the Chinese team management along with Deng, went into huddle the next day trying to figure out Kula's game and to identify a player with a style of play that was most potent against the seemingly invincible Kula, in preparation for the next Games at Shanghai. The game plan was to block Kula from progressing to meet Jiang at either the Semi-Final or Final.

Dan was sure that Kula would not be able to participate. Yet, he was taking no chances.

Someone suggested, 'Wang Long'!

Dan explained, 'Wang Long is a Marine in the Chinese Navy. Due to his professional training or the way he was born, he is hardened and sharpened like a Ninja sword. He would slice into anyone so finely that his opponent may never even know that he was being sliced, before he fell'.

Deng nodded in agreement and looked at Dan. Dan nodded while still in deep thought. He had other ideas too. 'I'm was not going to trust just one man to stop Kula on the way to the final. I'm going to throw a series of players at Kula at every round before the final, each with a different style of play and very competent at that. I have to ensure that Kula would not be meeting Jiang in the Final'.

The group appreciated. One mentioned Sun Yat Cheng and another, Qing Shan.

Dan was even thinking outside China, Hong Kong, to be specific. He suggested the name of Yuan Jun of Hong Kong. He had an unpredictable style, just like Kula and if he was trained right, he could be the one to beat Kula on his way.

'How do you get over the ITTF rule change that made it

difficult to include players from other countries'? Dan was asked.

Dan nodded, aware of the rule change that required that a player representing any country should have been playing in the country at least for three years before they could represent it.

'Yuan will train in China, but will play for Hong Kong. Let me handle that'.

The next question was how does one manage the draws in such a way that so many of the designated Chinese players get in the way of Kula at each step of the Tournament.

Dan and another colleague smiled at each other. 'Leave it to us', they said in chorus.

After the meeting was over, Dan and Deng's plotted further. The ITTF related tournaments are conducted with ratings R1, R2 and R3 and those played under Team formats. ITTF's ban on Kula and Jay is normally interpreted only for all championships with an ITTF rating R1 and for Games played under the Team formats, while they could still play the tournaments under R2 and R3 rating.

Thus Kula and Jay could participate in Tournaments with R2 and R3 like Kyoto and other such Opens that has rating R2. Dan would make unofficial moves at the IITF and reinforce and reinterpret the ban on Jay and Kula, so they could not play in R2 and R3 rated competitions too. It would not be extending the ban, but re-interpreting the ban to include R2 rated World Tour tournaments. The Chinese Federation has dominated the working of the ITTF for too long and it would not be difficult to push the ITTF.

But this strategy could misfire if the news of the pressure exerted on the ITTF was leaked to the media. Dan knew the risks, but what else were his options, especially with Deng breathing down his neck?

At the Prize ceremony Kula was interviewed by a Kyoto official;

'How did you feel after having tamed the 'Dragon's Dragon' at the Open?

'It was just another day out. I was confident and I won. I didn't see any dragon out there. I play with people who are and could be great friends both on and off the field. It was just another day out'.

It was Kula all the way at the interview, on the Newspapers, on all the TV channels in Japan. The demolished Saito was sparingly mentioned in the interviews and the great Jiang was suddenly the underdog well before the Games. The stage was set. Kula's popularity grew much bigger. He became the unofficial No. 1 and everyone looked forward to his official crowning at the next Games.

38 Pride of India

Jagadeesan was a Senior Officer at the National TT federation and was most excited on National Sports Mission's 'Pride of India Initiative', a brainchild of the new nationalist Prime Minister of India, NM, as he was known.

Bringing up Indian Sports and Games to a pride of place in the world was the mission through the National Sports Mission's (NSM) 'Pride of India Initiative'. Jagadeesan considered that the 'Pride of India Initiative' was the best thing to happen to the sport in India. The five sports and games selected under the initiative would be liberally funded by the Government with active sponsorship from Corporate Business Houses, to identify talent from across the country and groom them affording World Class coaching and facilities at District level. Various sports and games federations have been asked to present themselves to the NSM Governing Committee to consider their sport or Game to be selected among the five.

Jagadeesan was the silent brain and force behind the Joy-Li'll'y TT Academy and the recruitment model of the Academy could be credited to his sense of social responsibility. The model worked successfully in the 4 districts initially covered by the Academy. The last review of the performance of the Academy had shown that it had more than achieved its objectives. Due to the Academy, TT had caught up with significant number of youngsters as their primary sport and about 120 of them participated in the various district level Joy-Li'll'y Home TT Open Challenge tournaments'.

'Eight of the top players were selected to compete at the State level competition and the Academy players cornered most of the top prizes at this Indian Federation tournament. It was time for the Academy to extend the success of the Academy to the entire Tamil Nadu; at least 12 districts in the next phase.

Jagadeesan had bigger ideas; to expand the concepts developed by the Academy to the national level and make TT a sport of the masses in India. Of course it was not feasible to expand the Academy's reach to such levels immediately. But the Government could do it, especially under the NSM. His idea was simple; if more youngsters took up the game, there would be a better probability of success at the top level. That is, we could perform better at the international competitions.

Jagadeesan had received a call from the Secretary of Sports, 'Please prepare a presentation for including TT as a 'Pride of India Initiative'. This is your chance. Your boss, the bearded fellow has gone on leave, sick. As the PM is heading the committee, it better be good', he said.

Jagadeesan liked the performance and accountability expected of him. It was decades since any one asked him to be accountable for what he did and also to be warned that there would be penalties. He immediately discussed with Mahadevan, who in turn messaged to Kula, 'We have to prepare a convincing presentation to the committee headed by the PM himself. I trust you to prepare a professional presentation that will impress the committee'.

Kool saw the opportunity too. This was to be his best bet to help him with Joy and his restoration in the Indian Team. And TT could make it to the 'Pride of India Initiative' too.

Kool, with Joy had completed the presentation within two his days of landing in India from Kyoto. Mahadevan saw it and was confused.

This was not a regular presentation he was used to and so he had forwarded to Jagadeesan without any comments. Jagadeesan acknowledged that the presentation was the best that he had seen in his career, but it could be scandalous enough and could trigger a bitter diplomatic war, if the contents leaked out. He wasn't sure if he could risk presenting the same to the PM. So he prepared a plan B presentation.

39 'Assassins'

The first two presentations from two different Games Federations bored the PM no limit. He did not find that something he was looking for in them. He ordered to stop the next. He found a typical bureaucratic style in what he saw. Dreary facts and figures, charts, budgets, numbers, past achievements, current rankings, coaching needs, infrastructure needs, funding needs, and organisation charts etc. There was no trace of winning spirit in the either of them. The PM asked the Sports secretary, 'Is this the bunch of movers and shakers that you could assemble'? The Secretary mumbled something. Even he was not sure what the PM was looking for. Luckily, Jagadeesan and Mahadevan saw that. They murmured into Kula's ears to get ready.

But by that time, the PM also got ready to leave, rescheduling his meeting, 'I am not at all satisfied with your ideas. This will not take the sports to the heights we expect them to reach. I hope to see the Vision, Mission, Pride and the hunger to win, when we meet again'.

As the PM walked towards the nearest aisle leading to the nearest exit, he saw a young man and a young girl rushing into the aisle almost blocking his way, laptop in their hands. The security officers around the PM considered them as 'threats' and reacted fast. Two of the PM's body guards tried to block them. The young man dodged them as though they didn't exist and spoke loudly looking at the PM's eyes.

'SIR, WE WANT TO PLACE INDIA ON THE WORLD MAP OF TABLE TENNIS'. We have something to show'.

From the security drill that kicked off at the sudden appearance of the young man and the girl, the PM was led to believe that he was facing assassins and their bullets. The PM looked at the young man, in his eye and saw pride in it. Assassins don't have that. Even as he wanted to see and hear this young man, a protective ring was formed around him and he was ushered, rather carried to the nearest exit. It happened so quickly that even the PM could not defy his security. Without waiting for the PM to react, the young man quickly climbed on to the stage and grabbed the mike, followed by the girl.

The PM tried to look back to see what happened to the boy and the girl and saw both the young man and girl being overpowered by his security commandoes. He heard the boy's laborious, but determined voice that the security could not overpower.

The PM heard his voice as broken sentences through the speaker, 'WE PROMISE... INDIA'S FIRST TT GOLD... NEXT GAMES AT SHANGHAI... NEED TO SHOW YOU SOMETHING'.

'How dumb? This was the 'Pride and Passion' that I came here to see and hear and had wasted all my time today looking for. Instead of meeting them, here I am, the PM, being dragged away from him... and the young man and the girl are being hurt. Is this the heights of paranoia...'?

40 The Presentation

Kula's presentation for the PM started with videos of the 4 minute video of Jay's match against Meiling including her accusation of sorcery and witchcraft, especially targeted at the Bindi the Dot and Kula's sacred ash smear on his forehead. Then there was a slide displaying in text the face saving partial reversal of the ban on Jay and the match referee still ordering her not to wear her dot (bindi) for the rest of the Games and also banning Kula from smearing the white sacred ash, as it had 'the effect of distracting the and mesmerizing the opponents.

The nationalist PM, who rode a wave of success of his party that was considered to represent the Hindu religious right, winced. That was a rare show of emotion he showed till almost the end of the presentation.

Then next he showed a 3 minute highlight of his Quarter Final demolition of Deng, where the Chinese opponent's face was in shock and disbelief at great strokes played by him.

Next was a 3 minute video of the wrong refereeing decisions made against Jay and in favour of Zhen Zhen; that of a victim of treachery. Then he showed the picture of Jay in tears placing the Bronze medal at the feet of Zhen Zhen!

The next slide presented the final status of the two, himself and Jay and their unceremonious exit from the Games. He had directly accused the Chinese Team Management and also had named the two Indian officials of orchestrating the exit of the two from the Games and their ban by the ITTF and the Indian Federation.

Kula's next slide just cried out Loud and Bold,

'Humiliation'
For all Indians
PM Sir

In the next few slides, he talked about Joy-Li'll'y TT Academy's Mission to discover, recruit, coach, and develop world class talent from the small towns of India, starting with 4 districts, with a firm determination to make TT a mass movement and to challenge and defeat the Chinese; **AT THEIR GAME** - In The Dragon's Lair.

In the next two slides they described their selection process and funding model. Then they shared their big success so far with the Academy so far at the Tamil Nadu State Championship.

The next two slides he spoke about the support he wanted from the Government…

- We want the Indian Federation officials to be free of corruption and selfish agenda. They should be committed to growing the game. Only have officials who retired from players and not politicians or bureaucrats.
- We want the Government to help us mass base the game. The real talent is out there in the small towns. These most talented youngsters have not seen a TT racquet, ball and a table yet.
    - Discover this talent, pick them up, train them, incentivise them, Coach them to world standards and let them play against the best in the world. Of all these, 'Discover' is the problem that defies a definition and a set process.
    - As I said, 'Discover' is easy said than done. How do you discover talent? We distribute TT racquets and balls among the interested and get them to start playing!
    - But how do you distribute the TT tables? – Simple provide them nets for the youngsters to convert their home dining table into TT tables. It worked for us. That's how we, Jay and I got initiated into the game, while still in school. It works now for the Joy-Li'll'y TT Academy and is the first stop for our discovery of talent. We conduct the first level of talent hunt when they compete on the Home Dinning table.
    - Yes! We have successfully implemented this Model with a conversion ratio of 25 percent of the youngsters taking up TT as their prime sports…
- On the Policies, Organization, Processes, Implementation, Recruitment Methodology and Budget required etc.: Jagadeesan Sir will continue the presentation.

Jagadeesan rose to fill in. But the PM waved him, 'Later', he gestured…

Kula concluded.

Questions Please

Questions there were aplenty. Kula was relieved. Questions means that people were listening.

Question 1: An old committee member of around sixty five years of age demanded, 'Don't you think it is madness for asking the players to play on the Dining table, while expecting them to beat the Chinese'? Then he looked at PM for his reaction and approval.

The PM remained stoic, without betraying his mind. He gestured to Kula to take the question. He was listening.

Mahadevan rose to help Kula, as he gestured his coach to sit down and took the question himself. 'Sirs, with great respects to your experience and age, the Football great Brazil, the talent is fed from the street Football played by youngsters from the age of four. Not from Academies or the best Schools.

Closer home in India, until the late 1970's, cricket was a game of the chosen few, who could afford an all-white uniform and whose schools could afford a cricket gear. Till then India held an ignominious last place among the Test playing nations. But now, after when the Gulley Cricket, a phenomenon, kicked off, cricket in India has acquired a cult status'.

'Not only is it feeding a continuous stream of winners for the districts, for the states, for the nation to pick up from, but also the quality of cricket and the players have improved by leaps and bounds. We had Shewag, Yuvaraj and others staring into the eyes of Brett Lee and Michael Johnson and hitting them for back to back sixes. Nobody told these guys who were from the 'Gulley Cricket Party' that they are lesser cricketers than the ones that were produced spic and span from the elite schools and that they should not dare to dream, to win. No Dhoni, No Dhawan, No Ashwin, No Kohli, No Jadeja - if there was no Gulley cricket'.

'Yes, Dining Tables have their limitations. But what is the other model to take TT to the masses? Are you planning to provide at least one table to every school in each district? Are we prepared for the costs, even if the NSM is ready to spend, what is the cost benefit? Do you know that my school had a TT table? Due to the great demand for time and space at the tables, the school merrily raised the fee and only the most privileged had an opportunity to touch it. Most of them who had the passion, who had the game, left the table for other street options. I was lucky to pursue my interests at the Dining Table and look what I have achieved. Look what Jay, here with me, has achieved. We are no flashes in the pan. We have been trying to create a model and replicate our success. Our Joy-Li'll'y Academy identifies talent from among the 'Dining Table maestros'. You are right Sirs; once discovered, we do wean them away from the Dining Table game and train them on world class tables. It just takes them four weeks of practice on the regular tables for them to reorient and move on. We have been on the path of success. Our academy, as already presented, has bagged more than half the medals at the TN State Championship'.

The PM Clapped, his next show of emotion during the presentation. The rest of the questions were easy.

Finally, the PM asked, 'How confident and committed are you to win the Gold, both of you at the Games in China'?

Kula, replied, 'Absolutely Sir. We live for the 'Cold Gold'. We have a point to prove to the world. I want my vengeance. For the sake of Jay, who was disgraced! For our own sake, as we were humiliated. For the sake of our country's honour. I want to win the Gold. So wants Jay. Jay walked up to the stage and held Kula's hands and raised it high. 'We will bring you Yellow Metal from the Shanghai Games later this year, Sir', they both said in chorus.

The PM was thoughtful. He asked again, 'First, what do you want from the Government, for you to win. And Second; as reward, if you win? Name it and you will get it, whatever within the powers of this Government'.

'First; we both want an opportunity to play for India at the coming Games. Please remember that we both were unceremoniously exited and banned by the ITTF instigated by the Indian Federation for three years and that our ban would be still effective when the next Games are on. The PM turned to the Sports Secretary and asked him to prepare the actions for their exoneration and to reverse the ban. 'I don't promise', the PM said. 'If what I heard is true, I don't see why you shouldn't play for India at the

Games'.

'Regarding, what we want as reward is a place for TT in the 'Pride of India Initiative'.

Back in his office the PM scribbled an instruction on the report for Ramaswamy Shastry, Chennai, to verify certain facts and report to him in confidence. Shastry visited the Joy- Li'll'y TT Academy in the guise of checking on the admission process for his grand-neice. He had a long chat with Kula and Joy and asked several questions. He personally saw the commitment and fire in Jay and Kula's eyes. He was satisfied.

The next day, Jagadeesan received a message from the PM's office through the Sports Secretary. 'Congratulations, you have earned a place for TT in the initiative. The PM is proud of the youngsters'.

Part 5: Home Coming

41 Fragrance from China

Kool and Joy were on cloud nine following the meeting with the PM and as they were assured of his personal attention. It was like God's will being on their side. If they still did not get their exoneration, then it should be construed that their fate is stronger than the will of their Gods. Kool started trusting that both his and Joy's luck that had deserted them briefly at the heights of their career, was gently revisiting them. It was up to them both not to let go their fortune by another display of stupidity.

They both chatted incessantly on their flight back to Chennai, two days later with Mahadevan admiring their youthful energy and cheerfulness. This flight was a happy contrast against their flight back from Shanghai, when they spoke little.

As they took the morning flight back to Chennai, and reached around 12:30 PM. They both rushed to the Joy-Li'll'y academy, to share the news. The security at the gate alerted them that they had a surprise waiting inside. Probably the news of their successful meeting with the PM, travelled ahead of them and the members were in a celebration mood. But as they passed the playing hall to Joy's office, they found little evidence of any celebration, not a single person walked up to congratulate them. Surely, the news of TT figuring in the 'Pride of India Initiative' had not reached them yet.

As they reached near Joy's office, one of the players excitedly said, 'A foreigner has come down to join the Academy'.

It was a fact that a lot of foreigners especially from the Asia Pacific, who had seen the rise of Kool and Joy against the Chinese, had been showing interest in joining the academy. The Joy-Li'll'y Academy was yet to decide if they wanted to take such recruits in. Probably one such aspirant has come down to meet them personally.

Joy entered the office first with Kool climbing the stairs not far behind her. Joy screamed as she opened the door and pounced inside, shocking Kool, who rushed to her help. Kool saw a foreigner trying to get up from her chair, still with her back to him.

Joy pounced on her with a scream… of joy… 'Li'll'y'!
Joy shrieked in delight and she hugged her from behind almost toppling her. There were tears of joy. Surely, the Gods were with them that day.

'It is a long story', Li'll'y said on how she came into India and why she did not intimate them beforehand. By then almost the entire team rushed to the outside Joy's office drawn by the huge commotion. They heard the stranger telling Joy and Kool 'What's between friends? You know, I don't to even knock before entering'. The entire team got introduced to the Li'll'y of the Joy-Li'll'y TT Academy and also knew good times were flowing into the Academy.

It was already late for Li'll'y's lunch, who, they knew maintained strict meal times. Kool asked Li'll'y, 'what would you like to have for Lunch? Chinese, Indian, Continental, Pizzas, Burgers'?

Li'll'y felt too pampered. 'Come on Kool, Don't treat me like a guest. I'm not. Let me check out what Joy packed from home. It should be delicious'.

She picked up Joy's tiffin box to find a few idlies with some spice powders soaked in oil for seasoning. She ate all of them, with tears due to spicy heat welling up in her eyes.

'Delicious! Now where do you want to take me for 'your' lunch'? she asked.

'I will take you home. My mother will prepare something good for you.

Li'll'y jumped with joy, 'Let me meet Mom first. My lunch is done. If you want something, we will carry something home so you both can eat, so that Mom doesn't have to cook again'.

Joy would have nothing of that sort. She called her Mom, 'Mom, I'm bringing you a surprise guest. Better prepare some of your best food for three. Oh! The idlies? Just got eaten by a hog'.

There was no stopping her. Her sister was back!

They reached Joy's home in about half an hour. Mom welcomed her 'daughters' with a an 'Arathi' from a silver plate, smeared a dot on both their forehead with a vermillion liquid, poured out the contents of the plate outside home and asked them both in and insisted they put their right foot forward into their home. It was Mother's turn to hug them both and cry. She took Li'll'y, whom she had never met before, to be her own daughter; God's return gift to her and to Joy. She, just like Joy, would never again grieve for the daughter they lost several years back. For Li'll'y it was homecoming of a different kind. She was overwhelmed by the love and affection of Joy's Mom. It was the most poignant moment in her life in several years.

Kool was touched by the emotional family union, but having been forgotten by the ladies, stuck his head in the middle, as if to demand a dash of vermillion on his forehead too. As the Lady of the house had dispensed the same outside the house before entering, she planted a motherly kiss on his forehead and laughed and welcomed him too.

Li'll'y, in jest pulled Kool towards her and kissed him on the forehead and cheeks too. Joy, had an urge to pull Kool to her side and kiss him too, but stopped herself. It wasn't in her character. Her mother did not fail to notice the absurd urge in Joy to compete with Li'll'y with respect to Kool. She remembered Jay and Vaijay in their happier days, when they competed between themselves for their mother's lap and their father's shoulders. She hoped this was something as simple as that. She also noticed that Kool was embarrassed with Li'll'y's freedom with him, in front of elders.

She couldn't fault Li'll'y, as she was from a different culture and the sensitiveness of male-female relationships in India may not be known to her.

'Yet, she could have been discrete', she thought.

She trusted Joy's sensibilities in her relationship with Kool. And she trusted Kool equally not to take advantage of his freedom and proximity with Joy. She also trusted Kool to maintain a decent distance with Li'll'y. Mother prayed silently that none of the three should get hurt within a warped relationship. Nobody seemed to notice that mother went silent as she served lunch, while they chatted without care.

The three continued sitting at the dining table chatting away stories of years between them the whole afternoon, till late in the evening.

First, Li'll'y narrated how she landed at Chennai. She was one of the two TT coaches that were sent to Sri Lanka on a sports exchange program. When the Chinese coaches arrived in Colombo, they found that they had landed too early for any meaningful coaching assignment, as the Academy in which they were supposed to coach was still in the formative stages. Most of the trainee players were still in the process of being selected and the local coaches hadn't been recruited yet. It would take three weeks or more to complete the process.

The embarrassed Sri Lankan Government had offered to send them on a guided tour around Sri Lanka for three weeks. The two travelled for 2-3 days and there wasn't much else to see and wanted to go back to China. Hence the third option; a holiday in India for 2-3 weeks! Li'll'y's friend was more interested in a Buddhist cultural tour in India. So they planned to send the other girl coach on a Buddhist cultural tour starting from Bodh Gaya, in India, where the Buddha attained Enlightenment, followed by Rajgir, Nalanda, Patna, Vaishali, Kushi Nagar, Lumbini, Srivasti – Sahet & Mahet, Lucknow, New Delhi and back. Li'll'y excused herself from it. She preferred, she said, activities like trekking and Yoga at the foot of the Himalayas at her own pace.

Both the girls landed at Chennai airport before her friend boarded her flight to New Delhi on the way to Bodh Gaya. Li'll'y chose not to board her flight to Darjeeling for trekking and walked out of the airport. She browsed for Joy-Li'll'y TT Academy and dialled the number for directions.

'I am from Singapore. I want to join the academy', she introduced herself.

On reaching the Academy, she was so happy to visit such a successful academy that she shared her own name with. She told the gatekeeper that she came to meet Joy or Kool as she wanted to join the Academy. It had a profound effect on the middle aged Gatekeeper. He showed so much excitement like a school boy and shook hands with her for whole minutes.

'Madam, Delhi. Come one hour', proud of his English and walked her to Joy's office.

She settled at Joy's office deliberately facing away from the door to extend the surprise for a few milliseconds more.

In the evening, Li'll'y made a serious request, rather a command, 'Most important, no pictures of me in Chennai with any of you on any of our mobiles. I don't want another 'selfie' scandal that would push me behind bars forever. Even Cheng would not be able to save me the next time'.

The next two days, they spent a lot of time with the team at the Academy. Li'll'y interacted with the members. She played with them and gave them advice. She introduced a new style that the team wasn't aware of. They found that her game had such depth, only to be equalled by Joy and Kool.

'India is like no other country in the world', Li'll'y said. 'Somehow, I find God and religious rituals in every one of your talk and act! God is in your mind and heart!

'Yes, There is an anecdote, I would like to share…' said Joy.

'Someone from the west, who had closely observed India during his lifetime, had commented to one of his political friends, 'If God does exist, I am sure He exists in India…"

'His Indian politician friend had felt so happy at the acknowledgement of a foreigner and beamed proudly, 'Yes! We are sure God is with us because we are always morally and ethically superior to the rest of the world".

'The Westerner smiled and said, 'You seem to celebrate too early. Why don't you ask me for my reason for such an observation'; at which the Indian Politician, looked at him askance.

'The foreigner said with a chuckle, 'India is my living proof that God does exist. Else, how can one explain that people not only live happily, but also love their country and their politicians; in spite of all the corruption and apathy from the political class that rotted this country from inside"?

'The Politician was grounded'!

She stayed with Joy at her home and shared Joy's room. She tried Joy's Sarees, Chudidar's and loved to sport the 'Bindi', the Dot. Li'll'y twinkled at them both reminding them of the 'selfie'. Joy was embarrassed and chased her around the table in mock anger.

The three criss-crossed Chennai, with no destination in

particular on a hired three wheeled autorikshas, in the evenings until late into night. Li'll'y enjoyed every minute of her stay.

Kool asked her cautiously if she would like to visit his parents at Mathur, his hometown. Li'll'y was delighted, of course.

42 Mathur

They drove to his hometown in the car borrowed from Mahadevan, who was away in New Delhi for the next week. The country side was very beautiful and reminded Li'll'y of her village in central China. The people looked the same, except for their colour and costumes. They reached a huge dam across the River Cauvery. She was surprised at people venerating anything that moved or flowed, the Sun, the Moon, the Cow, the River, the Snake, the Monkey, the Elephant, the Eagle and even the lizard. There were even temples for each of these forms! Though there were parallels in China until century ago, as they shared common cultural and belief due to Chinese adopting Buddhism that propagated from India, the intensity of such faith among the Indians surprised and impressed her. She was seeing a different dimension to human life, something she has never experienced before, though she has travelled to several countries for her TT tournaments.

The River and the Dam seemed the lifeline of a whole lot of people as the country had not still moved out of its dependency on agriculture to employ its people. She did not compare India with China on any aspect of life and living. She felt they are two different worlds all together. India was easy, spontaneous, truthful, contended and slow. China was suspicious, dutiful, fast and always thirsty. She enjoyed her stay in India but loved China as her motherland.

Krishnan, who was waiting to see his 'second daughter', as his wife proposed to call her, found it difficult to believe her.

How could a friend from a faraway land that Jay had met just for two weeks become his daughter? And take the place of his dear lost daughter? He shook his head all morning while they were still driving from Chennai. But his eyes moistened when he laid his eyes on Li'll'y. He hugged them both and shed tears of joy, as though he had known this Chinese 'daughter' all her life.

The dining table at which the two youngsters discovered their

TT talent lay at the same place. It looked much older now though it was sparingly used. Kula touched to feel the table on an impulse as though he was touching his mother who brought him to earth. Only, he was not a dramatic person, else he would have hugged it. That's exactly what Jay did as tears moistened in her eyes.

Krishnan was grateful to Kula, who he heard had bravely held the Indian Team Managers 'by their scruff', in support of Jay unmindful of his own TT career and probably risking the rest of his life in a Chinese jail. He loved his daughter very much, though he did not find enough opportunities to see her these days.

'Did Kula love his daughter as much too'? He asked himself.

'Yes, what's wrong with it', Jay's Mom spoke quite loudly, as if in answer, though she was replying to a different question asked by Jay that was in no way relevant to her husband's thoughts.

'How did she read my mind? Am I so obvious'? Jay's Dad slapped himself at the back of his head in a half smile.

Krishnan remembered the day when Kula visited his home with Chandra while Jay was grieving and brooding over her twin sister who was no more. How he initially schemed on some of the days to keep Kula out of his home!

But later, when Jay opened out to Kula as a natural friend and started playing TT with him, forgetting her grief, how he had reluctantly permitted their friendship to take roots! Later to his surprise, how both of them carried home their respective school TT Championship trophies and won his heart and trust! And how Kula had steered her career in TT and life as well, and became her friend, mentor, guide and guardian! How well they supported each other to become the highest ranked players in India and world beaters at that, till bad times struck them in China!

'Would Kula make Jay's ideal husband too'? thought Krishnan.

'Why not, we all would love the idea', said Jay's Mom aloud, again in response to another question from the young ladies and nothing to do with the thoughts on his mind.

Krishnan patted himself at the back of his head again and smiled a full smile this time.

It was lunch time and Kool was invited, but he chose to excuse himself to see his parents and sister who came down for his visit. It was homecoming for him, who rarely visited his parents due to his frequent travel abroad. They only knew he was doing good, both in software and in TT. They also knew that he had been cheated and dumped and could not play again in international competitions by some Chinese 'enemies'. They were sceptical when he told them of his visit with his Chinese friend.

His father questioned, 'Did he not pay for his friendship with some Chinese already'? Why one more experiment? The Chinese are untrustworthy. They could back stab as they did to Nehru saying all the while, 'Hindi, Chini, Bhayee, Bhayee'!

His mother was persistent, 'I'm determined to caution my son against his Chinese friend, who I'm sure, 'is a spy of some kind'. I would politely ask Kula's Chinese friend to leave his company and save him from further trouble and ignominy. If she was a true friend, she would leave him and now'.

Kula's sister, Lakshmi was pleading, 'Do not to worry as Kula knows everything. Don't talk or do something very stupid in front of his friend. That would be a sure way to lose Kula, who already doesn't visit home often'.

But the parents were plotting their move against his Chinese friend and weren't in any mood to heed to Lakshmi.

After a sumptuous lunch, he lay on his mother's lap and slept like a child. His sister switched on the fan and not satisfied, she took a hand fan and breezed him with it. His mom picked up another hand fan and sang a lullaby, as if he was three month old baby.

Kula's father was thinking of his wedding.

He spoke in a hushed voice to his wife and daughter, 'As he is planning to stay for a few days, shall we ask my maternal grand uncle's, brother's granddaughter's sister-in-law's daughter's hand for him? I saw the girl at a wedding reception; she is beautiful as a Princess. She has studied Engineering and she worked for a while and now has left work to be at home in preparation for her wedding; learning to cook and keep the home.

His mother replied, in equally whispering mode, 'Why, I know the girl and all of them', with a scorn.

'Her mother is too talkative. I believe the girl would also have such qualities. Why can't we look at my Shobha aunty's cousin's granddaughter's sister-in-Law's sister'?

Kula's father said impatiently, 'I know that you can't sleep if you don't say something improper about my side of our relatives. I knew well before I started, you will veto whoever I suggest and you will suggest someone from your side'.

Kula's sister hushed them up. 'You are not only going to wake him up from his sleep, but also going to drive him off to Chennai. Can't you keep quite? Don't quarrel about his future wife. God must have already picked the right one for him. May be he has already met her', she said in support of Kula.

She was thinking of Jay as the right one for Kula. Kula smiled in his sleep.

That evening Kool wanted to take Joy and Li'll'y to his house to meet his dear family. But something wasn't right about his plan. How would Li'll'y respond if she found his house was very modest by any standards,

'We eat sitting on the floor? There were not enough furniture, no sofas, not enough chairs, no proper beds, only straw mats rolled on the floor. You still have to walk into the backyard to wash your hands and legs from plastic buckets and mugs as there were neither porcelain, nor running water'.

'My mother wouldn't have spoons for guests and if one was required, she would pull one from the pickle bottle and offer it. She has never seen a fork and never heard that Chinese eat out of chopsticks'.

He wasn't about to educate his mother about table etiquette in this haste.

'But still, if Li'll'y was a true friend, she wouldn't mind anything'.

He remembered how she devoured Joy's idlies laced with spices soaked in oils, with her bare fingers. He had never seen her eat with her fingers, until that day. He hoped that Li'll'y's friendship would transcend all these shortcomings of his and that they would still be as good friends at the end of the day. He would take the call later in the evening, may be after consulting Joy.

The three youngsters drove up to the banks of River Cauvery and walked together. Joy shoulders were rubbing against Kula's arms, and they weren't aware of themselves. It was a full moon and it was rising in all glory. The breeze was fresh. Li'll'y walked a step behind in admiration of their togetherness, though she had an urge to hold Kool's other hand.

She did not have a mind to play any of her pranks on Joy today, though. It would have to be another day. They walked for one full hour without anyone uttering a single word.

He dropped them both late at Joy's place and walked back to his house leaving the car behind, when he realized that he had not discussed with Joy on the question of Li'll'y's visit to his home.

43 Mother

Kula slept fitfully for the best part of the night and blissfully quite early in the morning. He had the full moon of last night in his dreams. But, what's this? Why are there two moons? And why is one of them eclipsing the other? Was it a bad omen? He was shaking violently. He felt he was being shaken out of his reverie while he was still searching for explanation for his two moons. He realized it was no dream thing any longer. His sister, Lakshmi was shaking him wildly.

'Get up, hurry up; come out. They have come', she spoke in cryptic clues and walked out adjusting her hair and smiling big. Kula, still not wanting to let go his ominous dream, was in no mood to wake up, wondering who it was that came at this early hour.

Then he heard their voices. He sprang up, off his straw mat bed and rolled it up quickly. He adjusted his dhoti and combed his hair. He ran into the back yard to wash his face and pulled some cloth on a line to wipe his face dry, threw it where it hung earlier and rushed into the house. It was still semi dark.

'What were they doing at this hour'? He stepped on to the front of the house as Jay and Li'll'y were standing in the front garden, smelling the flowers. He saw Li'll'y first, like he had never seen her before. Fresh and fair like morning dew.

He whispered softly, 'Li Li(ng)' as he took a deep breath. He smelt the fragrance of fresh Lilies surrounding and pervading him as the cloudy mist that passes by you on the hill.

Li'll'y exclaimed, 'Exactly, yes! This is exactly how to pronounce my name'!

'You had been a bit rusty and course, while in China. Now that you are back with family, yes, this is how to'!

By then the whole household had been swept off their beds and the entire beds swept of the floors. His sister helped his Mother to quickly dump all the clothes and things strewn around behind the only cup board they had. The bare top of his father was stuffed into a wrinkled though clean white shirt and seated on a straw mat with an old newspaper thrust into his hands as if to give him an air of 'intelligentsia' on his morning news scan. The mother's unkempt hair was brushed quickly, gracefully tied and folded into a ball. She was sent into the kitchen to make tea for the guests. All in a few minutes under the leadership charge of Lakshmi, who in her own right was a Bank Officer's wife in a bigger town.

She then rushed out to receive the guests, only to find a mesmerized Kool taking a deep breath and invoking the fragrance of the jasmine.

When she realized that he was only calling Li'll'y's name, she pondered, 'Has he gone mad? That too while Jay is watching'? She shook her head at this impropriety. She will reprimand him later.

Next, Lakshmi looked at Li'll'y and was too stunned for words at the pristine beauty, as if chiselled from ivory and shone like fresh snow in golden sunlight against a blue skyline. It was her turn to be overwhelmed by the morning lily; by her freshness and fragrance on a cool moist summer dawn. She had so many words to describe the beautiful Li'll'y swirling in her head, but could not find a single word to welcome her into her home.

Li'll'y was rushing in to meet Kool's Mom. As she walked past Lakshmi, she surprised her with a peck of a kiss on her cheeks and walked straight into kitchen past Kool's father who was engaged in pretention and hardly looked at her. He wasn't instructed to.

Li'll'y found Kool's Mom struggling with the kerosene stove kept on the floor, sitting beside it on a flat wooden plank. Li'll'y pulled a second plank lying nearby and sat near his Mother, hugged her and rested her head on Mother's shoulders.

Mother, who didn't expect her closeness, was dripping with her sincere affections for Li'll'y. She tried to say something, but could not. What language should she talk in? She held her face with both the palms of her hands for a while looking closely with Motherly warmth.

She finally asked, 'Mummy… Daddy…' she could not get farther than that with her limited vocabulary and gestured with her fingers and eyes 'good'?

Li'll'y conveyed in a sign language she devised on the spur of

-the moment, 'Mummy... died... child'. Daddy... died... four years'...

Mother was genuinely sad for Li'll'y and tears welled up in Li'll'y's eyes.

'Brother... sister'...? all in signs. As Li'll'y shook her head to say no, she began to sob.

Mother who had no knowledge of the one child policy in China that robbed all the children of their brothers and sisters before they were conceived, hugged her close and kissed her on her forehead.

She consoled Li'll'y, 'I am your Mother, I'm here for you. Kula is here and Uncle is here. Lakshmi is here. Jay is here. You are not alone. You always were my child. That's why you came all the way from your land to see me and placed yourself in my arms. Shouldn't weep, I am here, your Mother', all in Tamil, the local language.

Li'll'y understood every word that she uttered as their hearts that talked needed no burden of a language.

Li'll'y, found it hard to explain her tears.

The more she tried to rationalize, the more she sobbed and the more she moved closer to her new found Mother and rested squarely on her bosoms. She remembered the last time she wept in memory of her Mother was when she left her hometown with her Dad, while she was still six. She never returned to her home since then. Her father, the only family she had, visited her regularly at Shanghai and poured lot of love and affection on her.

She never cried in memory of her mother, when in Shanghai, not even when her father visited her. She wanted to show her father that she was strong. There were humpty Mothers of her friends in Shanghai she had bumped into. But no one ever held her face close with their palms and looked into her eyes with genuine love. This was the first time she was deeply reminded of her Mother's love in about fifteen years. She didn't even weep when her father died a few years back. By then she had learnt to conceal her tears. In the society around her, it was not fashionable to show one's grief and in any case, her tears had been frozen for too long as she had no warm shoulders to pour her sorrow onto...

Kula, Jay and Lakshmi watched the heart-rending drama in tears of their own for Li'll'y.

'How inconsiderate and selfish of us'. Kula and Jay thought in tandem.

'We never recognized that Li'll'y had so much sorrow pent up in her. Only Mother's genuine love could unfreeze her anguish and bring it out, though they didn't even speak the same language'!

Even Kula's father, came behind them near the kitchen door and watched the solemn get together of 'Mother' with 'daughter' and had moist eyes. Mother held her close with all love, till Li'll'y was spent on her bosoms at this humble home, but full of love.

Li'll'y recovered quickly, though clinging on to her mother, helped her prepare tea and some of the finest snow white, lily soft idlies prepared from hand ground batter that Mother had prepared the earlier day and coconut chutney to go with it. Li'll'y made all of the family sit in a row and served the entire family, including Mother, as if she were the host and they, her guests. She waited for Mother to finish her breakfast and insisted on Mother feeding her with her own hands, as she leaned on her shoulders without a care. She was determined to enjoy the privilege of Mother's love and family, as long as it lasted. This family offered her all that she longed for.

As the sun shone from overhead, the neighbouring ladies and children swarmed around Kool's house at the doorsteps, while some of them ventured inside. Jay was very beautiful too, but she was old time. Li'll'y was the fresh flower that interested them. Some of them were content at just looking in astonishment at her skin tone, freshness and softness. Some of them ventured to touch her on some pretext or the other. She offered chocolates for all, young and old. The older women dutifully handed over the chocolates to their younger children or saved them for the ones still at school. Li'll'y blended not only with the family, but in the entire neighbourhood as though it was her natural domain.

She heard whispers in Tamil, the native language in Chennai and Mathur, 'The girl is so charming'.

'The girl is unassuming'. Jay was translating the tit bits of whispers to Li'll'y and enjoyed the warmth and success that Li'll'y was showered with in the neighbourhood. She did not care that Li'll'y had grabbed all the attention that she was used to in this family and the neighbours. She wasn't jealous. She was in fact proud of Li'll'y.

She heard the next set of rumours in whispers, also in Tamil, 'Kula is planning to marry this Chinese Girl'!

At which another neighbour woman whispered back, 'Which caste does she belong'?

'I think Chinese Iyer. Look, how fair she is'.

'Whatever; she would be so ideal for Kula and of course for the family'.

'Will Kula go to China with her'?

'Why not? Let him go to China with her and let him live happily with her. He will get kids with such fair skin'.

At these last pieces of conversation, Joy closed Li'll'y's ears with her palms as if she didn't want her to hear, half jealous and half in mock anger.

Li'll'y gestured with her eyes, 'What about'?

Joy gestured back with her eyes, 'Later'.

It was evening and time to leave. Li'll'y had presents for everyone. A beautiful silk Saree for Kula's Mother, A silk Dhoti for Father. She purchased both at the Chennai Airport duty free and a beautiful Chinese talking Doll in ceramic, she brought all the way from China for Lakshmi. Her Mother, as was custom in India, gave the girls, bright red Kum Kum powder for them to wear as bindi, the dot. Joy accepted it and put on the centre of her forehead, just between but slightly above the eyebrows. Li'll'y had seen Jay's mother and Kool's sister and a few other ladies wear the same Kum Kum powder at the edge of the parting line of hair and she chose to apply the same there.

Kula's sister rushed to clarify 'Only married girls should wear the Kum Kum on the parting line of hair. Unmarried girls should wear only in the centre of the forehead' as she pointed out to Joy.

Li'll'y laughed at the detail in the custom and said, 'Let me get married. She pulled Kula to her side and asked, 'Kool, Please marry me'.

There was shock in everyone's mind, but they chose to cover it with embarrassed smiles. Joy moved first.

She tugged at Li'll'y and walked with her out towards the car, and murmured, 'Before you make more fool of yourself... Marriage and this Kum Kum are so sacred in India that it is sacrilege to joke about it'.

Li'll'y who realized that she had taken her prank too far, followed her to the car.

'Is it blasphemous'? asked Li'll'y innocently. 'No not blasphemous in the way we hear of edicts from other religions. Hinduism is more tolerant. It is sacred, that's all. It's just improper to make jokes on it', explained Joy still tugging her toward the car.

Li'll'y teasingly said, 'I was not joking; about marrying Kool. You know I was serious', with her twinkling eye.

Jay retorted rather angrily, 'That's why I can't permit you to make more a fool of yourself than you have already done'.

Li'll'y then remembered something and ran back to the house. She asked Kools's father and Mother to stand side by side and fell at their feet seeking their blessings. She had prepared herself well for this trip, watching a few Tamil movies and browsing several picture books, while in Colombo. His parents were most glad to bless her.

Kula's mother wished in her mind, 'Hope she would become part of the family, through a marriage with Kula'.

She hugged Li'll'y and said aloud, 'God bless you and may you be showered with all the sixteen riches a girl should enjoy in life'.

'This is the life I had dreamed of at home with 'my' family, with my Mother. I was lucky to spend the whole day today with Mother and I will remember all my life', she said as a matter of fact, her eyes welling as she turned to leave.

44 Banks of Cauvery

The next day Kula wanted to visit his high school. His friends and teachers had wanted to meet him and he had gladly agreed to meet them at the School. Kula had been the most successful and popular of the school alumni and his friends wanted to be with him on that day. For the present school children, Kula was their own star, within touching distance, to watch, shake hands and to feel the energy.

The Principal introduced him to those assembled amidst high decibel applause. He also introduced Jay, who he had heard of, but never met. The surprise package in this visit was Li'll'y, the fairest of them all.

Kula chose to talk a few words, 'I had played my first TT in this school. I won my first School Championship in this same hall. I could not afford regular membership subscription to play, so had to be content most of the time watching my friends play, from the side-lines of the table. It's a long distance I have travelled since then. I recall the help I received from the school and my friends in my formative two years of my TT journey. Of course, I should say I had the greatest support from Jay, who is sitting near me and her family. So far we have had the opportunity to journey together. We have some final objectives. We are striving to put India on the World TT map. So we have started an Academy named Joy-Li'll'y TT academy at Chennai, which also operates at Lasem. Some of our school students are also members of this Academy'.

'This is my friend Li'll'y, from China. She is on a visit to India. She is a great TT player herself. But her current hobby is trekking and yoga', and then winked at Li'll'y.

The audience wanted a match between India and China right then. They wanted to see their Indian Hero beat the Chinese opponent. The request was too heavy and Kool didn't want to disappoint them. He looked at Li'll'y.

Li'll'y rose up, smiling at the challenge, as always. 'This will be a friendly though. Moreover competitive Sport is not played in these settings. Let me tell you. Kool can beat me any day in a competitive tournament. But when countries' pride is at stake, we carry tremendous responsibilities and the will to fight and win. The rankings don't matter any more and more frequently than not, we have upsets. In such cases, we fight for much more than a cash prize. It all depends on who has the will to beat, on that day. It is true of me. I can beat Kool, if I am determined to fight for my country's pride. But remember, there are others in China, who are the people for Kool to beat. Knowing Kool's game, he could be a world beater. But the fact is that he hasn't beaten the best... yet... I don't know if he will, but he can. I wish he did'.

The friendly began. Kool won the first game. Li'll'y fought hard and won the second. They shared honours. Kool handed out his racquet to Joy. Joy played and won against the hard fighting and tiring Li'll'y. The spectators had an opportunity to watch great, world class games.

The Principal had arranged for lunch and Kool asked the girls if they would mind if he stayed behind to spend some time with his friends. The girls didn't mind and were glad to have some personal time between them and Joy jumped into the car with Li'll'y.

Joy had in mind to visit her school too. But she had something far more important. She took Li'll'y to some of the spots she liked and had enjoyed while Vaijay was still alive. She had been avoiding these spots, since her sister died and had been burdened by the memories of her sister.

She had to view the same spots in the company of Li'll'y and to reiterate to herself and the void around her that her sister was back and alive.

First they went to the Ganesh temple under the shade of a peepal tree and beside it was a serene lily pond. Li'll'y could not relate to the Gods in the temple, but followed all that Joy did. Joy liked to ring the bell and so did Li'll'y. Joy remembered how Vaijay and she used to pester her Dad to pick up lilies for them from the pond. This time the water lilies had a more significant reason to be picked. They had their namesake, Li'll'y to please. Joy insisted on wading waist deep in the water and pick up one of the lilies for Li'll'y. Li'll'y had never smelt an Indian water lily before and she tried it with the excitement of a child, only to be put off by its odour and she showed it by contorting her face.

Joy laughed and picked up the flower from her, closed her eyes and invoked, 'Li Li(ng)', as she smelt it with a deep breath and coughed… pretending to be choked by the odour. They laughed together.

Then they reached the waters. They cooled off their heels dipping their legs in the river sitting on a rock. Joy narrated the whispers that the neighbours had, while they were at Kool's home, with a tinge of jealousy and a lot of giggle.

She told her 'The neighbours expected Kool to marry you and proceed to live in China with her and also to have fair children just like you'. They both laughed.

Li'll'y found Joy was excited every time they mentioned Kool.

'How much do you like Kool' asked Li'll'y.

'So much', Joy showed the extent of water in the Mathur Dam reservoir that filled the horizons in front of them; and then the sky entirely; and then the land behind them. 'All together; that much'!

Li'll'y had never seen such excitement in a girl about her boyfriend before. The way Joy blushed, she knew that she had been untouched by Kool's hands.

'Your first romance'?

Joy nodded as she blushed again. Li'll'y knew intuitively that Joy had conceded to herself too for the first time. Joy was glad that she had a sister to share her first definition of love and to reinforce her love. She never shared her thoughts on Kool with anyone else; not even to Kool.

'Is it love or just 'like''? Li'll'y asked, to help Joy make up her mind. Joy blushed again,

'Love'! Joy blushed, with such embarrassment and shyness that Li'll'y felt Joy was much more tender than the lily flower that she herself related to.

Li'll'y was confused. How can she be so shy and coy when they had always given company to each other, had travelled together so much, stayed close and had their intimate moments? Joy's coyness like a schoolgirl in her early teens and on her first crush, baffled her.

Li'll'y asked, 'Does Kool know? Have you told him of your love for him'?

'No', shaking her head strongly as it would be heart-breaking task for her.

'Do you think Kool loves you, like you do'?

'I plain don't know. He never told me and I'm afraid to ask. I don't want to break his heart and mine too', Joy replied; the first coherent answer from her.

From shyness, she has moved to the next emotion, fear; fear of being heartbroken.

Still confused remembering something between them, Li'll'y was wondering if Kool was taking advantage of her innocence. For the first time Li'll'y saw Joy as a sister; a timid sister at that, who needed protection and guidance. 'The world is bad'. She didn't want anyone to take advantage of Joy, even if it was Kool; and especially if it was Kool. It would amount to betrayal of trust.

'Has he ever touched you in any way to arouse your feelings'?

'No, Kool is a gentleman'.

Not sure, if Joy understood her question, 'Has anyone else touched you with such intentions'?

'No', Kool would have killed him'.

She understood the question all right, Lilly was convinced and comforted. Still it didn't sum up.

'How did you feel or what would you do when Kool hugged you in the privacy of your room', Li'll'y was fishing for words to make Joy understand the point she was coming from.

Joy was living her own world of silly crush and shyness. Did she understand that love is serious business, not just about tender emotions, holding hands and a few blushes? How come Joy doesn't know yet, when she is all of twenty one that Love is union of hearts, minds and bodies, yes, physical bodies; it's certain vulgarities included?

That touches mean different between different sets of people. It is distinctly different; innocent between friends, brothers and sisters, while it is an extremely joyous, exciting, and sensual and a heart fluttering event between lovers. That same touch with similar intentions could be just beastly and toxic, if there is no consent? Doesn't she know or is she pretending not to? And why would she pretend?

'What happened on the day I found you both sleeping together, Kool shirtless and you hugging him? And I joined you both too for a selfie'?

Li'll'y got an unexpected explanation. Joy narrated her nightmare of her being shot on her bindi. She called in Kool for her safety, who rushed in drenched in rain and cold. Kool removed his shirt to dry himself. She was shivering out of fear and he was shivering due to the cold. She sat close to him for security, clinging to his arms and she realized later that she had dozed off on his shoulders; hugging him for security.

'What did Kool do then? Did he touch you and arouse your feelings'? asked Li'll'y in disappointment.

'No, Kool is a gentleman' Joy retorted as if it was forbidden to think of Kool in those lines.

Now it was Li'll'y's turn to think of Kool, 'If he needed some help or practical lessons'. A beautiful young Joy lying on his bare chest all through a cold autumn night in the privacy of her room and he does nothing! Not even try!

Li'll'y shook her hands in dismay. 'What fools you both are? Do you know what I would have done, if I were in your position? I wouldn't have lost the opportunity to let him deflower me. I know Kool acted as a saint. But I would have sent his sainthood packing on that day. What an opportunity lost. I had believed that you both had a great night together and do you know… I was jealous'!

Joy thought it would be scandalous to think so and wanting to switch the topic, cautiously asked Li'll'y, 'Do you love somebody'?

Prompt came the answer. 'Yes, Kool!' with her twinkle in the eye; teasing her. Joy's eyes streamed and she sobbed.

'Just kidding', said Li'll'y. Joy was half relieved that Li'll'y was just teasing, while her sobs continued.

'Yes, I'm in love', Li'll'y said to Joy, shrouding Kool, who lay in her heart and her mind, from Joy. 'Not the kind of love that you have', Li'll'y replied trying to console her.

'There can't be two types of love for your man', Joy sobbed again.

'Yes there can be, there can be love for someone that you know will never get fulfilled', said Li'll'y as tears welled up in her eyes too. She wiped them off deftly, before Joy could see. 'My love is one such'.

'Why so', asked Joy innocently.

Li'll'y wanted to cry out loud, 'I have a sister, who loves him as much as the river before us, and the skies above and then the land behind us, all together; everything that there is and has spaced me out'.

But she just could manage to reply, 'I was too late.', as her tears streamed and she wiped again.

It was now Joy's turn to explore what lay in Li'll'y's heart. Her tears showed that she was mistaken about Chinese girls and that she had generalized. She had thought that Chinese boys and girls or for that matter all others outside India, lived and loved for the day. That they were addicts to variety and that they had nothing called love in all its purity, in their hearts. They lose their innocence, enjoy the pleasure side of the touch early in life and never can roll back to innocence. The happiness is lost along with the ability for pristine love and mere crude pleasure remains.

Her tears had just reconfirmed that she also had a heart as tender and beating for her true love. That it was her duty to help her gain her true love back in China or wherever he was, just as Li'll'y promised help for her to fulfil her own love for Kool.

Why did she say that her love will not be fulfilled? She wished and prayed her God that her love for her boyfriend, whoever it was, ends in their wedding.

Joy asked her, 'Are you still in love with this guy? It's my duty to help you join him'.

Li'll'y nodded and shook her head at the same time,

'She is evading my question', Joy thought and wasn't ready to give up, 'Who is this? Can you show me a picture'?

'Oh no, not this time, I didn't bring any pictures and no selfies too. You know that', replied Li'll'y.

'Ok send me the picture of him, when you can', suggested Joy. Li'll'y just nodded.

Now with a twinkle that was characteristic of Li'll'y, Joy asked teasingly, 'Has he ever touched you'?

'No', she shook her head.

Joy was not prepared for such an answer. She expected real sizzling answers. 'Never'?

'Never'!

'What are you waiting for? You just told me that you have a boyfriend. Is it not normal for boys and girls to… she hummed for the right words, but gave up as she didn't find any to match the delicate mood they were in.

'Yes. It's quite normal for this generation in China. But I am special! Like you'!

'Like me'?

'Yes, like you! What are YOU waiting for'?

'For Kool and me to get married'.

'What if it's not Kool that you would get married to'?

At this Joy burst into tears and sobbed, 'Don't say such a thing'.

Li'll'y hugged her onto her shoulders till her sobs stopped. 'I won't. You will get married to Kool. You will be touched by him. Only don't wait to tell him your love'.

Joy nodded. 'I had tried several times; but could not. What if? What if? Too much fear. Why doesn't he tell me that he loves me? That would make it very simple. I know the answer, though! He doesn't want to break the trust of my parents. In the process he is breaking my heart and mind. I think I will go crazy, soon. I think he will tell me when the Games are over. Yes, I too understand it wouldn't do us any good if he tells me any time before the Games'.

It was now Joy's turn, 'Yes, what are YOU waiting for'?

'For my only and true man, just like you do. As I told you, I am special, Extraordinary. I am waiting for HIM', and laughed!

Joy asked cautiously, lest she offends her, 'This is your first romance'?

'I have had crushes before. But love! This is my first'!

'How long? When did you meet him first'?

'Less than two years'.

Joy thought her Li'll'y was more childish than her, though she was twenty one, just like her. Still she could not believe that she had not been touched before.

As if reading her thoughts, Li'll'y replied, 'Yes, I'm a virgin. I will offer myself to the only man I love. We may not be wedded then; that's not my concern. It's not a moral issue back in Shanghai. But he will be my only man. I will be glad if he touches me, even if it's only once. Wedding, these days, is a luxury and complex, back home. I may not be so fortunate', she concluded.

Li'll'y asked Joy, wanting to change the direction of the conversation, 'What about your parents. I understand that the parents play a big role in India to marry off the children. And even in the selection of the spouse'.

Li'll'y continued. 'What would you do if your parents want you to get married to someone other than Kool'?

'I only hope and pray that my parents too love Kool as they do me. They know that Kool much more than deserves my hand! I hope Kool's parents know that I deserve his hands too. Else, I don't know. I will plead', said Joy. 'And again... It's going to be very difficult I don't think I will forget Kool. I can't give up my parents either. I think Kool would face the dilemma too; that is, if loves me too'!

They had spoken enough and poured out their love for the same man of their dreams and ended up in their own insecurities. Both of them, wanted to move on to a different spot and needed to cheer up. Then Joy took her to her favourite spot, still on the banks of the River Cauvery. There was huge banyan tree with roots hanging from the tree. Joy explained that these are prop roots that hang from the branches and that they eventually support the tree as it grows in spread. Li'll'y nodded; she had learnt in her science class. She was still amazed, as it was the first time she had ever seen a banyan tree.

Someone had many years ago woven some of the prop roots together to make a 'swing of roots' and it was swinging in the breeze.

Joy and Vaijay used to swing seated on it till her Dad and Mom said, 'Enough for today, we will come here another day'. Joy and Vaijay never had enough of the 'swing in the breeze'. They pleaded for more time, every time. Sometimes they got more, some they didn't. But they always dreamt of 'swinging in the breeze' all night under the moonshine. After Vaijay passed away, Joy had been avoiding this spot. Her parents had brought her here several times. But she screamed and refused to step under the tree. Most of such days, she had nightmare as though the prop roots strangled her, just like the dhuppatta hanging from the fan did to her Vaijay. She had never talked of her trauma to her parents.

Joy found that the roots that used to be tied together were in tatters due to either years of use or disuse and that the swing was very weak. In any case she was too grown up and too big for 'swing of roots' that she used as a child. So on that day, Joy just clutched on to the roots hanging from the branches and clung to it with both her hands and swung in the breeze and Li'll'y followed suit. She exclaimed to Joy, 'I had never been such a fool before, ever' and laughed.

Li'll'y had thought that she needed some unwinding after the trauma of her Shanghai 'Home', but had to get into coaching in a haste. She had to or she would become irrelevant quickly and took the first opportunity to get back to life and TT. Moreover she needed to earn for her upkeep. She had no support system. She couldn't afford the space and time for winding down since then. But here with Joy and Kool and the easy pampered life that she came to believe only India could offer, presented her the best chance to loosening up. She wasn't ashamed of having broken down on Mother's shoulders the previous day. She rejoiced playing the TT friendly at Kool's school. She had never played such a relaxed game. She had never thought she would love hanging on the roots of a banyan tree like a monkey. She was doing it.

When Joy wanted to move on to show something else, Li'll'y protested, 'I want to 'hang on to this life forever''; both literally and figuratively.

Then there was a tree full of mangoes. The low hanging fruits had all been plucked by passers-by. The ones that were hanging from the high branches were tempting. Joy and Li'll'y braced themselves by tying the Dhuppatta tightly around their waist and ventured up the branches, cautiously. They ate a few mangoes still perched on the branches. They climbed higher when Li'll'y slipped and hard landed on the ground from the branch with a thud. In the shock of the moment, Joy too slipped and fell too, landing hard and directly on Li'll'y's right foot. Li'll'y grimaced in pain. She could not take one step further. The leg was swelling like a balloon. The car was at least five hundred metres away and limping all the way was out of question. Joy called Kool on his mobile. He rushed to the spot with his friends on a mobike followed by more mobikes and a car. Kool carried Li'll'y gently with both arms as though she was a child. Joy felt a pang of jealousy. How cool she rests on Mr Kool. Hope it were me and not her!

The x-ray revealed a fracture at the ankle. Kool felt that Mathur was not the best place for her treatment in this case.

45 One Life is not Enough

Within the next hour, all of them were packed to leave for Chennai. Joy's mother was attending to her packing and did not say a word, though she was very sad that her second daughter had such a misfortune when she visited her house. She wasn't too sure if this house has been afflicted by some evil eye that was harming her daughters and causing accidents and unpleasantness. She would consult an astrologer or a priest for a remedy, she promised herself.

On the way, Li'll'y wanted to say good-bye to Kool's Mother and sister. Kool's Mother was ready at the doorstep and had prepared for a small rite for the entire families of Kool and Joy. She brought out a chair and seated Li'll'y facing east. Then the entire family members were asked to stand behind Li'll'y as though it was a group photo opportunity. But instead, she brought out a plate with a vermilion coloured Kum Kum and turmeric solution in it and a coconut, dry red chillies and a lemon cut in half that had Kum Kum powder smeared on the cut faces.

She lit a camphor on the coconut and walked around the group with the plate, muttering some chants in Tamil and trying to invoke the Gods to crush the evil around their entire families and give them pleasant lives. After three rounds of walking around them holding the plate, Mother took the plate some distance on the streets that she thought was some sort of a boundary to keep the evil out. She dropped the red vermillion liquid in the centre of the street, crashed the coconut so hard on a rock on the street that the coconut burst into pieces.

Next she picked up the halves of lemon and the piece in her right hand, she threw quite far on her left and the piece on her left hand, she threw far on her right side, as if the evil that surrounded the families was cut into two pieces that bled red and was destroyed by throwing them far away on opposite sides, without giving them an chance to come together and start again.

She said, 'It's over now. You can feel free'.

Joy's Mother thanked Kool's Mother for being thoughtful in

warding off the evil eyes. 'I was about to ask my astrologer about how we can ward it off', she said.

They were ready to go. Li'll'y was enjoying the mystical practices and all the attention the families bestowed on her. She felt that with this ceremony, the two families came together as one and that she was accepted as one among them with the privilege of being seated in the centre.

While on the way to Chennai, Li'll'y thought of something and seemed much relieved. She now has an alibi for her stay in Chennai without raising any questions back in China. She shot an email back to her office, 'I had an accident that has made me immobile, while in Darjeeling. As there were no good hospitals near the mountains, I am flying back to Chennai, where, I heard, are good hospitals. I could reach Colombo as soon as she gets well'. Later, she clicked a number of pictures of her admission slip, x-rays, getting splints applied on her ankle region.

'Now I can stay in Chennai legitimately', declared Li'll'y. I can photograph myself, but not in the company of you both. From the next day, she moved around in a wheelchair. Joy was very happy to push it around, sister like. Li'll'y's routine was to have breakfast, pack lunch and settle on a wheelchair at the Academy and spend the next several hours coaching the students from her wheelchair.

Kool had explained the changes they had made on the TTSM. He expected Li'll'y to be appreciative of the work. But Li'll'y though appreciative of the innovation, was apprehensive. She in fact thought that… that… she struggled for words. 'I know its strengths and limits. All of you know its strength. I will tell you its weaknesses; actually it becomes your weakness. You will not apply yourself. Restrictive? No… doesn't let you think! Not even that..' she scratched her head. Her apprehensions were lost in translation.

Joy's mother took care of her as her own daughter. So it was not just lip service; this daughter thing. She was her cook, she was her nurse, she was her house maid, she was her teacher, she was her reading club, she was her night attender, she shouldered her effort to the washroom and most days washed and dried her hair as well.

She was her Mother.

During this period Li'll'y experienced the basic difference between Indian and the western and pseudo western societies of the modern East. The concept of Family. Families still existed in India and they were its greatest strength. Families rally around the members in good and bad times. They share the pleasures and pains. Sharing is not just sending a 'get well' card or greeting Mothers and Fathers on specific Sundays of the year. Sharing was being together in pleasure and pain, caring and supporting.

One day, Kool's Mother and sister arrived unannounced to see Li'll'y and to stay with her to take care of her. Li'll'y liked the 'What's between friends approach'. She also liked the way Joy's Mother greeted and welcomed them and made them comfortable as if it was their own home. Kool's Mom suggested that Joy's Mom could visit Krishnan Sir, if she wanted too, for a week or so, while she took care of Li'll'y and Joy. But Jay-ma, as she called Joy's Mother, did not budge. She had got her second daughter back recently and she wanted to maximize the pleasure of staying with her and serving her.

Kula-mma, as Joy called Kool's Mother, agreed, 'You should have been struggling to let go the overflowing love for your second daughter and now is the opportunity to bathe it with that love. But give me an opportunity to server it too. It came to me and sobbed and sobbed as if I were its late Mother. Even if I hold its hands all my seven lives, how can I replace its real Mother? It has put a huge burden of love on me. I hope I do at least a fraction of what it expects from its real Mother' and wept.

She continued, 'It is a God's gift to any family that win's it'.

From that day, both Mother's shared, no doubled the care given to Li'll'y.

Lakshmi was also was fussing around taking care of Li'll'y like she owned her. She also did lovely Mehndi on Li'll'y's palms, arms and feet and Li'll'y was very excited about them. Li'll'y compared the elegant Mehndi designs to the harsh tattoos of the Chinese and western world and she felt that the Mehndi designs enhanced the beauty and serenity of the girls, whereas tattoos brought out a discordant note in them. In fact amidst all the euphoria between the senior ladies, Joy and Kool found themselves out spaced, yet they did their best to fill in. Li'll'y felt pampered like a Queen. Even Queens may have just paid attenders to look after them, but they don't get to have multiple Mothers and sisters vying to serve them.

Li'll'y felt she was the most fortunate Chinese girl that ever lived. "India shines bright because of the Magic of Family. Family Life is the 'Pride of India'", she concluded.

Just as all good things come to an abrupt end, Li'll'y's stay came to end with an e-mail from her Coaching centre. Her place in Sri Lanka has been replaced by another coach from China and that she need not have to report back to Colombo. She was expected to report to Shanghai and not stay at Chennai forever.

She was reminded of her duties to her *zǔguó* (Motherland - precisely, the land of ancestors) and of her duties to the Coaching Centre. It was difficult to overlook these emails as she was indeed conscious of her duties to her Motherland and her Coaching Centre. Even having to be reminded of that pricked her conscience and she instantly got ready to leave.

There were a couple of arrangements and agreements that Li'll'y wanted of Kool and Joy. 'Due diligence', she called. Kool arranged for a receipt for her stay with her as a paying guest during the entire period of her stay in Chennai from one of his female colleagues. No emails, no phone calls no social media. No exchange of pleasantries, even when Kool and Joy land in China for the next Games. They re-checked and found no trail of their staying together in Chennai.

'But we need to meet in Shanghai, when we are at the Games at a confidential place. We don't want to communicate before the meetings or we would give ourself away', said Joy.

'You are right', said Li'll'y. 'Let's meet at the Bristo Bar, every Tuesday and Friday, evening 8:30 PM while you are in Shanghai for the Games, unless all of us have Games on those days. If one of us can't make it, don't worry, the other two will meet'.

This sounded sensible. 'However, please check your backs, sides and front to ensure that we don't have anyone following us or watching for us'.

All nodded and Li'll'y felt safe.

By this time, Li'll'y had recovered much and was able to move around using crutches. It was hard for her to believe that having been born in a remote village in central China, she would discover her family in a remote part of Southern India. Was it pre-ordained and designed to be this way. Was this connection something that extended from her previous life, as insisted upon by Kula-mma? Her scientifically and rationally trained mind refused to accept this idea. But there were no rational explanations either.

'I will be back one day to see you all', she said streaming tears, as she felt the hollowness in her words. In all certainty, she will never see them, ever.

She left with the feeling that 'One Life is Not Enough' to savour the pleasures of Family Life in India.

Part 6: Heart Stops to the Games

—

46 TT Federations

When Kool and Joy came back from their shortened vacation at Mathur, they realized they had completely forgotten about the things to take forward after the meeting with the PM. First they had to write to the Indian Federation to request them to review and reverse the ban, which they felt was unjustified.

Incidentally, the two Indian Team Managers who had wrecked Kool and Joy's life at Shanghai had in the intervening years had grown up in stature with the tall fair and bearded official becoming the President of the Indian Federation.

The Indian Federation asserted itself as an independent body and not as an arm of the Government, chose not to revoke the ban on either Kool or Joy. The President knew too well that if the two were exonerated through this review, it would bring to view the skeletons in his cupboard, and make his own position in the Indian Federation untenable.

Then there was a shocker, the ITTF had extended its ban on Joy and Kool to the World Tour Open Championships, courtesy, Deng and Dan. Dan had earlier vowed immediately after the Kyoto Open that he would try and interpret the ITTF ban to extend on the two for the R2 ranked Tournaments too that included all the World Tour Open championships. The extension of the ban that he helped trigger had just then reached Kool and Joy through the Indian Federation. 'So much for the support of the PM, sulked Kool, unable to understand politics of the Federations. That's the price of democracy that we pay for. 'Too much demo'crazy"!

With the chance of participation in any competitive TT tournaments completely evaporated, Kool and Joy practiced between themselves and with the other team members at the Joy-Li'll'y TT Academy. He had a library of video of the Top 10 players that he expected to meet at the Games that could be used on the TTSM X to analyse the games of potential opponents, but realized they were all old files. Jiang, Deng and Ding Xiang should have been improving their Game every day.

It was just more than three months to the Games at Shanghai. The Shanghai Games entry would close in less than four weeks. There was no sign of the Indian Federation relenting on their stand. And then there was no indication that ITTF was going to soften their stand either. The PM was busy on his foreign tours. The Sports Secretary confided to Jagadeesan that the delegation that had visited China along with the PM visit had appraised the Chinese delegation of the injustice meted out to Kula and Jay and were assured proper redemption for both.

When the PM sat at the next review of the 'Pride of India Initiative', just after his Moscow visit he was upset that nothing happened to overturn the bans.

Later that night, The PM called Shastry in Chennai, from his personal phone and spoke to him in detail.

47 The Protector

Ramaswamy Shastry was the PM's trusted lieutenant and he could be entrusted with the most complicated and urgent of all problems. Shastry had a towering presence and a great deal of Goodwill in any company or any committee or any group. He overwhelmed his opponents by his disarming and genuine smile. He could also terrorize the hardened criminals with his scornful silence. He was the modern day Chanakya. The PM unofficially announced Shastry as the 'Advisor' for the Pride of India Initiative at his request.

What the Sports Secretary could not achieve in over four months, Shastry achieved in less than two days. He invited the Indian Federation President to Chennai for some urgent issues. The Indian Federation President who had been side-lined till then on the PM's 'Pride of India TT Initiative', in favour of Jagadeesan, saw his chance to put his fingers in the pie. He knew how he would use this meeting to get back in the game. First he will have to put Shastry in his place. He had a cultivated disdain for the non-official power centres, like Shastry; he called them brokers! He, primarily a politician distinctly different from a professional or a bureaucrat or a sportsman, assumed the haughtiness of the 'Lord of all that he purveys'.

"Yes Shastry! How are you"? And punctuated his words with a contemptuous laugh, without letting Shastry's scornful smile and silence sink into him. I came to Chennai for an important meeting and we have a gala party tonight. I will have my secretary send you an invite... You should join the party as 'my advisor''.

'You can use the privilege, while The PM and I think you will be useful'. Booze would be flowing... Enjoy yourself...' He rose to leave having made his point that Shastry was only 'an advisor and at his call'.

Shastry did not miss his skills at superimposing himself, even from a point of hopelessness. Call it the audacity of hope!

As he reached the door, Shastry called him back, 'Mr President, I have not spoken yet... The purpose of today's meeting, that I called'.

The President, who had put up pretty good show elevating himself high above Shastry and believed that he had the game in his control, wasn't sure if he had to get back. But something in Shastry's modulated voice told him, he better do so and he got back, slowly.

Shastry's voice changed back to normal and said, 'Mr President, please take your seat', to the person, who was in hurry to flee. But as he was addressed as Mr President, it gave him some hope.

He spoke with an unmistakeable but quiet tone, 'Mr President, I have evidence of some of your misdeeds that I have to act upon today. I could have you arrested'. He laughed and continued after a pause that let it sink, 'You can choose if you are going to walk back free by choosing more dignified options'. The President didn't understand what Shastry was talking about, but was angry and cautious.

Shastry picked a puffy spongy cover, bound and sealed by thread, marked 'Confidential' threw it on the table.

'There are several allegations against you in here, tapping the cover, fourteen to be exact with evidences and proof of your misdeeds. The PM considers two of the allegations as inexcusable and he is in no mood to forgive you for those. Let me explain one of them. Do you remember the Indian players, Kula and Jay, who you dumped in favour of the Chinese and hounded them out of China and abruptly cutting off Kula's chances of victory over the World No. 1'?

'This DVD contains two videos recorded by one of the players; the evidence of your treachery'.

The President, protested, 'Who said so? The girl was officially banned by the ITTF and you know we don't have any say. The boy was violent and assaulted me... The matter went up to the Chinese Police. The Police were about to arrest the boy. We saved him from Chinese jail and sent them both back to India. We, the Indian Federation had to follow the ITTF ban and ban him too. I will talk to the PM myself'.

Shastry just smiled and continued, 'The second one relates to a list of assets that you have gained illegally and I am marking to the CBI for further investigation.

At this the President had a shock. His face drained off colour. Though he wasn't worried about the Shanghai Games incident, he was surely perturbed by the three letters - CBI. He changed to being conciliatory, with a tone as casual as he could get, spoke of his exploits in China during the last Games.

'We came after an extended week of privileges! The next Games in China, just months away, I could take you with me. This is your chance to visit a foreign country. I know of a lot of fun activity there. For one; Gambling. You can bet on anything. The hosts ensure that come back with loads of money. No taxes. No questions. No guilt. I have a lot of friends in power in China, whom you will get to know. Some 'homely' girls will accompany us, wherever we go'. He was throwing in all kinds of baits, wondering which of them, this bas**rd would fall for. 'Privileges. Only for the very special! You can use them while you still can. You are my 'Advisor' and why not? So you are special too. You are 'my 'friend'!

Shastry was recording all that the President was saying, both mentally and digitally.

Finally, when the President had nothing more to say, he thundered low, 'So I have heard you. All that you said has been recorded too. We are also aware of all the privileges that you were accorded by your Chinese hosts, including, the two stinking girls that gave you company'.

Shastry lowered his voice, and said, '...including the colour and pattern of their silky, laced lingerie.' slapping his forehead lightly as if in shame. 'Everything is in here; two videos, he tapped the sealed cover.

The President was bewildered. The mobile phone recording was with the Chinese Police Officer and the Chinese Team Officials had assured that the Video would be destroyed permanently.

He said boldly, 'Sorry, what videos? I don't understand. You are talking of some girls. I don't know anything'.

'May be they are the 'homely' girls that you just talked about, who show off their lingerie to privileged guests'? Shastry shocked the President to silence!

Then, Shastry quietly produced two sheets of paper, typed

neatly. The President stared at the first, wherein Shastry had typed his resignation. The second had a list of several assets properties, houses, farms, lands, company shares, deposits, Gold and silver purchased from various shops, Swiss bank account marked XXXXX with the date of opening the account etc. The list also mentioned the names of 'benami' persons in whose name each of the properties stood with the relationship; wife, son, daughter, Mother in Law, Brother in Law, niece, sister, brother, friend etc. The last two entries were

'Mistress 1'

'Mistress 2'…

'I have earned all of my assets by inheritance and hard work and business. You have no right to touch them', shouted the President.

Shastry, cool, said in a very low, but effective voice said, 'I happened to know your inheritance. At the age of 17, before you got into politics, you were a small time pick-pocket in and out of jail. Your net worth was less than Rs. 5000/- and you lived in a thatched hut, rented for Rs. 50/- per month. At the age of forty two you became a councillor in the Panchayat elections. Now your assets have been assessed to about Rupees 148 crores, 23 M in Dollar terms. Can you recollect your inheritance? Have you paid taxes on these properties? First, where did they come from'?

'Of course, Mistresses, normally are listed under liabilities, except when they each own seven to eight crores worth of properties that you gifted to them'.

'Mistress? Who? I don't even know any woman other than my wife. I have treated all of the ladies I know as my own mother and sisters I will sue you for defamation'.

'Don't humiliate your Mother and sisters. It looks like, you will not agree easily.' said Shastry contemptuously.

He continued, 'Ok. Look, the enquiry is over. It's judgement time, now! I give you two options'.

'One, you can keep your position as President of the Indian Federation, till the law takes its course and I send today, this copy of the list and evidence of all the ill-gotten wealth you have earned this far to the CBI along with the videos'.

'Two, you will resign your position as the President now and sign a confession statement. I will hold the list from the CBI until you get to meet the PM and let him decide what to do'.

'You will decide on either option in five minutes. Else, the third kicks in automatically. You will lose both. I will leave this room and the Police will walk in'. The CCTV screen was showing among other pictures, the outside of the building where two Police Jeeps were waiting with seven to eight uniformed policemen, swarming around. There was one plainclothesman, the Officer-In-Charge. He looked mean.

The President felt for his Mobile in his coat pocket and his pants. He had to make urgent calls and have this crazy ba****d step off this case. He is going too far. 'I will show him who I am'. But he couldn't find his phone.

'You had handed over your mobile to the security that whisked you at the door', reminded Shastry.

The President enraged, shouted, 'Behave like an Advisor. I have seen so many like you. I am not afraid. You don't know my powers. The PM calls me his brother and has had lunch in my home. You will regret all this when the PM is back in India. Don't threaten me'.

Shastry said unperturbed, 'I am doing this on the PM's behalf. He can't be standing witness to the arrest of every scoundrel like you', and laughed.

When Shastry provoked him calling him a scoundrel and laughed at him meanly, the President reacted; he rushed to and grabbed him and was about to hit him.

Shastry politely said. 'Thanks, you have given me the final reason to proceed against you for obstruction of justice. Remember again. The Camera is watching'. The voice was polite, yet steely.

He looked at Shastry's eyes. They were not fiery hot. But freezing cold. The President shivered as he was plotting his next move. He really didn't have any options, without his Mobile. And there were policemen waiting outside for him. Should he accept either of the options and get out for now? He could always fight back while in New Delhi. Buy time, find this bas***d's weakness and kick him on his balls. When he wanted to 'kick one in the balls', he remembered his friend and deputy, who actually enjoyed kicking people at their vulnerable points and who shared all the President's sins. 'Where the hell did Amin go'? he demanded to himself. He hadn't seen him in the last two days.

As if in reply, Shastry's mobile rang. He picked up and answered, 'Good. OK. Fine. Very Good. Ready for confession? Excellent. That will fix the President… Approver? Yes! We can work that out… Immediate… Scan, Email...' Turning to the President, 'Your friend is singing. The statement is getting ready. Will be signed in the next 20 minutes…'

The President could not believe his ears. 'Not Amin, I suppose'?

Shastry replied, 'They said the short and stocky one, whoever he is. You will know soon'.

'How dare he? He was the one who in a drunken daze that agreed with the Chinese not to appeal against the girl's ban and now he is turning approver'?

Shastry was enjoying the conversation and said, 'Right, I agree, he was too drunk and you were drunk too, but a shade sober'.

'But wrong; he said, 'Jai Hind' and you said 'Hindi Chini Bhayee, Bhayee', and got him to repeat it, both still in the arms of those gorgeous Chinese women. Everything is in the video files'. He remembered the details from his conversation with Kula.

Shastri's mobile rang again. Shastry spoke and confirmed to the President that his colleague just signed the confession.

'Mr President, the game is up. Don't make a fool of every one, and all the time. Let me tell the whole story. We are Government. We have sources. We have got the Videos from a Chinese source and we even know his source and his. We ran the videos through the forensic lab and found they are genuine. There's no way to escape. Now your Amin wants to be approver and already has signed the confession statement. Your five minutes expired long ago. Either, you sign now or I leave; leaving you to the mercy of those men, who will take you into custody', pointing to the CCTV.

The President was dumbstruck. 'Where did this fellow collect all this information? Though all the assets aren't true, some of them are; and then one of the mistresses is also true'.

The other one had left him a few months back and is now a mistress of a minister in the state of Bihar. She is still fond of him and helps him with his affairs in Bihar.

'They are enough to roast my buns. I can deny all that he has just said. But not now. I will have to consult my auditor and lawyer to provide a coherent reply. I may get into trouble if I say something without advice as this ba****d is recording everything'. He weighed in the options. He was resigned to his fate.

'I will resign', he was thinking aloud, just when Shastry reached the door.   He scribbled his signature on his readily prepared resignation sheet and the confession. Then looked up at Shastry, 'I have resigned, though I made no mistake, but because you have held me against my will and threatened me, under duress', addressing the camera.

Shastry smiled, locked up the signed letters, 'You are, of course free to tell the world, what you just told me. I also get the freedom to send all that I know to the CBI. You can make up your mind. If I were you, I won't throw stones at others from my house of glass'!

Then turning considerate, 'I can hold your letters for now. I'm sure the PM will be pleased if you reverse the ban on Kula and Jay by your Federation and get them participate in the Games, to correct your own injustice. But your responsibility does not cease there. I know you have tremendous influence on the Chinese National Team Management. You will still have to get the ban revoked by the ITTF in time for the issues to be considered resolved. Else…!

The President did not let him complete the sentence and agreed angrily, 'I will do', sensing that he had no options after all.

For the first time the President, in awe and fear of Shastry asked, 'Sir, Who are you? May I know'?

Shastry replied nonchalantly before walking out of the room, 'I'm God, the Protector of the meek'!

48 Young's Exploits

Li'll'y, in China, was similarly frustrated that there was no progress in her acquittal that could help overturning her unofficial ban by the Chinese federation. Thankfully the ITTF was not involved and if the Chinese Federation was ready to overturn her ban, it would be good enough. But the chances of the Chinese Federation considering her appeal were very remote.

The last date for her nomination to ITTF by the Chinese Federation was just less than two weeks away. There was still no light at the end of the proverbial tunnel. She was depending on Cheng to help overturn the ban. Cheng tried cajoling some members of the Chinese federation. Having failed, he tried buying the support of some of them, It didn't work for reasons obvious to Cheng; Deng!!

Deng had a stranglehold on the Chinese Federation and all those who promised much, while outside of the federation meetings turned silent on the face of Deng's faction, during the meetings. Then Cheng tried to threaten some members, who had committed petty misdeeds. Who didn't? It was easy to find.

One had taken a mistress. Cheng had videos of another, who was at a nude party that turned into a scandalous orgy. Another had built a huge secret mansion on the seafront with ill-gotten money. Cheng had extracted such information and evidences on the misdemeanours and threatened to expose them. This strategy did not work either. The members threatened by Cheng and party were resigned to their fate and begged that Cheng forgive them rather than confront Deng. Cheng gave up.

The only half a chance was the video of Chinese officials offering material incentives and carnal pleasures to Indian Team Officials to keep the Indian players out of the Games. Cheng wasn't too sure for his own reasons. Firstly, it should contain such sensitive information that Kool claims to have in it. Next, he would have to decide on its 'Scandal Value' or at least if it has a 'Scandal Potential' to cause enough fear or discomfort in the minds of the members who the trail will eventually lead. He will decide if it had, only after looking at the video. Lastly, he had to use such light evidence cautiously, yet exaggerate the threat perception, to make it work and to ensure that he doesn't make a fool of himself. Having convinced himself that this was the only chance, though a slim chance, he decided to work on this line. He had promised to help Li'll'y and he was desperate to keep his word.

It would be tough to convince his network to help him in finding the video files or on the necessity and objectives of this mission. The network officially would not do anything if foreigners were to benefit against the Chinese system for obvious reasons. So he was not getting anywhere closer to the mobile phone or the video files. He decided to handle the search by himself with close friends in the network in a personal way. It would be risky as he would have to surface over ground now and then to move forward, making him vulnerable to detection by authorities. The challenge was exciting.

He walked up to Lee, the Police Officer, who he remembered, as per Kula, was the one who had confiscated the Mobile phone. He felt vulnerable and could get quickly arrested if he made one small error. He had done some homework. Cheng had been at a funeral of someone doing social work and died the previous week in an accident trying to save someone else, as the group was providing relief to the flood hit in Central China.

He was the hero of Shanghai all of last week. He had seen Lee at the funeral, in tears. That gave him an idea and here he was.

He introduced himself as Young. In the course of his association with the Network, he had taken several 'avatars'. His favourite was the avatar of Young, a journalist, a freelancer. Young wanted to write and obituary to the hero, who gave up his life for his countrymen.

'I want to know more of the dead Hero', he paused, 'from the living Hero' and smiled.

Lee looked at him suspiciously, 'I don't trust any person who praises me'.

'Of course, you are a Hero, my Hero', Young stressed. 'Being a journalist, I have a good knowledge of the inner workings of the city. The Police work done here is extraordinary because of you. I know you are one of the most sincere and upright of the Police in Shanghai. Don't need to trust me here. But I carry the trust and opinion of the general public. I represent the public'.

There was some truth in what Young spoke. Young looked at Lee and he smiled.

Lee looked like he had taken the bait. 'What can I do for you'?

Young repeated, 'I want to know more of the dead Hero. I can see you are busy with your work', looking around casually.

'Any time you are free, any place. May be over a cup of Coffee... may be a drink'? Young knew he made the right impression. 'How about today evening. You may call me'. He produced his card.

'Can I have your Mobile number too'? Young knew that Lee was still evaluating him, though his face was smiling, as he scribbled his number on a piece of paper and handed over to Young.

'Good to know you Mr Lee. Hope to see you soon... Obituaries are like funerals, can't wait...' he dragged.

Lee nodded trying to recollect as Young turned to leave. He had seen him somewhere, but wasn't a journalist then, Lee knew for sure. These freelancers keep doing so many things to occupy themselves.

'That's why they are freelancers. That's why we are bound', Lee thought as he tried to shake his thoughts off.

Yet Young kept popping in his mind all day. 'That's why I'm a Police Officer', Lee smiled to himself.

A day later, Lee messaged Young. Not just to talk about his friend, the Hero. He wanted to confirm something about Young. He knew he wasn't a journalist then, not even a freelancer. But there's no law that a freelancer can't have his first job. He had nothing against Young; nothing yet.

'We will meet for Coffee at 6:00, at the Mei Ma bar, near my Office, if it suits you'.

Young confirmed. He had a feeling something wasn't right. But he had waded too deep and too far. Trying to get back in haste could muddy the water. So he will play.

They went into a private room for a chat. Lee started briefly about the Hero. Young thrust his voice recorder at him, 'like a professional'. The hero story was done in five minutes.

Lee asked casually, 'Tell me about yourself'. He had effectively disarmed Young.

Young was prepared for specific questions. But this could be a trap. He wouldn't know where the bait would be.

Young dragged about it in general terms, without getting into specifics, Been there, done that, been here, done this, overall experience was good.

'Now took up journalism recently. Wanted to cover this Hero, as I always liked my Heroes. I know a few tabloids and they promised to publish my story, if it was good. I better make it good'.

'That's why this interview with you, another Hero in real life. My next interview is about our own Sports Heroes'!

He felt relieved as he could push the conversation into sports and games.

'Did you watch last year's Games? I had the chance to watch most of the matches'! If he was pushing too fast into this lane, he wasn't sure. But he seemed to have got both; some comfort and some control, when Lee called the waiter and asked for;

'A pitcher of draught beer; two glasses'.

Lee never probed. He seemed to take Young's words at their face value. The topic moved into favourites at the coming Games.

'Jiang'! declared Young, the best that there can be. Ever to be born'.

'Jiang' Lee raised his glass and Young clinked.

They emptied the glass in silence, as if each of them was weighed down by some burden of memory. Young was thinking of Deng's match against the Indian, 'What's his name'? He always had difficulty in remembering the boy's name. 'Whatever... he could beat Jiang on a good day'.

Lee was thinking of the last Games and the early morning incident at the Indian quarters of the Games Village. He remembered the pressure from senior party officials at the behest of the Chinese Team Management to have the boy arrested, and that he called the boy for an enquiry and let him off; rather saved him. He also remembered how badly the Indian Team Management wanted the boy's arrest. He was shocked then and still is. He then felt compelled to get to the bottom of things. Instinct had told him that there was more to the events than had met the eyes, hence he had chosen not to approach the official forensic agency to decrypt the file.

He had links, friends, among a hacker group due his profession, with whom he worked occasionally, when he needed some unofficial support. He had finally decrypted the two files on the mobile with the help of a youngster, just fourteen.

Lee had watched the Video and had been ashamed. He had saved the files into his laptop and he let the hacker friend corrupt the original video files on the mobile. He sent the mobile to the official forensic agency, who had returned it promptly sealed, and with a sticker on it, 'File corrupted, unable to decrypt'. Lee had recorded the same 'facts' following due procedure with the date and time on it and placed the mobile in the official locker.

He had since, taken an active interest at the matches that were played at the Games. He had asked for and received all the official tapes in HD for his view. 'Security screening', he claimed; it was quite routine. He saw for himself the demolition of Deng. As a natural follow through he had watched all the matches of the Indian girl, Jay. Her overpowering Meiling, though the latter was declared winner and Jay's pathetic loss to Zhen Zhen included. He saw real tears in Jay's eyes as she placed the bronze medal at Zhen Zhen's feet. He was moved. The girl had played like true champions and pride was written on her face, even in defeat. Had he not been involved in the incidents at the Men's quarters at the Games, he would have appreciated the Chinese domination at the Games. Now it sounded hollow. Ever since he watched the game of the boy and the girl, he had been bitten by guilt at any reference to the Games and to China's dominance in TT.

Young thought Lee's expression had softened and was considerate. He did not know what was on Lee's mind though. But he knew it was time to strike. Lee realized that he had let emotions take over him and hoped Young did not see through his mind.

Young ventured out a little bold, 'As a journalist on prowl for stories, I heard something unsavoury scandal about the last Games…'! he dragged. Lee was afraid that this guy had read his mind somehow. To ensure that Young didn't take advantage;

Lee cracked, 'Now Young, what were you doing at the Club'? Young knew the game was up. He was fiddling for an answer. 'Club...? Club...! Oh, yes you know! I was the manager at the club. But after retirement, as I just told you, doing this and been there. But I want to get back to some active life. That's why this journalist stint'.

Lee demanded, 'Is it a cloak for something more sinister? Why did you change names'?

Lee said in all sincerity, 'I heard it's best for Journalists to work in anonymity, to get at the right stories. A popular journalist, doesn't get stories, I was told. People avoid them as they bring trouble. Have I done something wrong? I didn't realize it was a crime'. Young knew it was time 'to cut and run'. The video files wouldn't come through Lee, he almost concluded.

Lee saw that his crackling voice had the desired effect as his control and comfort restored and had Young cowering, brought his voice to normal.

'What scandal'? commanded Lee. Young, jolted a few minutes back, wanted to play along, though cautiously.

'Heard some matches were fixed, I think some Women's matches involving an Indian girl being fixed. And another Indian – a semi-finalist at the Games was forced to concede the match... something like that... I thought you would know...' He had to leave the Indians out. Indians don't matter in the Chinese system. In any case, his real interest was Li Ling; Li'll'y, if the readers have forgotten.

'I heard that one of the Chinese Women's team members stood up for the Indians and was jailed for the same'.

Lee jerked up. He wasn't aware of this. He was glad that a Chinese national, a young girl at that, had stood up against injustice; something he could not do, in spite of being a Police Officer. He was proud of the girl. By inference, he was ashamed of himself. 'The girl was jailed'? he asked unable to conceal his interest and shock.

Young was encouraged. 'The girl's name is Li. Was a member of the Chinese team. Was representing the Singles team for China in the Games. She wasn't jailed, but was pushed into 'a Black Jail'', he whispered, afraid of laying bare a state secret – the existence of Black Jails!

As Lee didn't show any signs of annoyance, in a way, confirming the existence of Black Jails, Young continued to whisper, 'Reason for dumping in Black Jail: Though no evidence against her, the authorities still sought to punish her. They are still in hot pursuit and are trying to dump her in the dungeons for treachery against the nation. For them, she knows something and could be a living bomb that needs to be de-fused in time'!

Young cautiously ventured back to the Indians, 'The Indian male player was about to be jailed. He was let off by some fair Police Officer, I was told… Put on the flight back to India, the same day. I heard the officer faced a lot of flak for the let off, but faced them bravely and gracefully'.

Lee thought about the Indian boy and girl. The girl had reacted like a Champion full of pride, honour and dignity at the podium, though it wasn't exactly what the world liked. The boy had protested, as chivalrous as a young man should and could be, in these circumstances. He still remembered the boy pleading and offering himself to be arrested. 'Please put Jay back on the flight back to India, even if you have to arrest me', he had begged.

Young continued, 'I believe there are some Video files doing the rounds… two files to be exact. Those could be potential time bomb. Somebody I know claims to have watched the videos. But I don't trust he has. They always claim that they had seen this or that assuming an aura of self-importance. But I do believe that there are enough copies of the files that are doing the rounds that could potentially expose a lot of officials and the Chinese Team Management'. All the while he looked through Lee's face to read his mind.

'How do you know all these'? demanded Lee, trying hard to hide his interest behind the façade..

Young replied, 'A lot of freelancers are working on this story. So we talk. I don't know whose story it will be and when it will be out'! He thought it was time to go as Lee became thoughtful. If he wanted any more, it would have to be another day. He waited for Lee to make the first move to leave.

Lee was wondering how the video files could have slipped

from him and doing the rounds? He thought he had an airtight grip over the files. He suspected his friend, the hacker. They are known to pull out copies of 'confidential files', without any purpose and just for the fun of it. 'Digital Kleptomaniacs'! Or did someone who knew of the files, dared to hack his laptop? He wasn't sure. The incident did not seem to die out as he had believed. If there was fallout of this incident he was afraid that he could be made the fall guy. If so, then this file would be his only defense.

Lee was visibly impatient but then asked Young politely, 'Is there was some other way I can help'?

Young knew this conversation would continue soon, at the request of Lee and it would be safe to continue. His instinct told him that Lee had the files tucked up somewhere and he might be checking the files tonight, with the interest he had created. He was pleased with himself.

49 Consensus Lost

The overturning of the ban by the Indian Federation and a request to reconsider the ban on Kula and Jay was received with mixed interest at the ITTF HQ. Most members at the ITTF committee, believed that the ban was forced by the overbearing Chinese TT Team Management also understood that the girl, Jay, who lost at the Semi Final to the eventual Runner Up, Zhen Zhen had all the reasons to be aggrieved, both on and off the field.

Further sympathies for Jay poured in when someone raised a need for the committee to sober down, 'We should look at this case in the light of another similar incident that rocked the Sports World. I'm referring to a precedent from the Asian Games at Incheon a few years ago. One Sarita Devi, a boxer', with a well-intentioned pause, ''again from India', who aggrieved similarly, reacted likewise. She refused to accept her Bronze medal and offered it to her Semi-Final opponent and Silver medallist, whom she had lost to, saying, 'That's what she deserved. I deserved better'. It happened in Incheon Games, South Korea'.

'The case was similar, poor umpiring decisions partial to the host nation. We have to consider that AIBA had taken a sympathetic and lenient view of Sarita, and had banned her for just 1 year'.

Someone else in the committee laughed and said, 'I think we should not blame Jay for her outburst. I think it is in her national DNA and hence we should review her punishment'. Everyone laughed.

Another said earnestly, 'It probably is a reflection of their collective self-esteem or a lack of it, especially in sports. Let us not be too harsh'.

Another member spoke with conciliation, 'I don't think anyone here supports the indefensible behaviour displayed by Jay at the podium. But we have to realize that the umpiring during the Semi-Final was substandard and was the trigger point for the later incidents; that Jay had suffered enough for her inexcusable, but immature behaviour having gone through the ban for over 21 months; it is imperative for the ITTF to correct the wrongs and set things right'.

The consensus was evolving, except for the Chinese representatives in the committee. The other ITTF committee members knew that unless the Chinese members were brought around, their opinions would not count. So there was extended discussion on the subject and small groups were trying to help turn around the Chinese opinion. Everything looked positive.

The next day, something unexpected happened. The Chinese members, after consulting their National Federation, tabled a motion; to penalize the Indian Federation for going against the spirit of the Games and the ITTF, for unilaterally overturning the ban on the two players. The rest of the members were unpleasantly surprised. This was not what they spent a day deliberating on and evolving consensus for. But the clout of Chinese National Federation within the ITTF was so strong that the consensus of the collective rest of them was broken. The matter was debated for just five minutes, put to vote and decided before the morning tea break.

'The ban on Kula and Jay stays and the Indian Federation would be penalized with a heavy fine, for supporting indiscipline of the players'.

When the news that ITTF had rejected the reversal of the ban on Kula and Jay and had imposed a punitive fine on the Indian Federation reached India, the President of the Indian Federation was terrified.

If he did not get the ban reversed, his good life would be destroyed with the kind of list and the Videos that Shastry possessed. He was counting on the Chinese Team Management to help reverse the ITTF ban.

The President was also angry that the Chinese Team Management let him down so badly, by not finding the video files and destroying them as promised. Now it looks like the copies have surfaced threatening his very existence. His only hope was that the Chinese Team Management also realized that they were in the same boat as him and that they would only sink together. The President tried to contact Chou to find the status of the videos and to destroy them as quickly as possible. Chou was the Team Official, who negotiated the deal with Amin and him at Shanghai on that day. But as Chou didn't respond to his calls for more than a week, he panicked.

'What if he had changed his phone number? Or if he had moved out of the Chinese Team Management? Or if he was dead'?

He didn't know how else to contact him and he was his only point of contact to the Chinese Team Management.

'The bas***d and the CBI are breathing down my neck'.

Chou was actually on a vacation in the Bahamas for two weeks and it was a matter of time before the President could get in touch with him.

50 The Emissary

A Special Emissary of the Indian PM, Shastry, had an official meeting scheduled with the Premier of China, who was the most powerful after the President. Shastry presented his case for 15 minutes. He showed a 4 minute video of the 'friendly' match between Jay and Meiling, where Meiling makes a claim of sorcery.

'The incidents against the 'Bindi' on the girls forehead isn't isolated, but part of a conspiracy. This ridiculous claim from Meiling came after an earlier threat by one of the Chinese team members against Jay, not to use the Bindi ever again. This Bindi, while one may ignorantly, yet sacrilegiously call it a 'Dot', is but very sacred for us. It is a symbol of the vitality, feminity, fertility, compassion and Godliness; or simply 'Shree', embodied in the woman who wears it. The happenings not only shows disrespect, but is an arrogant affront to our culture, our values and faith, apart from being a direct assault on the young player'.

'Strange' he said, 'How the umpire and the Match referee first gave in to the Chinese girl's sorcery claim though they partially reversed their decision and only under pressure'.

He showed clips of the headlines on various news channels and newspapers. 'Not Friendly!', 'Shanghai Shames', they claimed, a rhythmic pun on the Shanghai Games.

Then he showed the clips of the same newspapers on the reversal of the decision. 'Not enough', 'China partly wipes its shame face, as it licks its wounds inflicted by 'friendly' Indians', some of the credible newspapers reported.

Next, Shastry opened a 4 minute clip of the Joy's game against Zhen Zhen, but did not show it for paucity of time.

But he showed the newspaper clips, related to the match that were equally critical of the Chinese conduct of the Games. 'Shocked', 'Truncated', 'Miscarriage of the matches and the stillborn Games'.

Shastry showed a picture of Jay in tears, laying her medal at Zhen Zhen's feet in protest. Shastry then showed one of the prominent Sports papers put up an obituary column, with a photograph;

'Jay in tears and in mourning; lays wreathe to the scandalous Games that breathed its last at the feet of Zhen Zhen. May the Games RIP; along with the Chinese Pride'!

Shastry continued. I'm sorry. I can see you shocked. That's a good sign. But our woes aren't over yet. There's another equally perturbing dimension you should know; that of Kula.

He showed a short 1 minute clip of Kula's game against the then No. 2, Deng, in which Kula wins the match point. In this video, Deng was seen clenching his fist and swinging menacingly at Kula, within inches of his face and walking out without the customary handshake after the match.

Then he showed clips of some of the news headlines;

'Cool Kula tames the Menacing Deng, The match starts now';

Somewhere inside the column, the author says, 'Jiang should be in hiding, after Deng takes a hiding'.

When it was announced that Kula was withdrawing from the Semi-Final due to sickness, 'Sickness save the day for Jiang and China',

And when the official ban on Kula for three years was announced, 'It is evident that it was not sickness, but sick minds that saved the day for China and Jiang. It doesn't seem to be just a passing sickness. There's a deeper malice and disease than meets the eye'.

The columnist vows to find the truth behind the incidents and expose the misdeeds behind the Jay and Kula ban. 'If the decay beneath the Chinese Table (Tennis) is not identified, if it is not cured bottom up, TT as a game would disintegrate.

Shastri continued, 'There's much more to it than we can see. The Chinese Team Officials, please don't mistake me, not the Chinese Government, were not sensitive to the adverse worldwide comments of the Games on very creditable news media. Else they would have not have urged the ITTF ban on Jay and Kula. Of course, the few unpleasant comments were submerged in a sea of goodwill the Games generated for China. But please beware of a few drops of poison in your pot of milk.

'It's a pity that the Indian Government has woken up to the injustice meted out to Jay and Kula very late. But now that we know, our Prime Minister, NM is very keen that the justice be delivered. I am carrying our PM's personal message to you as Chinese Premier'.

The Chinese Premier spoke cautiously, 'There seems to be something seemingly at fault and I would do whatever required about this', without any commitment.

Shastri not convinced, replied 'Mr Premier, It's just not 'something seemingly at fault'. There are serious misdeeds by the Chinese Team Management which we are raising. Our PM expects that China takes responsibility and to act quickly and before the coming Games. At a minimum, he wants the ban on both our players to be quashed and they be allowed to participate in the coming Games. We agree that the Indian Team Management was involved too. It was a joint conspiracy. We are taking suitable action at our side'.

But the Chinese Premier trying to hide his annoyance asked, 'Why…? Your Government took almost two years to come up with your response. And there's no evidence. This has to be investigated. We have this year's Games in a couple of months. We can't afford to rock the boat this late. I can't set the officials on a wild goose chase and send my Chinese Team Management packing, without any hard evidence'.

'I assure you that there will be a full-fledged investigation, but it will take time. We will have to wait till the Games are over. I hope you appreciate'.

Shastry cool as ever, said smiling at the Premier, 'Exactly, it's about this year's Games. We are also stakeholders in the international TT fraternity. We are also interested in TT as a sport to flourish, not languish at the feet of Zhen Zhens of the world. We are keen as well that the Games should be conducted respectably and responsibly. We are also keen to participate in the Games, if we are convinced that our Team will be treated fair. But, we aren't convinced, at this point. If action to correct is not immediate and visible, Indian contingent will be withdrawn from the Games. The reasons will be obvious to the world. The news will be lapped up by the correspondents, reporters and senior columnists, who already are determined to expose the Chinese conspiracy at the last Games. What else can we do but to share the same evidence on our hands and to expose the deceit'?

'About the Evidence, Mr Premier, We do have hard evidence. We have Video files that our Team member Kula has recorded that exposes the nexus between his own Team Management and your Team Officials and their devious deal, Shastry placed the DVD that he fished out of his brief on the table. 'The entire conspiracy is captured in great detail. A copy of the video files rests with your Police Officer, Mr Lee, serving in Shanghai. Now several copies of these video file are known to exist and the story could break out anytime on Primetime News. I also have the confession statements signed by the two Indian officials involved in this plot. They have named the Chinese officials too and the two girls of disrepute that were used as honey traps'.

'We are not targeting the splendid Games or the Chinese Government. We are only trying to help you stem the rot in the system that unfortunately spread over to our side too.

The Chinese Premier seemed genuinely worried, though he looked impatient that he had to spend his time on this episode; more time than he should and could afford. He was also concerned that if one of the several copies of the Video files floating around as claimed could land on the wrong hands or the media, the episode could tarnish the reputation of the Chinese Nation and of the Games. He replied with caution, 'I can at best order an investigation and it would be up to the investigation team'.

Shastry was convinced that the Premier was sincere and that his job was well done. 'I will hand over the evidence to competent investigators, you officially name'.

51 The Ping of Death

The competent investigator appointed by the Premier was a retired Lt. Gen. Ping Ling. Lt. Gen. Ping was no nonsense Lt. General, PLA and he was known in his circles to brook no indiscipline. Everyone had to follow all three; political, moral and legal correctness, with equal importance; all except him, that is. He could excuse himself of the processes on the grounds of his personal integrity and sense of fairness.

He had been the longest serving member of the Court Martial Jury and he had been the toughest in the Jury to please. He had awarded over two thousand deaths by firing squad in the five years he was part of the Jury, including members of the PLA, Government officials and civilians. He has now taken over the mantle as a Prosecutor as he found several accused being let off without the commitment of the prosecutors.

As a prosecutor, he had a successful conviction rate of over 95% and death sentence rate of over 50%. One could just toss up a coin and see if he would be killed by a firing squad, if their case was up to Lt. Gen. Ping.

He had earned a nickname 'the Ping of Death'. He was also referred to as the Sun Tzu of modern China.

Shastry arrived to meet Lt. Gen. Ping at his swanky office suite.

The office was too large for just one man, in Downtown Shanghai. The office was glass and spotless stainless steel. The chandeliers were crystal. The furniture were French décor created for modern royalty. Though there were huge impressive stations for a Secretary and a posse of officers, there were no signs they were ever occupied.

There was a Renoir decorating the walls with a spot light on it. Must be original.

On the far eastern side, beyond a barrage of glass enclosures, clear as crystal, he could see an impressive and sparkling office room; should be Lt. Gen. Ping's. He could also see that beyond his office was a view of Shanghai Downtown, with equally imposing buildings and glittering offices, each vying against the others for a place in the sun. Surely, the average Chinese thought and accomplished everything in grandiose scale and Lt. Gen. Pings of China helped lift the average several notches higher. In India these would be called profligacy on a vulgar scale. Yet, Shastry appreciated the mind and technology behind all the glitz and wondered, 'How many years would India need to catch up'? And again wondered, 'Is it necessary to catch up'?

Lt. Gen. Ping looked like a business man in a pin stripe Armani suite He was a sharp contrast to Shastry in decent, yet, down to earth white cotton full shirt and black trouser, who chose not to wear his navy blue blazer and tie; Shanghai was still warm and pleasant that he did not need the extra baggage. Both shook hands and instantly communicated their suspicion of each other, as they stared into each other's eyes.

Both settled in their respective seats opposite each other, with a discussion table between them. They studied each other in silence as if they studied the positions on the chess board. Their respect for each other grew as their dislike scaled down. Yet the suspicion for each other seemed to grow more pronounced.

Shastry opened his laptop to make the presentation. Lt. Gen. Ping spared him the trouble of repeating an elaborate speech. He watched the entire presentation by himself. He asked pointed questions, very laconic. Shastry answered tersely, without wasting any words, mostly in monosyllables.

Finally, Lt. Gen. Ping asked, 'Evidence'. Shastry repeated what he told the PM on the evidence using as few words as possible, this time. Lt. Gen. Ping was convinced of the incidents. He was convinced that there could be such video files lying with Lee. May be there are more copies. His intuition told him that there were no such files in possession of Shastry, though he bragged about them tapping a DVD; probably blank. Shastry instantly knew that Lt. Gen. Ping knew about the blank DVD. But both did not mention this. This is a mind game between Chanakya and Sun Tzu. Not of mere mortals.

Lt. Gen. Ping asked, 'How long can you wait for the reinstatement of your team members by the ITTF'?

Shastry had a ready-made demand, 'three days maximum or

else our team would not be able to meet the deadline to participate in the Games.

Lt. Gen. Ping confirmed, 'Three days? Done! What else do you need from us, the Chinese Government'?

Shastry replied, 'Fairness and confidence has to be restored'.

Lt. Gen. Ping replied, 'Done. I invite you to be a guest of Chinese Government for two months, till the Games are over, to help us watch over the Games as an impartial observer. We need people like you to enhance the prestige of our Games'.

'I have no doubts about the fairness in the future Games with persons like you in the lead. I will assist your investigation till full reinstatement in the next 2-3 days. Whatever you need from the Indian side, will be provided'.

Lt. Gen. Ping replied, 'The investigation is over. There's nothing more to know. If you are thinking of the video files to deliver to me, I know you have 'reasons' for not giving them to me at this point. I have my reasons for not asking for one. May be someone of you have modified the content to please someone or to fix someone else'.

'I now know the video files exist within our Government. I will get them myself. I will be fair to everyone. We will get ITTF reverse and welcome your players. I will take an independent view on Li Ling and she will be reinstated, if she deserves to be. It will take time to cleanse the system for the future. That can't be done before the Games for sure.

Shastry nodded in satisfaction. 'Of course, I will be at the Games. Not to protect my team. I believe they would be safe and that you would be fair. I accept your invite; will be here as an observer and let the world know either way, under proper protocol from the Government of India.'.

Their handshake was warmer than before. It could even be termed friendly.

52 The Evidence

Cheng wasn't the type to set a trap and wait for the tiger to fall. He wouldn't catch any tiger at all, all his life, that way. He believed in hunting for the tiger; deep in the forest; whenever and wherever they might be, in spite of the risks. He suspected the files to be tucked away in one of Lee's personal home systems. It could be his home server, desktop, laptop, personal mobiles, sometimes you keep two or three, or his pen drives or his external hard disks. It could be in his 'drop box' or somewhere. He asked one of his hacker friends a personal favour.

'Nothing to do with the Network or Movement', he had explained.

His hacker friend obliged. It was his chance to return the favour to Cheng, who had done so much for each of them personally and risked his very life for the Network. None would refuse a personal favour for Cheng. Not this friend! Cheng passed on several images of Kula, frozen from the Games HD Videos for the hacker friend to identify the files that contained this face.

Later Cheng corrected himself, 'You wouldn't find this face on the files, as he was recording the video',

Instead he gave him the context, 'To look for two young gorgeous escorts getting out of a car with two Indian gentlemen… 'Oh, not this guy'.

'Some video of interior or exterior of 'Paradis' hotel, with or without the same group in the frame… you may find photographs of the exteriors, interiors and Lobby of 'Paradis' from it's webpage for identification… Another file taken inside a scantily furnished apartment, like a guest house… the same two Indians fully drunk and tripping all over… same two ladies and two Chinese men...

'Date of file creation'? asked the youngster.

He seemed to get interested as this was getting murkier with foreigners involved.

'That's none of my business', he subdued his interest.

Cheng consulted someone on his mobile, before he replied, 'The 'Paradis' thing should have been Oct, 24th 8:00 PM or later, a day before the Men's Semi Final. The apartment video file should been several hours later October 25th 2:00 AM to 5:00 AM'.

That night, at 11:00 PM, the young friend called Cheng, 'There were a number of files that matched the face of your target. Mostly playing TT at the Games, I think... Wow, what a game. Who's he by the way? And on other videos is a young cutie girl, again who plays a great game too. Who's that? Can I meet her? Would like to ask her for a date. Would you mind'?

Cheng laughed and said, 'You youngsters have no reverence! Where did you find these files'?

His friend replied, 'Mr Lee's home PC. Right now the Wi-Fi is shut down. Who would want to shut down the Wi-Fi anyway? The guy seems to be paranoid, smelling hackers around him. He is cautious. I thought the Police Officers were dumb'.

Cheng said, 'Good news so far, 'Keep a watch; for all the gadgets that sync with this desktop and for all the gadgets that are networked, even briefly. Also check all the memory cards and pen drives and hard disks, you know it all, that are plugged in. It's a successful day, so far'.

At 4:15 AM the youngster called again. No response from sleeping Cheng, who had a long day.

Again at 4:32 AM and again at 4:50.AM. Deep asleep. No response.

Finally, Cheng woke up to an impatient long ring. There was a marked excitement in his young friend's voice, 'I think I got them from his Laptop; two video files matching the description; two bi**chy ladies, two Chinese men and two Indian men; same date-time range. Pick up from my Dropbox and confirm, if they are the files'.

He had messaged the link to his drop box and the credentials. 'Quick. The party is on the laptop checking emails and browsing. Probably thinks that this is the safest time to keep hackers away. Better be quick. I may have to look again for the files before he completes sync-ing his laptop with his PC and or switches off the Wi-Fi, if these happen to be the wrong ones'.

Ten minutes later, Cheng called his friend and said,

'Congratulations and Thanks. Exactly, what I wanted from you. We will meet this weekend and you can ask for your reward'.

'Reward? OK. What else? Can I ask the Indian girl for a date? Would you mind'? He sounded so serious and so it was out of place to joke about it.

Cheng delighted with the files, was in a mood to promise, 'I will introduce the girl, when she comes to China for the coming Games, if I have a chance'.

Next minute, Cheng passed a cryptic message to Li, 'Paradis beckons' is now available at the Video library... Active... Copy is good... Working on next steps'.

53 Lee's Troubles

Lee called Young early at 7:00 AM from a different number. He sounded angry and desperate. He wanted to see Young and then. 'Same Mei Ma bar… The bar would be closed at this time… But you would be allowed inside; same private room'…

Young confirmed 'I will be in the bar in 45 minutes'.

Lee needed help; desperately. 'I'm under investigation… No, not until today. I knew of it only when the authorities swooped in on me at my apartment and impounded my laptop and desktop. What they are investigating? Who they represent? I have no idea yet'.

I have been asked to report at 9:00 AM at the Police HQ with a certain Mobile phone I had confiscated earlier. I am in a rush".

Young listened to Lee carefully and asked him with confidence and politeness, 'I don't know how I can help you, but please know that I will do as well as I could. As I told you, you are my Hero'. Lee tended to believe Young this time about the Hero stuff.

Lee explained, 'You talked to me about some files doing rounds somewhere. I want you to find those files for me. Urgent'.

Then he confided to Young, 'I'm afraid I could be in trouble related to involving the Indians and the Chinese girl during last Games that you mentioned of yesterday'.

As if reading Young's mind, 'Yes, I'm the brave and graceful Police Officer, you spoke of… I don't know your sources. You had been right by and large'.

'So the video files you mentioned yesterday should be lying somewhere. I'm sure you could access them, if you worked on it'?

Whether it was a question or statement, Young wasn't sure. Yet he nodded, still trying to understand why Lee needed the files so badly.

Just twelve hours earlier, Lee was the owner of the files and Young, who wasn't sure if he had them, wanted them badly. Now, the tables were turned. Young owned the files and Lee without knowing it wanted them desperately. Call this the cycle of life? He could afford to smile today, though to himself.

Lee continued; 'Please go after the files straight away. You will have costs, of course; let me assure you, you will be paid generously. If you may need my support sometime, you will have it'.

He stepped out of the room to leave. Then as an afterthought, he stepped back in and said, 'In case, I don't return from this meeting, say, if I'm detained, please continue and find them; for my sake. I may need the files more urgently than ever'.

Lee added thoughtfully with a lot of hesitation, 'If you have any interest in the girl, Li, I will be with you helping her. If you have interests in the Indian boy or his girlfriend, please count on me to help them too. May be it's neither of them that you need help about; it may not even be about those Games or the incidents that you spoke about yesterday. It could be any other issue too. For instance, you may want help for your network or for your support to the Hong Kong democracy friends. I am not threatening or blackmailing you. Let me say, we have common friends...' His voice trailed off.

Young was bewildered. So, when did Lee know about his connections with the network? Young was satisfied that Lee wasn't threatening or blackmailing. He could trust him. He was sincere after all, as he poured out his troubles.

Young had his motives and objectives. Now he had Lee with him; both caught in a tango and needing each other and the files. Only, Lee didn't know that Young didn't have to look for the files! How could he use this situation to help Li for sure and Lee, if possible? Is it feasible to help the Indians in the process? In a way, Young saw that all the objectives merging into one; that of Li, those of the Indians and now that of Lee. He holds all the aces for today.

The pressure on Lee had come from the Chinese Team Management courtesy 'Godfather' who acted through the higher Police Officials. They grabbed Kula's mobile phone that he retrieved from the locker giving him no opportunity to copy the corrupted files for later usage. He didn't even try for he feared he may be monitored.

They demanded to know, 'Why had you not taken any steps to decrypt the files'?

Lee showed them his records.

They checked the Mobile in his presence; found the seal intact and sticker of the forensic agency to be authentic with print; 'File corrupted, unable to decrypt'. Other records also pointed out to Lee having followed the procedures.

But Lee was still scared. He knew his game would be up soon, when they found the video files on his Laptop; something he shouldn't have saved the files in the first place. He waited for the eventuality.

But... to Lee's surprised his Laptop, and Desktop PC and all devices were returned to him while he was still with his Senior Officers. 'No such files found'.

Lee was off the hook, even as he was perplexed 'Where did the files go? I had checked the files just a few hours earlier, hardly an hour or so before the swoop and played them briefly on my Laptop!

'I will worry about the files later. I'm safe for now'!

The Senior Officers demanded, 'So where did the leak occur and how? The Indians seem to have a copy and we hear there are copies out there in the cloud'.

Lee protested his innocence, 'How would I know'? He continued, 'May be, they could have been leaked from the Forensic Agency. It could not have been from me, because, when I got the Mobile phone back, it was already declared 'brought dead' by the Agency; 'corrupted'..

But Lee knew by instinct, 'I'm still not above suspicion and have to be careful'.

He volunteered and vowed to his higher officials, 'I will get to the bottom of it and find the culprits. They need the highest level of punishment for playing with files that are of highest importance for China'.

This final rhetoric earned the trust of his Senior Officers and saved him for the day.

The Senior Officers huddled within, 'Who would you entrust to find the files, if not Lee? Already, there is a leak and we don't want more Officers in the know and snooping further around. Lee looks committed to find the files, any way'!

Before dismissing Lee they gave him a deadline. 'Find them before early next day, or else'… they warned,

On the way home, he called Young from his car and informed him 'The crisis has passed, rather paused for now', and as an afterthought, he said, 'But go ahead and pursue the files from the cloud as soon as possible. They're more valuable now than any time before. I will call you soon for an update'.

As Lee reached home, he tried to recollect, 'Did I accidentally delete them after I watched the video'? He searched the recycle bin, but didn't find any.

Lee wasn't aware that Cheng's hacker friend had tiptoed into Lee's system while he was checking emails and browsing between 4:30 AM and 5:30 AM. The friend wasn't sure if Cheng wanted him to delete the original source files after copying or if he wanted them to be left as-is. He had called Cheng three times around 5:00 AM and as Cheng did not respond, he chose to permanent delete them.

'If required, I could always sneak back to replace the files in the same folder', he had concluded. He had forgotten to mention of the delete when he updated Cheng.

In any case, Lee was happy to have deleted or lost the file, even if by accident. Else, he would have faced sure firing from his job and possible jailing for retaining and hiding sensitive contraband. He breathed a sigh of relief that the problem drew to a close.

Even before his sigh ended, the doorbell rang in a hurry. A gentleman in a pinstripe Armani suite announced himself on the door camera, 'Lt. Gen. Ping Ling'.

Lee's face turned white, 'What's the 'Ping of Death' doing here? Was this the ring of the doorbell or the knell of Death'?

The conversation was brief. 'I have information that you are holding some confidential video files on your laptop or desktop or wherever, It's in your interests that you hand over the files immediately and destroy any copies that you have, with a report to me'.

Lee was worried. He did not want to say something that could be held against him. When it was the Ping of Death, there was no rolling back what you said.

He swallowed a gulp of air, 'I don't have any files, Sir'.

Lt. Gen. Ping clapped and two men stormed into Lee's apartment. They scanned the entire house for 10 minutes. Lt. Gen. Ping used this time to extract a story from Lee.

He told him, 'There is a complaint and I'm investigating'.

'I have acquired a copy of the video files and that I want to make sure that it tallies with the original ones that you have in your possession'.

Lt. Gen. Ping partly confided in Lee to get the truth out of him. He wasn't suspicious of Lee. He had known Lee to be an upright Officer and expected him to be truthful.

By this time Lee felt, "This 'Ping of Death' has better demeanour than his Senior Officers he had met a few hours ago and that he could trust him more, if he had an option".

Lee explained again, 'I don't know anything about the files. The files were encrypted when I checked them first and later was certified by the Official Forensic Agency as corrupted. As I had not much choice, I had left the Indian's mobile in the office locker, until today'.

Lt. Gen. Ping demanded, 'Then, handover the mobile phone'.

Lee informed him, 'Just a few hours earlier the mobile was taken over by my Senior Officers, who had also got hold of his Laptop and Desktop that had just been returned'.

Lt. Gen. Ping exclaimed, 'Oh sh*t', and bit his tongue as if it was out of his character.

'A true blue blooded Gentleman', thought Lee.

'Then they have possessed the files already? I guess I'm a little late'.

Lee found his chance to reiterate, 'No Sir, they wouldn't have these files, at least not from my system. I never had them in the first place and the files on the Mobile were corrupted'.

Lt. Gen. Ping considered this and nodded, 'Are there any chances of finding the original files? They say there are copies in the cloud'?

Lee agreed, 'Yes sir, they say there are copies in the cloud. I am already looking for them, as my Senior Officers have ordered me to'.

Lt. Gen. Ping replied, 'That's good. If you find them, get them to me; not to your other Senior Officers. They are also under my investigation. From now on, I'm your Senior Officer'.

'Yes Sir, understood', in a state of confusion. 'I will report to you when I get the files'.

'Any other way to get the files'?

'Yes Sir, if we could have the Mobile, there are some experts, who could rectify those corrupted files. We can try. But we need to first get the Mobile from the other Senior Officers', confident that the young hacker who corrupted the files should be able to remove the bug.

'I will get them. When I do, can you get help to rectify them, quickly'?

'Yes Sir, I will do my best'.

'This isn't the end of this investigation, We will have a follow up meeting soon', Lt. Gen. Ping said to Lee, as he and his men walked out with his laptop, desktop and every scrap of digital devices and storage, including his wrist watch.

Lee looked faint and reported sick for the day.

54 Destiny of Nations

Lee didn't want to stay in his apartment for even a second. He was being chased from too many directions. If he tried to please one, he may end up being hostile to others. He picked up his few things and got into the car and left for the countryside to nowhere in particular. His regular office mobile and his private mobile phones were picked up by the 'Ping of Death' but he could save his 'very private number', as he had hidden in the boot of is car, not visible to Lt. Gen Ping's commandos!

Only his wife and one of his most trusted colleague and friend, Zhu could reach him on this 'very private number' number from their own very private mobile numbers. These three very private numbers weren't registered in their own names. Hence none of the calls could be traced to him through these numbers. He eventually drove towards the home of Mia Hua, his ex-girlfriend. He was left with no other place for privacy. None, including his wife and his friend and colleague Zhu, who were the only ones to have his 'very private number', would suspect him of going there. He had completely broken his relationship with Mia ever since he had married another woman.

Mia lived alone. She wouldn't get along with any other man. Lee was her life then and now; no other man interested her since then she loved him; she respected him. Though she felt let down by Lee, she didn't feel humiliated. In a way, whatever he did saved them both from trouble with the authorities.

Lee had circumstances that he had to marry in haste; anyone other than Mia. Lee recalled the fateful week.

Mia's cousin was discovered by the Police from underground. He had several cases of treason against the Nation and Lee had to act against him. His relationship with Mia was well known. Though Lee was upright and was determined to act against Mia's cousin and Mia supported him, he was being watched and any slip by him, would have been treated as an act of treason in concert with the enemies of China and probably both Mia and he would have had to go to the gallows with her cousin. He had to cleanse himself of his relationship with Mia's cousin and hence his relationship with Mia. Lee got married to a different girl, quickly. In a way that removed the spotlight on Mia too and Mia left him in peace with his new family ever since.

Lee slipped into Mia's home unannounced. He was welcome warmly. Mia embraced him like they were always together in the last fifteen years. He hadn't changed much, she thought. So did he think about her! She didn't ask why he was in suddenly. She offered him the comfort of home. She did everything a dutiful wife should do when her husband looked to be in trouble. She massaged him. She bathed him. She offered herself completely, the way even his wife never did. When Lee was spent, his mind was clear. He had always shared his problems with Mia. He could trust her. She was the only one in the world he could trust so completely.

Lying lazily with his head on Mia's lap and feeling her bare bosoms invigorated his mind. He could think better. He analysed his problems aloud. There are three lines to the story converging on the video files.

'One: My senior officers are chasing me to retrieve the video files'.

Just then his 'very private mobile' rang. It was Zhu. He demanded to know, 'Where the hell are you'?

Lee replied, 'On a very critical investigation and would like to keep away from sight'.

Zhu understood and asked 'Awara DVD'? Referring to the old Indian movie 'Awara' that was the biggest hit among Bollywood movies in China during the early 60's, before the war; their code word for the video files on the Indians'.

Lee's silence was interpreted as yes.

'Then I have some more interesting news. One more customer wants to buy the 'Awara DVD'. His name is Chou and he has approached me through a friend of a friend of a friend. But let me warn you. The connections are too powerful and may be dangerous for us to ignore'.

'Tea business'? asked Lee in code, for the powerful Chinese Triad.

'Yes. Chou is desperate to get the 'DVD rights' and is ready to set up a shop in 'Macau'. Our common friend of a friend says in confidence that he is at least partly financed by someone who is current the Indian Federation President. Looks to be partners-in-crime'.

Lee 'googled' for Indian TT Federation President without any expectation and was surprised to see a familiar face. The guy was the senior of the two Indian Officials, who had been attacked by the Indian boy and the one he had seen him recently on the video. He recollected that one of the Chinese officials, who had been caught in the video, had introduced himself as Chou.

'For the first time the persons on the tape are surfacing', he explained to Mia. They are not just asking for the 'video', but also for the 'video rights', which means they want the originals and all the copies that existed, probably they want them destroyed.

Mia guessed, 'If you happen to be on such a hot video, you may want to destroy all copies too'.

'Ready to set up a shop in Macau means ready to pay $1M. Here is my chance to make 1M and escape to South America or become a permanent tourist in Pattaya with you. But where are the files'? He smiled sarcastically.

'I thought I had enough trouble with the files on hand. Now I'm having offers when I'm without them'.

Lee was first scared at the new interest and confided to Mia, 'Chou's connections, the Triad, are more menacing than my own hostile superiors who swooped on his home earlier today. But they were definitely less dangerous than the 'Ping of Death'. However, since Mario Puzo's Godfather, all Gang's without exception have been talking of 'Offer you can't refuse', while serving ultimatum's. The Triad is well known for 'executing' their 'threat, if 'offer' not accepted'.

Mia shuddered and his body shuddered too in resonance!

Lee requested Zhu, 'Can you find more on their interest and if Chou was representing the Chinese Team Management. It may be possible that the Team Management having lost their effort to get the video rights through our Senior Officers, were trying to bribe or intimidate through the Triad. In that case, we better beware, the shop in Macau could be a bait'!

Zhu assured him, 'Chou has already poured his trouble out to my acquaintance, someone in the friendship trail, well before the bosses demanded the DVD. So this should be an independent story.

He continued after a pause, 'I have reasons to believe Chou represents a sub group, one comprising of the Indian and Chinese actors in the Movie'.

'Give me your reasons', asked Lee.

Zhu replied, 'Chou seemed to have approached his bosses, the Chinese managers, at the insistence of the Indian Federation President. But to his dismay he heard from his friends from within the Chinese Federation that if the video files got leaked, they would dump Chou and let him take the blame'.

The story prepared by the Chinese Team Managers and ready to circulate, ran like this; 'Chou is a part of a group of gamblers, who had betted a huge fortune on the Chinese to win both in the men's and women's semi-finals and finals'.

He continued, 'Earlier they had betted heavily on the Chinese team to win the last sixteen and the quarter-final too against the Indians and lost heavily. They were bracing for more losses due to Kula's menacing form'.

'So to cover future losses and recoup their previous sufferings, they had got into a deal with the Indian Team officials offering them carnal pleasures, riches from the gambling den and also a number of goodies promised to be delivered in India, past the nosy Indian customs in return for help in blocking Kula and Jay from further matches. Bookies either linked to Chou and group or unrelated to them could also have been behind fixing the umpiring in favour of Zhen Zhen; may be the Meiling match too. That Chou had acted independent of the National Federation and should be punished'.

By this time Lee and Zhu forgot to refer to the files and persons in code names.

'The story is flawless'! said Lee derisively. 'Dirty minds at work! Looks like the Chinese Team management will extricate itself from the fallout of the tapes that could surface any time'.

Zhu added, 'Chou also mentioned that the Indian authorities may have a copy of the video files. He is desperate to watch the videos himself at the least to prepare a proper Defense against it when the leak occurs'.

Later, Lee sulked to Mia, 'Somehow the video files that evaporated from my Desktop and reached the clouds are raining copies everywhere! Raining within the reach of Cheng's pals; raining within the reach of the Indian authorities and raining within the reach of the 'Ping of Death! It seems they could be found everywhere, except in my laptop'!. 'Where did we leave'? Lee asked Mia, still playing with her bare bosom.

She filled in dutifully, 'Story-line - One: Your immediate higher ups are chasing you to retrieve the video files'!

He laughed out loud and said, 'Yes, They represent a cross of the Chinese Team Management officials, the likes of Dan and my higher ups are trying to pressure me. They seem to have a flawless cover-up story, but may be worried that the story may not stand the scrutiny of the Ping of Death. They don't seem to have any copies with themselves. They also believe that the leak had happened, if at all, through me and want me to retract the copies and find those in the cloud and the persons who placed them there. They also still suspect that I have a copy and they want to lay their hands in time and to and destroy it. They will come back to harass me'.

'Two', he continued, 'I'm being chased by Lt. Gen. Ping; says he has got the Videos already and he wants to compare the same with the original. His doesn't seem to want to destroy the files. What motive can he have? He represents the Chinese Government for sure, which probably is acting on the complaint of the Indian government... who else would complain at that level'?

'He may be an investigator or better special prosecutor and could book those who were involved. I can see a number of half-dead men already'!

Lee continued, 'Three: 'Cheng was probably looking for the video files too. There are too many holes in his journalist act. He definitely isn't a journalist. Did he come fishing for the files? If so, who is he representing? The above threads leave only one person out, the Chinese player, Li Ling, he casually pushed into the conversation. It sounded deliberate, then'.

'Possible, unless there are more actors than I know. How do these files fit in to save Li'?

'Li', he mentioned, 'was punished for supporting the Indians. Why should she have done that? How did she know them? Or she just could be a type to stand up for injustice anywhere; in that case, she would be a misfit to live in China. Better she finds a safer harbour'.

Lee googled for 'Li Ling, TT Player'. Nothing much in the last two years. He checked with Zhu.

Zhu came back in just fifteen minutes from the official archives. 'Li has been unofficially banned from playing for the Chinese team. She was lost for nearly seven months from a few days before the end of the last Games, almost same dates when the Indian boy and girl from India were caught up in incidents, to be very specific, just a day earlier. She had in fact been in detention for a month before being acquitted; No evidence. She was then sent to the 'Home' for six months. Looks like she had survived it'.

Mia imagined the rest of the story-line for him, 'Li's own incarceration must have been closely linked to the fate suffered by the Indians. She should have been aware that the Chinese Team Management had hatched and executed a conspiracy to prevent the Indian players, who were potential Champions at the Games, including fixing of matches against the Indian girl. Li bravely voices her protest against her own Team Management that landed her in jail. Next the Chinese Team Management tried to have the boy arrested for knowing too much and recording evidence on video'.

'We are aware it's true as you also had been under pressure to have the boy arrested. When that ploy failed they had threatened him and forced him out of the country in haste, along with the girl, before his match against the World No. 1. Li may be aware of the existence of the video files and desperately needs the video evidence; the only way she could extricate herself. Cheng is a friend or a relative of this girl, Li; or may be an investigator; or a committed activist or a paid small time criminal, commissioned by her to look for the files. He takes up her cause and is looking for such evidence based on leads from Li. He is fishing for the video files from you as also from the cloud'.

'Perfect, Mia. You make a good investigator'. He could not stop touching her at sensitive places and getting thrilled. 'You have summed up the whole thing as though you have watched the video tapes'.

Lee let Mia complete her summary. 'So Cheng is searching for the video file and when he gets it, Li may want to get back to the team or at least clear her name for the rest of her life. If the incidents are connected by their friendship to the Indian boy and girl's case, she may get the acquittal direct and easy, now that the Indian and Chinese Governments seem to be involved. If they weren't related and if it was just a coincidence, then Cheng may have to arm-twist the Chinese Team Management to get the acquittal quid pro quo'.

'Mia my darling, you are a genius. However, my genius, how does Cheng know I have the files or that the files existed? Neither Li nor Cheng were in the picture on the day the boy's mobile was taken. Probably by the dates that Zhu gave me, Li must have been in detention already when the videos were being recorded'.

Mia answered after a thought, 'That settles it. As Cheng himself said, Li stood up for the Indian girl, when she lost the match by wrong umpiring. They were friends already. It was not as though she stood up for a stranger. Now it's two years since. They should have been in touch and exchanged notes. You, the mobile and the video files were in the notes'.

'You are right. In that case, Cheng is looking for the files, not to destroy, but to use them, concluded Mia. Lee nodded.

Mia intervened, 'I think you now have one more line of story to the three lines you already have'.

'Yes, Four: Chou's looking for the same files. He is representing the Indian Federation officials and himself; all the faces that are on the video, except probably the 'elite' Chinese escorts'.

'Who knows, they may be in the racket too'.

'They have taken the help of the Shanghai Mafia linked to the deadly Triad. Ill-gotten money is flowing freely, both Chinese and Indian', concluded Lee.

Lee said, 'Then there is one more line to the story'!

'Story-line Five; It's me. I am also hunting for the files. If I get my hand on them, I will keep my Senior Officers at bay'. Declared Lee.

'So there are five story lines around the same video files. The interest groups all converge at one place; on the files that were in my Laptop till today morning and they were real. The files, known to be in the cloud are all unreal. They are virtual. They don't exist. They can't have slipped my cordon', he claimed emphatically.

But he wasn't so sure, when Mia reminded him, 'Don't be so confident. Your files 'did go' missing from your Laptop and they 'did slip' out of your cordon'.

But he still liked the idea that the entire world was converging on 'his files'; claiming ownership of the files.

'Yes, I'm central to the resolving of the problem, as well. None of the actors in any of the other story-lines were even aware of the all the other story-lines and the players acting in them. I'm the only one who knows all the interest group, their motives, their strengths and weaknesses, and their relative depths of desperation'.

'I'm the only one, who has watched the videos till date and know it's potential to raise a stink...The destiny of nations, two of the most populous nations, economic giants in the making, the destiny of the relationships with each other as nations, the destiny of their TT Federations, the destiny of their TT teams, the destiny of the individual players in the team, the destiny of the individual members in the Team Management, the destiny of the Games and its reputation, the destiny of other actors like me, all our collective destinies are bound to the files. I will be the central person who would decide on these destinies and so I have an immense responsibility, to act conscientiously and boldly. I vow to do so'.

At the realization of this responsibility, his fear vanished, and he was ready for the challenge. For now, he needed some sleep.

55 Gordian Knot

In Gordium, by the Temple of the Zeus Basilica, was the ox cart, which had been put there by the King of Phrygia over 100 years before. The staves of the cart were tied together in a complex knot with the ends tucked away inside. An oracle foretold that he who untied the knot would rule all of Asia. Many people tried to undo the knot but all to no avail.

In 333 B.C. Alexander the Great had invaded Asia Minor and arrived in the central mountains at the town of Gordium; he was 23.Having arrived at Gordium it was inconceivable that the young, impetuous King would not tackle the legendary "Gordian Knot".

Alexander climbed the hill and approached the cart as a crowd of curious Macedonians and Phrygians watched intently as Alexander struggled with the knot and became frustrated.

Alexander, stepping back, called out, "What does it matter how I loose it?" With that, he drew his sword, and in one powerful stroke severed the knot.

That night there was a huge electrical storm, which the seers interpreted to mean the gods were pleased with the actions of this so-called Son of Zeus who had untied the Gordian knot.

Courtesy: http://www.alexander-the-great.co.uk/gordian_knot.htm

Lee needed a partner or an assistant and he zeroed in on Cheng as his partner. He would be useful. He would do the running and carry the torch if he was de-capacitated, say, arrested'. He included Cheng in his very private mobile phone contacts and called him.

Just 48 hours before the official closing of the entries to the Games, Kool was backing up his latest photos from his iPhone up into the iCloud.

He had just heard of the ITTF decision to penalise the Indian Federation for revoking the ban on him and Joy and including them in the Team for the Games. He was bitter. He gave up on the Games as he saw no miracle to get him onto the games with Joy.

He suddenly remembered something like a flash. It could be Joy and his ticket to the Games. He remembered vaguely that he had set his last Android mobile phone seized at Shanghai, on auto backup so that any new photos or videos taken with the phone would automatically be uploaded on Google Drive. So there was every chance that his video on that fateful day also could have got auto backed up. The auto backup should have worked till the battery was charged, that was at least 48-72 hours from his last use, if the phone wasn't used otherwise or switched off by Lee. His daily backup should have got kicked in comfortably.

YES! He found his videos on the Google Drive. Why did he not think about this earlier? What a relief! Had he got this video earlier, he would have saved the TT lives of all three of them and probably got on the Indian Team in time for the Games.

He quickly backed up his videos in a dozen sites in the cloud and hardware. He also sent out the video to his important friends, with a caution to keep the files safely backed in their laptops and on their cloud and be ready to pass it on to him, if or when he needs them. He now gained the power to twist the arms of any number of the Indian Federation Presidents, especially with NM and Shastry on his side. He would also pass on the same to Li'll'y to get her informal ban revoked and to find herself a place in the Chinese Team.

But was he too late for any meaningful action? It was just more than a day and what could he achieve. Even if things get done at Godspeed, he would lose the deadline by a mile.

But he was a trier. He rushed the email to Jagadeesan Sir and Mahadevan Sir. He spoke to them over phone to ensure they passed it on to the Government secretary or Shastry, who had met him a couple of times and enquired in detail about the incidents at the last Shanghai Games.

But try as he could, he couldn't connect with Li'll'y. Her known email ids were bouncing off. He was careful to use the ID's of his friends, working in the US and there wouldn't be any suspicion at all. He wasn't sure of how to reach Li'll'y and pass on the Video files to her.

Lee waited for Cheng at a restaurant on the outskirts of Shanghai, far from the Highway that led to Mia's country home.

After a handshake, they drove off together in Cheng's car. Cheng brought the files on a DVD. He was careful to have made several copies earlier and had them stashed away safely. Lee played them on his laptop, while in the car and found them unaltered and was speechless. Cheng saw that Lee was greatly relieved, in spite of his silence. Lee narrated his interactions with Lt. Gen. Ping.

Cheng asked in disbelief, 'Lt. Gen. Ping? Who? The Ping of Death'? Cheng wanted out of this game as he wished to live.

But Lee convinced him saying, 'Lt. Gen. Ping could be helpful, if we trusted him and approached him with clean hands. We may need his help as we are under attack from several directions. We need to trust someone; big and powerful. I have a feeling that the game isn't about winning or losing TT matches. I think the Indian boy and the girl had been incidentally caught up in the Power Games of the high and mighty. I am being used by my Senior Officers as just a pawn in their games and could be tactically expended for them to gain a strategic advantage'.

'The files that you just armed me with, is my protection, my bullet proof vest or a suicide vest. My Senior Officers suspect that I have the files; that's an advantage. They would be afraid that that if I'm miffed, I will not go down without causing maximum havoc within their midst. But they will still try to prise the files from me by force or otherwise. They are haughty and mad and it is a sure death situation for many of us. I hope I will live free another day to save myself. I had effectively bought some time with these files. I have to buy my Defense next'.

'I'm sure that Lt. Gen. Ping plays for the powers that be that are trying to fix their opponents. I am glad that he needs these files for the fix. He will be my Defense and I have to pay for it with these files. I can't thank you enough for them. You probably saved my life'.

Cheng considered Lee's logic and saw some truth in it. He also needed to reach the top layers of the Government or the Party to be able to arm twist someone more powerful than the Chinese Federation, to be able to reinstate Li in the Team; and quickly enough. He had less than a day! Nobody could help like Lt. Gen. Ping would, if he saw that they both were genuine. But, Cheng knew he was taking high risks and his identity as a member of the network could surface and he could get into trouble. On the other hand, he saw the best opportunity to get Li back into the team and was prepared for the risk. He would simply hide behind Lee and let

Lee do the talking, including covering his interests to reinstate Li, while meeting Lt. Gen. Ping. Lt. Gen. Ping did not sound death after all!

While they drove, Zhu called Lee, 'There is good news. The customer, the Shanghai mafia, has deserted Chou high and dry, the moment they knew that the 'Ping of Death' is involved'.

That was a good sign. That meant, One down, three to go and with Cheng, who was partner now and on his side, two to go.

Lt. Gen. Ping was in a terrible mood as the deadline he had promised Shastry was nearing. He had just a few working hours to get the ITTF revoke the ban on the Indian boy and girl as he had promised Shastry. He wanted to keep his word, as always. He checked his diary to see if he missed something.

Day 1: Morning, he had promised Shastry.

Day 1 Evening, he had a pending work from a previous assignment and was complacent. He, however figured out in his mind on the home work he needed to do and how and where he would find his files and who would be involved or threatened in overturning the ITTF ban.

Day 2: Morning, he had entered Lee's home and grabbed his systems only to find the expected files were not on his system.

Day 2: Afternoon, He had ordered Lee's Senior Officers to see him in his Office. The Senior Officers were playing for time. No, they did not have the Video Files. They did not find any from Lee's laptop or the desktop PC, corroborating what Lee had said. 'Yes they did have the Mobile Phone in their custody. They have to check something, before they can release. Lt. Gen. Ping sensed that they weren't very enthusiastic about returning the Mobile, for obvious reasons. This is the first time that an official did not cower before him in fright. This experience was new to him; such was his reputation and the power he wielded.

He had to remind them, 'The investigation has been ordered. You have a responsibility to report to me and to cooperate with me in the manner I wished. If I do not get this Mobile untampered, by the end of the day, I would be forced to act on you both'.

The Senior Police Officers assured him, 'We will surely hand over the files by today evening', and left. Lt. Gen. Ping sensed that they would not.

He suspected they had protection from a 'Godfather' and was trying to guess who he was. This was getting murkier. He may have to use higher fire-power than he intended to.

Day 2: Afternoon. On the strength of the assurance that he will receive the Video files from the Senior Police officers, he had ordered the officials of the Chinese TT federation and the Chinese Team Management to his Office. But without the video files, he could only give them a dressing down and held them responsible for the incidents. He had ordered the arrest of Chou and another minor official at the Chinese Federation for investigation. He took care not to arrest either the Senior Federation or the Chinese Team Officials as it would have an adverse impact on the Games and would raise uncomfortable questions around it and on its credibility. But without the Mobile phone and the video files, he felt shabby; a snake with just a hiss, but no pangs.

Meanwhile, unknown to Lt. Gen Ping, the Senior Police officers, the Officials of the Chinese Federation and the Chinese Team Management had banded together and got their Godfather to act, with the demand to put off all investigations into the last Games to later than the current Games. The Godfather, a Politburo member, was close to a member of the Politburo Standing Committee and fourth in the Chinese hierarchy, who had a great clout with both the President and the Premier.

The Godfather spoke to the Premier, 'There is no evidence of wrong doing except hearsay spread out to malign the games, by the Indian the boy and the girl; now supported by the Indian Government, to embarrass China. Even the Indian Team Officials and the Indian Federation recognized the complaints as malicious and were in full support of the Chinese Team Management.

Day 2: 8:00 PM: Lt. Gen. Ping had late evening call from the Chinese Premier, 'Please play it low and slow'.

Lt. Gen. Ping assured the Premier, 'I am also careful about the conduct of the Games' and confided, 'Neither the Chinese Federation nor the Chinese Management Officials have been harassed or arrested so far. They would not be, if they cooperated', he assured.

He also updated the Premier, 'I have promised my Indian counterpart that I would get the Indians participate in the Game. It is best for the investigation and resolution to proceed as planned'.

The Premier, advised him 'You may stop any further investigations that I ordered and do not bother about the Indian request for now'.

Lt. Gen. Ping demanded to know, 'What about the assurance, you as Premier had given me that I will have total independence'? He was incensed that the Premier was reneging on his word.

Premier, who also respected Lt. Gen. Ping spoke to him just as politely as he could get, 'By our constitution, the Party is the all-powerful. By virtue of his leadership of the Party, the President is supreme. So we all have to wait in this case, as per the will of the President'.

Lt. Gen. Ping fought back, 'What if I get my evidence'?

The Premier confirmed, 'Yes, you may proceed, 'if' you do get your evidence'; the stress was on the word 'if'.

Lt. Gen. Ping had, till his conversation with the Premier, believed that the resolution of the problem would be as easy as cutting the ribbon and leading the Indian players and possibly Li, the Chinese player into the Games, once he had his evidence. But the Premier's call had made him uncomfortable. He wasn't used to being told, what he should do, even if it were the Premier. With one call, the Premier had messed up the plain ribbon into a messy knot. He smiled to himself, 'If the Premier has presented me a Gordian knot, I am ever ready for the challenge! He was determined to undo this Gordian knot in his own indomitable style and in time, though he didn't know, how. Yet!

He smiled an audacious smile.

Day3: Morning: Lt. Gen. Ping was in a foul mood. He had been blasting everyone on his phone. Lee and Cheng who were waiting at his Office for him, didn't want to get caught in the cross fire, and fled out of his Office and planned to return an hour later.

Unaware that the evidence was waiting outside his Office to meet him, Lt. Gen. Ping was plotting his next moves considering that he wouldn't get his evidence in time. He asked for a meeting with the President. He intended to take the services of the Director General of the Political Department, Central Military Commission with him to drill sense into the political establishment. He hoped that he doesn't have to force the situation thus. But if he had to do it, he would do it. He was not known as 'Ping of Death' for no reason. When he saw justification, he just did it, without bothering about the process or niceties. The President was in the middle of deep deliberations with the EU Chairman, on the Infrastructure Bank, China had proposed. So he gave an appointment to meet him at 7:00 PM, over dinner.

Day 3 Morning: (Just then): He received an email from Shastry, 'Dear Lt. Gen. Ping,

Since our last meeting, I have verified the copy of the video files that the Indian Forensic Agency vouches for its authenticity, that are central to the investigation. I felt it my responsibility to hand over a copy of the verified files. I'm sure that you have your copies. But I thought that you would like to have authenticated copies to compare with your own. As we all know the importance of the files and that there are a number of groups ready to subvert the process, I would like to hand over the files through a confident you can assign to collect. I'm still in Shanghai as your honoured guest at the Shangri-La Hotel.

In just two hours, Lt. Gen Ping was checking the video. The contents did shock him, but he was greatly relieved to have this copy in the nick of time. While he will live his shock for later tonight, he called to thank Shastry for his gesture after he received the files and he assured him that the restoration of the two Indian players would happen as required and within the deadline that is the morning next day.

Now that he got the evidence, he could have gone ahead and run amok without having to refer back to anyone. If he did so, he knew that he would upset the Premier.

He preferred to deliver bitter medicine without pain. The best way to hang someone for his crimes is when the whole mass of people is rooting for his death. That was his style. It had been his duty to present the case in all horror for the stakeholders at all levels to realize there were no other options.

He was exploring such subtle methods. He did not want this executed through his normal Government channels, being very sensitive. He had taken private agencies in confidence before for his investigations and to twist arms to get hard evidence. He was thinking hard, 'Who among the several of his men would be right for this job'? He had little time till tomorrow morning. Of the possible eight or so hours he had, he would be travelling for about five hours to Beijing and back; to be stuck in an unproductive conversation with the President for another two hours.

Lt. Gen Ping was pacing in his office, thinking hard, when he found Lee with another companion at his front Office. He was wondering what news Lee brings. May be he could use it. He ushered Lee in and he had also brought the Video files on a DVD. Suddenly there were too many copies of the files floating into his hands. He could use the new set of video files no more than he could use the video files given to him by Shastry and were still playing on his laptop. He had just 45 minutes before he should drive off to the airport.

His intuition told him that he could use Lee for his subtle method. From his interactions with Lee, he found him dependable, intelligent, knowledgeable and bold. Lee also trusted and mortally feared him as well and so would not do anything to cross him.

Lt. Gen Ping did not know who the other person was and looked at him and then at Lee.

Lee took cue, 'He's Young, a freelance journalist, the one who got us the files'.

Lt. Gen Ping thanked him and asked Lee if there were any costs, he would pay.

Lee replied, 'Sir, there are no costs. But Young himself has been on the lookout for these files believing that it could be used to acquit his God daughter, who had been unjustly punished by the Chinese Team Management Officials and detained. She also has been thrown out of the Chinese TT team as punishment'.

'I heard so. One Li, I suppose'? Interrupted Lt. Gen. Ping.

'She was later acquitted for no evidence, though she had to go through the horror of the 'Black home'' Lee whispered.

Lee continued, 'Her unofficial ban by the Chinese Federation stands. She is one of the top women's TT players and should have had a rightful place in the Chinese team at the Games. But she is languishing without an opportunity and in disgrace. Young seeks your help to overturn her unofficial ban and to let her find a place in the Official team; only on merit. That's how and why he found the files'.

Lt. Gen Ping thought for a while. There was a convergence of motives between Young, Lee and him. If Young was good at picking the files from the anonymity of the cloud, probably by hacking, he could also place the file anonymously on the cloud in a limited and controlled public view to activate his subtle option. He grilled Young to satisfy himself that Young wasn't a Trojan horse planted to spy on and subvert his plans.

Lt. Gen Ping laid out his plan to Lee and Young. Lee wasn't sure, but Young replied enthusiastically, 'It's doable',

'Who would you engage'? he asked.

Lee answered and let Young keep a low profile, 'As a Police Officer, I have access to certain harmless technical persons who are experts in their field and would do my bidding for some hard cash or a small return favour. You know that we have to use their services for several investigations, where we get into a dead end. I assure you they are harmless, reliable and very discreet. In fact, we had used them to find the files'.

'I don't deal with people underground' said Lt. Gen Ping sternly.

Lee was struck for an answer. Young who had a strong opinion reacted in Defense of people underground, 'They operate at just sub-ground, not underground, and Sir! They love their country'.

Lt. Gen Ping laughed aloud. 'That's a smart definition. I guess you are part of them too? You seemed to be sensitive about your ideology! Are you really a journalist? Is your name really Young'?

He laughed like thunder, the kind of laughter that froze both Young and Lee. Young feared that Death was teasing him'.

The silence said it all as neither Lee nor Young ventured, struck in fear. Lt. Gen Ping watched Young closely. He saw his face pale, continued, 'Never mind, we have work to do; as I said, I wouldn't deal directly with people underground. That's why I engage folks like you. We don't have time to deliberate between 'sub-ground and under-ground'. But beware, I will be watching. Don't cross your limits, ever'.

Had he seen Young's face redden instead of pale, his response would have been different and dangerous for his visitors.

Now it was time for Lee to display his competence and his absolute loyalty to Lt. Gen. Ping. He produced a sheet of paper to Lt. Gen. Ping and said, 'I have a statement signed by Mr. Chou and also a video record of his statement. Mr. Chou is the Chinese TT

Federation official seen in the Videos. He has independently corroborated everything in the video and also our suspicions, without watching the same. I have him in my private custody and at your service'.

There was determination and pride in his voice... his way of getting back at his Sr. Officers, who harassed him. He was intent on buying his defence and protection.

In the next sixty minutes one of the video files was uploaded on to Youtube and was placed for view under invitation only.

The invitation was passed on to the personal email boxes of the President of China, the Chinese Premier, the President Chinese TT Federation, the Chairman of the Games Committee and Dan, the official Chief Coach of the Chinese National TT Team. The message was;

Sirs,

What's happening to Chinese TT and the Games?

Innocent players, Chinese and other nationals, have been dumped, fixed and haunted. We have waited for justice. As Chinese citizens overseas, we also have huge stake in Chinese Development... also are concerned that the Chinese reputation is taking a beating. We find that the last Games had become a subject of ridicule. Adverse comments from World news media have been ignored. And those within the country have been suppressed. Where's the Chinese pride? Have we stooped so low that we can be a dominant nation in such sports like TT, only by fixing matches and cheating? Yes, we are sorry to say so... Cheating?

We have uploaded two Video files on You Tube that we possess as evidence of what's happening to the Chinese TT. These videos directly reveal the conspiracy of the Chinese officials along with Indian officials during the last Games that we know you are already aware of, but have done nothing about. Until now, these files have been placed for view only by invitation. You have the honour of viewing these files, by our invitation and to ACT. If someone in the crime trail still defends by cooking up a mock-up story, remember, we have a videographed statement of Mr. Chou, with us. 'Who's Mr. Chou'? you may ask. The answer is, 'Everybody in the trail knows and Mr. Chou regrets what he has done on behalf of the team management. Don't look for him, he is safe with us'.

Please restore parity in 30 minutes. Else, this video will be published for all to watch... 30 minutes – 1800 seconds!

We also understand the risks. We are taking might of Chinese Government. You could easily shut us down. But if you do so, there would be thousands of sites that would automatically host them in the next 30 minutes for public view. These sites are hydra headed!

Similarly, you may identify me through my email and being Chinese, you could harass my dear ones back in China, even if you can't lay your hands on me.

But again, I am not I. I am we. We are hydra. Cut one of us, a thousand more heads will appear.

Chinese Hydra.

The email carried the power of a 10 Ton nuclear device ready to detonate in the hearts of Shanghai and Beijing. The entire establishment buzzed up. Phones, emails, faxes, wireless, hotlines, were all busy in the next thirty minutes. Everyone was trying to locate Lt. Gen. Ping, but he was nowhere to be found. His office phones were silent. His Mobile phone was switched off for three full hours.

Later, when he reached the President's Private Suite, along with the General of the Central Military Commission, he was mobbed by Officials and calls. He didn't bother to explain where he had been or why his mobile was switched off.

Lt. Gen. Ping 'learnt' from excited and anxious Officers, 'There was a serious threat to the Games and the reputation of the Chinese Nation, posed by a video posted on the Youtube. Everyone was looking for you to resolve the issue, while you were nowhere to be found.

He also heard, The President's and the Premier's Office buzzed for you incessantly; that the Premier called and was irritated that he could not be reached anywhere'.

'Finally the President ordered two hours or so earlier, 'LT. GEN. PING BE ASKED TO CALL ME WITHIN 10 MINUTES, FROM WHEREVER HE IS'.

'But as there was no clue on your whereabouts and as the issue was so critical, the issue had to be resolved by the intervention of the President himself'.

Lt. Gen. Ping called the secretaries of the President and the
zPremier and passed identical messages to them, "I understand
that there was an urgent issue related to some postings on the
Youtube on the Games and you had been looking for me'.

'Unfortunately, I was on a Flight to Beijing to meet Mr
President. I could not take the Military helicopter and had to take a
civil, commercial airline'.

'I was considering this another normal day and didn't think
twice and switched off my Mobile in deference to the rules on
passenger flights. I regret my lack of anticipation of this issue. I
thank Mr President for taking his time off to resolve the issue,
which would have been my prerogative on this day. I appreciate
and support Mr President's decisions as always and I'm available
for any further brief and actions in this regard'.

Lt. Gen. Ping didn't ask how it was resolved. The Secretary to
the President volunteered;

'Dan, and two Senior Police Officials have resigned', whispered
the Secretary. Dan has been asked to continue as the Chief Coach of
the Chinese TT Team till the Games as it would be too difficult to
replace his services before the Games'.

'Chou, a member of the Chinese TT Federation Management
was dismissed from services, arrested and an inquiry ordered into
his role'.

'One Li Ling, who had been left out of the Chinese TT Team list
as submitted to the Games Committee earlier is included, and a new
list was submitted to ITTF, today by the Chinese Federation.

'The ban against two players from India has been revoked by
the ITTF after a Chinese recommendation. The ITTF penalty against
the Indian Federation has been reversed and their original Team list
with names of two Indian players has been approved to participate
at the Games'.

'The video on the Youtube has been removed voluntarily by the
protagonist. A head hunt has been ordered. They couldn't be traced
yet. They would be soon'!

Further whispers on the corridors of power informed him that
one Deng, World's no. 3 TT player opted out of the Games Team,
but was persuaded by the Chinese Team Management to continue
his services at least until the Games, at the behest of the President.

One Zhen Zhen, runner up at the last Games, was hospitalized for food poisoning. Information from the hospital indicates that she consumed poison to commit suicide. She had taken care that the quantum of poison was well below the lethal dose level and so she survived and a lot of sympathy was flowing in for her and her place in the Chinese team was intact. One Meiling collapsed while practicing and has been in hallucination ever since. She has been claiming that she was affected by black magic. Her place in the Team is said to be doubtful due to reasons of her health, both physical and mental.

56 To the President, His Men and their Girls

The dinner meeting between the President, the General - Central Military Commission and Lt. Gen. Ping went well. There was no mention of the Video files on YouTube that caused so much anxiety a few hours earlier at the highest levels of Government in China… and its resolution. The President did not seem to remember that Lt. Gen Ping had been invisible for over three hours and that he had been annoyed with him, just a few hours earlier.

Lt. Gen. Ping proposed toast 'To the President of China! – *gānbēi*' meaning 'Empty Cups', equivalent of the English, 'Bottoms Up', *gānbēi, gānbēi*, there was chorus as the glasses clinked.

'To the President of China'!! – there was a chorus as they chuckled, *'gānbēi, gānbēi, gānbēi.*

Lt. Gen Ping ensured that his glasses were lower than the President's as he clinked, so as to respect his position. As he tried to do the same with the General (Lt. Gen. Ping retired one level lower than the General), the General lifted Lt. Gen. Ping's glasses with his palms from the bottom and positioned it equal to his as he clinked his own. That was the Generals way to show his respect for Lt. Gen. Ping, who, though retired one rank lower than him, was his senior and superior in the current power structure in the Government and was a great friend.

Lt. Gen Ping noted that there was something less cheerful about the President on this day. His mood wasn't as vibrant as it usually was.

'To the General! – *gānbēi'*, proposed the President. It was his honour for the Officer.

'To the General!! – *gānbēi'.*   The General of Central Military Commission was known just as 'General', between them. They laughed, and clinked before they gulped.

'To Lt. Gen Ping, the Ping of Death! – *gānbēi'*, proposed the President louder and with more cheer, in his effort to bring Lt. Gen

Ping on par with the General, unofficially. 'To Lt. Gen Ping, the Ping of Death'!

The General hailed generously noting the importance the President had bestowed on his dear friend Lt. Gen Ping, without any jealousy – and they all echoed, '*gānbēi, gānbēi, gānbēi*', amid so much laughter and cheer.

'To the Games' – *gānbēi*'. 'To the Games, *gānbēi*'.

'To the Chinese TT Team! – *gānbēi*'.

'To the Chinese TT Team!! – *gānbēi, gānbēi, gānbēi*'.

'Do you think the Chinese will be beaten by the Indians at the Games'? The President was really concerned. The General stared in disbelief. How can the Chinese TT team be beaten? Lt. Gen Ping confided with them both. 'No such thing would happen. The Indian boy and the girl are good, no doubt. But they can't best us; WE ARE CHINESE', he boasted.

They all laughed and had a lot of fun around the table, with the world's finest liquor flowing into their cups every time they bottomed up.

They talked of the crisis brewing in the South China Sea and the Daiyo islands. The President had strong views and said, 'We are preparing very unconventional, yet a strong claim on the *Nánshā* islands (Spratly islands)', and hinted 'creation of artificial islands around a group of other islands claimed by Phillipines, bolstering our claim to the islands and blocking others' claim to them'.

'Someone has nicknamed it as the 'great wall of sand'. I like it'! he exclaimed in delight. There was also a discussion on the US based newspaper reports claiming that China is building airstrips on some of the islands.

The President just shrugged off the reports and concluded, 'We do what we need to do. We don't do something's just because someone speculates that we do and we don't stop doing something just because someone demands that we don't'.

The President mentioned in passing that he wanted to discuss with Lt. Gen. Ping about his steely intent to crackdown on corruption, privately. The President's sweeping anti- corruption campaign had already netted a number of Political Heavyweights and light weights. He was expecting a strong backfire. Actually, the fire had started and he needed Lt. Gen. Ping's immediate attention to the source of the fire. Lt. Gen Ping who was part of the President's fire fighting team, in fact wanted to update the President on the signs of the revolt that he had information of. But the President waved him off; not then! He seemed to want a detailed and serious discussion on it, the next day.

Then they chatted about their good old days they had spent in the military camp together, sneaking out to the exciting company of their girlfriends late nights. Having been got caught one night, they had to do one thousand push ups each as punishment.

'My arms are stronger by the push ups', the General, showed off his muscular arm.

'I would have done two thousand just for seeing my Liu, the next night', laughed the President. His mood drastically changed at the mention of Liu.

'Does Mrs President know Ms Liu'? stammered the General mischievously.

'I would be toast, if she gets to know some day. She's the only person in the world, I am afraid of, other than...' laughed the President.

'Then let's drink - To Mrs President! – *gānbēi*'.

The room echoed several times, 'To Mrs President!!! – *gānbēi, gānbēi, gānbēi*'. This time they hugged each other, and clinked several times before they gulped. As the 'spirit' was rising, the formality was wearing.

'Wherever is Ms Liu, Mr President'? asked the General innocently. 'Shhh' the President gestured, finger on lips and winked.

'Not to leave out my Ms Liu, wherever she's now? She's in my heart'! pointing to his chest proudly.

The President continued, 'Let's drink to Ms. Liu!!! – *gānbēi*'.

'To Ms. Liu!! – *gānbēi, gānbēi, gānbēi*', the chorus was getting louder and less sharp. By this time, the glasses that clinked were not in sync with the hierarchy. They weren't even seated. They were hugging each other, spilling their drinks and tripping around and helping themselves with some seafood and pork.

'To my girl on the night at the Military camp' said the General... 'Forgot her name! – *gānbēi*';

The others repeated; 'To my girl on the night at the Military camp. Forgot her name! – *gānbēi, gānbēi, gānbēi*', the echo was shriller.

The General corrected them, 'She was my girl and not yours. You have to toast saying, 'to your girl.....', and passed out... before the others could echo him.

'To my girl on the day at the Military camp...' said Lt. Gen Ping and thinking of his girl, managed to propose – '*gānbēi...*' before he passed out on the table.

The President was quite sober after the bouts of – *gānbēi!!* He summoned the security and said, 'Drop them off. Be careful. We had a serious and important meeting and they are exhausted.

The next morning during breakfast, the General asked Lt. Gen Ping, 'What was it for that you asked me to join the dinner with the President. I didn't see any discussion'?

Lt. Gen Ping replied, 'I wanted to tell the President that the only way to undo the Gordian knot is to cut it'.

The General asked, 'You didn't mention that; whatever the Gordian knot was?

Lt. Gen Ping replied, 'He knew, when I presented the challenge to him; he had cut it without bating an eyelid, even before I landed in Beijing. So there was no discussion on it'! and smiled.

The General knew that if Lt. Gen. Ping chooses to play 'hide and seek', he wouldn't get anything out of him. He was enjoying the pleasure of having cut somebody to size. He knew Lt. Gen. Ping would volunteer all the details during the next meeting, when things cooled off. So he said, 'Don't worry. We had a great time remembering our girls at the Military camp. The dinner with the President was just great', and bid goodbye.

Lt. Gen. Ping understood that the President wanted to discuss something in confidence with him during the dinner that was urgent. Lt. Gen. Ping re-read the story on the last edition of Nikkei Asian Review that he had browsed on his flight to Beijing from Shanghai. The story ran thus;

'...Although the drive to stamp out palm greasing has won the President plaudits with the citizenry, he seems mostly concerned with

keeping the formidable 'economic factions' -- rival centres of political power -- in his crosshairs. The ... faction has wielded enormous influence for years, shaping top leadership changes at the party congress...

The President has claimed several important scalps already, even 'big tiger' Zhou, a former member of the Politburo Standing Committee, the party's top decision-making body. Zhou was sentenced to life in prison after being found guilty of bribery and other crimes.

The President has vowed to crack down on both 'tigers' and 'flies' -- top and low-level officials. The push to clean up the party and the government has also sent shock waves through China's corporate world, netting numerous senior officials at state-owned companies, including those in the auto and electronics industries, as well as in the oil industry, Zhou's old fiefdom. The President is trying to crush economic factions with huge vested interests,' adding, 'if you trace the major economic factions' family trees to the top, you will mostly find one elder...'

Lt. Gen. Ping was anxious yet excited as he could feel the huge storm that was brewing and threatening the President and his men and at the enormous power wielded by the 'elder' in the Politburo and the Standing Committee. He spoke to his confidante, his mole on the elder's side, to have the latest update on the fermenting revolt. He heard attentively for the next 10 minutes and then called the secretary for a meeting with the President.

Book II

Part 7: In The Dragon's Lair

57 At their Game – The Defensive Ring

Kula got through to the Semi Final at the Games with great difficulty, struggling, one must admit! He fought hard to break the Defenses of even lowly ranked Chinese opponents, right from the initial rounds. It looked like the Chinese had analysed Kula's game too well and had deciphered his game and every Chinese player had been trained to outwit Kula at his game. He played five rounds before he came up to the Semi-finals.

The first round was against Sun Yat Cheng, China, seeded twelve. Kula lost the first two games tamely. Then he pulled himself together to take the second and third and the fourth game, only to lose the fifth game by a whisker. He had to win the next two else will be packed off in the first round. Then Kula reeled off four points at a stretch to reach parity at 4-4 and went on to win it to stay in the hunt. In the decider Kula took an early lead and wrapped up the game against his Chinese opponent.

In his second round match, Kula started off to a strong start against Kato, the fifth seed from Japan. He ran away with strong leads in each of the four games and gave no opportunity for the Japanese opponent to catch up. He wrapped the match in straight sets. The Third Round was against unseeded QingShan, from China, who was hailed in the media as a giant slayer as he had demolished the seventh seed Peter Wilkstrom of Sweden in the first round and the fourth seed Saito of Japan in the second round. Qingshan almost killed Kula as well. But Kula managed to get past him in a six game match.

One of the Sportswriters Liza Martin had analysed the draw of the Men's and Women's singles and conjured up names of players to watch as favourites to reach the final from a Chinese Team Management perspective. She assumed, just a hypothesis, that the rest of the Chinese team with different skills were preselected in an engineered draw, to commit hara kiri 'Do or Die', trying to stop the potential challenger in various rounds. The players that were to form the defensive ring around Jiang, were thrown at the potential challenger at every round in a bid to stop him dead! Liza mentioned at least four Chinese players, Sun Yat Cheng, QingShan, Wang Long and Yuan Jun, who were thrown at the potential challenger.

Wang Long, a Marine in the Chinese Navy, who lived by the sword, was one of the players, who was slated to stop the challenger on his tracks.

'However', she wrote, 'Wang Long, who lived by his sword also perished by his sword, in a round earlier than his potential meeting with Jiang's potential nemesis'.

The Chinese Team scoffed off her analysis as pure imagination of a fertile mind and said that it wasn't worth commenting about.

But Dan secretly wondered if a leak occurred somewhere.

The bookies silently and heavily voted in favour of Liza's analysis. The potential challenger, as per her analysis, turned the bookies favourite to win, overnight, after languishing much lower before her analysis was published. No prizes for guessing who it was; he was 'Kula'.

Kula's Fourth or the pre-quarter round was against the American, Henry Middleton. Henry had a sharp game and was considered TT's most promising star, just as Kula was considered as the hottest challenger to the Chinese domination of the game, immediately after the Kyoto open. But after the ITTF prevented Kula and Jay from participating in The World Tour Open Championships too, the media wrote off Kula as rusty citing lack of match practice.

The arrival of a rising new challenger, Henry from the US excited the collective attention of the world media and stole the front pages, while Kula barely managed to languish as short single column news on the periphery of the sports pages, in spite of his three consecutive wins at the Games; until Kula tamed Henry in straight games with ease; that is.

The mainstream media buzzed again in excitement and expectations on Kula. The verdict was that Kula was improving the game by every match. Will his game hold and improve enough and in time when he faces higher ranked Chinese players; the likes of Deng and Jiang?

58 Listening Posts

Ru was born in the North East Indian State of Assam to a Chinese father and an Assamese mother. The family later moved to Hong Kong where his father was in business; importing timber, primarily high quality teak, lentils and gemstones from Burma, Thailand and Malaysia into China through Hong Kong.

Ru, was educated in Hong Kong. When he was sixteen, the Chinese mafia in Hong Kong that identified Ru's family to be wealthy, expatriates, and an easy target, kidnapped Ru for ransom, and held him in the forests near the Vietnam border. In spite of Ru's father paying the ransom, someone in the Chinese establishment had either panicked or double crossed him and so Ru wasn't let go and his life was at stake. The episode got caught up in political quagmire as the local Chinese establishment wasn't ready to take on the fearful Mafia and quickly disowned Ru and his family.

Ru's father remembered his roots in India and ran to Shastry, an old acquaintance for help. Shastry, then a senior functionary in the RAW had convinced his friends, ex-Vietcong Guerrillas, to undertake a private rescue of Ru from the Jungles in a daring night raid on the hideout. The Mafia didn't know what had hit them at the hideout and had no reasons to suspect either the Vietcong guerrillas or the Indian brain behind it. The rescue was a huge blow to the pride of the Chinese Mafia, but earned huge respect for Ru's father within the Chinese establishment. They respected his daring against the Mafia and feared his invisible powers.

Ru volunteered to help India in general and Shastry in particular. His initial tasks were to influence Chinese officials and help Indian businesses that were stuck in deals with Chinese companies or Indian nationals, who had got into a mess with the Chinese authorities for overstaying etc. Slowly he got drawn into more heroic stuff, snooping for the Indian Government, especially at the request of Shastry initially in Hong Kong and later in China, where he had several business interests from Timber, Furniture, Real Estate and Media and Entertainment. He liked the challenge and the flow of adrenalin. Ru subsequently was inducted as a listening post for RAW in China and Hong Kong. He was tasked with three activities.

Activity one was to understand the undercurrents beneath the Government Policies and its impact; to read between the lines and understand the real intent over the content.

Two; he had a political responsibility; to analyse political significance of events and dumb it down for the masters back in India. He had to understand the Power Structures, the Power Centres, their heirs apparent as also the heirs behind shadows. Ru smelt the scandals involving those in Power, like who was supporting whom and on what expectations, who was backbiting whom and who was b**ching with whom, before they became whispers, much before they became rumours and long before they became news.

Three: To make sense of the country's International Power Play and what they meant to their relationship with other countries, especially India.

All the three activities, though seemingly different converged at the corridors of power. Ru had ascended as one of the most popular event managers in Shanghai and Hong Kong and that gave him a decent access to the corridors of power and he could eavesdrop on the conversations first hand.

He had also established a strong network of sleuths, journalists, political analysts and journalists, who were happy to share information with him in confidence for mutual benefit. He did a wonderful job of reading the political weather charts of the Far East, even before seasoned political analysts could.

His current Project was deciphering the internal one up-man-ship war between the President and the 'King Maker'. Shastry, had his information that all wasn't fair weather in Chinese internal Politics. He was here in China to reconfirm the story through his own channels. Ru was one of his channels.

Shastry met Ru at the washroom of the Hotel, where Ru was assisting an event conducted by the Games Committee in honour of the official Guests at the Shanghai Games. Shastry was one of the guests. Ru handed over a few laser printed sheets of paper to him in confidence that carried a story about a Chinese King and his concubines. Shastry did not read it through and it was evident that he wasn't interested in the story.

Shastry left for the Indian consulate, where he picked up a few old fashioned, code templates with hundreds of punch holes, and placed them one by one over the sheets of paper he received from Ru in a particular orientation. The templates revealed a different story on the pages than the Chinese King and his concubines. Shastry got the names and the story he was looking for. Satisfied that the story was consistent with his suspicion, he burnt the papers and the template to ashes and stepped out of his office.

Next, he entered a coffee shop at the ShaanXi Road Metro, where he met his second contact, Watanabe, who worked for a Tour Operator that specialized in Luxury Liner tours between China and Japan.

Shastry shared a great friendship with Watanabe for nearly 50 years, since they were very young. They shared and continued the friendship fostered by their fathers since the Sr. Shastry's days at the Subash Chandra Bose's Indian National Army (INA). Bose had personally assigned the elder Shastry a role as an analyst and strategist, considering his intelligence and analytical abilities. Watanabe's father was his point of contact and mentor on the side of the Japanese Imperial Army.

Jr. Shastry and Jr. Watanabe, coincidentally had similar careers, following their fathers' footsteps. While the former retired recently as a senior functionary at the RAW (the Indian Intelligence Agency), the later was entrenched till recently in the Public Security Intelligence Agency of Japan and was a Military Strategist of Modern Japan. After retirement, Watanabe took up position with a tour operator for Luxury Liners wooing Chinese tourists into Japan and vice versa. The position was a clean cover for his covert operations as an agent in China for the Japanese Military.

Watanabe handed over his tour program brochures for the next 3 months to Shastry. Between the sheets, Shastry found what he wanted. Some of the background papers on the stories that he had earlier read on the Nikkei Asian Review. Watanabe was known in certain circles as an undercover agent and as a journalist in others. The series of recent stories that had appeared in the Nikkei Asian Review, which Shastry wanted to dig deeper into had been authored by Watanabe, though were published under different pen names to protect the source.

Shastry paid him a wad of US$ bills and Watanabe promptly issued an official receipt and a ticket for the amount, booking Shastry for a Luxury Liner tour to Japan and back from Shanghai starting the subsequent week. Later, Shastry tore up the receipt and the ticket and threw them part by part at various dustbins along the way.

That evening, Shastry dispatched an encrypted email to NM that read as follows;

Sir,

It's true that the Chinese President is under intense attack from his detractors, who want him to step down. Some stories of a possible assassination attempt and a potential coup against the President continue to pop up and they may be true. In fact, even the tea being served to the President seems to be monitored and tested (tasted) before it is consumed by the President. The President has antagonized several power centres in the Politburo in his fight against corruption.

The allegation that the President is targeting his opponents in the garb of fighting corruption is gaining ground and may be partially true as well. A majority of the public are supporting the President in his fight. At the same time, it has to be understood that the public opinion means nothing in China. Only the support at the Politburo and the Politburo Standing Committee is anything to go by.

A senior member of the Politburo Standing committee, considered as a 'King Maker' is mentioned as being annoyed with the President.

The power struggle is expected to intensify in the next weeks.
Shastry.

59 Taming of the Shrew

Li'll'y had found her place in the Chinese Team, the moment her unofficial ban was relaxed by the Chinese Federation. The Chinese federation President had orders to find her a singles place at the Games. During the run-up to this Games she was welcome to play in the various World Tour Open Championships, as she wasn't officially banned by the ITTF. But she could not raise enough money to attend them. She couldn't find sponsors as the best of them wouldn't antagonize the Chinese Federation. In spite of these constraints, she did participate in a couple of Open Championships, including one in China. She had burst her bank account and used all her savings. She had almost a similar practice level like Kula and Jay, just above rust level.

Li'll'y was progressing in style, in her own right and reached the Semi Final. No one predicted a possible Jay – Li Final... Yet!

The Games were poised interestingly with the Semi Final round to be played in the Women's singles. In the Men's singles, the Quarter Final was to be played.

On the other side of the spectrum, it was 'Jay', who, as per Liza, was seen as a threat to Wen Qiang, the current World No.1 and the top seed. If one went by Liza'a analysis, 'Zhen Zhen was thrown at Jay at a very early round, even in the round two and the Chinese planners wanted to stop Jay for good, right at the entrance. Moreover, they had planned to draw one of the players with a style similar to that of Wen Qiang for the fourth round, to sweep Jay off her feet. If true, this would mean that the Chinese played a lot of brain games well before the Games began'.

Before the second round match, the media whipped up huge expectations as a 'rematch' for Zhen Zhen and a 'revenge' match for the Indian. Whatever, Jay breezed past Zhen Zhen in the second round.

At the post match interview Jay replied, 'I did not consider it as a 'rematch' or as a 'revenge' match. It was just another day at the table'.

'Believe me', she continued, 'I am neither under nor overwhelmed by any one. I wouldn't have recognized Zhen Zhen if she had walk past me off the court yesterday and I wouldn't recognize her if she walked past me tomorrow. I would be happy not to', with a tinge of scorn, unusual for Jay'.

She refused to be drawn into the controversy of her placing the bronze medal at the feet of Zhen Zhen. She simply quipped, 'I hope and wish that in future the dignity of the podium will be respected and only those with matching dignity should deserve to ascend it'.

It was fair redemption for Jay as, one of the TV reporters telecasting live described Jay's win as 'Taming the Shrew', while others picked up the lead and repeated the interview several times the next few days by all mainstream TVs regularly. …

Jay's next match against a Chinese was to be in the Quarter Final. The girl with Wen Qiang style was defeated in her third round and failed to reach the appointed fourth against Jay.

Liza, who seemed to be gathering followers for her excellent and unique analysis of the Games, commented, 'The third round match that the girl with the 'Wen Qiang' style lost to her German opponent, was so one sided that it looked as though the Chinese girl was asked to give up by the Team Management after a quick rethink. Reason: denying Jay some quality match practice against the 'Wen Qiang' style of play'.

Thus, Jay met the tough German in the Quarter Final. It was the only match that Jay had been in starting trouble, unable to fathom her opponent's game. Once, Jay got the rhythm, there was no stopping her.

60 Mirror Image

Li'll'y was watching Kool's matches and was afraid for him. Though she was glad that he had scraped through to reach the Quarter finals, she knew that his game wasn't good enough to hold against the top Chinese players like Deng, Ding Xiang and finally Jiang. They all could beat him down mercilessly at the level he played. The worst was that though Kool seemed to know that he was having a problem, he hadn't diagnosed the cause. While all other analysts and experts, including Mahadevan thought he was improving his game in each round, Li'll'y dreaded that he was moving more and more away from his natural style as he 'improved' his game in the un-natural style.

Kool was playing as though he was trained to be a robot by another robot. He was repeating the moves he had learnt like a military drill, without applying his mind to it. He had become over reliant on his training with the TTSM and had been converted into a robot like itself. One of the features that Li'll'y recalled about the machine was that it also tells one how best to respond to each stroke. The return shots one makes against the machine's serves are captured by it and analysed on its trajectory for various coordinates and other attributes before the machine tells you, which of the strokes that you took was the most ideal by giving a rating on a scale of 10. One can set the TTSM to serve the ball repeatedly till you hone your strokes and gain higher ratings.

Li'll'y had earlier tried to explain to Kool while she was in Chennai at the Joy-Li'll'y Academy. She could define it in Chinese; 'Kool had become 预测'; pronounced Yùcè. But she had never got the right English word to explain to him.

She fumbled with words like forecasted, projected etc. But they did not convey the right meaning. Her effort had been 'lost in translation'. The previous evening, she was reading an English news column on Kool's Pre-Quarter Final victory against QingShan, which said that 'Kula had become very 'predictable' to the Chinese, who should have been practicing hard against his style.' She re-read the passage.

She discovered the word; Predictable!!!

She had to convey this to Kool. She went to the Bristo Bar that Tuesday and soon Kool and Joy joined her.

Li'll'y knew she didn't have time. She got onto business quickly. She showed him three video clips each less than two minutes.

The first clip was from the previous Games, An unnamed Chinese player smashes a powerful forehand topspin and the ball that tears through the air, low over the net, suddenly dips further on contact with the table and tends to dive below the surface of the table just beyond the table's edge like a programmed missile. Any player on the opposite side would have have been bewildered at the sheer pace, dip and dive and would have had just time enough to scamper below table height and if lucky enough to touch the ball, would have would have sent it sky high.

The standard Chinese style of play would have been just to play defensive for such a complicated shot, position oneself, kill the spin and return as best as you can, and save the energies for a later double offensive to overwhelm the opponent. But not Kool! He was seen to be ready for the ball well ahead, as though he had observed the ball saunter along its low trajectory and had seen it spin wildly, yet slowly towards him, had seen the ball dip and dive, all in in slow motion. He seemed to have all the time in the world to position himself, bend low to not only scoop the ball from its near grave, but also to effectively kill the spin, smash his favourite backhand top-spin - left-side spin combo loop and send the ball crashing to the right edge of the table all in one expert stroke that he made looked easy. His baffled opponent, who did not anticipate an out-of-the-depths loop culminating in a strong offensive shot, was caught on the wrong foot and just managed to meet the ball that flew into his face. For Kool in such situations offence was the best form of defence.

In the next clip, Deng had sent out a similar powerful forehand topspin and the ball whizzes past the net keeping low and further dipping on contact at the table, tending to dive below the table surface. A cool Kool, who seemed to have watched the ball topspinning at great speed and in slow motion and having visualized the dip as it happened, rushed forward, and before it could dive, whipped it forehand, enough to kill the spin and loop drove it with a wee bit of topspin to the left corner; The mighty Deng, who seemed to have studied the response of Kool in the previous match, prepared himself well ahead and moves to the right edge of the table, only to be deceived, as he watches the ball streak past the left edge. Kula had improvised both the shots with precision on the spur of the moment and had Deng as baffled as the other unnamed player, in spite of his preparation.

Li'll'y observed that Kool in the last edition of the Games, did not play to any rulebook or follow any specific style during the last Games. So it was difficult to predict his game.

In the third clip taken from the current Games, against Qing Shan's-similar-in-character stroke, Kool smashed a confident return that he had had well trained himself on TTSM. So, Kool's return while great; but Qing Shan's anticipation of his defensive return was even greater! He had positioned himself well for Kool's 'by the TTSM recommrnded return' and blasted back a beauty from a strong position that Kool had no chance at all and lost the point. It was evident, the stroke as timid and uncharacteristic of Kool, and more in line with the suggestions of the TTSM –' don't risk… put the ball back into the game' stroke.

Li'll'y smiled at Kool, who realized his mistake.

In the pre-TTSM days, he would have played his return in a dozen different ways, devised on the spur of the moment, rather than follow a text book move borrowed from a Chinese library that made him predictable and vulnerable. Now he knew he had corrupted his game beyond recognition.

'So far I had played like a dumb robot, playing shots mirroring the TTSM and its limited, programmed shot making capacity, in effect pitting not me, but the machine against my Chinese opponents. Definitely, each one of the Chinese player, who had practiced against the TTSM, would be able to beat it hands down and thus, me too. By extension, when I play against Deng next, all my actions would be visible to him just as a mirror image of his own, for he had designed the machine, which ironically, today I personify. He just would have to lie in ambush for me to play my 预测 (Yùcè - predictable) strokes', Kool conceded and shook his head to shake off the scare.

He had to un-train whatever he had rather desperately conditioned himself in the last few months.

Kool recalled a story that he read several years back in his mind and laughed as he narrated it to the girls. 'A conman on a cruise ship challenges two International Chess Masters, his fellow passengers to play simultaneous chess games with each of them and bets he would either win over at least one of them or at least play creditable draws against both'.

'Before the start of the games, the International Masters had agreed to his condition that each of them and the respective audience would be seated in a different room and would not step out of it or communicate with others till the games were over, while the conman himself would be free to step in and out of the rooms to play each move'.

He accomplished the feat by playing mirror images of each of the moves made by each International Master, against the other, in effect pitting one International master against the other and held each of the popular Chess Masters to a creditable draw, taking everyone by surprise.

'Looks like by playing as a mirror-image of my nemesis, I had been effectively conning myself! Kool ridiculed himself.

61 The Chinese Meal

As soon as Li'll'y took her cab, Joy suddenly realized, 'Oh! I'm famished'.

The Games quarters was at least an hour and a half away. She being a strict vegetarian hadn't ventured into any Chinese hotels even for a snack. Kool an occasional vegetarian, who avoids meat on Fridays and on specific religious auspicious days, appreciated her concerns.

He volunteered and boasted to her. 'I know a good Chinese restaurant around here and I know the chef too! I can talk to him and get you the best of Chinese vegetarian food'.

Joy wasn't convinced, 'I'm not taking any chances. I will rather wait till we reach my room. I have some bread and yogurt. I have read of frogs, snakes and what not... I am sure of the shape of things that would be served. I have heard enough to know that they have only one 'ism' that is communism... they simply don't have an 'ism' called vegetarian'ism'.

Kool confided to her, 'Li'll'y had taken me to this nearby restaurant and had got the chef prepare a good vegetarian dinner once. I remember the chef quite well too'!

Joy relented at the mention of Li'll'y. Call it the Li'll'y effect!

Kool, who was confident minutes before, wasn't too sure as he staggered into the street. The street looked so different from his memory of it and the face of each restaurant had changed. The only thing that didn't change was the mixed meaty, umami and fermented smells emanating from these restaurants that was surely appetizing. But it was enough to cause a sickening sensation and upheaval in Joy's gut. She stopped at the corner of the street, as Kool staggered along to find the object of his boast. He found one nearest to the description in his mind and lo, the chef looked the same as any other on the street.

His pride didn't permit him to back-off and so he led Joy assuringly to the chef, who definitely didn't remember him.

Kool described in sign language, what a vegetarian dish is, as much as possible to his Chinese host, who was busy, but polite and honoured them - special guests from a foreign land, with his time and patience. When words failed, Kool scribbled sketches of what looked like a hen, a goat, a fish and a cow and struck them off and said, No'. Next he picked up an egg from its tray and gestured a big NO. His host smiled affably and bowed and nodded. Then Kool followed through with the demonstration holding a cauliflower, a carrot, a beetroot and a cabbage picked up from around the chef and gestured 'OK', thumbs up. The gracious host smiled and hugged him with one hand and gestured a thumbs up sign with the other. He left walking backwards bowing to Joy several times, as he left.

The other patrons of the restaurant didn't miss the fun and were entertained by the dumb charade, though it embarrassed Joy. At the end of the act, Joy wasn't sure if the host understood, but out of pity for the caring and relieved Kool, she sat at the table, waiting anxiously.

When the food arrived, steamy hot, she even liked the flavours that she once detested, partly due to her hunger and partly due to the friendly nature of the chef. The meal was served neatly laid and with appetizing colours and flavours. Joy was overwhelmed and bowed to the chef, thankfully.

She struggled with the chopsticks and couldn't pick up any food. As Kool tried to guide her to hold the chopsticks right, she experienced many a slip between the chop(stick) and the lip. There were no spoons and forks in the hotel.

Her hunger further exasperated her and she was ready to use her hands and bare fingers as she would do back in India, but avoided it here. As she scrambled her neatly laid meal by her experiments with the chopstick, she found amid her vegetables, something that looked less like a vegetable and could easily pass for a piece of meat. Kool assured her, 'No it can't be. May be he used a soya based mealmaker, a Texturised Vegetable Protein as they call it, that has a meaty texture'.

To reassure her further, he asked the chef in a sign language. The host smiled, waved them to wait and rushed in only to bring a large plate covered by an equally large bowl. Then he proudly and gracefully lifted the cover with the countenance of a magician revealing an unexpected rabbit under his hat and looking re-assuringly as if to say, 'This is the best there could be - for my special guest'!

And most unexpected it was… a semi-conscious suckling baby piglet!!!

Joy fled out to avoid throwing up on the restaurant table.

Kool later conceded apologetically, 'I didn't draw the piglet'!

Joy screamed, '…and the whale… and the Tiger… and the cat… and the cockroach… and the bat'!!!

The next day was Kula's Quarter Final against Yuan Jun, who hailed from Hong Kong, seeded sixteen and had trained intensively with the Chinese National team. It was to be a lucky break for Kula as Yuan Jun's game was as natural as his. Kula settled for a technique where he had to play each stroke without any predetermined style. He enjoyed the Game against Yuan Jun. Kula prevailed in the match in a seven game marathon lasting over two hours. It did him good to play naturally against Yuan Jun and helped him at least partially get out of the shackles imposed by the TTSM and its Chinese brain. At the end of the match, Kula felt that his nerves and muscles were liberated. They were aching and all in knots, as he had been playing his unnatural style for the last couple of months.

He will play Deng in the Semi Final after a day's break.

The Day's break came. He practiced against Joy and was making significant progress by the end of the day. Kula got confident and was eager to face Deng.

Deng was eager to face Kula too. After Kula's first few rounds at the Games, Deng and Dan, were surprised too; pleasantly surprised. 'Looks like Kula had taken a secret Chinese coach' Dan observed and Deng nodded. Both were unaware that a prototype of a TTSM, sold to a scrap dealer in Shanghai found its way to India.

'No one can beat or better the Chinese by playing in the Chinese style'.

'Yes, if Kula had to be beaten then this is the chance'.

Moreover, while Kula was struggling to scrape through each round against Chinese players, with great difficulty, Deng had been winning his matches with such authority that it seemed Deng could make no mistake. He was harbouring hopes of upsetting Jiang in the finals too.

62 Gorgon's head

Gorgons refers to three sisters, daughters of Gorgon and Ceto. Medusa, like her sisters, was a winged human female, with a hideous face and had hair made of living, venomous snakes. She also had a horrifying appearance that turned those who beheld her, to stone. While two of the Gorgons, Stheno and Euryale, were considered immortal, their sister Medusa was not. She was beheaded by the demigod and hero Perseus, who thereafter used her head, which retained its ability to turn onlookers to stone, as a weapon until he gave it to the goddess Athena to place on her shield.

... Greek mythology

Deng's capitulation was a short affair. After a hard fight in the first game that he lost 11-9, he surrendered the second game 11-2. Kula won the next two games as well, 11-4 and 11-3 and sailed into the Finals with a straight win.

Kula was proud, yet looked humble and extended his hand towards Deng, while his adversary gleamed at him viciously with all the contempt he could muster. As Deng fell, absolute silence blanketed the stands of the stadium. Had Kula beheaded the feared Medusa and held her head by the serpentine hair for the entire stadium to see, the state of the crowd wouldn't have reacted much different; the spectators just turned into stone at the gaze of the Gorgon's eyes that were still alive and raging. Even the Indian side of the stands were struck into silence in fear of the icy cold eyes of the vanquished Deng and missed the celebration. It looked like the acridity dripping from the mutilated Gorgon could scorch the air around Kula and consume him in the next moments.

Kula, who beat Deng without much thought, was enjoying the moment and was saved from being petrified; from the fear of consequences of winning, as he didn't see Deng as anything other than human; he had just called the bluff called 'Deng', the second time.

All the calculations of Dan and Deng and their confidence were proved to be just pre-match boast. Kula had switched to his natural game without any inertia.

Deng was crestfallen. He did not attend the post-match interview. He did not participate in the post-match team analysis. Jiang would have loved to have some inputs from Deng at the analysis, for he had to face a resurgent Kula.

Liza Martin wrote that Jiang could be the chosen Chinese challenger, to try to stop Kula; not the other way around. 'The mood in the Chinese camp' she wrote 'would be that it was not who won, but who would stop Kula's golden run'.

It would be Jiang's first match against the 'fickle player from India', as Dan preferred to describe Kula. However the analysts chose to term him as maverick, who not only challenged the collective intellect and arrogance of the Chinese team, but also was just one step away from upstaging it.

After the post match analysis, Dan found Deng in his quarters pacing in double circular loops of 8, like a wounded, angry, lonely, hyena confined in a small cage, looking mean through his bloodshot eyes, ready to pounce on and tear apart any life that comes its way with its dreadful, barren teeth... In happier times, after every successful match, he could be seen celebrating in the company of young girls, who were willing to lose their innocence to him, a herd at a time. But that day, he found solace in rage, unable to come to terms with the humiliation that would stay with him forever. He wanted his revenge.

Dan entered silently, waited for him to notice him and handed over a letter that accompanied a photograph without saying anything. Deng was irritated at his showing an irrelevant photograph, while he was burning in anger and humiliation and tossed it aside without looking at Dan.

Dan spoke, 'It's OK Deng, you had a bad day, that's all...'

Deng picked up his gun, pushed Dan against the wall by his neck and pressing the metal on Dan's temple and screamed, 'One more word...'!!!

Dan pleaded, 'Do you want to see Kula behind the bars? We have a strong case against him'.

Deng's eyes lit up and said 'Yeah the ba****d has to be cracked. But don't play with me'!

Dan showed him the photograph again that looked like a frame of a machine, he had received from Jiangsu Sports Equipment Company again and read out the letter from Jiangsu, 'One of our Software Consultant, a contractor has smuggled out a frame of the TTSM from China. The part has been established to have been dismantled by a scrap dealer from the prototype that was scrapped. The person who smuggled the part had claimed it to be a part of laundry equipment at the customs. As the name plate on the frame bore the stamp of Jiangsu Sports Equipment Company, the customs officer suspected some foul play, photographed the part and informed us. We have already made a complaint with the Police. The case is being investigated by Officer, Mr Lee. We want to keep you informed as you are the sponsors of this confidential project'.

Deng demanded, 'How do you link it to Kula'?

'It is emerging that Kula is the one. He had come to China as a Software Consultant and has worked for Jiangsu'.

Deng saw his big chance and with a spring in his feet and voice, questioned, 'Why Lee? Is he the same Lee'?

Dan nodded, 'Unfortunately it comes under Lee's district'.

Deng cursed, 'The ba****d! He had let off this guy last time. I won't trust him. Our own Senior Officers have also resigned, due the 'Sh*t of death'.

Dan added, 'Last time we had a light case. This time; it is a strong one'.

Deng was encouraged.

'We will have to talk to 'Godfather', said Dan. 'Let's do our homework first'.

63 Ladies' Day Out!

Then there were two excellent Semi Final Games played by Joy and Li'll'y against their respective opponents at the Games. Joy played the first Semi-finals against Lan Fen. Lan Fen was a timid girl with a great game. She was seeded second to take on Wen Qiang the number one in the Finals.

Lan Fen's aggressive game was in stark contrast to her nervous demeanour and rattled Joy in the first game that she won 11-5.

Kool normally gives tips to Joy during these situations. But for reasons unknown to Joy, Kool was nowhere to be found on the side-lines. She wasn't aware that he was facing a brutal enquiry at the Police Station. Had she known, she would have either broken down or would have been provoked to walk out of the match at the Semi-Finals stage causing another furore at the Games.

She meditated on the side-lines, with Kool in her mind to guide her. He would have asked her to respond to Lan Fen's characteristic Game, with her own natural Game. 'Not to do anything funny. Study each shot, and each return, service and placement. Don't let her repeat the same trick again. Don't let her spin deceive you. Watch her movements and footwork. Judge her strengths and weaknesses. Most importantly 'watch' the ball'.

Lan Fen, thought Joy, moved slightly slower to her left, when moving backward, when Joy had played two strokes to the edge of the left flank. Joy recalled she had taken both the points. She heard the whistle and got ready for the next game.

She had to win the next games or lose at the Games. As she walked past Lan Fen, she smiled at Lan Fen and she smiled back. It was a nice and positive feeling.

She asked herself, 'If I lost to a particular shot from Lan Fen?

And replied to herself, 'Yes, I did',

As Lan Fen served for the next point she got a demonstration of the shot.

Lan Fen could combine topspin and sidespin the ball at great speed. She said to herself, 'The spin was bafflingly effective, deceptive enough and I have lost a few points in the last game and the first of the current game. I need to position better next time, anticipate the spin and then make my return'.

'No... Anticipation is not the word. I have got to look at the ball as Kool would have done. I have to see the ball as though it was shreds of glass pieces flying in slow motion against me and that my life was in great danger'.

It was difficult at first to see the ball that spun at the speed and deftness at which Lan Fen shot the ball. She focused hard and got herself the view.

Yes! She was able to see the ball side-spin and deflect, as it touched the table top and move lazily away from her, in slow motion. That she sighted the subtle spin and swing was enough for her to anticipate, position herself and kill the spin as she slammed the ball back to Lan Fen. The first time Joy slammed it back, she found Lan Fen unready for the ball and was completely caught off guard. Joy knew that her opponent was normally so confident of her stroke, a unique one at that, she never was prepared for a return and a winning return at that.

Joy didn't find any more arsenals in Lan Fen's armoury. She was a one trick pony and once Joy saw her trick through, wasn't a threat anymore. Of course, Lan Fen was a great fighter and fought for every point in the second and the third, but was always trailing Joy.

Joy wrapped up both the games and the fourth and fifth as well in style and walked on to the Finals. She would have to face the winner of the second semi-Final, either Wen Qiang or Li Ling.

The second Semi-Final between Wen Qiang and Li Ling (Li'll'y) would start in the next 30 minutes. Joy was excited and prayed all her favourite Gods to bless her friend Li'll'y. Her Indian team mates were wondering, why Joy had so much stakes in this match. She wasn't even so tense in the minutes before her own match against Lan Fen.

They asked Joy, 'Do you prefer to meet Li Ling to Wen Qiang, as she would be an easier opponent to play in the Finals'?

Joy just smiled and let them decipher her smile themselves.

The battle between Wen Qiang and Li Ling was the fiercest fought battle ever in the Women's TT. It was evident that Li had limitations in her game against a towering opponent like Wen

Qiang. She fought hard and won all hearts, but lost the match 10-12, 15-13, 16-14, 17-19, 9-11, 10-12. Joy cried for her friend. She wanted to run and hug her and console her. But she had to keep away, keep her emotions in wraps lest she trips someone's resentment like last time.

Joy was glad to have watched the Li'll'y – Wen Qiang match as she had trained extensively with Li'll'y, it was easy for her to visualize Wen Qiang game transposed against her own, rather than that of Li'll'y's. She would discuss her Final match with Kool, tomorrow evening as her final match was scheduled a day later than Kool's Final match against Jiang. First they would discuss Jiang's style of play and an effective counter all of today.

Two years earlier, when Joy had some doubts about Li'll'y's intentions towards Kool, she had wanted to express her own love for Kool ahead of her, lest she loses Kool in the race between 'two sisters'. Joy had decided during the last Games to just kiss him lightly on his lips; a light brush of lips when he wins the Semi-final against Jiang, in front of the crowd and all the camera's and media.

Joy had had a fear that the less inhibited Li'll'y would propose to Kool first and walk away with him at the cost of perpetually waiting Joy. But her exciting plan had been short circuited by Deng and company.

Two years later, that is now, after their heart to heart talk with Li'll'y of her love for Kool, on the banks of Cauvery the previous year, she was less concerned. But she was overcome by an urge to express her love for Kool and in style. The same dilemma, the same settings, the same excitement after two long years.

This time, Joy decided to Kiss Kool on his lips and lock him into her heart - a Kiss with a capital 'K', like in a Hollywood movie. She hoped that such daring, in full public view of the world, just after his Final against Jiang, would pre-empt anyone else from getting close to him or crave for his affections. He would thence forward be her own; nobody else's. She prayed that her parents would understand.

64 Waves of Attack

Lee, had established that Jiangsu had hired Kula, without checking his background. Questioning the scrap dealer did not help.

The dealer pleaded innocence and profusely lied, 'I had dismantled the entire machine immediately and scattered the parts around so that they can't be traced back to the TTSM. I do remember that one foreigner came looking for some scrap parts for his parts business. He was sold just one part, from the machine that had been just dismantled and scattered, this frame, after he was informed that it was a part of laundry equipment'.

He also told Lee, 'The person had purchased not only this part, but also other parts from other laundry machines. I can vouch that the person was not looking for the TTSM machine or its parts.

Lee asked, 'Can you give me a list of parts that this person purchased from you'?

The dealer replied, 'Sorry, I wouldn't remember. I don't keep track of his scrap sales inventory'.

'Who did you sell the parts of the TTSM machine to'?

'I wouldn't have been able to remember the very next day also, sir. After I scattered the machine parts to different bins, it would have been difficult to identify which parts belonged to the machine'.

'How long do you save security camera records'?

'No Sir, I don't have surveillance camera covering much of the parts warehouse. We don't track the sales or stock much. I don't expect anyone to steal these parts. They are zero value, may be negative'.

The investigation could not proceed beyond that. In any case, it was six to eight months earlier and nothing of evidence value could be found.

The dealer tried to cover his own as* and life, when he lied convincingly. In the process, he covered Kula too.

He prayed, 'I only hope the Indian would corroborate my story or else both of us will walk to the gallows in company'.

Lee had sympathy for Kula. But he definitely would not excuse him if he had smuggled a 'Secret of China' in a clandestine manner and would never let him get away with it. His investigation of the scrap dealer produced a dead end. He was struggling to figure out the story. He had visited the Indian Quarters at the Games village to question Kula.

Kula had a shock and did not know how the Authorities had caught up with his misdemeanour. He understood that the Chinese machinery was very efficient. It could be very brutal too. This had happened several months ago and he had almost become complacent.

He kept most of his answers to; 'I don't remember the details'.

Lee reported, 'Though it is established that it was Kula who purchased at least this one part and took it outside China, there was no clue on his motive for purchasing a weird looking steel frame that was supposed to have come from a laundry equipment. Given his access to the TTSM design, he would have been motivated to reconstruct the machine from whatever machine parts he could lay his hands on at the scrap dealer. But could he? There's no evidence that he purchased more than just a steel frame. Motive unclear, so not suspect'.

Deng charged that Lee was soft on Kula. Under pressure from the 'Godfather', Lee had to concede to have a parallel investigation officer, Hui Qing, who would also investigate along with Lee.

The new officer known to be anything between harsh to heartless summoned Kula to report to Lee's office. Hui Qing dealt with Kula downright brutally, with the conviction that his hard ways would force a softie like Kula to accept his crime. In the process, Kula was bruised badly on the head, forehead, arms, back, abdomen and thighs. Kula held his nerve and didn't concede anything that could be held against him. He knew any admission of guilt would be his last free word. He managed to compose himself to answer coherently and not make contradictory statements that could point to his guilt.

The summary of Kula's story was that a friend of his, back in India runs a used parts business for laundry machines.

He had requested, 'I have heard that due to the use and throw culture prevalent there, a lot of used parts could be sourced very cheap; dime a dozen. Could you please find some of the parts I need for some of the laundry machines models'?

Kula continued, 'I had purchased mostly programming controls that were dismantled from washing machines models that were popular in India'.

'No, I do not recall what else I had purchased'.

When Lee showed him a photograph of the metal part, he knew where he had slipped. It had been at the airport.

'I had purchased most of the controls I needed. I came across this frame among the laundry parts. I was interested in the name embossed on the frame. It said Jiangsu Sport Equipment Company. I was curious if Jiangsu makes laundry parts too? Not as far as I knew; but could be'.

'But why did you buy this metal. It was not something you came looking for, I suppose'?

Pat came the answer, 'Oh, I saw my company name embossed on it. I thought it was souvenir to take back home; to show my friends'.

Hui Qing was surprised as he coughed, 'Souvenir! That is an odd story'!

But the quick and cool shrug from Kula, made them both think, 'Why not'?

The spontaneity of the reply and the natural 'shrug' should have convinced Hui Qing. Moreover, Kula's story was consistent with that of the dealer. In spite of the violent methods of Hui Qing, he seemed to be fair. He informed the higher authorities and signed off reporting, 'There is nothing suspicious' and left.

Kula was happy to be let off with some bruises. It could have been worse. But the incident, just a day before his Finals match against Jiang had shaken him badly. Was he in a frame of mind and body for the Final? He doubted it as he reached the quarters. Mahadevan and Jay along with the other Indian team members swarmed around him. They were shocked at the treatment to Kula. Joy hugged him and sobbed on his shoulders.

She was helpless, 'Did we do the right thing to have ever come to China. Is the whirlpool dragon grabbing you again'?

Shastry appeared with an entourage of the Indian consulate in Shanghai and was visibly in rage. He called Lt. Gen Ping on his mobile and spoke to him. He insisted to meet quickly.

Lt. Gen Ping said, 'I'm away somewhere out of Shanghai and would not be back till the tomorrow evening. In any case as this enquiry relates to smuggling of 'State Secrets of China', I can't do much about it. The law will take its course'.

Evidently, Lt. Gen Ping was irritated that Shastry continued to disturb him even as he moved on to another flare he was fighting for his President and was not averse to show it. Shastri's rage increased and was visible like mercury rising when stuck in boiling water.

He subdued it with a gulp and said politely, 'This needs to be dealt with in private. I am having company. May be you have too. We shouldn't be playing to the gallery'.

'Shall we set up an emergency Video conference in the privacy of our space? I suggest in 10 minutes, 8:20 PM. I will get into my car that you provided for me as a State Guest, as a fair observer at the Games', Shastry taunted sarcastically.

Lt. Gen. Ping on the other end protested, 'I am in the South China Sea, on a Frigate, in the midst of a flare up with another country. I am simply not available until tomorrow evening. I don't have time or care for some petty criminal caught red handed, taking away Chinese 'National Secrets' and your pleas to save the boy'.

Shastry, got cooler as he gets more enraged, 'OK, if that's what you will. I'm meeting the international press at 8:25, who are already assembling in front of the boy's quarters; about 10 of them now and counting.

'Kula is an honourable Indian, a guest of China at the Games. He is our Ambassador of good will, and deserves a near diplomatic status. He has just beaten your world No. 3, on the way to Finals at the Games. Your Chinese Team Management has been throwing punches outside the ring to stop Kula from entering it, since the last Games'.

'I have enough dynamite to blow up the Games and the press is hungry for the story since the last Games and they will have a juicy story. The word will be from a 'Neutral Observer' invited by the Chinese Government. I will be expecting your call at 8:20 PM. If I don't receive it, I will be constrained to meet the press at 8:25'.

Shastry rushed to the car park. He expected the car would be bugged. So he stood about twenty metres from the car, 'you don't know how far these mikes can pick up the voice', and spoke to the Indian PM for five minutes and was ready for the call with Lt. Gen. Ping at 8:19 PM, when his phone rang.

Lt. Gen. Ping quickly, said, 'I was wrong about your boy being a petty criminal. I agree he is a guest of China, until the Games are declared closed; that is. I have ensured that all proceedings be suspended against the boy till then'.

'As you are an honoured 'Special Emissary of the PM of India, I would like to invite you to the special Gallery to watch the Finals along with the President and the Prime Minister of China, with appropriate introductions and protocol'.

Shastry made some quick mental calculations. 'It would be my pleasure'.

Lt. Gen. Ping also invited Shastry for a dinner with 'friends' after the Finals. Shastry wanted to say, 'Let me do a rain check', but thought the better of it, said, 'With pleasure'.

After the investigation officer, Hui Qing failed to arrest Kula, Deng with the help of his Politburo 'Godfather' did some more plotting. They sent a Special Police Officer, with an order to arrest Kula. When the Special Officer was ushering Kula out of the Indian quarters, he was greeted with flashes of powerful lights and cameras. The Officer wondered how they came in so quick. He ordered them off, thinking they were domestic Chinese press. But when he realized they were international press and that he was arresting the Finalist at the Games, the gravity of the situation sank into him. He thanked his own stars that he did not have this Indian hand-cuffed, though that would have been standard procedure. He called his Senior Officer directly, and asked him what to do. He could visualize another person, grabbing the phone from his Senior Officer at the other end, who he later knew to be Deng, who growled an order at him, 'Just arrest the ba****d; don't even ask'.

Just then Shastry returning from his call with Lt. Gen Ping saw the commotion at the entrance to the Indian Men's quarters. The press were clicking away pictures and videos streaming live. The Special Police Officer knew that his goose was being cooked in public and most well done at that.

Shastry stepped in to save the situation. He walked up to the Officer-in-charge and shook hands introducing himself.

'I can see what you are doing and that you are in a quandary. If you would listen to your Special Commissioner, who is much higher up than anyone who has ordered the arrest of Kula, I think, the situation can be defused'.

The Special Officer was in no mood to listen. He didn't want more pressures than he already had.

Shastry was already speaking into his mobile, 'Thanks for picking up amidst your busy schedule. One more crisis has raged that has gone against the spirit of our last discussion. Could you please talk to the Police Officer-in-charge, Lt. Gen. Ping'? and handed over his mobile to the Officer.

The Officer who was angry at the intervention of this person, Shas..?.. whoever, froze at the name of Lt. Gen. Ping. 'Death beckons', he thought to himself and took the phone. He spoke something in Chinese. At the end of the conversation, he was glad that he had his orders 'over his orders'. He was grateful to Shastry as he handed over the mobile to him.

Shastry smiled and spoke to the benefit of the mikes thrust all around him, 'The official version from the Indian Team Manager is', he pulled Kula close to him for effect, 'That Kula had an accident'.

'An incident', he corrected himself.

He continued, 'As you would have seen, he has bruises all over his face and body. This Police Officer on duty seems to have stepped in to enquire. A series of incidents have been happening against the Indian duo, Kula and Jay, since the last Games and we believe that they aren't happenstance. They seem to be orchestrated and there seems to be a lengthy conspiracy. A Special Commissioner of the Chinese Government spoke to me and said the Government is investigating the matter. He also assured all help and best treatment to Kula before the Finals and until it is curtains to the Games'.

'At his moment, 'All's Well! I would suggest we ignore the incident in the best interest of the Games, for now'.

'Thanks for coming'.

He had scattered enough live ammo in his little speech that he was sure the Press got the message. He could pick up the pieces left for them and connect the 'incident' to whatever Deng and his nexus were plotting at the closure of the Games.

Next, he discussed with Mahadevan on providing Kula ample rest and appropriate medical attention and get Kula ready for the finals.

That was about Deng's 'Final Gambit', or was this his final yet?

65 Climbing Mt Everest

Kool slept deep, sedated for over 10 hours. He woke up still drowsy and worse, a heavy ache all over his body caught up with him. After an hour at the Jacuzzi, he got into a light practice with Joy and quickly got into the rhythm. They both discussed the match against Jiang, to build Defenses against his strengths and ways to exploit his weaknesses.

Kool thought to himself, 'I do have a psychological advantage. The day I had beaten Saito at Kyoto, I had seen uncertainty in Jiang's eyes'.

He also cautioned himself, 'But that was a year back. Now Jiang had improved his game, while I have run out of match practice'.

Kool did not want to think more of Jiang than absolutely necessary. He knew that the quality of the game that he would play in the evening would count much more than his worrying about the game all day. He was getting ready for the match after a cold shower.

The Games Finals recorded the highest viewership in the history of TT. It was rated as the one of the most anticipated matches and whipped up frenzy in the media, the spectators and the viewers alike.

Kool did not realize what he was up against, till he faced the first few exchanges against Jiang. Jiang seemed to control the ball on its flight as though it were guided by his eyes and thought. If there were lessons on clear, crisp, sharp, incisive shots and returns, right on the spot that was beyond his reach; as deceptive as hell; Kool was taking his lessons.

Kool was known not to fall for the same deception twice. So he was clinging on. He scored against the same trick, whenever repeated. He was waiting quietly for Jiang to exhaust his arsenal of tricks and repeat some of his earlier ones. But the variety of library strokes from Jiang continued and he had deep pockets. Kool wasn't exactly 'faultering', but he was clearly lagging. In spite of his best efforts and touching the limits of his talent, he was failing to break

Jiang's cordon. He did not find anything in his skill that he could readily use even to nudge into a lead however slender, ahead of Jiang; forget, overwhelming Jiang.

Jiang was already serving 9-7. He would wrap up the game, before one could sneeze. Kool knew that he would have to raise his game and soon enough. Though this was a seven game final it afforded just no liberty at this level of the game.

He looked for weaknesses in Jiang. Nothing much. The small weaknesses, Kool did exploit and got a couple of points and got this close, trailing at 7-9.

'I have to raise the game. I have to focus on the ball. I have to see the ball ahead and with such clarity that I'm used to. Today, may be the hurt inside his head; may be the ache in every joint makes me cranky. May be the sedatives I have taken makes me drowsy; isn't letting me see the ball as clearly'. That was his diagnosis.

Now for the cure; instant cure. He took a timeout. He rushed to his corner, took a big sip of the herbal concoction that Mahadevan had prepared for him, that helped to clear his mind a bit, sat in padhmasana posture, closed his eyes and took deep breath, through each of his nostrils; Pranamaya, the shortest of yoga and meditation he could afford in the timeout break.

He jumped back into the play area, only to find a small commotion near the umpire.

Dan on the urging of Deng was complaining, 'He is using mind control techniques and hypnotism on our team'.

Mahadevan jumped into the fray defending Kool, 'Yoga and meditation are mental exercises, and nothing to do with controlling another's mind'.

The issue was referred to the Match referee. The match referee was under pressure.

Shastry thought it fit to interfere, but was caught up among the VVIPs of China and protocol.

Jiang saved the day, 'I have no issues with Kula's yoga. I discovered Yoga during the last Games, while watching Jay and am now a staunch believer; I even participated in the International Yoga Day last June', he declared as Dan deflated.

The match continued. Either the concoction or the yoga or the commotion kicked in to help Kool sight the ball better. He was at home now. The initial uncertainty was replaced by confidence. That showed on the score line as he served 'Sixteen All' first game, the first time he caught up with Jiang after their 'Love all'.

The rest of the game was see saw battle. Though Kool lost the first game against Jiang 20-22, his confidence soared.

Joy looked so forlorn and was busily tapping into the smart phone, without even glancing at Kool.

He was looking to meet Joy's eyes after first game and wondered, 'What's wrong with her? What is so important? Continuously typing something into her mobile, when it was time to watch the game and guide me with clues'?

The time was up so he returned to the table and forgot about Joy and her concerns.

The next Game was even tougher. Both were fighting equally hard for every stroke, every point. Eventually Kool took the second set 18-16.

The third and fourth set went one each to Jiang and Kool and it was equal position, thus far. The Fifth game was Jiang's, after a tough fight.

Kool took one more sip of the herbal concoction and meditated while at his corner whenever he could afford some time. He had to take two games in a row, else he would be history. He jumped into the fray determined to equalize – one step at a time. He slowly sweated out his drowsiness, as he purged out the residual sedative from his blood stream. He saw the opportunity to win as he could see the ball better and his aches were relieving. Though his body was tiring, he could still position himself precisely to take each shot.

He did win the next game, but only after a draining long fight with Jiang for each point. Now for the deciding game!

If Jiang too was drained, he didn't show. Kool hoped he could last just one more game and then he could permit himself the luxury to collapse. His head was still hurting badly, but fortunately, only when he was back at his corner. But while he was in the arena, he didn't remember any ache. He could focus.

The decider started and moved at a slow pace. The rallies were big as both of them were tired. Neither was taking any chances. The killer instinct was replaced by 'live, and let die' policy. Both were careful not to make any unforced errors. As they both ran all over to dig out every ball and expertly land it on the other side they were all the more exhausted from their effort. Kool promised himself, 'Just one more point before I collapse', at each point. Jiang seemed to reciprocate, 'So do I'.

Kool was leading 16-15 after several see-saw moments and was serving for the match and championship the second time, while Jiang had served two as well. But Jiang wasn't about to give up yet. One of them would be winner, when the other collapses out of exhaustion.

Kool thought of Li'll'y. He thought of Joy. He remembered Meiling; then Zhen; then Deng and Dan. Then the Bronze medal at Zhen Zhen's feet; Then Li'll'y's home experience, then the 'Paradis', then the treachery, and finally the silent last flight back from Shanghai. He remembered Li'll'y's calling Indians as wimps, at the Bristo Bar.

He felt a surge of Cold Blood pounding into and against the hurt on his head. He shook his head to shake out his slumber. Then saw the ball in slow motion, pacing towards him gently. He saw the ball growing bigger as it floated towards him. He saw it spin and wobble and heard it Whirrr... He was already gliding towards the ball with ease, his sights fixed on the ball. All he saw was the ball... and the position on table behind, where he intended to land his stroke and nothing else. He positioned well. By instinct he knew when, where, how, at which angle to whip the ball and which point on the sphere to meet with his racquet and at what velocity and what angular velocity to impart to the ball. He did by instinct. The ball that was whipped backhand, an attacking topspin that hurtled furiously just on on the far edge of the table and Jiang dived to his side and fell crashing on the periphery.

Game, Match and Championship Kula.

Kool permitted himself to collapse on the floor, something he had promised himself at the end of each 'next' point. He was still sprawled on the floor, when it sank into him that he defeated Jiang.

He looked around and found that Jiang did not make any effort at getting up. Minutes later, amidst dead silence in the stadium, Kool managed to walk up to Jiang and gave him his hand of friendship and pulled him up. Jiang hugged him and a mutual respect evolved between them.

It sank in slowly, as he heard the commentators hailing the new world Order in TT with the arrival of India on the scene.

Kool looked around and could not find Joy. What happened to her? He was expecting her to run up to him and hug him. At least he wished. He wished so on every win. He also wished to hug her after every of her win. He wished he possessed the guts to kiss her on her lips. Will today be the day? He wished he wasn't such a good a guy after all.

On the opposite side of the stadium; where was Li'll'y?

Mahadevan hugged him warmly and congratulated him. He looked around to see Shastry in the special Gallery celebrating his victory and accepting congratulations from the President of China, who tried his best to smile though shook his head across as he shook hands. Same routine followed with the Chinese Premier, then a host of unknown Chinese faces.

He was taken to the podium. The Indian National Anthem was heard for the first time in the history of International TT Championships anywhere in the world other than South Asia, during the prize ceremony. Kool had tears in his eyes.

The runner up was Jiang. The bronze medallists were the Ding Xiang and Deng.

Kula felt on top of the world even as he climbed down the podium. The mandatory interviews were next. Kool praised Jiang and said 'It was like having to climb the Mt. Everest to wrest the title. We mortals may climb the summit for our chance at glory. But Jiang is Mt. Everest. I learned a lot of lessons playing Jiang. It was a question of who would hang there longer after an exhausting game, both of physique and mind'.

Kool continued, 'My God, I was cold blooded; on the last shot. I am glad that I won. I dedicate this win to India, my beloved country and my friends of mine in my country and in China', without naming Li'll'y.

Jiang was equally effusive about Kula's game and his win, 'Kula's game today epitomizes the human spirit. To Excel Beyond One's Reach. He compared me to Mt. Everest. Yes, every one human being that conquered the Mount have stood taller than the Mount. That is the time that Mt. Everests of the world learn to be humble, while the Kulas of the world continue to stand taller long after they climb down. That's the human spirit. I wish I had been more humble in the years before the match. I could have learnt more from Kula and his game'.

66 On the Run

Once Kool stepped off the podium and finished his interviews, Joy, who seemed to have emerged out of the shadows hurriedly ushered him out down a deserted flight of stairs that he wasn't familiar with. Though he wasn't sure of why she was dragging him away from the crowd, he wished that she wanted to hug him in private; probably kiss him too! After all she was shy like him. He was full of anticipation. But he thought of the customary appearance before the Press. He hadn't met and thanked the organizers, all his teammates and supporters for helping him. Joy whispered so many things on her way. He wasn't sure if he heard her right.

Joy pushed him into a car and Kool found Li'll'y at the driver's seat. As she pushed him into the car, Kool fell back on the seat and Joy fell over Kool. Joy held Kool's face in her palms of her hands for a whole minute and sobbed.

She next planted a kiss on his lips and muttered, 'I Love You Kool', barely audible. 'Sorry, I'm feeling so bad that I could only manage to tell you this when you are fleeing for life'.

Kool was dumbstruck at this. He felt it was the fastest expression of love, in fleeting circumstances. He was wondering to himself, 'Who was fleeing from whom and why'? He couldn't make out anything.

As if in answer, Joy said, 'Li'll'y would explain everything on the way. Good Bye'.

She bent to plant a couple of kisses this time, one on each of his cheeks and turned away wiping her tears. Kool didn't react, as he should have. He was shell shocked by all this.

Next Joy rushed to Li'll'y's side. She kissed her on her cheeks and with tears streaming from her eyes. 'Take care of Kool. You will, better than I would'. Then she said, 'You deserve Kool's love and affections more than I do', as the car drove off.

Li'll'y was the only witness to the expression of love that Joy had been plotting to convey in full view of the world. She was happy for Joy to have expressed her love, after all these years, to

Kool. And she was sad for herself. Kool, who still in a daze, was driven out of the stadium by Li'll'y.

Joy on hearing footsteps and angry voices running down the stairs, hid herself behind the staircase. One of the voices shouted angrily at the car that was speeding away. Joy peeped out from behind the stairs to see Deng in the company of a Police Officer, cursing people in the car that was vanishing beyond the gates. If Joy had doubts that she could have over-reacted to Li'll'y's story, she didn't have any, now. Deng continued to shout behind the car, in Chinese 'xxx Kula xxxx xxxx xxx Consulate xx xxxx xx'.
'Oh My God, Li'll'y didn't think of this', feared Joy.
She was startled, when she felt someone breathe close behind her, while she was still crouching under the stairs. She almost jumped out of her skin only to find a handsome young Chinese man, who asked her, 'Can I help you? Your friend seems to be in trouble! You seem to be distressed! I'm your fan and a friend too! Please trust me'!
Joy trusted him as much as she would trust a King Cobra. 'What if he was one of Deng's men, or a maniac… either way, would itt make a difference'? She fled back the stairs, two steps at a time, fearing her safety. She had to see Shastry immediately. Only he could help.
She would wonder later who this 'fan' could be and how quickly things changed for Kool and her in the last 120 minutes.
But can the readers wait to know?

The 'fan' was none other than the hacker friend of Cheng, who had earlier requested Cheng to introduce her to him so he could ask for a date. Cheng had absented himself from the finals match, though he promised ro introduce him to Joy. He had positioned himself close to Joy at the stadium and witnessed a fervent dumb charade act between Jay and another Chinese girl on the opposite side of the gallery and had seen them rush and vanish into the restroom for a long time, while her friend Kula played the match of his lifetime. Evidently, something was amiss and should have been an emergency. So the hacker friend followed her as much out of curiosity as to help her and possibly to introduce himself and ask for a date. Of course, Joy wouldn't have known any of this and that he later cursed himself, for having scared her beneath the stairs.

As to how things changed quickly for Joy, Kool and Li'll'y, it had all started with Li'll'y's whatsapp message to Kool. Li'll'y, seated on the other side of the gallery hoped that Joy would pick up the message, while Kool wouldn't as he was already into his match with Jiang. Yes! Joy did pick up Kool's mobile as Li'll'y watched her from the other side.

The message read, 'In danger. Could be arrested... Take shelter at the consulate in Shanghai... Don't take the cabs; all should have been instructed to hand over'.

Joy knew the message was from Li'll'y. She sighted her in the Chinese gallery on the opposite side, who also nodded and typed;

'I can drive him out, I think that would be best'.

Messaging so, she pointed in one direction and walked towards the women's restrooms. Joy followed.

Li'll'y as she left, told a couple of friends that she was leaving for the day, excitedly, 'I have a date with Han' and winked.

Her friends were engrossed in the Finals. They could understand that her date with Han would be more important to Li than the Finals, knowing that she had been single for too long and probably still a virgin.

Li'll'y looked around the restroom, satisfied they were alone, fired off quickly, 'Cheng has information that Dan and Deng have got a warrant against Kool. They are getting ready to arrest him immediately after the Men's singles prize ceremony. Cheng knew through Lee. He told me, but asked me not to interfere. 'Matters of national security'; he tried to warn me'.

Joy replied with hope, 'Shastry had got an assurance that no action would be taken on Kool till the end of the Games, that is still two full days away and that Shastry was working to ensure Kool would walk free. He said he is talking to the highest level of the Chinese Government'.

Li'll'y replied, without much hope, 'Yes, Cheng told me about your 'Sashtre' is in touch with our Lt. Gen. Ping, who is feared by all in China. No one dares cross his path. No one would defy him. But looks like the belligerent Deng and his coterie have decided to defy him. But please understand, smuggling National Secrets from China is the highest form of offence and cannot be compromised. Deng and his men are aware that even the President of China cannot step in to save some one accused so. The President is answerable to the Politburo and Cheng says that Deng's 'Godfather' may have powerful friends in the Politburo. Lt. Gen. Ping will be in a soup if he tried to do anything to save Kool'.

She continued, 'Deng is vengeful, vicious and venomous like a King Cobra. I had the taste of his venom. I'm lucky I am still alive today and to have played at the Games. In any case, assurances don't mean anything in China'.

'Cheng would not do anything to help Kool this time. Probably Lt. Gen. Ping wouldn't too… that is sheer bad luck. I don't know how to save Kool'. Li'll'y was in tears.

Joy realized she was in tears too. Their discussion was interrupted by some ladies entering the restrooms and the two girls pretended to wash their faces in the sink, while they washed off their tears. But the group hurried off quickly to watch the match.

Joy and Li'll'y realized that the Kool's Finals that they were looking so much forward to was not in their mind or priority now. Li'll'y knew by experience, what would happen to Kool. She was arrested on the similar charges, 'betraying the nation'. She trembled at the thought of Kool going through the same… and certainly worse!

'I will have to help Kool myself', she said with determination.

Joy hugged Li'll'y and sobbed. She knew that Li'll'y was the only one standing between Kool and death; and that she is inviting death to herself.

'Is Li'll'y doing this for mere friendship? No, 'Li'll'y loves Kool as much as I do. May be more'.

'What have I done for Kool myself, except encouraging him and keeping him company as we both rode the waves of success? Here is Li'll'y stepping in support of Kool and me for the second time. Can I attribute this to just a week of friendship that blossomed between us? And her genuine tears…

'It is more than that. Li'll'y really is in love with Kool', she convinced herself, with a shudder.

Li'll'y explained her plan. 'I'm sure that the cars of the Indian consular members at the stadium would be swarming with Police around it. It would be a trap, even before he gets into the car. It would not be advisable for Kool to take a taxi to the Indian

Consulate; he would be a sitting duck. The best case is for me to drive Kool to the consulate, where he will have protection, legally'.

Li'll'y knew that the Police Officers would be lying in wait in front of the Consulate, if she ventured anywhere near it, though she didn't mention it to Joy.

She needed a Plan 'B'; if she found unusual Police activity at the Gates of the Indian Consulate, she would rush Kool some place, where he could be hidden safely and lie in wait till probably, 'Sashtre' finds a solution for him or she gets Cheng to change his mind and help him.

'It would be life and death between here and safety, while I have no plan 'B' yet', she thought.

They didn't have time to discuss any more. A flood of women rushed into the restroom. The match was over and Kool had won, they knew from the sullen Chinese faces and their bitterness. They had to leave. They got behind the stairs just for a few minutes, 'Pluck Kool from the crowd and bring him down the same flight of stairs leading to the exit, where I will be ready in my car to take him away'.

When Joy reached the arena, the prize ceremony was on. For Joy, the Indian National anthem at the ceremony was the sweetest music she ever heard and remembered. 'Congratulations Kool', she shouted on top of her voice after the anthem was over and hoped he heard her. She had promised herself that she would hug and Kiss him, Kiss with a capital 'K', when he won Gold at the Games. 'But not now', she said to herself. She had discovered someone more deserving than her for Kool's love and affection.

She had to pluck Kool from the ceremony and had to hide her tears before that.

67 Venus de Milo

After sending Kula with Li'll'y, and a brush with Deng and another maniac calling himself her fan, Jay rushed up the stairs to meet Shastry, who was near the podium. All were searching for Kula. The Chinese Premier had arrived to congratulate the Medalists and the Gold medallist wasn't to be found.

The Organizers announced that Kula, the Gold Medallist, had to be rushed out due an emergency - a clear cover-up. This being China, everyone agreed, though no one believed. The Premier nodded as well. The break of Protocol wasn't missed by anyone.

It looked like ages before Joy would get to see Shastry. He was with the Premiere and Lt. Gen Ping, as part of the prize distribution and the ceremonies that followed. Mahadevan also was too busy waiting on the team and could not be reached. When she eventually explained to Mahadevan, it didn't help much, except that Joy had a companion wringing his hands and waiting for Shastry. Shastry was freed of his protocol and became accessible only when the Premier left. He heard Joy's story and asked several questions and got the details he needed. He was glad that Jay had answers for most of his questions.

He was glad that this girl Li, 'Had a clear sense and thought like a professional. It looked like Kula was in safe hands'. But he had to act fast. Even Li can't hold Kula for long.

Shastry called Lt. Gen Ping on his mobile, 'I'm part of the entourage of the President's drive to the airport. The President had asked me to join for discussion on some matters of importance during the drive. I will call back in 45 minutes'.

'We still have the dinner meeting on; at 7:30 PM', he reminded Shastry.

The Consulate officers flew to the Consulate, just in case Kula gets to reach there. Also, to explore if they could somehow get him reach a safe temporary hideout, if he can't reach the Consulate.

Then Shastry called to update the Indian PM and added, 'The break in protocol when the Premier was around was actually an advantage. The whole world was now wondering, whatever happened to Kula'!

Li'll'y did venture as far as the Indian Consulate, with the hope that she could beat Deng and his coterie one more time and land Kool in the safety of the Consulate. But the road to the Consulate was already cordoned off and a car to car search was on. She slipped into the road leading to the right, without arousing any suspicion and drove in circles still wondering what to do. She hoped that she was still out of the picture with Deng's coterie.

As she did not have a Plan 'B', her Plan 'C' was, 'Deliver Kool and herself to Cheng at his covert hideout in the suburbs. She will land Cheng a hot cake direct on his palms, without any warning and let him decide if he will take the heat or drop the cake.

But before the long drive to Cheng's hideout, she had to pick up a few essentials from her apartment. The most important being, her id cards, showing her new identity as 'Daiyu' that Cheng had prepared for her long ago. She also had to pick up another mobile, not traceable to her, again courtesy, Cheng.

As they approached her home she showed an exceptionally beautiful mansion to Kool, 'Here lives Deng's most current mistress, who happens to be the reigning Miss China'! Looks like they are contemplating marriage.

Kula wasn't concerned about Deng and his mistress, but the grandiose mansion refused to fade from his mind.

Li'll'y found no police activity at the gates of her apartment. Yet she decided to take the fire escape. She entered her apartment in the dark. She drew the curtains before switching on the softest lights. As she was looking to pick up her things, she heard a knock.

She peeped though the sight glass on the door, 'Police'! She signed with her fingers on her lips and asked him to hide in the bathroom.

The police knocked heavily this time. She was about to walk to the door, changed her mind and walked into the bathroom instead with Kool still inside and closed the door. She asked him to hide behind the door and signed him to close his eyes, as she stripped herself to her lingerie.

When she heard the main door burst open she whispered, 'Sorry', stripped herself bare, off the 'lingering pieces twoo' and turned on the shower. Kool, mouth open, gaped at her nude figure between his fingers that were meant to be closing his eyes. He was watching a girl in the nude for the first time in his life and it happened to be the most beautiful girl he had ever seen and she was within his touching distance.

She shouted out as if to someone who had walked in. 'Hi Han, just a few minutes. I'm in the shower. I am sure you would love to join. But not today. Please wait till I step out. I'm sorry, I am late, Han'.

As an afterthought, she asked, 'Why did you have to bang the door open as you came in Han? Don't be in a hurry. I am here all for you. But you have to grow up too'; she chuckled loud enough to be heard outside the door.

Kool thought with wonder, 'She has one more talent that I didn't know; acting', still peering between his fingers at the delightful sight of a lily flower drenched in a drizzle of rain.

The Female Officer who stepped in with her subordinate, pointed a gun at the bathroom door that was closed and the subordinate officer followed her with her gun.

She ordered her subordinate to record a video. 'You don't have your mobile? Then use this', handing over Li'll'y's mobile lying on the bed nearby. The sub-Officer pressed the recording button and placed the camera at a vantage point on the bed, focused on the bathroom door, before she picked up a gun to provide cover her senior.

Then a thundering voice ordered, 'Open the door or I will have to break it open'. Kool crouched well behind the door. Li'll'y answered in Chinese, 'Who's it. I'm in the shower. You are not Han. Or is it you, up to your pranks'? Just a minute; I will cover myself'.

The bathroom door burst opened, even before Li'll'y could reach for her towel. She stood there stark naked dripping wet under the shower flowing all over her. She was frightened to see two a Female Officer pointing their guns. Li'll'y froze, before she moved to pick up her clothes.

She froze again, when she heard another thunder, 'Don't move' and a click as the safety catch was released'.

Li'll'y was prepared to show herself nude just for a second or so, to have an impact, if her act could save Kool. But the actual act of indignity brought tears in her eyes due to shame, embarrassment and fear. The officer did not fail to differentiate her tears flowing on her cheeks along with the shower water and softened a bit, but not enough.

Li'll'y sobbed, 'I thought it was Han', still frozen, too frightened, ashamed and humiliated.

She saw the seriousness of the moment that she didn't anticipate, was afraid; any slight movement and she would get shot, probably Kool too.

'Who's Han'? demanded the Lady Police Officer. 'My boyfriend… We have a date'.

The Officer wasn't ready to believe her and ordered her not to make any move. 'She could reach for her gun instead of her clothes', suspected the Officer.

She half stepped into the bathroom cautiously, the shower still running and Li'll'y still frozen, naked, just inches away. She peered across the door that was flung wide open to check the ventilator. From this position, her line of view covered the space just inches from crouching Kool. Did she realize the vague shadow on the wall to be Kool's?

Kool, who could hear the breath of the Police officer, within two inches of him and getting closer, hunkered backward to keep her out of his sight and held his own breath. He realized how much the lady had ventured close to him, just looking at Li'll'y's bare bosoms that were heaving to the pounding of her frightened heart.

Li'll'y had to do something as the Police Officer's eyes were still sweeping over Kool's shadows and towards him behind the door. She deliberately moved one step behind. The movement was enough to distract the Female Officer, whose eyes and gun swept back sharply to point at her, as she barked, 'Don't move'.

Kool feared Li'll'y could be shot and prepared himself to fling on her to take the bullet on himself and watched the trigger finger carefully. Li'll'y, who was terrified as well by the Officer's mean and angry outburst, froze in time and thanked their stars that neither the Officer pressed the trigger nor did Kool instinctively hurl himself on her protectively.

Having already satisfied herself that the ventilator fan was intact and running and none could have escaped through it, the Officer stepped back, out, her eyes still gleaming at Li'll'y and the gun pointed at her. She ordered the other officer to shoot, if she moved. She went to inspect the rest of the apartment for signs of the accused. Finding nothing suspicious, the Officer snarled a 'Sorry', and Li'll'y heard them troop out of the house.

Li'll'y ran out naked, still dripping, to close the main door behind them. Finding the door lock broken, she pushed a heavy sofa to restrain it from opening unless with a force, she ran back under the shower unsure if she should expect the uninvited guests again. After a few minutes of trembling, she was satisfied that the Officers had left for good and smiled out of relief at Kool.

The naughty twinkle in her eye returned she, still nude and wet and under the shower, held her arms invitingly wide open to Kool, 'I have nothing more to show my love for you Kool – and nothing less to hide! I'm all yours'!

Kool, still hunkering behind the door and watching her between his fingers, was pretending to close his eyes that were 'wide shut.'

He had seen the statue of the Aphrodite, Venus de Milo, during his last visit to the Louvre museum in Paris. Here stood Li'll'y etched in marble and wet from a drizzle of water, more beautiful than the Greek Goddess of Love and beauty.

Kool replied, gone giddy with her beauty, 'What else can a hu-Man do'? stepping into the shower with Li'll'y, who smelt fresh like the fragrance she epitomized. The door closed behind them.

Ten minutes later, Li'll'y was leading him down the fire escape. She had picked up her mobile that was recording the bathroom scene meticulously from its perch on the bed. Thank goodness, the Officers left the mobile behind. Else her video would have been visual feast for the vultures at the Police Office and she would have been subject to extreme humiliation.

She stopped on the stairs as Kula asked her, 'While you have a different identity, would it not be good to have a different car. Is it feasible'?

She ran inside back and picked up the keys of her friend's Motorbike that he keeps parked in her lot, for want of space in his apartment parking; He had two big cars and three motorbikes. She had ridden this beast before. So she could use this for today. Her friend would never realize that she was using it even if she did not return it for months together. He seldom used it.

They rode out of the apartment on the Motorbike, complete with helmets, jackets and gloves; he in ill-fitting ones. They felt safer. Her car would have been a target. Not the motorbike.

68 'Toxic'ated

Unknown to her, Deng's coterie was active at the Police Control Room, trying to trace whoever was helping Kula.

The first report was negative. The lady Officer reported from near about Li's apartment. 'Only a girl called Li, no sign of the accused'.

'There was nothing pointing at Li, yet. But I will get at her too', Deng sounded mean.

Deng demanded to know, 'How could Kula have known about his impending arrest after the Prize Ceremony? 'There's someone helping him from inside'.

They didn't suspect any one from the Police as a source. He continued, 'Lee was the only one who knew Kula and had sympathies, but would not go that far as to alert him. In any case, Lee wasn't involved in this arrest warrant. But Lee or whoever, would not contact Kula directly, would he? So there was someone, an insider leaking information and probably another, who picked up and passed on to Kula. Who were they'?

Deng questioned, 'Moreover, the arrest warrant on Kula was issued that evening hardly an hour before the Finals match, maybe two hours or so before the Prize Ceremony. How could someone pass on this information to Kula, while he was still into the Match, so fast? Did the Indians have a dedicated network that worked better and faster than the Chinese Police'? The officers with him didn't have a clue.

A check on Kula's phone's call history during the period revealed no calls on his phone during the period. There were a number of whatsapp chat messages exchanged between another Mobile and Kula's Mobile. 'Could this be'?

There was no time to get the hacking team to get at the actual messages. It would neither be feasible nor required for today.

They just succeeded in getting a clue. Assuming this as the point of alert, they tried to trace the number of the source of the messages and its locations, if only it was from within China!

****

Report 1: The number registered in the name of a girl Hiu, then a university student two years ago.

Location at the time of messages: Could be inside or just outside the Games stadium as the free Wi-Fi at the stadium was used. .

Current location: Attached a map with a star indicating the current location.

****

One of the officers pointed out that the current location was near about the place where the Lady officer assigned to check on Li Ling had reported from.

'So Li is the culprit and she is using a mobile with a fake identity', concluded Deng. This was a double delight for Deng.

He commanded, 'Arrest the bi**h too'. He 'laughed out loud', 'How both Kula and Li, as a habit, fell into the trap set up for the other, trying to protect one another. Call this love? Call this bi**hing'?

The lady Police Officer rushed back to Li's apartment and as she neared, a motorbike without lights was leaving the building. She could not note the number as it was too far and dark. She knocked, waited and broke open into the apartment second time that evening. A heavy sofa was set up restraining the broken door.

No sign of Li or that of Han. May be Li left with Han, who should have come in after they had left. She looked for the mobile on which the video was kept recording that her assistant had forgotten to take along with her. It was gone.

Within a few minutes she reported to the control room, 'No sign of the accused. May be, Li left on the motorbike that I saw leave, when I was nearing the apartment. Or she might have left with her boyfriend Han earlier, who she said, she was dating. I'm trying to find the janitor of the building to check the CCTV camera to get the motorbike number. I will pass on as soon as I have the information'.

Deng got excited. This chase gave him thrills. That Li was also

300

his 'game' with Kula, supercharged him and in a few minutes was rushing on his Ferrari towards Li's apartment, where the Lady Officer had told him that she had held Li frozen, nude for a full ten minutes under the shower, without any cover.

He was aroused at the thought of her and was obsessed at seeing the bathroom then, even if Li wouldn't be inside, nude. While in front of the bathroom, he visualized her and promised himself that soon Li would re-enact the nude act for him. Soon his mood depressed from 'in'toxic'ated' to 'toxic'ated as he was possessed by a maniacal animal urge to subjugate her in a beastly manner to whet his lust and in revenge.

Li'll'y drove up exactly on the opposite direction of Cheng's hideout home, where she would discard her old mobile before leaving in the forward direction losing herself to her 'followers'. She stopped after thirty minutes for dinner. She was famished. So was Kool. While they were waiting for their order to be served, Li'll'y spoke nothing, but watched the video that was recorded by the lady Police officers at her apartment.

Kool asked, 'What's the video about'?

Li'll'y suddenly shy, showed him with a twinkle, 'Nothing that you didn't watch in person'.

Kool lowered his eyes. He let her watch the whole sequence. May be she will derive some ideas from it.

Her shame, fear and embarrassment turned into anger, on Deng.

'First let me save Kool. Then I will plot a revenge on you Mr Deng', she vowed, unaware that now she was also a fugitive in the eyes of law, along with Kool.

She never had been photographed in the nude, not even a selfie that was so popular among her friends who were proud to circulate them among their friends, boyfriends included. She had never even been seen by any girl or boy in the nude. Though it was common among her friends to have group showers with other girls, sometimes boyfriends included, she could never be seen in such company. She was so angry and ashamed that she wanted to delete the file.

When Li'll'y was just about to hit 'delete', she smiled and with her eyes twinkling, she passed the video on to Joy with a winking 'smilie', by eMail under delayed transmission; she scheduled to be delivered to Joy after her Finals match against Wen Qiang.

69 Joy's Cuppa

Joy received an email when her worry about Kool and Li'll'y were at its peak, 'Was he able to reach the consulate? Or a safe hiding place that Li promised to find for him'? The email came with no text but just a video attachment and a 'winkie' as subject.

The video started with a Police Officer kicking a bathroom door, gun in hand and another covering her, gun in hand too, both their backs to the camera. As the door burst open, she saw Li'll'y freeze under the shower naked from head to toe. She heard Li'll'y begging to pick up her clothes and she genuinely sobbed and said something about Han and date. Was she making up a story to distract the Police Officers and away from Kool, with an alibi? But where was Kool?

Was he hiding somewhere inside her home or had she found a safe home already for him. But she was sure that the Officers were searching for Kool then. So Kool was safe, until this time at least.

'Did they catch up with him'?

Then, the lady officer stepped into the bathroom and searched inside. How mean of her? Would Kool be hiding inside the bathroom, while Li'll'y was taking her shower? At one point, she saw the Officer swing her gun sharply and almost shot Li'll'y. In any case, when the Officer stepped out of the bathroom, satisfied that Kool wasn't in, Joy also breathed a sigh of relief.

'How mean and paranoid'!

Then the Officer stepped out of view ordering her subordinate to shoot, if Li'll'y moved. 'How heartless. How cruel'.

Then they both left from the view. Li'll'y rushed out of the bathroom, out of the camera's view only to step back into the shower again. Joy was shocked as her friend was seen in the nude by the Police Officers, even if they were ladies, for the sake of Kool and more shocked that her life was under threat. One false move and she could have been shot. She wished she was near her so that she could have saved her chastity by rushing towards her and covering her with some clothing, even at the risk of herself being shot.

Just then the unbelievable, most shocking event happened and she felt giddy as though lightning struck her.

Li'll'y opened her arms and said addressing someone, 'I'm all yours, Kool'...

Joy felt faint, but continued to watch.

And Kool stepped in from behind the bathroom door and hugged her naked body, saying 'What else can a hu-Man do'? Then the doors closed behind them.

She couldn't believe herself. So Kool was behind the door watching her shower all the while. She wished that the earth parted below her feet and consumed her that instant. This betrayal was more than anything that Deng or the Indian Managers perpetrated on her. She hated Li'll'y. What an opportunist? She hated Kool. She never ever wanted to see them again. She threw her phone in disgust and flung herself on to her bed, burying her face on the pillow and sobbed.

It was the same evening that she had kissed Kool on his lips to say, 'I Love You'. How could Kool do this to her?

She sobbed again. She didn't want to continue living. But she didn't know how to die. Then she remembered that she had neither spoken of her love to Kool until this day.

'Was it too late and too little'?

'Were Kool and Li'll'y already in love'? Joy remembered that Kool stayed in China for over a month and Li'll'y had given him company.

By the time Li'll'y finished her dinner, Joy had replied to her email.

The message was terse. 'Thanks for the video message'.

Li'll'y was surprised, rather taken aback. 'How come'? Did the message scheduling not work and was the email delivered instantly? Joy should be in a rude shock and all tears before her Finals. What a cruel joke on her'.

Li'll'y cursed herself for not waiting. Her prank has gone all wrong the second time.

Li'll'y checked for Joy's number with Kool and 'ping'ed her on whatsapp immediately. Joy who had composed herself just minutes ago, had her submerged love for Kool flowing and the feeling of betrayal overwhelming her; her tears and sobs returned. She felt betrayed, though she couldn't decide, who betrayed her more.

Her terse message to Li'll'y, 'What'? showed her bitterness and grief for a lost cause; but not at all accusing Li'll'y, who could virtually hear Joy's sobs on her messages.

Li'll'y asked in confidence, 'Did you see my video? with a naughty winkie, supposed to assure her, 'Not meant to hurt her' and to raise Joy's spirits.

Joy answered with a resignation, 'Thanks Li'll'y for saving my Kool, I mean our Kool, I mean your Kool', she said undecided and incoherent. 'And congratulations! Kool is all yours now. I am happy for you for the incident that you just sent me a video of. I hope you meant it as a parting gift. But, you should know that you just killed my spirit'.

Li'll'y felt as though Joy screamed at her and felt pangs of guilt and shame.

Li'll'y, listless, explained, 'I am sorry, what happened. It was an accident, not an incident. I wanted you to understand. If I hadn't shared whatever happened, I would have been guilty as hell. So would have Kool. Of course, the timing was dead wrong. I should have explained to you in person, rather than sending you the video and just before your Finals match tomorrow. I had actually sent a time delayed email, It's evident it landed ahead of schedule'.

'Yes, I understand it was an accident. I saw the whole act before the Police Officer. You were so brave. That's why you are the right one for Kool, while, I am not'.

She continued, 'I am not angry with you Li'll'y. I know you had done the right thing. I don't fault Kool either.

'What could a Man do', she continued sarcastically, 'when such a beautiful girl presents herself dressed in just a running film of water under the shower. I was charmed by your beauty myself. Why would not Kool? Congratulations and how was your experience'? with a wry smile on her face and a smilie emoticon on her message, just to make it easy for Li'll'y.

Li'll'y could feel the tears streaming on Joy's cheeks.

'My dear little fool, are you imagining something happened after the door closed'? chided Li'll'y.

'No, I am not so cheap to imagine the acts of boys and girls behind closed doors, under such circumstances', Joy replied.

Li'll'y asked, 'Do you trust me'?

Joy replied, 'It's not about trust. I trust you. If you had done something like that to seduce Kool, then it would be a breach of trust', remembering though, that it was Li'll'y, who opened her arms and invited him. She continued, 'I believe that you asked Kool just to tease him. But Kool is a Man. He could have closed the doors without your invitation, in such situations. It isn't even important, who invited whom, any longer. No Li'll'y, I am not angry'.

'Just that I am a bit jealous. That's all. I am jealous that in all my several years of friendship and companionship with Kool, we never had such an intimate opportunity present itself to us. Not that I would have used such an opportunity. You can trust me here. Not that Kool would have used one. I trust him too. My parents trust us both too. Hope I have the right to be jealous, at the very least'!

Li'll'y, desperate, asked her, 'Do you trust Kool'?

Joy said 'Hmm… yes, of course'.

That was enough of an opening for Li'll'y. 'Then you should trust him, when I say that he did nothing to me under the shower. Not even a kiss on my cheeks'.

Joy was perplexed and sent an '!!!!!!!'.

'Do you want to know what happened inside'? asked Li'll'y.

Joy now was getting back her colour, 'Yes', she urged.

'I thought you didn't want to know, not even imagine, the acts of boys and girls behind closed doors! That would make you cheap, wouldn't it'? It was Li'll'y's chance to assume an air.

'☺, it's alright to know, nothing happened', - Joy.

'Do you trust me, that nothing happened', - Li'll'y

'Don't tease me, don't build the suspense. My head will explode. Go ahead, tell me all', - Joy.

'Let me explain, if you trust me', - Li'll'y still fought for her trust.

Joy, impatiently, 'Yes. I trust you… Please go ahead. I don't care even if something mischievous happened. After all it's you, my dear and I wished you well already with Kool. Just tell me the truth, the whole truth and nothing but the truth'.

Li'll'y explained, ''Kool stepped under the shower, saying, 'What else can a hu-Man do'. Then he gently hugged me by my waist and pulled me closer, electrifying both of us. He brought his lips close to mine'.

'Then as if he remembered something, he paused and closed his eyes'. Li'll'y paused her conversation with Joy to watch Kool, who was deep in guilt and in thought.

Joy could not bear the anxiety, 'Please tell me all. I beg you'.

Li'll'y continued, 'Closing his eyes Kool said, 'I promised Joy a long time back that I will remember her, when I see you. For which, I asked impatiently as hell, 'Yes, you did; before your last trip to China? What of it now''?

'Kool replied, 'I remember Joy, as I see you now. I remember her first kiss, though, just a brush of her lips on mine, just an hour ago. She even managed to tell me, 'I love you', after all these years. I love her too. I can't do this. My heart is with Joy and she trusts me. I will never betray her, now nor ever'.

'She loves you too more than as a friend; as a sister. She trusts you too, especially with me. You should not be betraying her'.'

'I just agreed, with tears rolling down my cheeks. I had been selfish, just minutes earlier. I opened my arms to him as a joke, as a prank, to tease him this time, as you rightly believed. But I was carried away when Kool acceded and stepped into the shower holding me for just a moment. I had been selfish and impatient for his touch and more. Then he proved to be a REAL MAN, not just another hu-Man; not the selfish hu-Men you see all around. He kept his promise to you, though unspoken to this day. Just like my dear father kept his promise to my mother'.

'Kool did lose a real opportunity here. He did not take me, though I offered myself to him, unconditionally, without any commitments. I offered myself to him, the only man I was waiting for all these years. Just this once would have been enough for me, for all my life. I will forever remember his touch as he pulled me close to him, hugging my naked body. I was not fortunate for anything more than his touch'.

'I hope you will permit me this memory forever. Don't plead with me to take this feel of him away from me. I would lose more than I ever did and ever would. That's beside the point. What matters is that Kool proved he was more than hu-Man. He gave me lessons on Love and Trust, under that shower that I will never forget, ever. I hope I will never ever again betray my sister's trust'.

There was dead silence from Joy. 'I trust you Li'll'y, she messaged at last. 'I'm sorry, really'.

Joy realized that Li'll'y had been in love with Kool from the beginning, though she wouldn't admit. She herself had known this fact all along, while she wished and pretended to believe otherwise.

'Why doesn't she take Kool away with her, when I consented once? Why does she return him back to me and betray herself'?

Joy realized that her love for Kool paled in comparison with Li'll'y's great sacrifice that had just unfolded to her.

Just a few minutes earlier, I thought I wanted to die because of Li'll'y and Kool. Now I pray God the Great, 'Please let me die so that my Li'll'y can have her Kool. She was once again ready to sacrifice Kool for Li'll'y, and 'If I couldn't die, I would remain a virgin all my life. May be I will take up social work or become a saint'!

Li'll'y continued in Defense amid Joy's protests that she heard enough and was convinced, 'Please check the video further. We opened the door and stepped out within two minutes and I was fully dressed'.

'Yes…' realized Joy. 'the two were behind closed doors, for two full minutes'.

Then she wondered to herself 'How long would a boy and a girl take to do funny acts behind closed doors'?

She did not know. It had never occurred to her before and she didn't want to know, yet. She will cross the bridge, when Kool and she would eventually do such acts behind closed doors. She blushed and smiled to herself, shaking her head shyly.

Li'll'y replied herself, without waiting for Joy to repeat the question, 'He turned off the shower. His dress was wet, so he removed his shirt quickly and squeezed the water out. Poor thing, he wouldn't remove his pants in my presence and chose to wear the same dripping wet pants in the near freezing autumn cold and is riding with me on a motorbike and in an ill-fitting jacket, exposing him to the elements'.

'He is still shivering and he wouldn't even hug me tight for warmth, as I drove; the natural thing to do while on Motorbike. I think he is thinking of you and still in a in a state of guilt'.

'I hope not that I save Kool from Deng and gang only for him to die of pneumonia'.

'I trust you Li'll'y, but please don't say any such harsh word about Kool', she said, now her joy flowing back into her as tears.

'I sent this video file to you just in jest; just to tease you and make you jealous. I wanted to take my own sweet time to explain to you later, if I happen to live'.

Li'll'y continued, 'But I never expected you to sob like a jilted teenager and grieve like a loser. Don't worry. Kool's all yours. If something had happened between us, I would have been guilty as hell. So would have been Kool. Would either of us have had the nerve to share the video with you'?

'Thank you Li'll'y. Thank Kool on my behalf', But I have something to say, 'There are two damn fools in this world that I know. One is Kool, of course'.

'The other one is you'? asked Li'll'y.

'No, maybe I'm the third, way behind you. But you are the No. 2'.

'???' Li'll'y messaged.

Joy explained, 'What an opportunity? What a fool to miss it? And for whose sake? A sister? Let me tell you, If I had a chance like that, I would have wrapped myself around Kool and never let him go till he… till he… touched me... touched me...', searching for words, 'touched me… deep'!!!

Satisfied with her vocabulary, she winked with a 'winkie'.

Smile and shine returned to her face for the first time that evening and Li'll'y sensed it and was glad for her.

'Got the point! What a fool had I been! I'm planning to take him back into the shower. He's still with me, right'? replied Li'll'y, again with a 'winkie'.

'Oh My god! No! was just kidding. I now know I can't trust a sister. I am better off trusting Kool', pleaded Joy.

'Don't trust him too much. He's just opposite me. He looks like he too is regretting the opportunity lost. After all he is hu-Man too. You were lucky once, just about. Don't push your luck too far'.

Joy surrendered in mock shock, 'Oh yes! I learn that I can trust a man just once; a sister, not more than just once too, if at all. Please give Kool back to me in full, my 'Silly Li'll'y'. I love him; you know. Now, I know he loves me too! You know that too'!

They laughed together, 'LOL'. Kool was restored back to Joy, with love from Li'll'y. Li'll'y had tears in her eyes, but didn't show.

Li'll'y wished Joy, 'Go for your Gold'! Do get some sleep tonight and be ready for tomorrow's match', she said with genuine concern.

Just then, Cheng called. He was angry. 'What are you doing? I asked you to lay off the Indian boy. You should not have made contact with either the Indian boy or girl using this mobile. You have exposed your Mobile and positions to the Police. They are tracking and chasing you now'.

She wanted to say, 'Yes, I knew the risks. But I had to have this conversation, having triggered Joy's tears'!

But... all that Li'll'y could do was to say 'Sorry'.

Cheng was annoyed, 'Your sorry doesn't help. Actually our entire network phones have to be changed now. It's not difficult though. It happens sometimes. But you will go to sure jail for helping someone who stole 'Chinese National Secrets'. You know what it means. I can't save you this time. It's a lost cause'.

She picked up courage to tell Cheng, with determination, 'I am willing to go either to safety or to the gallows, with Kool. We are inseparable'.

After a pause, he asked, 'Where are you planning to go next?

She explained, 'To your hideout in the suburbs. I don't know where else to go to. Please help us'.

After a minute's pause that seemed like eternity, he said, 'Let's plan on next. Destroy this sim card. Destroy the phone too. You could be tracked by the IMEI number too. Use the other phone. Don't call anyone yet. I will call you first after the entire network is synchronized with new numbers'.

He called her again on the newly synchronized numbers. 'Where are you'?

She explained.

'I will reach there in an hour or so. Wait there, if you reach earlier. Check all the way if you are being followed. I don't assure any help. But let me try. In any case, how are you travelling? Don't use your car'. Li'll'y explained, 'I'm on my friend's bike. I should reach your place in around two hours'.

Cheng commanded, 'Run, before it's too late'.

A few minutes later, the Lady Officer landed at the hotel they had just left.

'Damn', exclaimed the Officer, finding the accused had fled just a few minutes earlier, from the CCTV recording. She got the motorbike number that tallied with the number she got from the janitor of Li's apartment and informed the Control Room.

The number was religiously transmitted across all Police stations and road blocks were set up around Shanghai and suburbs to catch the 'criminals'. She updated the control room and rushed behind the fugitives. Deng kept constant touch with her and followed her.

Li'll'y believed that they had shaken off the Deng's gang for good and relaxed her speed. An hour later the lady Police Officer was closing in on the motorbike.

Part 8: Matters of State

70 A Nation in Denial

Shastry was enjoying his dinner with Lt. Gen. Ping and his friends. Lt. Gen. Ping was a great host. After some introductions and some gānbēi… in honour of those assembled, Lt. Gen. Ping excused himself and took Shastry to a private lounge, both carrying their drinks.

Lt. Gen. Ping asked, 'What makes this urgent call'? Evidently, he wasn't as sober as Shastry would have liked him to be. May be he had a few drinks with friends before he had reached their table.

Shastry had to explain the issue again. "There was an agreement between us that no action would be taken on our Champion boy before the end of the Games and that would be 48 hours from now. We were supposed to discuss the issue between us and resolve before then".

'So, that was the agreement. What is the urgency now'? Lt. Gen Ping asked, ignorant of the arrest warrant.

Shastry was partly relieved that the warrant did not come either on the orders of or with the knowledge of Lt. Gen Ping.

'Lt. Gen Ping could still be on my side', thought Shastry.

To Lt. Gen Ping, he asked, 'Then why this arrest warrant to be effected immediately after the Prize Ceremony?' demanded Shastry.

Lt. Gen Ping sat up, 'What? Arrest!? Who? When'?

'Not yet. At least we don't know. We have credible information of the arrest warrant and the boy had to be rushed to safety with the help of some good friends. We could not take him to the safety of our consulate as it was cordoned off in search for Kula', said Shastry sternly.

'Lt. Gen Ping laughed, "Credible information'!!?? I didn't expect the Senior Emissary of the PM of India to rush to conclusions, based on rumours. When I give my word China sticks to it', he boasted and continued, 'I thought Kula's win over Jiang would give hallucinations to the Chinese, but not to our Indian friends. Go out, forgetting the rumours and celebrate! Enjoy! You may not have this chance again at the next Games. By the way,

Kula's game was extraordinary. He has become my personal Hero. I will not let him down'!

Shastry noted sternly again, 'You have given the second word without verifying the facts and status of the first. Please check and let me know. If there's no arrest warrant, let's go out and celebrate our Hero of today together. If there's a warrant, please get it annulled and let's have a late night party. But for now, please check before it's too late'.

Lt. Gen Ping made a few calls. His face changed to 'concerned'.

He did not see Shastry in his eyes as he always does when he spoke, 'There's some mistake! The issue is that the boy is now being dealt under the National Security laws and not civil laws and the Officers follow and refer to different protocols and different masters. Hence the warrant was not visible to me. Moreover, as you know I had moved in the last two months on to something more critical than the Games, from a Government point of view and lost touch with the issue. I understand now that the adversaries have been persisting after the boy'.

He then went into deep thought. 'I am worried that the earliest I can get this mess evaluated is tomorrow. I'm still not getting at who is handling this. There are so many Security Agencies and several teams within each of them. Each one works independently and in confidence of the others. I need to understand what evidence they are working on. If they have fair evidence, I'm afraid; I won't be able to help. National Security is prime in China and it can never be compromised and investigators can never be over ruled. But give me a day. I will have this clarified by tomorrow. My word is a word'.

Shastry realised that this wasn't time for politeness or for being laconic.

He went on the offensive, 'I am wondering if your words are getting to be just that; just 'a word', without any substance. I have heard that it's common in China to give a word, without thinking first. So much for the word and so much for the, 'I will not let my Hero down' rhetoric. Ok. Let me tell you. This is a witch hunt against my boy. I showed you clearly in my videos last month how our 'Champion Girl, Jay' had been harassed and hounded out, for challenging the Chinese might during the last Games. You know pretty well that they had succeeded in stopping Kula from entering the ring to meet your Jiang on false charges and packed both them on a Flight back to India. Last Games, the Indian players had been alone and without any support from us. They had been left without protection, to the mercy of the unruly mob manning your Federation and the Team'.

'This year we are seeing history repeat itself. Had your Government cleansed the stables before the current Games, the coterie would not have resorted to re-establish the supremacy of the Chinese team through dubious and ridiculous means. Instead you had rewarded the conceited men and they have grown large enough to challenge the final authority. Now you seem to be cringing and crouching behind them'.

'When the International Press was assembled yesterday, your Police Officer had stepped into our quarters to arrest the Champion. The press was agog with stories; most of them half true. Sometimes half-truths could be more incisive and damaging than truths'.

'One word of truth shared yesterday with those eager to hear along with substantial evidence in our possession would have consigned the Games and its glory to the dustbin of time. We, the victims, saved the blushes for China, with a cover up, on your behalf, to save the prestige and reputation of the Games and hence the Chinese Pride. We believed that Kula would win Gold at the Games. So we took the option to fight and win the Finals. Also we think ourselves as partners in progress with China and we wanted our TT potential to grow at the Games and with the Games. We could have brought the Games down with just a whisper. But we didn't. Anywhere in the world, it would have been called sportsmanship and the hosts would have responded with gratitude'.

'Today, a Chinese Official mob is paying back by the only way it knows – Vendetta. Those who could not fight and win the game at the Stadium are pushing for Kula's death sentence, misusing the privileges handed down to them by your Political structure'.

'I have waited for two hours since the new Champion is on the run from such desperate, insecure, vengeful renegades of civil society. I waited for these two hours, risking my child's arrest, as I saw a man of action in you and that you would keep your word. I want him saved before he is arrested. India will not permit its honourable citizen to enter Chinese detention even for a minute… And be prepared! This issue will resonate in the international corridors either in less than hundred minutes from now or on the arrest of our Champion, whichever occurs earlier'.

Lt. Gen Ping was taken aback by the polite use of forceful language.

He chose to be offensive. 'There are charges of stealing of National Secrets and the boy has admitted to the same'!

Shastry retorted, now angrily, 'Let me answer one question at a time. National Secrets: forgive me for being impolite and for lack of decorum and magnanimity after an Indian win. You saw your 'National Secret' bite dust'.

'Kula has been hailed by the experts and media for playing and winning not by learning from your 'National Secret' aka, the Chinese style. So what did your National Secret do to your own likes of Deng and Jiang? Kula personifies a new style, the natural style and that's the new International Secret'!

'Next, stealing: Who stole? It could have been at best planted into Kula's baggage, by anyone who wanted to fix him. Haven't you heard such stories'?

Lt. Gen Ping intervened, 'Your boy has signed a statement'.

'No! The boy has clearly denied the accusation, in spite of your most brutal assault in custody to have a statement extracted from him, he has held his nerve and the truth. He never signed a statement. If there's one, it is clearly a concoction of your devious officers', Shastry fired back.

'You could see his bruises prominently during the Finals and so could the Press! So, have your Officers fabricated a statement too? Disgusting'!

'I think you are in a denial mode now; much different from your yesterday's mood. I'm afraid you are the only person I have ever met in the Chinese establishment that is sensible and fair. But if you chose to beat retreat at the slightest resistance from Deng and his coterie, I am afraid again that we both would be working at cross purposes. We are a sovereign nation and our citizens are free. We don't crouch before your mob.'

'Please note that the world outside China has a reasonably fair legal system and the Press is free. You will find there are limits to our magnanimity and that the International Press is less merciful. The opinion of the world outside China counts, if you care. If China chooses to position itself along with the authoritarian regimes like North Korea, where the inner Coterie rules, rather intimidates, you would have stepped back by ages, well into the stupor of the Middle Kingdom'.

'It is time you step into modern times, contemporary times. I hoped that fair and prudent citizens with powers like you do would lead China out of this insensitivity'.

Lt. Gen Ping was at a loss for words. So he remained silent. He was thinking.

Shastry continued, 'The hundred minute count down has started six minutes ago. You could choose to continue to be in self-denial and face the inferno the international press is going to start tomorrow, aided by nothing more than a small spark from me. Believe me, it would not be the glorious fireworks you have planned around the stadium during the Closing Ceremony. It could be a fire that could burn the Games down and the Closing ceremony would be like a fitting funeral'.

71 Diplomacy

Lt. Gen Ping had underestimated the determination of the 'rogue' Deng and his coterie and was surprised at the Godfather's keen interest taken against Kool. He believed it was Deng's story, at least in the beginning. And it was becoming clear that the 'Godfather' has adopted the story and was authoring a dreadful sequel. He realized the Godfather's real motives and the events around the Indian boy fitted in line with his larger conspiracy. A pattern was visible as he connected the dots and soon a clear picture would emerge. He would fix them later. He knew how. For now, he wanted Kula out of their crosshairs.

He called a few numbers and spoke hastily in Chinese.

Shastry looked relaxed and was casually flirting with his mobile phone seemingly uninterested in Lt. Gen Ping's telephone conversation, wholly in Chinese. He scribbled three Chinese names on a sheet of paper and kept it ready.

Lt. Gen Ping dragged after a couple of calls, 'We need strong reasons to effect the release of Kula. China, contrary to what the world believes, isn't an authoritarian regime. Even our President is accountable to the Politburo. We have an effective opposition from within and the voices could embarrass the Government of the day, especially if it is to do with 'National Security''.

Shastry put it straight, 'Are you looking for 'face' saving'?

Lt. Gen Ping looked at him silently not responding to the crude verbiage.

Shastry continued, 'Would 'three faces' be enough'?

Lt. Gen Ping looked annoyed, 'What's it'?

Shastry passed on the sheet with three Chinese names that he kept ready as he casually mentioned, 'Between yesterday and today, the Indian Government has picked up three Chinese nationals who were engaged in espionage on behalf of the Chinese Government, one near the Cochin Shipyard building our own indigenous Aircraft

Carrier, and another near our Kalpakkam Nuclear Power Station and another near the Monastery of the Dalai Lama. The last of the faces was held with a cache of arms with Chinese markings. It looks like he was there to assassinate the Dalai Lama, whom India and the world hold in great reverence. The other two are being investigated for stealing 'Indian National Secrets''.

'They were monitored for the past two months and the Indian Police have recovered dossiers of classified information from your nationals and a few of their sources within India have also been secured. They will be formally charged in the courts tomorrow. If they are charged in the court, then there is nothing that even our PM can do to let them off'.

'Just for your information, the second on the list happens to be a Chinese Olympic Athletic Gold Medallist, who also doubles as one of your secret agents', said Shastry.

Lt. Gen Ping recognized at least two of the names and took a deep breath to get over the shock.

'So, what exactly do you want'? asked Lt. Gen Ping after considering the names in deep thought for a while.

Shastry gave him three names, this time Indian, scribbled on a different sheet of paper. 'As the situation we are discussing with you is time critical, I will straight jump into the demands of the Indian Government. I hope you appreciate'.

Lt. Gen Ping nodded.

'I need the three Indians to be released from your investigations. One of them is Kula. Another, who was an innocent bystander during the Honk Kong Occupy Central agitation and the third, is an Oil Industry expert who was consulting for a Vietnamese Oil exploring company engaged in exploration in the South China Sea near the Spratly Islands. He was picked up by your navy from a Vietnamese vessel and held hostage on trumped up charges of espionage. These Indian citizens have been picked up over a period of one month. This would be a Government to Government deal, for the sake of securing their respective National Interests'.

'I am sure that your Politburo will understand this language and this deal of securing 'National Interests', he said, sarcasm written in every word.

Lt. Gen Ping nodded, 'Understood. I will get back to you in fifteen minutes'. He spoke to someone animatedly for about five minutes. He read the names from the two sheets of paper. During the conversation that was primarily in Chinese, Shastry was meddling with his mobile phone. Or was he?

He was using an app that translated spoken Chinese sentences into English sentences and presented them on the screen as default (you could set the app to present the English output as voice as well). Either the speaker was too fast or the app was too slow in picking up the Chinese sentences, or both, it could succeed only partially in its English translation and only a few half-baked sentences were available from Lt. Gen Ping's conversation along with a plenty of garbage. The most sensible of them were;

'Let's not complicate matters more than they already are and save the Games from the gang...'

'Yes, I am digging and found skeletons... No not _____ (garble... garble...)

...if they gun for us on this cause, it may be our best chance to outgun _____ (garble... garble...)

_____ have chosen the wrong issue against us...

...should encourage them to walk into the trap they set for us...

When Lt. Gen Ping finished his conversation, they left to join the 'Friends Party', to the chorus of gānbēi... Within ten minutes, Lt. Gen Ping had a call. He tipped his last gānbēi... and rushed out to speak in private, nodding at others, who weren't even looking at him. Shastry was enjoying the fun. He was already tipsy even though he had participated in less than half of the gānbēi campaigns the others diligently went through. These campaigns seemed never ending and never drying, until people passed out. There was no sign of any one passing out yet.

A waiter at the table asked Shastry to join Lt. Gen Ping in the other room. Lt. Gen Ping said in a monotone, 'There's a consensus on the deal, the exchange'. After a brief pause, 'But procedures have to be followed. We need to verify facts about the Chinese citizens and the Indians in custody. So we have to keep the entire proposal in wraps for these couple of days. Till then I can't interfere with due security processes. We could be raising an alarm and disturb the plan'.

Shastry said casually, 'OK. So be it. We too have some due processes planned and they have to be put in place immediately as per the countdown I already cautioned you about. This is not blackmail. The Indian Government considers the safety of its citizens, especially the new Champions at the Games a top priority and cannot compromise their wellbeing. He checked his watch for time. Our due process starts in about seventy five minutes and that would be, when as I reach my Indian Games quarters. I need to be excused as I have an 'International Press Conference' arranged…

Lt. Gen Ping remarked, 'You should understand that it takes time to complete such a deal and that Kula cannot be let off without its completion'.

Shastry said, 'Fair enough. Let's agree on various time bound intermediate actions or a protocol that both Governments would follow till the deal is executed and our respective citizens are released. The exchange should happen four hours before the commencement of the Closing Ceremony of the Games. If any of the agreed intermediate steps or the final exchange that we would agree, is delayed even by minutes, I will have the liberty to add the spark. We from the Indian side will work twenty four hours a day to get this deal through. You could do so too if you will'.

'But to start with, there should be a minimum commitment, call it confidence measures, from the Chinese Government that we should agree on that you should execute it in the next seventy five minutes. The confidence measures that we are looking for are; One, that you should ensure Kula's safety from the gang and find him a safe sanctuary, verifiably, till the deal is complete and he is put on a flight back to India. Two; all investigations against him cease with immediate effect. All this within seventy five minutes! Else I meet the press after then.

'Just over an hour! Too short a period', protested Lt. Gen Ping.

'It's not too short for the Chinese Government with strong administrators like you. We also have a time constraint. One, I'm not sure how long Kula can hide from your Police dragnet. If he is arrested, then the deal is off'.

'Two, We want to strike when the iron is hot. The Games is poised at a critical point, just after the Men's Finals and just before the Women's Finals. The entire international press is agitating on the real story behind Kula, Jay and a Chinese girl. Now the iron is at its hottest. Two days later, the curtains on the Games would be down and the press will disperse to assemble later at a different Game on a different continent. We can't afford more time. I hope you understand it is time for action and not to keep bargaining interminably'.

Lt. Gen Ping nodded and shook hands with him and stressed impatiently, 'Well, in seventy five minutes then! Before your press conference...'

Lt. Gen Ping called the President seeking a Presidential order for a couple of things to handle the crisis that was getting out of hand due to the gang. 'We have let the gang too far. Yes... That's my responsibility... I will take care... I will be sending out a request shifting of the case from the Ministry of Public Security (MPS) to the Ministry of State Security (MSS), where the other two cases of espionage by the Indians are being investigated. Yes; the same names that appeared in the list; so the three cases could be dealt together. That would also pull the rug from under of the feet of the gang immediately and by surprise'.

He also wanted a quick acting Officer, to work on this case at the MSS. Just any Officer at MSS wouldn't do. He wasn't aware of the depths of the coterie's influence in the MSS. He wanted his own confidante on the case. He called for the General. But the General was on a Mission to Argentina. He had left the previous evening.

Then he asked himself, 'Why not Lee'? He patted himself. Lee knew the case so well and he could jump on it immediately. He would have a head start, while anyone else will need a few hours brief and another few hours of inertia at least'.

'A few minutes would be a luxury in this case'. It would mean that Lee would have to be transferred to the MSS quickly. He clubbed this transfer posting request along with the Presidential Order transferring the case.

Meanwhile, he was briefing Lee on his new assignment. Lee was thrilled. This was a powerful position.

'The first assignment is', Lt. Gen Ping explained, 'finding Kula, who is on the run in the city and the suburbs, possibly assisted by a Chinese national;

'_______'.

'Yes, you know! Li Ling'!

Two: To secure them before Deng's men or the police lay their hands on them. To keep him in a totally confidential location.

'_______'.

No, definitely not the Indian Consulate! You will never get across the Police dragnet. These are crazy times.

'_______'.

No, Not the Black houses for sure. Hide them in your private but absolutely safe custody. And wait for my instructions.

Lee asked, 'How many days do I have'?

'Fifty minutes! Max sixty', was the reply. He could hear Lee gasp, as he replied, 'I will do my best'.

'Let your best be good enough. Sixty one minutes - we will have a lost cause'!

As he was completing the brief for Lee, he received the presidential order by email, within fifteen minutes of his request. He forwarded it on to Lee first, even before he read through himself. Lee was already in action. He suspected that Kula should be in the company of Li Ling. He checked with Zhu, who was peripherally involved in this case, while he himself was robbed of the charge.

Zhu confirmed his suspicion, 'A warrant has been issued for both of them'.

Lee called Cheng, naturally.

Cheng confided, 'I would be meeting the two at a confidential location in about forty to fifty minutes', without mentioning where.

'Excellent', Lee said. Please, 'could you take them to some safe hideout in the next forty minutes'?

'Forty impossible. But fifty, may be'. – Cheng.

'Should be good', said Lee.

72 Corridors of Power

Wu Zetian (624 – 705 AD) was the concubine of Emperor Taizong. After his death, she married his successor – his ninth son, Emperor Gaozong, officially becoming Gaozong's huanghou (皇后, empress consort, title for the reigning emperor's main consort) in 655, although having considerable political power prior to this. After Gaozong's debilitating stroke in 660, Wu Zetian became administrator of the court, a position equal to the emperor's until 705.

Empress Wu was once described as hated by "gods and men alike." She developed a reputation for ruthlessness, leaving behind a legacy of intrigue. Wu also broke a barrier by becoming China's sole female ruler…

N. Henry Rothschild, Wu Zhao: China's Only Female Emperor.

Huajin wore a wicked smile! She had been giving finishing touches to the dream she had been working on for the last week or so. No ordinary dream this; to become Queen of China! The more she thought about it, the more she was 'drunk' with excitement!

She had always achieved, whatever she wished; thanks to Weimin.

'This wish would be no different', she knew! 'I would be Queen, when, not if, Weimin is crowned Emperor'.

A small correction; this being Modern China, and not the Middle Kingdom, she actually, wouldn't be Queen. But well, close enough… she could be the First Lady; Mrs President! That is, when Weimin is crowned President!

There was only one person, she believed, to be standing between her and her dream! She hated him.

Though her dream was a recent one, the growth (or the decadence?) of Huajin is a long story.

When Huajin left Bojin and married Shan Yuan, Bojin had committed suicide. Some said he had poisoned himself due to shame at the loss of his position as World Badminton No.1 to his friend Shan Yuan. Some said he poisoned himself due to the loss of

Huajin, to the same friend. Some said Huajin poisoned him to free herself in favour of the new World Champion. Whatever, Shan Yuan had a troubled conscience for a few days. But he convinced himself that all is fair in Love and War. He also told himself that a dead friend however dear, wasn't worth a fraction of Huajin, lying in his arms.

Within days of moving in with Shan Yuan and the death of Bojin, Huajin announced that she was four months pregnant. Shan Yuan knew it wasn't his child. But by then he was enslaved to Huajin's beauty and poise that he quickly claimed that the son was his to avoid the risk of annoying her. He was ready to lend his name to the child to be born to his wife.

Huajin always exercised such control over her paramours. They knelt, crawled and begged before her, so that she wouldn't leave them, every single night that they got to spend with her. She had the capacity to bring them to life. She had the capacity to drive them to death.

After her son, Deng was born, Huajin got into the social circuit quickly, getting back to physical shape and exercising all her charms on those who could shower wealth and status on her. She had all the fun at the expense and humiliation of Shan Yuan. In the next two years, she discovered what she really wanted from life. It wasn't money. She could get however much she wanted at her command. It was 'Power'. She toyed with several party members till she found the fastest path to the Corridors of Power; Weimin.

Weimin, as his name meant, was a People's Hero. He was thirty and thirsty, when she first met him and she was twenty three. Her son, Deng, was just two year old. Weimin soon became Deng's Godfather and it got him an excuse for his proximity with Huajin. Weimin was then the fastest growing power centre in the Party. He had ample help from his father, who was the right and left hand of the then President of China. The President owed it to his father for his position. The power of the father-son combination was such that, when Weimin showed his interest in Huajin, the thousand and odd eminent personalities of Shanghai that were crazy about her, deserted the streets that she strode, in fear and favour of Weimin. Those few that still eyed her and crossed his path were turned to naught and they had to desert the city, anyway.

It was no secret that Weimin and Huajin were living as

husband and wife, but never married for several years. During this time, they were known to have a son, who Weimin decided to register as the son of Shan Yuan and Huajin as it could complicate his earlier marriage and his political life, even as Shan Yuan whined in protest. All the three elders knew the truth and most of their friends and acquaintances suspected it.

They had named their son, Peng, who took to his mother and closely resembled Deng,
Shan Yuan was broken, first of his heart, then of his game, then of his money, then of his health and then of his mind. By the time Weimin and Huajin decided to wed, Shan Yuan had become a mental wreck, was drunk all the time and became worthless as a junk. In this condition, he protested and would not free Huajin for her to marry Weimin. He even slapped her once and humiliated Weimin in public. Shan Yuan made two mistakes that that became fatal to him; crossing Weimin's path and becoming a nuisance to Huajin. His death was recorded as 'illness of the heart".
'A few days later, Weimin and Huajin married and went on their honeymoon to Hawaii.'

Even after Weimin became stepfather, Deng continued to speak of him as his 'Godfather'. Peng mechanically followed whatever Deng said or did. So he spoke of his father, Weimin as 'Godfather' too.
Deng could have followed either father but he chose to follow both. As Shan Yuan was the father who gave Deng his name and brought him up, was a sportsman, Deng became a sportsman too. At eighteen he won his first Chinese National Table Tennis Championship, though there were better players than him in China that year; Huajin took care of that. At twenty he became World No.1; again there were better players than him in his native China, and by extension, the World, as China dominated the world of TT; Huajin took care of that too. He held the position for nearly four long years.
Just as his path to World No. 1 was littered with a number of fallen potential champions; fallen to the conspiracy of his mother, his successful stay at the top was equally destructive for his rivals. A good number of better players were shuffled out of his path so he

could reign as Champion for that long.

Deng had lost his World No. 1 position to Jiang two plus years earlier and he was the Official World No. 2 during the previous Shanghai Games. He could not reconcile to the erosion of his position and that even his mother could not help stem. His frustration grew and he became contemptuous and resentful. When he moved one position behind as World No.3 after the Kyoto Open, he became aggressive. During this downward spiral, he aged ungracefully; he plotted, schemed, continuously conspired day and night, to run down his opponents in and out of the TT court, either to stop them before they met him or as revenge after they beat him on the court. He had become maniacal!

Another path Deng followed was - Politics. He had acquired enough powers courtesy his Godfather and felt it was a natural privilege of the Weimin clan. Deng had been ruthless and extremely aggressive. He terrorized everyone to submission and made things happen his way. Deng could walk into any Government office or Police HQ and take over the control of the office as though it was his personal fiefdom. The senior most Officials at those offices used to cower in front of him, something they didn't need to do even before the President of China.

Deng's step brother Peng, who was four years younger to him adored him and tried to emulate him in sports and the use of political power. Hidden in an elite school and without the care of parents, he had taken to drugs and girls at an early age. He lost interest in studies and when he habitually misbehaved with other girls in the school, the school decided to throw him out, but did not carry out the threat due to the power and influence of Weimin. Peng's name stayed in the school's registers long after he dropped out of it and he was ceremonially promoted to higher grades. He had tried sports, especially TT, but he neither had the discipline nor subjected himself to the rigour like Deng did. Also due to his drug habits he could not focus on the ball and didn't even pass the initial tests. Sports just wasn't in his DNA.

On the power side of politics, Peng had ambitions like Deng. Weimin, who wished to pass on his mantle eventually to Peng, when he grew up, found he wasn't growing up in the right direction and he was tarnishing his name by his use of his brute force to ride girls everywhere and without their consent. Peng had a penchant for girls who didn't like him and he had a compulsive urge to overpower them on his bed. He ruined them body, mind and career with sadistic pleasure, if he found them resisting him.

Weimin who had no leverage with his son, watched him helplessly gravitate into this psychopathic behaviour. The reports that floated about his son were scary and were caustic enough that Weimin was concerned that the stray linkages between him and Peng could jeopardise his own political ambitions.

So at some point, he distanced himself from his own son and left him in charge of Deng. Deng liked his brother and tried his best to groom him and had him partially de-addicted from drugs, but not from his psychopathic tendencies toward girls. Once when Peng had forced himself on a girl, just 12, whose father had connections too, it came back to haunt Weimin, Deng shielded his brother, who was his look alike, by providing a perfect alibi and faced the charge himself. The star struck girl, who believed and was thus relieved that she lost her virtue to the World No. 1 and not to the drug addicted Peng, dropped the charges. She actually was known to have gained from such notoriety and became a top model.

Weimin had arranged to send Peng to a US school, to learn etiquette and English language. Deng had ensured that the Godfather's name was not dragged down by his step-brother's horrific behaviour overseas during the critical phase of his career. Deng shielded Peng and Weimin from each other and brought peace to both.

When Weimin was forty eight, he was a member of the Politburo and was considered the most influential among its twenty five members. He was strongly recommended for a position as a member of the Politburo Standing Committee, which was a select subset of the Politburo, with seven members and was more powerful than the Politburo itself. As his father, the Chairman of the Chinese People's Political Consultative Conference was already a senior member of the Standing Committee, Weimin couldn't be immediately considered for the position.

His father had offered to step down, without in any way diluting his powers, under a deal, in favour of his son. Weimin was promised to be elevated at the 'next available opportunity', by the then President. But four years since then, the opportunity never had favoured Weimin.

Weimin's father had been the kingmaker and the maker of all Presidents in the last two decades. He actually ruled China by default, whoever was President. Though the current President also owed his position to him, once elected he did not surrender to the Kingmaker's commands; as he demanded a much bigger price than the President could afford. He wanted the President to be subservient to his son too. The President, incensed, did not relent and plotted independently of them.

Huajin became ambitious and power hungry. She controlled the thoughts of Weimin. She had direct access to most Officials in most Government Ministries, including Home, Police, Finance and even the PLA, who were ready to do her bidding. They were corrupt enough that they needed the unwavering support of the future First Lady of China, who was known to control the mind of the future President. The corruption and the need for support was mutual and hence the nexus. She could recommend or even decide appointments to key positions in any of the Government departments, including foreign ministry's consular postings. She had amassed huge wealth in every country of her choice. She only had to speak a wish and Weimin would offer anything at her feet.

Deng was Weimin's executor and a ruthless undertaker and was used to silence his enemies, rivals and critics at lower levels.

He loved the raw power vested in his hands and executed his Godfather's will, his mother's wishes and his own whims, with pleasure. Peng, who had been hearing of all the powers that were vested in the family hands and growing, did not want to be left out of the action and excitement. He returned to Shanghai from the US against Weimin's wishes. Deng hid Peng from his father's views and selectively exposed him to the excitement and action.

Deng initially used his power judiciously, especially if he found the circumstances were right and called for display of his power. Later he lost his restraint and balance as he lost his TT World No. 1 status and as Weimin's powers and influence soared, became vindictive and brutal.

While the King Maker father ruled the minds of Presidents of China and Weimin ruled the Politburo, Deng grew to be the most spiteful and ruthless person known to straddle the middle and lower corridors of power in his generation.

At this stage, the Weimin clan was running a parallel Government in China. This parallel Government was developing serious hostility with the regular Government under the President.

Weimin had long ago decided that he wouldn't be just another Kingmaker after his father. He had decided to be the next President. During the last two years, towards this end, he had been conspiring with vengeance and secretly pushing his agenda and increased his sphere of influence in the Communist Party of China that appoints the Politburo, with the knowledge that with a majority of the Politburo members on his side, he could force a consensus in his favour. If Weimin, who already had a third of the Politburo behind him, could take his influence one notch higher, his powers would be limitless. He would be the next President of China.

It was then that Huajin had this dream and as casually as one would ask, 'I want mei for lunch', she demanded, 'I want 'his' head at my feet…'
'I want to be Empress Wu Zetian'!
Weimin shivered first, before a tingle of realization passed through his body, head to toe! It was very much in the realm of possibility.
He quickly re-oriented his mission and objective to comply with Huajin's demand - to place the head of the current President at her feet! And to immediately make himself President.
Huajin would be Queen, when, not if, Weimin would be crowned Emperor, after all! It was a foregone conclusion.
The entire country was about to tremble at the consequence of her dream!

Weimin went on warpath; on an undeclared war on the President! He was too impatient to wait his turn for Presidency and considered himself as the de-facto President of China. He chose to confront the President on matters of importance for him. Due to the frequent confrontation, the President looked weak and destabilized.

The President has been trying to consolidate his powers in the last two years, but had been finding it difficult to overwhelm the Weimin-father duo. He was looking for an appropriate issue and timing to strike at Weimin and his support base, while he continued to entertain the clan.

The President had a trusted lieutenant, whom he had personally chosen as his Commander, a terror in Uniform, also known as the 'Ping of Death' to quell the rebellion of the Weimin clan.

73 In the Crosshairs

'Why is it difficult to swat a fly'?
"Now I can finally answer," says Dickinson, Esther M. and Abe M. Zarem, Professor of Bioengineering at the California Institute of Technology (Caltech).
Using high-resolution, high-speed digital imaging of fruit flies (Drosophila melanogaster) faced with a looming swatter, Dickinson and graduate student Gwyneth Card have determined the secret to a fly's evasive maneuvering. Long before the fly leaps, its tiny brain calculates the location of the impending threat, comes up with an escape plan, and places its legs in an optimal position to hop out of the way in the opposite direction. All of this action takes place within about 100 milliseconds after the fly first spots the swatter.
"This illustrates how rapidly the fly's brain can process sensory information into an appropriate motor response," Dickinson says.
https://phys.org/news/2008-08-scientists-flies-hard-swat.html#jCp

Shastry sent out his next encrypted dispatch to the Indian PM, NM, after a couple of clandestine meetings with his contacts;

Sir,

This is in continuation of my last dispatch.

The most serious challenge to the President comes from the 'King maker', about whom I had discussed in one of my previous reports. A leader in his own right he was the power behind the making of the current President too, but somehow the relationship fell out soon. The other groups at odds with the President are rallying around the clan and against the President. A revolt is brewing!

The rebel group has been scenting victory and have even started identifying their cabinet, and the bureaucrats to run their command.

Though the President is seen without hope, it would be in Indian interests if the incumbent President continues in his current capacity as we have established good rapport and communication lines with this group. We have to appreciate the realities and desist from any action or comments that would cause discomfort to the current President, even if we

The blatant power struggle is expected to see its first victors and victims in a matter of days; not even weeks.

Shastry.

PS: The Chief Investigator appointed by the Chinese Premier is sympathetic to our Kula and Jay and is willing to go the extra mile to fix the unruly elements within their establishment, though may be for internal political reasons. It is now known that the rebel Political Leader has taken a strong position in support of the Chinese TT Team management and against the Indian players. He is known to have strong prejudices against India and in favour of Pakistan. We could see hostile reactions against India from day one of his likely ascension to the Presidency.

Fortunately for Li'll'y and Kool, they were ahead of the roadblocks being set up everywhere to detain them, until they reached the suburbs and were coasting towards Cheng's hideout. Then they were alerted by the siren of the Police car far behind them that was catching up fast.

Li'll'y was exhausted from the day's challenges and was too tired to handle the beast of the Motorcycle at that speed. Kool sensed this and offered to drive. They quickly changed positions, and lost minutes, while the police car gained on them.

Cheng called and warned Li'll'y, 'There are police checkpoints ahead and the patrols have increased. You would have to reach safety somehow. If you find police activity, stay clear. If you get caught, message me the location; make sure to delete the message. Delay being taken; argue, take washroom breaks, something. I will be there as soon as possible'.

Li'll'y was concerned, 'But what could Cheng do'!

Kool turned the accelerator hard and the sporty Motorbike engine revved up energetically and they gained speed and a small distance ahead of the police car. Then there was a gunshot. The bullet grazed his jacket before it shattered the right side rear view mirror. Li'll'y screamed and hugged him closely and urged him to speed on. Kool drove zigzag in anticipation of the second bullet that actually hit the metal frame. Kool stopped before the third shot was fired…

Li'll'y urged him. 'Speed up! Speed Up! Speed Up'!!!

Kool threw his hands up, 'I don't want you to get shot. I wish you were driving and I am at the pillion… anyway our game is up'!

Not before long, the Lady Officer was covering them with her gun as she was updating her actions on her mobile and taking instructions. Li'll'y was disappointed that their fate was sealed so close to their potential safety, as Cheng's hideout lay hardly 15 minutes away.

Soon they were taken in the Police Officer's car, onwards till they saw a makeshift roadblock, a temporary police checkpoint using only a Police car parked against the flow with lights flashing and a couple of policemen standing. It occurred to Kool that the checkpoint emerged and sped towards them from the horizon at great speeds only to slowdown and stop just a few metres in front of the car, as the Lady Officer slowed the car to an eventual stop. He saw everything as a negative developed on a photographic film.

One of the policemen, the short one walked up to the Lady Officer and introduced himself, 'I'm Inspector Lee of the Ministry of State Security, looking for two fugitives Kula, an Indian National and a girl called Li Ling'.

The Lady Officer was annoyed, but nevertheless stepped out of the car. She tried to check his badges, but it was too dark. The policeman understood her predicament and produced some documents.

The Lady Officer checked the order under the car headlights and wasn't satisfied and murmured, 'I know Mr. Lee'.

Lee smiled and clarified, 'Oh I'm Inspector Lee. I report to the Senior Mr Lee, who is in charge as per the Order'. As she reluctantly permitted them to check for the fugitives in her car, she was talking to Deng.

Deng wasn't pleased. How could the Indians get ahead of him, everytime? He ordered her, 'Break the cordon and fly past the checkpoint and if necessary, shoot. I am just a few minutes behind you and will take care of any fallout'.

As the Lady Officer wasn't willing to go that far under his instructions, he assured her, 'This is either a fake Presidential Order or happens to be the last one signed by the current President. In two days, Godfather will be the President. Trust me. You are in for a huge promotion'.

Officer Lee was in a hurry to wrap up the takeover of the fugitives, but the Lady Officer started an argument over the procedures and she wasn't about to give up easily. She was buying time. Waiting for Deng to surface in the promised few minutes.

The lights of the Ferrari emerged at the horizon, in the next two minutes, flew at a great speed and halted behind them with a screech.

One of the policemen was still checking the photographs in hand to identify Kula and Li, while the other, Officer Lee, who was wrangling over the procedures with the Lady Officer was watching Deng's Ferrari closely undecided if it brings a friend or foe. Foe, he was sure; he wasn't expecting a friend.

It was then that Deng raised his gun and shot at Kool, before the policeman could react.

For Kool, the gunshot triggered his brain into an overactive mode to help him protect him from the sure death situation. His watch became so intense that he could see the bullet leave the gun and clearly spinning lazily toward him in slow motion. He could duck just in time, as he watched the bullet whiz past him almost brushing his ear.

He next saw Deng point the gun at Li'll'y. Kool instinctively rushed forward to protect Li'll'y hoping the next bullet wasn't fired too soon, afraid that he wouldn't cover as much ground before the bullet would.

The short policeman rushed towards Deng in panic, shouting, 'STOP', reluctant to use the gun he just pulled out. Deng cursed as he swerved his gun at him and shot him, felling him with a hit on his right thigh. This wasn't in his script. But he was too maniacal to care.

Li'll'y stood shaking like a leaf in fear, screaming, shutting her eyes tight and closing her ears with her palms; a poise inviting Deng to train his guns on her, once again. He seemed to enjoy his power over Li'll'y.

The distraction from the policeman gave enough time for Kool to cover the distance and move between Li'll'y and the bullet, all the while watching the later blast its path towards her in slow motion, until it tore deep into his left arm.

When he recovered on his feet from the shock and stagger, he saw Deng's gun explode for the third time and the bullet racing slowly towards them slowly in a spin. If he ducked, it would surely hit Li'll'y.

He fell backwards onto her protectively, without losing sight of the bullet, knocking her towards the ground, ahead of the bullet that ripped deep into his shoulder.

Even as he fell all over Li'll'y, covering her to ensure that she would not be hit, the next bullet hit the ground inches before Kool, bouncing off it and got embedded inside his left ribcage, just where his heart was.

Deng clicked again to find his magazine empty. He had watched Kula collapse in pain to the ground, holding his left breast, covering a large blood drenched red patch, probably dead, seemed satisfied with himself and sped off, past the check point shouting obscenities that were to be his victory cry. The Lady Officer jumped into her car and fled from the scene, just a few seconds behind him.

The other policeman panicked, picked up the bleeding Officer and assisted him into the car. He forced Li'll'y at gun point, who dragged a bleeding Kool too into the car. His hands were clearly shaking as he abandoned the post and drove off quickly into the first side lane.

Li'll'y sobbed as she checked for Kool's breathing and heartbeat. She was greatly relieved that Kula was breathing, though with difficulty and that his heart was beating, albeit faintly. He wasn't conscious. She first checked the injury on his chest. Then she held her towel pressed to the chest that was bleeding most and hoped she wasn't hurting him.

His breathing became laborious and she could hear it.

'Don't die on me, Kool', she pleaded with him. Then she remembered Joy, who was too sentimental about saying or thinking about Kool and death at the same breath. She had pleaded once, not long ago, 'Please don't say any such harsh word about Kool'.

Probably, Joy would have prayed for Kool. Li'll'y had never prayed in her life. God just didn't exist for her, even during the toughest times.

Li'll'y felt she was Kool's custodian on behalf of Joy, and so she would do as joy would, to save Kool.

'I don't want to mess up with Joy's God, and so I would pray for Kool'. She prayed... only to realize with a smile that she didn't know how to pray, other than saying, 'Oh my God... Oh my God'!

So she started a positive chant, 'Live, Kool, live. For Joy's sake! For My sake'!

As she pressed the towel on Kool's chest a little harder, to stop the blood that was staining her towel fast, she felt something hard between his ribs.

'It should be the bullet', she thought. 'The bullet should not have got very deep. Thank goodness! A fraction of an inch closer and deeper would have punctured his heart.'!

She felt proud of herself, 'God has answered my very first and only prayer'.

As she pressed harder and at the right place, the blood had practically stopped oozing.

He was still bleeding from his shoulder and arms. She urged the Policeman to drive faster to any hospital in the vicinity.

She went silent, deep in thought as her fear changed to anger against Deng. But she felt helpless. She was resigned to the thought that their freedom run was truncated harshly and now they will wait for the law to catch up with them.

She felt for a second that Kool would be better off dead than be a prisoner, charged for treason in the Chinese system. But again, she didn't want to Kool to die whatsoever.

Kool regained consciousness and made an effort to smile at her, though weakly, to reassure her that he was alright. She remembered something, lighted up, and whispered into Kool's ears with a smile, partly with the hope to cheer him up, 'You did sight the bullet after all! I have never seen a more intense gaze than yours. You could have not only stopped the bullet on its tracks with such a gaze, but probably melted it to chocolate and bitten it too'!

Then she confided shyly, 'I will tell you a secret? I saw the bullets too! Thank you for training me'!

She kissed him on his lips as she whispered, 'This is my first and could be our last, before our final kiss of death, by the firing squad'!

First he was flustered, then responded by kissing her back. What kind of hu-Man would I be, if I can't love her back; this most lovable Li'll'y who has chosen death by my side and for my sake?

Inspector Lee, who had lost a lot of blood and was in pain, recovered from his daze, turned back on his seat and asked, 'My dear Li, Are you OK? It was brave of you, Champion friend, to save Li. Thank you. Please don't die yet, I am getting help soon!'

Kool faintly tried to relate the familiar voice to a face he recalled and was confused as it didn't fit, even as Li'll'y screamed, 'Cheng'! She jumped forward, hugged him and sobbed.

Cheng called Lee in the next twelve minutes. 'Sorry, I made a miscalculation of time'.

Lee shook his head in frustration. 'So when can you, earliest'?

'I think you misunderstood me. I already have them in my custody, ten minutes ahead. I chose to intercept them on the highway, rather than wait for them. There was a big drama at the point of interception with Deng who chased them on his Ferrari, gun in hand and shots fired'.

'The boy hit on the left chest, and deep in the right arm, the shoulder and bleeding heavily. The shot close to his heart isn't deep, and my doctor says he will live, if we could rush him to an equipped medical care…'

'Undergoing first aid to stop his bleeding. He's very faint. I have engaged a doctor for first aid, a friend, who will need immunity if something goes wrong. I will update you later, on the details… We will be on the move, once the first aid is done…'

'Sorry! I can't tell you where… Just let me know where I should take them… Ok… We will be there in not more than forty minutes. But you need to get a safe surgeon soon to remove the bullets when we arrive there… It will still be emergency, and could turn critical, if we delay by more than an hour'. His voice was getting fainter and wanted to hand over his charge to Lee as soon as possible.

Lee dialled Lt. Gen Ping. Lt. Gen Ping congratulated Lee and said he was mighty pleased at the quick work, but was concerned about Kula's injury from the gunshots. But after satisfying himself that first aid was being administered, he called Shastry. He still had three minutes to go, when the call connected.

Lt. Gen Ping confirmed, 'The boy is in my custody along with the Chinese National who assisted his getaway. Unfortunately, there were gunshots and he is bleeding, but not critical. My information is that decent first aid is on and is still emergency. I'm yet to verify'.

Shastry was in shock and turned silent at the turn of events. All he could manage to say was, 'Could I talk to him'?

In the next few minutes Shastry was speaking to Kula on a conference video call, found him in a serious condition and traumatised by the gunshot injuries.

'Bleeding has been stopped and he is conscious'!

He also took the opportunity to thank Li for her help. 'We appreciate your courage. Congratulations. You fought like a tigress at the Semi-Finals. You are now doing the same for your friend. You both will win this time', he said.

Shastry appealed to Lt. Gen. Ping, 'Please rush Kula for emergency medical care'.

Lt. Gen Ping assured, 'The best of care will be provided. I am taking care, personally'.

At the Press conference that started after five minutes delay, Shastry spoke, 'I'm sorry about the delay. Several things are happening. First the Good news! We were in a mood to celebrate India's first Gold Medal in International TT competitions. That it happens to be the Games is all the more gratifying'.

'Now the bad news! 'We are told that Kula has been rushed out on an emergency. We don't know what the emergency is and where he is, yet. We are also told that he has been badly injured. We are awaiting information on the nature of the emergency and the injuries. Everything is a mystery, till this point. We are most worried! I'm only glad that I have been promised official cooperation from the Government of China'.

He had said enough to keep the iron hot! He could strike at the time of his will.

Kula and Li were transferred to Mia's country home by Lee to ensure their safety from the hands of Deng's coterie and an expert surgeon with his assistant was already waiting to take care of Kula.

74 End Game

The next two days were the most turbulent days in the last four decades of Modern Day China and of course the most challenging days in Lt. Gen. Ping's life after his formal retirement. Unknown to the rest of the world, China witnessed two days of political upheaval as a result of a fratricidal and internecine war declared by the Godfather against the President of China. Most Chinese people did not notice the shudders that passed through the spine of the nation that the ruling elite tried hard to contain, especially by the quick and daring actions of the 'Ping of Death', who by his master skills had orchestrated several events across China as if he conducted his favourite symphony.

Some of the significant events of the two days were;
Day 1:
Jay won her Gold at the Games in style 12-10, 8-11, 11-4, 9-11, 14-12, 6-11, 14-12, in a gruelling Final against Wen Qiang.

Li Ling the second bronze medallist was missing from the prize ceremony. The officials were squirming uncomfortably.

Their version was that Li Ling was unwell and could not attend the Prize Ceremony.

There was booing from some sections of the spectators that suddenly stopped, followed by a raging silence among the crowd. The press corps desperate to know the truth, in the absence of it, were intently typing away rumours...

Joy missed Kool and Li'll'y at the Prize Ceremony and wept in joy and in sadness, knowing that Li'll'y and Kool had been safely stashed away from harm's way, a secret shared only with her by Shastry. She dedicated her win to her Chinese friend, without naming Li'll'y. Lt. Gen. Ping stepped in carrying wishes from the President and personally congratulated her too.

Cheng was being treated for the gunshot injury in his secret hideout without arousing suspicions and sympathies of Lt. Gen. Ping. If Lee knew about the injury, he didn't talk, not even to Lt.

Gen. Ping.

Cheng, who had several months ago promised his hacker friend to introduce Jay during the Games and had forgotten about it, was surprised, when his friend reminded him of his promise.

'Seriously'!? asked Cheng at his friend's request and reminder. But the friend found Cheng was in no physical shape to be able to do so. Moreover, Cheng apologetically said, 'I'm cooling off after exposing myself and the network to save some friends and it would be inopportune time to surface now'.

The friend, who appreciated the position, still insisted. I would still want to ask her for a date, even if it means I have to travel to India with you!

Cheng was perplexed and lamented, 'Can't understand the youngsters at all'!

Lt. Gen Ping had known from his sources that Deng had vowed to find and finish off Kula and Li, as per the 'dictates of his Law', as he unleashed all the powers that he could beckon. Weimin had a broader and more sinister agenda; to overthrow the incumbent President and to be the sitting President in the next couple of days.

He had serious issues with Lt. Gen Ping, acting at the behest of the President, as a challenge to his fiefdom and he knew that he was the one that could happen between him and the Presidency. So he assured himself the 'Death of Ping', rather than the 'Ping of Death', even as he took on the President.

Weimin saw the issues raised by Deng; the stealing of National Secrets by Kula as a serious issue that could hurt the President and Lt. Gen. Ping. If he handled the issue right, he could have the President impeached!

Weimin could not let go the gift of an opportunity that the President and Lt. Gen Ping presented to him and claimed that they were supporting foreign nationals especially from arch rival India to get away from stealing 'National Secrets' of China. He made a hue and cry claiming that the President was supporting Anti-National activities, at the behest of Lt. Gen Ping, who he claimed was the defacto President and the 'Virtual Power Centre' that was running, rather ruining the country.

He also claimed that Lt. Gen Ping was actually an agent of the United States of America and 'has an Agenda to break up China like

Gorbachev did to the erstwhile Soviet Union to please his masters in the US'.

Whoever he was, Weimin's speechwriter was making the right noises that whipped up 'National frenzy' amidst his target audience. Whoever the original speechwriter was, Huajin edited them finally and the final speeches had her stamp of approval. Huajin and Deng were busy floating rumours consistent with Weimin's claims, through his coterie spread across China at a grass root level.

'There's no smoke without fire', Weimin claimed. He listed a number of 'Official Secrets' that had been reportedly transferred or smuggled out to US and other countries including India, Australia and Japan that had ganged up and called themselves the Quad, to contain China within its shores.

Weimin, his father and a small number of hard line supporters got into intensive parleys among the Politburo and the Politburo Standing Committee members through both the front door and the back door channels and were garnering support for immediate action. 'If we fail to act now, we would regret the fall of China soon', they urged. Weimin had effectively declared a war on the President and was gathering mass. He had also got together a group of powerful voices within the PLA, who felt that the President should go.

Lt. Gen Ping took Weimin and his war cry head on and shielded the President from any fall out, like a true soldier. He faced the war inside the Politburo and outside it. He took the war to the PLA and the party that Weimin had power to influence. He had earlier in the day, spoken to the 'General' on a Mission to Argentina, who immediately decided to cut short his mission and return to Beijing.

In the meanwhile, Shastry and Lt. Gen. Ping tied up a deal between the Indian and the Chinese Governments to release their respective captives and return them to their respective countries without charges or further investigation. Kula's case was closed by the end of the first day evening, just immediately after Jay's win in the Final. The other two Indian captives were released simultaneously against the three Chinese captives released in India were handed over to their respective consulates at Shanghai and New Delhi, for further procedures.

Kula was driven to the airport directly from Mia's home by Lee. Jay joined them in the company of Shastry and Mahadevan at the airport. Jay burst into tears when she saw Kula wounded and heavily bandaged in the shoulder, arm and abdomen. Lt. Gen. Ping had promised to join them during the drive, but had excused himself at the last minute; 'Matters of State', he said.

But however, Lt. Gen. Ping appeared at the airport to the surprise of all, in time to witness the most poignant friendship between Kula, Jay and Li, as Jay clinged on to Li and bade adieu in tears. He hugged Li and declared her a 'National Treasure of China' and pronounced her as his 'God Daughter'.

Lt. Gen. Ping left for the military airport and flew to Beijing in a military copter. There he rushed to a secret camp to meet the top PLA brass along with the 'General' who had returned from his truncated Argentine mission. They had several parleys with the leading heads of the PLA. Then there was one conference, attended by the group addressed by the Top General of PLA through video conferencing. At the end of the day, Lt. Gen. Ping was convinced by the support he received and updated the President on the developments.

The President ordered him to declare war on the Weimin clan.

75 Check and Mate?

Antony:
Friends, Romans, countrymen, lend me your ears;
I come to bury Caesar, not to praise him.
The evil that men do lives after them;
The good is oft interred with their bones;
So let it be with Caesar. The noble Brutus
Hath told you Caesar was ambitious:
If it were so, it was a grievous fault,
…

…
He hath brought many captives home to Rome
Whose ransoms did the general coffers fill:
Did this in Caesar seem ambitious?
When that the poor have cried, Caesar hath wept:
Ambition should be made of sterner stuff:
Yet Brutus says he was ambitious;
And Brutus is an honourable man.
You all did see that on the Lupercal
I thrice presented him a kingly crown,
Which he did thrice refuse: was this ambition?
Yet Brutus says he was ambitious;
And, sure, he is an honourable man……
…

Second Citizen
O noble Caesar!

Third Citizen
O woful day!

Fourth Citizen
O traitors, villains!
…

All
We'll mutiny.

First Citizen
We'll burn the house of Brutus."

Julius Caesar, William Shakespeare

Day 2

Lt. Gen. Ping addressed the emergency late evening session of the Politburo;

'We have a deal... between the Chinese and the Indian Government to exchange our mutual captives. We have made this deal in our National interests'.

It wasn't about this Indian boy at any point in time! It is never about the Indian interests! It's about us; it's about our interests; about our agents, who unfortunately, had been foiled in India as you will know soon...

First he gunned for the TTSM, 'though was claimed to be a "National Secret', TTSM is one of the biggest failures ever of Chinese National Projects; a National Disaster'.

'TTSM was a highly hyped up machine. It trains our Players to be Super Zombies who believe that the machine would bring them the Gold if they followed it orders on how to play - ridiculous. It stunted our players and imparted in them a predictable, monotone game. We saw the results in the just concluded Games. The introduction of TTSM was by itself a serious strategic error and if I have my way, the sponsors of the machine and those behind our forgettable outing at the Games would be held accountable. But fortunately for them, it is not the purpose of today's discussion'.

'Yet', he added, 'I am with every one of you Honourable Members of the Politburo here that wants to hang the boy, for he stole Chinese National secrets'.

'Please make no mistake... We have worked out a favourable exchange in our own interest. But let us separate facts from self-serving myths, solely created to whip up passions. As I said, it's never been about the two talented players from India, though they had showed their superior game at the last Games and again during this Games. We ignored the events, stage managed by our own TT Team Management during the last Games and thus we failed to improve our competence. This encouraged the same management to hatch elaborate conspiracy to keep their competitors away from this year's games too and shamefully, it almost worked'.

'It's not a surprise though! The shameful events are reminiscent of the ways one of our world champions and his mother plotted to reach the top and ruled from there for a good four years, subverting real talent that challenged him, but lost out to their machination. It is again appalling that same ex. No. 1 is the brain and force behind this conspiracy too. This time he chose to subvert able competition from outside China… and here we are – on the defensive'!

'But, thankfully for those who stage-managed those events and brought disgrace upon us and the powers behind them, today's discussion isn't about them', Lt. Gen. Ping explained.

'Even assuming that the Indian boy stole the single part, even assuming that he successfully reconstructed the equipment back in India using whatever he stole and benefitted from it, while there is no evidence that he did, it should have been an independent effort – no conspiracy. Our competent investigation agencies have not found any evidence of sponsorship by the Indian Government or other agencies.

'Yet, I am with some of you here that wants to hang the boy. He could have stolen the Chinese National secrets'!

'But today, it's all about, how the most important of our secret agents, with high knowledge of our clandestine operations, including names of our other agents and doubles was exchanged for a small time standalone 'thief' – the Indian boy Kula, who 'could' have stolen our secret Machine. Our agent was sponsored by our Government, four years ago. He also happens to be a Top Chinese Olympic Athletic Gold Medallist'.

There was a big gasp among the Politburo members, when he spelt out his name. This information changed everything.

Lt. Gen. Ping continued after a well-executed pause, 'We had to save our most important agent by letting go this small time Indian Medallist 'thief'. Are we just pleasing the Indian ego? No, we do this all the time to bring back our valued assets from abroad, as do all other countries'.

'We also have taken advantage of this situation and could take back two more of our agents on clandestine assignments for more than an equal exchange'!

'Yet, I am with anyone of you here that wants to hang the boy, who think the boy stole our critical National secrets! Alternatively, you could support the deal and help bring back our brave men'.

Lt. Gen. Ping paused to let the murmur among the Politburo members subside, before he spoke again.

'The august sub-committee of three within the Politburo Standing Committee had been appraised of the Government to Government deal, before we assembled here. I request the head of the committee to share the views of the esteemed committee.

By referring to the matter impromptu sub-committee, Lt. Gen. Ping had effectively evaded the views of Weimin's powerful father, also a member of the Politburo Standing Committee. Weimin rose to speak. But everyone's eyes were on the member of the sub-committee who rose as well. Ignored totally, and without any visible support, W had to sit again.

The member of the sub-committee had a short discussion with the other two, who just nodded in answer.

He summed up for the benefit of the others, 'The committee has heard from both sides. We are convinced that China gained a ROOK, a BISHOP and a KNIGHT in exchange for a ROOK, a BISHOP and a PAWN'.

The entire Politburo, well almost, except four of the staunchest supporters of Weimin, nodded and raised their hands together in support of the deal. Lt. Gen. Ping's address was accepted without further murmurs within the Politburo and especially majority of the members of the Politburo Standing Committee, who mattered most.

Lt. Gen. Ping concluded, 'Thank you for your approval of the deal'.

As Weimin and his father were isolated, panic spread among their supporters. The father-son duo had bitten more than they could chew and now would choke.

'Check...' pronounced Lt. Gen. Ping!

76 Justice for Shan Yuan

Weimin and Huajin were arrested on charges of murder at the wee hours, just later than midnight and within an hour of the end of the emergency Politburo Session. The case was heard by a one man Military Tribunal, a 'General' of the Central Military Commission, who incidentally had flown back to Beijing from Argentina just 12 hours earlier. Lt. Gen. Ping would be the Prosecutor arguing the case. The case was heard for two hours, the same night.

'This hearing is about the Hunger for Power... No... imposing raw political power over an unwitting Nation and its people... The Power Play included thousands of treacherous acts against the Great Chinese Nation; hundreds of murders of innocent people of China, swindling this Great Nation and her people of its wealth and prosperity, for the sheer delight of those who imposed their will.

'However, I want to focus on only one of the most despicable act committed by the two. This hearing would be about a gruesome murder of a National Hero, Shan Yuan, our former Badminton World No. 1, who incidentally happens to be the ex-husband of Ms Huajin', pointing out to Huajin, to satisfy the lust of the two accused, who were the centre of the Power circle that I just described; Ms Huajin and Mr Weimin'.

'This murder was all the more ghastly that it was planned meticulously and executed using a few rogue officials of the Chinese Administration that bent before them. Worse, the investigations into the murder were interfered with and the honest investigator was threatened with dire consequences'. '

'He had dropped the investigations that he had already completed, resigned his job out of guilt and found peace by going back to his home province; but not before he placed copies of the evidence and his aborted investigation reports out of reach of his successor, whose integrity had been compromised'.

'We have the CCTV recording of the events leading to the death of Shan Yuan and the original autopsy report of the Investigation Officer twelve years ago, who had been forced to drop the investigation by the then powers that be. Actually he had backed it up on his 'Yahoo! Briefcase' service that was prevalent about 14 years earlier, something of a precursor of the Dropbox of today. Though the service has been closed, I could get a copy of the same from the Yahoo! servers, with some effort', claimed Lt. Gen Ping.

Lt. Gen. Ping first presented evidence of poisoning on an autopsy report on the recently dug up remains of Shan Yuan.

'This report matches with the original autopsy finding', he said producing an extract of the original autopsy report created some fourteen years ago.

The CCTV video files had recorded several events.

Scene 1 (The First Day - Wednesday, Time: 10:30 AM): Shan Yuan and Huajin have a big argument at their family home. He slaps her angrily. She holds his shirt and shakes him and vows, 'I will kill you' (as read from her lip moments, and reported by the Official Forensic agency).

Scene 2: (The second day – Thursday, Time: 6:30 AM): The camera at the porch records a team of hospital staff arriving at Shan Yuan's home on an ambulance and carrying an empty stretcher into the house.

Scene 3: (The second day – Thursday, Time: 7:41 AM): Shan Yuan was being carried out on a stretcher, by the staff into the ambulance parked at the entrance. He is still alive, but looks to be in a critical condition. The Ambulance leaves at 7:47 AM.

Scene 4: (The second day – Thursday, Time: 7:51 AM), Huajin steps out onto the porch of the house talking into her mobile, business as usual. She doesn't seem to be very concerned at all. In fact, she seems happy. She says something into her mobile as she stood with facing the direction of the camera with a grin, unusual for a lady whose husband has been rushed to the hospital on an ambulance. The lip reading experts report as; 'I have finished off the 'pain in my back'. Now take care of the hospital autopsy. We should not have any trouble with the investigation. I need a vacation when the funeral is over'.

Lt. Gen. Ping continued; 'We could trace the mobile phone call Ms Huajin made on the fateful day at around 7:49 AM and the talk time is 4 minutes. Here's the Telecom Report as evidence. She was talking to Mr Weimin, standing beside her over there'.

Scene 5: (The second day – Thursday, Time: 7:56 AM): A young boy, aged around twelve steps out of the house and shows her two bottles of infusions, both empty. 'Mom, you forgot this', again by lip synchronization. There was pride in his face. His mother now back against the camera, pats him. Lips not recorded. But later she turns around, the bottles in hand and pushes them inside a bag quickly.

She was recorded by her lip movement as saying, 'Don't get involved in this. It is the game of big people. And don't worry too much. He was not your Dad, in any case'.

The boy gestured in protest, 'Why should I be left out of the action? OK, if you want it that way. Let me know, if you want me to help'. He seemed happy that he could help, as they move away from the view of the camera.

'The boy is Deng. Her son', says, Lt. Gen. Ping to the Jury, pointing out to Huajin, who was standing in the box unconcerned and actually smiling, almost devilish and full of arrogance, 'We want Deng questioned too. We need a warrant. He is absconding'.

The Jury agreed to issue the warrant.

Next he showed the zoom of the bottle of the infusions in the hands of Huajin. The print reads, 'Potassium Chlo....., 30mmo...... Bretshneid...

'Here's the pathologist's report on the effects of the drug that had been injected into Shan Yuan. The doctor is your witness to explain the report'.

The pathologist reported: 'We found high level of Potassium Chloride in the body and the heart. Potassium Chloride is given in high doses to temporarily stop the heart, say, for performing a bypass surgery. It is administered only by a team of experts'. He described more...

Lt. Gen. Ping: 'That describes why the Ambulance Team, who came at the request of Mrs Shan Yuan were inside the house for over one hour! To administer the drugs to stop Mr Shan Yuan's heart. The key witness is Mr Shi Hong '.

Shi Hong explained that he was one of the junior hospital staff on duty at Ms Huajin's home on that fateful day. 'Dr Zhao Hui who administered the drug died four years ago. We administered Potassium Chloride drug, normally given during a Bypass operation. I was new to the hospital then. I learnt later that this drug is administered to stop the heart. I used to wonder why it was given to the gentlemen, on whom no by-pass surgery was performed... I just assisted the Doctors who administered the drug and I am not an expert on medicine and my role is to follow instructions'.

'Mr Shan Yuan was drunk, but looked healthy. When we administered the drug, he collapsed fitfully on the bed. We carried him off. He was declared dead on arrival at the hospital due to sickness of the heart. This lady, pointing out to Huajin, guided us to his room for the procedure. And stayed by us during the entire procedure. She came to the hospital an hour of her husband being declared dead. I don't think she was worried. In fact, she was smiling when the procedure was performed at their home', deposed Shi Hong.

'I have also submitted to the Honourable Jury, Mr Weimin – Ms Huajin's marriage certificate dated five days after Shan Yuan's funeral. I have also submitted a voucher from a Hotel in Hawaii that the couple spent their Honey Moon days, immediately following their wedding. Actually you could call it Bloody Moon as the couples' moons on those days were soaked in Shan Yuan's blood'.

Lt. Gen. Ping concluded his arguments: 'It is very evident that Mr Weimin and Ms Huajin conspired to eliminate the victim who slapped her in anger on a particular day. They took the help of Dr Zhao hui, who is no more now and assisted by other hospital staff to administer a medicine normally used at lower dosage for temporarily stopping the heart during by-pass surgeries. After administering the drug I excessive quantities on Shan Yuan, they then lifted the victim to the hospital to declare him dead on arrival due to 'illness of the heart'. Mr Deng, her son of just twelve years helped them conceal the evidence that makes him co-conspirator in the cold blooded murder of Mr Shan Yuan's murder. The victim happened to be Ms Huajin's former husband and was believed to be Deng's father. However, by the conversation that was recorded on the day, Ms Huajin is known to have conceded to her son that Mr Shan Yuan wasn't his biological father'.

'The motive for the murder is evident; to eliminate the victim for furthering her prospects of marriage with Mr Weimin. Theirs was shameful story of lust and power. This should not be seen as an isolated case of a murder driven by lust, given the national stature of the victim, who was a National Hero and a World Champion and the Power wielded by these two who perpetrated it. The two also have brazenly misused the power vested in their hands by the nation to bend the investigation and to escape the laws of the

Nation; this should be treated as an inexcusable crime against the society and the nation'.

'Though I had promised to focus on the murder of Shan Yuan, I cannot but highlight the serious charges of several other cold blooded murders that the two had ordered, corruption that the two were being investigated against, under the new Presidential effort to crack down on both 'tigers' and 'flies', in his fight against corruption'.

'So far under this crackdown the Central Commission for Discipline Inspection headed by Wang Qishan, a member of the Politburo Standing Committee, has caged Xu Caihou, Zhou Yongkang and Ling Jihua. Mr Weimin is just the next on the list. Mr Wang Qishan has signed a decree ousting Mr Weimin from the Politburo and ordering his arrest a few hours ago; before the start of this hearing'. Lt. Gen. Ping producing a copy of the decree signed just two hours ago.

Lt. Gen. Ping also produced a list of properties and assets that the Weimin Family are known to have amassed within China and another list of the same in various other countries. It totals around US Dollars 20 Billion and still counting. By the account submitted by him, the Weimin Family has foot prints etched in over 27 countries with their huge ill-gotten Assets and Estates.

He continued, 'The decree passed by the Central Commission for Discipline Inspection has ordered the confiscation of the ill-gotten assets of Mr Weimin and Ms Huajin in the list and to be returned to the People of China'.

That's all your honour.

How much of the evidence was genuine and how much was made up, only Lt. Gen. Ping could say. But the Honourable one man Jury lapped it up all, without casting any doubt. When the Jury asked the accused for their Defense they just laughed at him. The prison authorities had earlier ensured that both had been administered enough morphine and smoked enough grass to keep them in induced hallucination for a whole day.

Someone, who had experienced smoking cannabis knew that eating sugary candies during the smoke induced the person to laugh incessantly and uncontrollably, had helped both Mr Weimin and Ms Huajin take enough of the candies too.

Mr Weimin and Ms Hua both continued to remain hallucinated

and were known to have been laughing, even as both of them were executed by a firing squad, that was effected within four hours of their arrest, and before the first rays of the Sun hit the Chinese land the next morning and well before the Golden Indian team touched down at Chennai, India after a quick transit at Singapore.

'… and Mate', smiled Lt. Gen Ping!

Weimin's father, the Chairman of the Chinese People's Political Consultative Conference and a Senior Member of the Politburo Standing Committee resigned his position almost at the same time of Weimin and Huajin arrest. His earlier letter to the Communist Party General Secretary, a position since taken over by the current President, that he was ready to quit the Politburo Standing Committee was accepted and acted on. It may be recalled that Weimin's father was ready to relinquish his position, though in favour of his son. The letter was used by the President to exit him from his powerful position, before daybreak. Weimin's father knew the game was up and immediately lifted a flag of truce and negotiated a deal with the President. The President agreed to let him live, but under house arrest for the rest of his life in the remote countryside of a small western province, to satisfy his loyalists in the Politburo.

A large number of Officials that stood in support of Weimin and his coterie were all arrested and discharged from duty the next day. This was the largest purge of the Chinese Government Officials on a single day, since the Gang of four were eliminated in a purge in the mid 70's.

This time over 2700 Government Officials from the Administration, the Police and a few from the PLA were charged and discharged removed from their positions. They were to face investigation for various crimes including; intimidation, assault, assisting murder, bribery, favouritism, nepotism, helping grabbing of Government properties, unauthorized use of Government resources and position of power for personal gain and under many more sections of the criminal code. Most of them were executed silently in the next 4 weeks.

Deng went into hiding. Li'll'y went missing.

Part 9: All in the Family

77 Love's in the Air

The wedding preparations were on in full swing. Less than 48 hours remained between Joy and Kool, who were enjoying the late morning sunshine in the privacy of an old shed in Kool's backyard that used to be a part of the demolished old hut, still left standing. The shed was covered by the shade of a few coconut trees and had a thicket of shrubs all around. A small dis-tributary of an irrigation canal from the Mathur dam flowed close by the old shed. This inland cove offered a perfect foil for a private romantic, intimate getaway. Kool and Joy were dipping their legs in the canal, splashing water all over each other. Joy was lying on Kool's lap and they were enjoying their closeness in ways they had never experienced before. The privacy, the natural coolness under the shade of the trees and the canal full of flowing water heightened their sense of pleasure.

Joy and Kool recalled, how they came to tell their parents of their love for each other and win their approval. Joy, for whom it had been quite difficult to express her even love to Kool, and could do it only under the intensity of the situation; her last opportunity before the world was about to crash down on Kool, immediately after his win at the Games. Kool had expressed his love for Joy in a more scintillating situation under the shower with Li'll'y and had proved worthy of Joy's love and trust. But expressing their mutual love to their parents for their approval was getting to be even tougher. Today they could laugh merrily as they retold their stories, may be the hundredth time, of how they did it.

One day, about three months ago, Joy's mother showed her photographs of some eligible boys.

Joy was taken aback and protested, 'What's the need for marriage now. If I get married, who will take care of you'?

This was a standard false rhetoric of girls of her age, normally shy, when the wedding plans and alliance search begins for her. But her protests weren't taken seriously by her mother. She just laughed them off.

'You should get married now, as you are 24. When I was 24, both of you girls were already in school'.

When Joy could protest no longer, she had to pretend to look at the pictures of the boys as she hadn't yet formed in her mind on how to introduce the subject of Kool and wasn't sure, how her parents would react. She was praying that they would respond well and not react, when she gets to talk about him.

Two days later, the photographs were still on her table as mother waited for Joy to return for lunch. As she was tired, she lay down to rest her aching body on Joy's bed and went into a deep slumber, without knowing it. Joy came back and found her mom sleeping in her room, tired. Joy finished her lunch quietly, stepped into her room and checked the photos. She 'mind-voiced' her views on each of the boys, without realizing that Mom happened to just wake up, though was lying still with her eyes still closed, too exhausted to swing up.

'Kool has larger shoulders', Joy said of the first boy.

'Kool has better eyes', she said of the second, 'this boy has some kind of …

'This boy looks rough. Kool is gentler', she said aloud.

'Oh my, he is too frail and stooping, fair and handsome though'. She compared the fifth boy with Kool and said, 'Kool is more cool and athletic'!

Next she found a Doctor's photo. A Doctor? Not for me. Why not an Engineer and a Sportsman like Kool, so we could eventually build on the Academy'?

The next day, Joy was narrating the pressures on her at home to Kool.

'I am concerned my parents are pushing me for my marriage I have been avoiding a discussion. I don't know how long I could keep avoiding them. I am unable to raise your topic with my parents. Better you talk to your parents and let them talk to mine'.

Kula came to his parent's Mathur home that weekend. He had insisted on his sister joining him from Lasem. He was at a loss as how to open the topic of Joy with his parents. He was twenty six and was of marriageable age. His parents were talking of his marriage and were trying to find some good girl from a good family, preferably related to them and preferably from the city and preferably educated.

'He is a city bred boy you know'!

But they weren't taking any active steps yet.

He asked his parents, 'Why don't you shift to Chennai and we will all live together. I'm getting sick of living alone and eating hotel food. I need both of you for company. Even Lakshmi can join us all, once in a while, at Chennai'.

Lakshmi got the point, but before she could say something, his father replied saying that after his retirement he was taking part time jobs that was keeping him engaged.

'I will go mad doing nothing at Chennai. Moreover you have built a house here and we have a farm. I have to take care of them else they will all go wasted. I can't come. If you are particular, take your Mom with you'.

Mother asked his father in all innocence, 'What will you do for food'? Who will cook? Better for both of us to move to Chennai with Kula'!

Lakshmi was amused but commanded, 'Enough of this talk. Neither of you have to leave Mathur. It's time we get Kula married. Let's look for a girl. They both would stay at Chennai happily. He will visit you every month with his wife, Won't you Kula'?

Kula nodded gratefully.

Mother started, 'Yes, we are looking for a city bred girl, who would be suitable for Kula. We found two. One, your father didn't like. Another, I didn't like'.

She asked her daughter, 'Do you know someone else'?

Lakshmi started, 'I know a distant relative from 'his' side...' when Kula cut her short.

'Lakshmi, it will be a good idea to have some sportswoman, who has some international credits. Preferably in TT, and preferably a Software Engineer, as it would be easy for me to relate to her. She should be humble, pleasant, good looking, educated, bold and be a good friend and companion. Preferably from our district and better still from Mathur or nearby'.

His smart sister got the message. She said aloud, 'Would it also not be better if the girl lives at Chennai and runs an academy. Any wishes for the name of the girl, Kula? And wouldn't be better if her name mean's 'Victory', so that she will bring good omen of 'Victory' when you think of her during your matches', alluding to the fact that 'Jay' meant 'Victory'. 'Would this description of the girl suit, Kula'?

Lakshmi teased him and laughed heartily at having trapped him.

He was so embarrassed and annoyed that she could read his mind so easily, though, that's what he wished and pinched her on her arms till it hurt her.

She laughed aloud at his display of false anger.

Exactly at the same time, Joy's mom narrated the incident earlier that week to her husband, Krishnan, who was visiting them at Chennai for the weekend. 'Nobody seems equal to that boy Kula. We may have to find an exact replica of Kula and get her married to him, but where to find his double, like in a movie'? she lamented to Krishnan.

Krishnan got his daughter's message and his wife's intention.

Three days later, Wednesday, Krishnan and his wife got ready to visit the potential groom's parents in the same town.

They would visit the Ganesh temple by the river, before they went to the Groom's house. To their surprise, Kula's parents, sister Lakshmi and brother-in-law were at the Temple too, all bedecked in silk.

Kula's father greeted Krishnan and said, 'We are just on the way to visit you; just a courtesy call. It is wonderful that we met you at the God's home. All will be well'.

Krishnan liked the omens and prayed the deity in his mind for just a few seconds, before he spoke. 'Well, well… We also are on the way to your home. On the way, we wanted take the blessings from this Deity, so all would turn out well'.

Kula's father said, 'It doesn't look like a mere coincidence, but the will of God that brings us here. Let us talk in God's abode. Shall we'? Krishnan was delighted and agreed.

Joy and Kool were practicing TT opposite each other at the academy, when the calls came, confirming the parents intentions to get them both married to each other. They jumped up and met half-way around the table and Kula hugged her for the first time in her life. She blushed, looked around and making sure that no one was looking, kissed him softly on his cheeks and he returned her kiss on her forehead. After this day, whenever they met in private, they would always hug and kiss softly on the cheeks. They would reserve their first kiss with a capital 'K', for another day - till the day after their wedding.

Joy recalled the happy incidents, as she lay on Kula's lap in the privacy of the old shed by the canal behind Kool's home. 'I hope Li'll'y was here with us for our wedding. I feel guilty as she has got into serious trouble while protecting you from the gang'; Joy was in tears.

Kool looked at Joy lying so on his lap, so close to him; somehow he was reminded of Li'll'y. He remembered him lying on her, in close embrace, protecting her from Deng's bullets. He remembered Li'll'y kissing him on his lips as he lay injured by the bullets, on her lap, and his kissing her back. He remembered Li'll'y's flawless unclothed figure under the shower and shook his head, trying to focus on Joy's moonlike face. He shook his head again to clear Li'll'y's naked image that stubbornly stayed in his inner eye.

Joy looked at him anxiously and became silent.

Just then, they heard their names were being called out frantically from the direction of Kool's house.

78 The Gift

Eight months after the Indian Team consisting of Kula and Jay landed at Chennai with the Gold Medals in both the Men's and Women's events at the Games, Shastry stood at the airport waiting for a package; a gift.

A day earlier, Lt. Gen. Ping had sent an encrypted email, 'I'm sending you a gift through a known person. The gift item is most valuable and is close my heart. I have to pass on this package to a person I respect, and who I feel, would be worthy of the gift and the vice versa. I decided that you are the only such person, I know. The Gift would be delivered to you by Flight SQ 528 at Chennai, on Saturday. Please hold a placard 'Gift'.

Shastry was hanging around the Arrival hall of Chennai airport with a placard that said stupidly, 'GIFT'. Shastry knew that in spite of the terror that Lt. Gen. Ping could create in the minds of people he had a good sense of humour. He was curious to know what the gift would be, more than getting the actual gift itself, which may not be much useful to him, though would be valuable.

Just then a SQ hostess pushing a wheelchair bound girl walked towards him. The young girl on the wheelchair, probably a Muslim girl, veiled in from head to toe; not the standard black veil, but a fine white silk and cotton laced veil as if meant to wrap a beautiful secret. He wondered if the SQ hostess was helping the veiled girl, who looked sick, transit at Chennai. The SQ hostess shook hands with him. He guided her to a café, found an empty corner.

She handed over a small gift wrapped packet. Shastry wasn't in a hurry to open the packet.

Shastry ordered drinks for the SQ hostess, the wheelchair bound person and one for himself. The hostess tried to offer the drink to the chair bound person, removing the veil just a little, unintentionally unveiling a shock.

She was a pale and delicate girl, looked hardly 16-17 years of age, with a number of ghastly black scars on her face that were visible. Shastry, instantly knew that they were scars from cigarette butts and was shocked and enraged. The girl was staring blankly at yonder, without a sense of who she was or where she was. The sight shook even his battle hardened heart. After just a couple of sips, the girl would not take any more.

The SQ hostess smiled at him as if she was back to business with him. As he opened the gift wrapper, he felt there was a familiarity about the girl's eyes and tried hard to recollect without success. He found a voice recorder within the wrapper. Lt. Gen. Ping sent him a voice record and the reference to the gift was in the message that he played on his laptop. The SQ hostess dutifully handed over a password to access the voice record file.

'Hello Mr Shastry,

'My greetings. I am passing on a very valuable gift to you, with the trust that you are one person who would appreciate it most and feel worthy of it. My gift is Ms Li Ling'.

Shastry had faced enemy artillery and had been hit on his chest and had survived. He had watched his close friends torn to pieces as tonnes of bombs explode amidst them. But he had never felt more shattered as when he realized that the veiled girl was Li; the dear Li'll'y. He glanced at the veiled figure. The SQ hostess understandingly unveiled her face slowly to reduce the shock it could produce on him.

Lt. Gen. continued, 'You know that we had serious cleansing program in China immediately after the Games, which of course is an internal matter'.

'A couple of our prime Targets had disappeared, before we could lay our hands on them. And Li was also missing. Though we did suspect and link the disappearances and the missing Li, we didn't get any confirmation, until just about four weeks ago. We understood that this particular Target had taken Li as a captive to a very secretive location; it happens to be a private and unauthorized nuclear bunker and had constantly violated her sexually and abused her physically for over eight months. He had burnt her regularly with cigarette butts, as you would have seen. The doctors counted over one hundred of the scars, probably he had burnt her once every night that he violated her'.

'The horror she faced during confinement had caused a concussion in her brain and had frozen Li into a state of permanent shock. Nothing affects her any longer and none of the senses seems to work; touch, sight, smell, taste, hearing; nothing'.

'If she felt hunger or thirst', he continued, 'she licked her lips. She has a few sips of vegetable soup each day with a special concoction of proteins and cheese and copious water – sometimes a few sips of gruel or juice. In this condition, her staple is primarily glucose, saline, vitamins and Amino Acids administered as infusions.

Shastry continued to listen. 'The doctors feel that she could have been in this state for at least seven months. It means that the Target drove her to this state within a month of her being interred'.

'We captured this Target about a week back, trying to escape to freedom at the Shandong airport in disguise, as he collapsed at the departure Gates. He had high fever, intense pain, vomiting. The doctors later had diagnosed him to have rapid progressive jaundice, edema of the limbs, and swollen livers. Further tests on him revealed he had cancer of the intestine in an early stage and he would have died, in any case, of cancer in matter of months, if untreated'.

'We were led to his hideout by tracing back his mobile calls and the corresponding GPS positions. We found Li in the underground bunker. She was in a critical condition. We feared that she would die on us any minute, as we tried to move her to a hospital. Though she has recovered since and is out of danger, we found that her recovery was fragile and she remitted to her original state easily'.

'Cheng, her father's friend, came over on hearing her condition. She couldn't recognize him too and he felt helpless and was worried about the pain she would undergo. The Doctor assured him that she wouldn't feel any pain as she couldn't feel any touch, smell, or taste, or hearing'.

'They then showed her pictures of all of those she knew. Her friends, her relatives, her coach Dan, her Semi Final game against Wen Qiang. No interest. Then Cheng hit on the idea to show pictures of Kula and Jay, her new found friends. Cheng claims that he caught a slight glimmer in her eyes. But no one else did. If there was a gleam in her eyes, it wasn't strong enough to even be a sliver of hope'.

It was a surprise for us when the investigators told us that she may have nailed the Target before he tried to flee China!

'The theory of the investigators was that sometime during her confinement, abuse and violence, she should have acquired a singular obsession to punish or kill the Target, who wrecked her life and subject her to unspeakable miseries. Her ingenious idea to punish or kill the Target, in her current state, surprised all of us. She should have subconsciously planned her revenge carefully, without arousing any suspicion in the mind of Target and with very limited resources at hand. She should have made a huge effort to retain her mental abilities, and physical strength only for that singular mission; that is to punish or kill the target'.

'Li should have managed to poison the Target regularly for at least six months with small doses of poisons she had acquired during her stay at the bunker, enough to cause haemorrhage and severe damage to his liver before he collapsed. The most intriguing aspect was how she managed to acquire such poison, while she was still a captive and with near zero mental and physical abilities?

'We found a sack of raw peanuts stacked in the bunker along with bags of rice, other cereals and large quantities of supplies including dehydrated vegetables, probably to help the Target and his men survive a possible nuclear attack on China. She seemed to have collected sufficient quantities of the raw peanuts and hid from his view. She had isolated some peanuts with fungus and placed them in the heap, wrapped in with moist cloth and let the fungus proliferate; we found the moist wrap'. '

The fungus that affects the peanuts is known to produce the deadly 'Aflatoxin'.

'Aflatoxins are one of the most deadly poisons for animals and human beings and about a gram of the purified aflatoxin could be fatal for a normal sized human, if served in one dose. Daily toxin ingestions even in low amounts could cause haemorrhage and acute liver damage and cancer over a longer period. Larger dosage either single or daily spread over a number of months could be fatal. She should have harvested, rather scraped, enough of the aflatoxin from the fungi afflicted peanuts to spike his hamburger or noodles or whisky every night, with the hope that he would die one day and that she would have her sweet revenge'.

'The Target's health should have deteriorated due to slow poisoning and he was aware neither of his condition nor of the cause. On the fateful day for the Target, he should have packed his belongings to flee China with the assistance of friends'.

'Li should have overheard or just sensed his impending departure and should have collected as much of the toxin that she could and should have loaded the punch into his last and final 'goodbye drink' or snack. He managed to get past the check-in, immigration and security check, but couldn't get past the potion served by Li as he collapsed at the departure gates at Shandong'.

'On enquiry, we came to know that Li had studied a short course in Agriculture and Food Sciences during the time she entered Shanghai, with the hope that she would go back home to help her father in his farm someday. That explains her knowledge of the fungus and the toxin. But the rest of her plot is sheer ingenuity'.

Lt. Gen Ping questioned himself, 'But would a person in her state of consciousness be able to perform such acts'? He answered himself, 'Yes, it would be a medical miracle of sorts. And human history abounds with such miracles! The theory is still a conjecture and we may never know, until she regains her conscious self and confirms our understanding'.

'When she regained some strength in about a week, we decided to perform a surgery to remove the concussion in her brain. A few days after her surgery, something should have happened inside her and she uttered, 'Klamma'. This was the first 'word' she uttered since her trauma. It was a major improvement; she could talk; though could utter only one unintelligible syllable. She was struggling and the only sound that she ever uttered, once every few hours, uttered 'Klamma' and reverted to her restlessness. The Doctors couldn't make it out'.

'As 'mma' is a universal phonetic for mother, someone suggested she be taken to her mother. Cheng informed us that her mother had died while she was still a child. We were disappointed that we could not proceed. When we showed her mother's photograph, her gape didn't change and was fixed as usual'.

'When she said, 'Klamma' next time, Cheng suddenly raised his hands and spoke, 'She could be referring to Kula's mother and that she had claimed 'Kula-mma is my mother' after her India visit'.

'The Doctors didn't believe that their drugs and hospital care could help her further. 'She is looking for motherly love and that is hard to administer in the hospital'.

'Cheng requested me if she could be taken to India to Kula's mother for a while at least. It could help her. I nodded and sent the email to you about the 'Gift'. I didn't want to disclose her identity or her travel plans to India on email, as the target, her nemesis is still obsessed with revenge on her and has been vowing to kill her, even though he is now in prison. We also know that the target still is dangerous and could act through his friends and associates well entrenched in the system and could possibly hack our messages. She needs to be well preserved and protected; else she could be attacked or killed'.

'I am sending my daughter, if you remember, I took Li as my 'God Daughter' at the airport. I'm sending her to her Godfather-in-Law. I trust you will take care of my Daughter as your own and take her to Kula's mother and give her a chance to life. If she doesn't get better in reasonable time, please feel free to send my gift back to me. I will treasure her'.
Thank you,
Lt. Gen Ping

Shastry had tears in his eyes. So did the SQ hostess. He wrote a short letter to Lt. Gen Ping, 'Thanks for the greatest Gift, I would value all my life'.
'I will take her to Kula-mma, her adopted mother. I'm so happy she remembered and wished to see her chosen Mother in India even under such trauma'.
'India will treat her well. She will find more than her mother. She will find her family. Kula and Jay are already her family. Now all of us join her as family'.
'She will have the best of medical care. Will keep in touch on her progress. Will make arrangements to let her join her Mother soon, when she is physically fit to travel'. Shastry sealed and handed over his reply to the SQ hostess, who promised delivery by early morning next day.

Shastry visited her morning, afternoon and evening for the next two days with Mahadevan. Shastry postponed Li'll'y's travel to Mathur as Mahadevan reminded him that Kula's wedding with Jay was just a week away.

The doctor opined, 'It would help Li'll'y if she could visit her chosen Mother after all. If she could be part of the wedding celebrations, it would do her a lot of good. She may even recover! The celebrations and the festive atmosphere could activate some of the dormant memories deep in her and could activate some of her innate senses too'.

When Shastry asked Lt. Gen Ping for his advice, he replied, 'Cheng would be visiting Chennai shortly. You could take a decision together'.

Cheng flew in the next two days. He was excited about the idea. 'It could do a lot of good for Li', he agreed.

'Let's not pass up an opportunity for Li to be at the celebrations that she could relate to. In any case, it wouldn't do her bad'.

They wanted to keep this a surprise. 'Surprises could jolt Li back to her good health'.

Mahadevan and Cheng took Li'll'y in a car. Half way to Mathur, Cheng panicked, 'I'm not sure if it is right to impose Li in her condition on the families in the middle of a wedding'.

He was carrying a huge emotional baggage and was going to trust Li'll'y's fate to two families who he had never met, but heard so much about from Li. Of course he had met Kula and he trusted him to stand up to resolve any issue, if the emotions went out of hand and into unexpected lines.

But neither of them were prepared for the quake in Mathur that would upturn lives of those involved, in just one evening.

79 Family – The Pride of India

When they heard their names being called out frantically, Kool and Joy jumped up and walked towards the sounds cautiously, afraid that something was bad enough. It was! As they entered the house, they heard his mother wailing from inside.

'Is anybody very sick, or dead? My sick old grandmother'?

Then as Kool entered he saw a young girl draped in a white veil, her back to the door and his amma hugging her and weeping inconsolably. Who was she? Then he saw Mahadevan sir, who nodded and 'Who was this? A fair face! Chinese..!!.. Cheng. What's he doing here'? Cheng nodded at Kula as a solemn greeting.

'Who is she? Li'll'y'? What about her? Why is Mom weeping instead of celebrating her arrival'?

It was a surprise, but not a pleasant one it seemed. Everyone seemed to be in a state of shock. Only Kulamma had broken down past the shock and was weeping. He went on his mother's side to check what about the girl that his Mother wept for.

He had the biggest shock of his life. He sobbed, 'Li'll'y', and cried.

He forbade Joy from coming near her, 'Oh no, you can't stand the look of your dear Li'll'y' he cried.

But Joy rushed to Li'll'y, not heeding to Kool. On seeing Li'll'y's face, she fainted. Everyone watched Joy collapse and fall forward in slow motion at the feet of Li'll'y. But Li'll'y sat there looking at the yonder, oblivious of the turmoil around her, like a statue of 'Veiled Rebecca' at the Salarjung museum in Hyderabad sculpted out of marble. She, this partly unveiled 'Statue of Marble, the Venus de Milo', sat there with her face pock marked with round pitch black scars of cigarette burns; about ten of them could be counted on her visible face and arms.

Cheng explained the misfortunes that Li'll'y had to go through as a captive and he narrated with pride, 'Li'll'y's ingenuity in bringing down her nemesis', whom he mentioned every time in a hushed voice; 'though it is just a theory'. Cheng continued, 'He is sure to face the firing squad due to the courage and genius displayed by Li'll'y'.

Joy's mother and Krishnan were also there. She cried, 'How cruel of God to have brought such misfortune to my child? Was she destined to go the same way of Vaijayanthi the moment we thought of her as our own? Was fate so horrid to harm my child so, even if she were the beautiful and loveable Li'll'y? Had we known such a fate persisted with each of our 'second child', we would not have recognized Li'll'y as our own. Did we bring about her misfortunes'? They didn't have answers.

Li'll'y lay as a heap with her head rested on the laps of her Kula-mma, who was squatted on the floor with her legs stretched long and leaning against the wall. She was holding Li'll'y's face with the palms of her hands and shedding silent tears, unable to console herself and unmindful of the story that Cheng was narrating. Joy recovered from her faint, released herself from Kool's embrace, and laid herself on the lap of Kula-mma, close to Li'll'y, tears flowing non-stop from her closed eyes. She was listening to every word Cheng said in rapt attention.

'How brave and strong willed of Li'll'y', she thought and was proud of her sister, who lay as a wreck beside her.

Kula-mma was running her fingers through the hairs of Li'll'y and Joy with love and both of them slept with the comfort of mother's touch.

The whole neighbourhood was watching with tears in their eyes. They had all seen Li'll'y as fragrant as a fresh lily on a cool, dewy and misty morning, the last time she was here. Now they weren't able to reconcile to her misfortune and had no words to console the families of Kool and Joy.

The entire homes, the families and the neighbourhood that were celebrating the wedding of Champions were suddenly reduced to sorrow for their dearest one that came from far away.

Someone suggested that the wedding be postponed. The families were confused. There were arguments and hushed discussions. They all knew that Kool and Joy will take the final call and waited for them.

Just around dinner time, Joy met Kool in private and could have been heard talking, 'No Kool, we have to do this. Remember, she is my sister. She has almost given her life for you and me. I have to ensure that she gets back her life, before mine. Our wedding, as planned, would rob her of our care... Sorry, I don't believe anyone else can take care of her'.

Most of night Joy was arguing with her parents. 'She is my sister. She's your child too. Would you argue like this, if she was Vaijayanthi'?

'I can't leave her like this to deteriorate further. She needs care... Only Kool and I can. It has to be only between us. I don't trust any of you to take care of her', with such firmness of heart that there were no chance for a reply.

'About Kool's family? They have to accept once Kool makes up his mind. It's my responsibility to convince Kool. He will convince his family. I will talk to Kula-mma and Lakshmi. Kool will not refuse my request'.

Early morning, Joy went to Kool's home. Kula-mma was sitting at the same spot on the floor all night, leaning against the same wall, eyes closed, with Li'll'y lying on her lap, blissfully staring at yonder. There were dried streaks of tears that ran through the night on Kula-mma's cheeks. She had never been inactive as far as Joy knew; was always working at something. But on that day, she was totally lost about a daughter who lay frozen on her lap.

Kula-mma hugged Joy and cried, 'My eye, see what this cruel God has done to my lovely child. It had wished and reached my lap just a few months ago, the only mother it had recognized'.

For Kula-mma, there was a lifetime of responsibility for a daughter, she didn't beget.

She continued, 'The last time it came down from China, we knew that we were connected, mother and daughter by an invisible bond. But this time, I heard that it had saved Kula's life, almost giving its own and reducing itself to this vegetable state. It has become my family deity that protects Kula and you and will continue to protect Kula and his family in future, long after I would be gone. How can I return the love, this little darling child had for Kula? I will take care of it in this lifetime as my own daughter and in the next and in the next. I only pray that it is born to me as a daughter or gets wedded to my son, in each of our seven lives, so I could take care of it and repay all my debts', Kula-mma grieved.

Encouraged by the grief of Kula-mma, Joy ventured and whispered the changes she had resolved on the wedding and asked, 'Please agree to this change in plans for the marriage. We can't proceed with this marriage as planned. Li'll'y comes first'.

Kula-mma was stunned at the request. 'Is this a girl or a Goddess'? she wondered. 'No my sweet child, you should not sacrifice even a day of your life with Kula in this lifetime. I will take care of this child. It's mine'.

'I will never give it up to someone else's care. You should be rightly wedded to Kula on the rightful day that will be tomorrow. I'm proud of you dear; so much of sacrifice in your young mind and your heart should be of gold. I am so grieved that such beautiful girls of heart should undergo so much of tragedy in their early lives. Grieve no more. You all have sacrificed so much for each other. Sacrifice no more'!

But Joy was determined to push her convictions. She talked for an hour and convinced Kula-mma.

Kula-mma conceded at last, 'Before you came in even I was thinking, even wished, on these lines'.

'After seeing you, I changed my mind, 'Why should this child bear the burden of it's unfortunate condition, when I am all alive and strong as a stone, ready to take the complete responsibility for it'.

But Joy by her determination convinced her that Li'll'y was the responsibility of Kool and herself and only they should be authorized to take the final decisions about their marriage and on Li'll'y's care.

With Kula-mma reluctantly agreeing with her, Joy knew she won the most influential heart in favour of her decision. She was delighted and hugged and kissed Li'll'y, who stared still lying on Kula-mma's lap.

As she lifted her lips away from Li'll'y's cheeks, did she see her smile? Yes, she did! Li'll'y did smile her twinkling smile absentmindedly while her eyes still stared frozen at a sight beyond her. But she did smile and twinkle. As Joy jumped up with joy, Kool came into the hall that was bearing his mother, Li'll'y and now Joy. Kool didn't miss Li'll'y's twinkle of a smile as though she was teasing them both. She was rushed to the Hospital at Lasem, to monitor her other conditions and to see if the progress could be sustained.

Joy and Kool waited by Li'll'y all day at the hospital. If there was any progress or movement from Li'll'y they wanted to be the first to know and be delighted.

Yes, Li'll'y progressed much on the day. She smiled her twinkling smile more often. She could open and close her eyelashes, though slowly and less frequently than she should, considering her eyes were drying frequently. She could move her eyeballs form one side to the other initially, may be in anticipation of seeing someone; or may be a voluntary movement without being conscious of it. But Kool and Li'll'y saw a pattern in her opening her eyes, moving the eyes sideways towards them and smiling that twinkling smile at them. They were all delighted at the progress Li'll'y was making.

Cheng was witness to the magic of family life in India. He could not believe his eyes and ears. He didn't in his wildest dreams, think of such a teary welcome to Li'll'y who was never a part of this family and the competing responsibility and charge each one took of her in her vegetable state. He felt Li was blessed.

Cheng met Joy in a glass walled cabin near the Intensive Care Unit where Li'll'y lay, to thank her for all that the family was doing for Li'll'y. Soon she could be seen as the one talking. Though whatever she said was not audible across the glass panels she could be clearly seen pleading with Cheng and that he was taken aback. He in turn seemed to plead with her shaking his head. She was smiling and persuading him. Finally he seems to have conceded to her, blessed her and kissed her on the forehead.

Late in the night, Cheng didn't sleep, still worried if he made a mistake of bringing Li'll'y on the eve of wedding celebrations and did he unwittingly turn the wedding plans topsy-turvy? He had no answers. He left it to God's will. Though a hard core communist, who never believed in Gods, he was willing to go an extra mile that day to fulfil the will of the Gods. He recalled TV advertisements on some parts of India mentioned as 'God's own country...'

'True', he said to himself.

80 The Wedding

Early morning the whole of the Mathur town assembled at the venue covered by shamiana, to see their local, Gold Medallist Heroes' wedding. This was an opportunity of their lifetime. The District Collector was attending with his paraphernalia. Shastry was in, carrying personal message from the PM for the couple. He explained to the District Collector how the Games was won and the trouble faced by the couple and another Chinese girl called Li'll'y, whom he would introduce to him later. Everybody who was somebody in Mathur and Lasem District came to bless the couple, and to have a glimpse of Li'll'y, mostly uninvited. So much, for the simple wedding that Kool and Joy's family had planned.

The groom was seated on the decorated floral stage behind the ceremonial fire - 'Agni'. Joy, bedecked in gold and flowers like a Hindu Goddess, was walked to the stage flanked by a matchingly bedecked but veiled and wheel chair bound Li'll'y and Lakshmi pushing the chair.

Li'll'y's fixed stare at yonder, as she graciously accompanied Joy, was suddenly broken for just a minute by an expression of fear, concern and anger, in that order. Did she see a shadow of someone, who was the last person she wished to see on this day, just a shadow that disappeared behind the crowds? Her fear and anger stricken eyes wandered in the next moments searching for the eyes that she could never forget. But as she fixed her stare on him, the person's eyes met hers and he walked away quickly and vanished into the crowd. It took several minutes before her eyes stopped staring at the point where he vanished, and before her mind eased.

There were whispers everywhere. The story of Li'll'y being adopted by Joy's family was now folklore at Mathur and almost all of Lasem district. The look of Li'll'y evoked strong emotions in the crowd and the students from Kula's school, who had met her during her last visit started a chant;

'We Love Li'll'y'! 'We Love Li'll'y'! 'We Love Li'll'y'!

The chant become bigger and bigger until it brought tears in everyone's eyes.

It was Joy's turn to see a face in the crowd, something in him that sent a shiver in her, by merely looking at him. She had seen him once before in a much stressed circumstance. She searched her memory to identify the face. But she couldn't fix the context. But clearly, someone she identified with their common nemesis. Was he was around to harm them? She looked around for the face to reconfirm. But she found none. Was this one of her typical nightmares? She smiled at herself, confused.

As Joy reached the side of Kool, she removed the flower garland she was wearing on her shoulders and placed it on Li'll'y's and positioned her wheelchair beside Kool. All were wonder struck at this drama that just unfolded; like in a movie. None among the crowd could tell what was happening. It seemed like a change of wedding plans; Joy seemed to have given up her place to Li'll'y as the bride. The drama seemed to be happening in full agreement of the families involved. There was pin drop silence.

Pari, who was at the wedding was in shock, for he recalled that he had mocked Kula with his harsh tongue several years back, 'His love would never be consummated' drawing comments if it was intended to be prophecy or a curse! Nobody could tell, then. Nobody could tell, now.

He ever since, had felt sorry for having spoken those words then; just to impress his friends. Now he truly regretted it, but didn't know how to consume back his curse.

The silence was broken by a string of firecrackers that burst outside the marriage hall, when Li'll'y's eyes gleamed for a few moments. It was followed by the reverberating music of Nadhaswaram and Kettimelam to which, Kool tied of the 'mangalsutra' around Li'll'y's neck. The bride, whose veil parted a little sat there like an angel, revealing a lot of marks in black, all over her face, staring at yonder. Kool recalled Mahakavi Kalidasa, a great Sanskrit poet of ancient India and his verse, 'Small black marks do enhance the value of a person in terms of beauty and pleasantness just like the black marks on the face of the moon do'.

He saw moonlike beauty in Li'll'y's ravaged face.

Joy bent down from behind her and whispered into her ears, 'You Silly Li'll'y, you are a boyfriend grabbing fiend, after all'

Silly Li'll'y, opened her eyes wide, turned her face towards Joy, though with an effort and smiled that twinkling smile at her. Both Kool and Joy were delighted at the progress she was making.

Joy held Li'll'y's hands in her palms, pulled up Kool's hand and placed on Li'll'y's and said to them, 'He is my wedding gift for you, my dear Li'll'y and she's my gift for you Kool... Please take care of Li'll'y like she is your child'. Saying this she wiped her tears.

81 Rewind: Events on the Wedding Eve

Joy had through the wedding eve, argued with Kula and each of the family members that Kool should wed Li'll'y.

When Kool protested, Joy recalled and reinforced, 'Think of Li'll'y's great sacrifice to protect you and me and both of us owe our life to Li'll'y. Without her, probably you would be languishing in a Chinese jail today and I would have gone wasted in your memory or done something stupid to myself. The only way we could repay is for you to marry and take care of her all her life'.

Kool shed tears, confused and torn between the love of his life and his responsibility towards Li'll'y.

Joy teased him next, with the hope that some humour could help him overcome his confusion. 'Don't say you don't love Li'll'y. I have seen it in your eyes'!

'Yes, I love her as a friend. But not the same way that I love you'!

Joy laughed at him teasing him further, 'When you went to China you promised me that you will remember me when you see Li'll'y. I know that you kept your promise. But on return to India, I can find you seeing Li'll'y, when you see me'! with a twinkle in the eye teasing and challenging him.

At this Kool dropped his eyes, unable to reply. So she had noticed! After a minute of silence he said, 'It was a distraction, just once. I am sorry and you know that. It may be how the man's mind is wired. You have reason to be angry. But don't punish me for that... and don't punish Li'll'y too'.

'Oh! Sorry. I didn't mean it that way... just kidding. But I do feel that you should marry dear Li'll'y. She needs you more than ever... And I will help too'.

Kool still protested strongly.

'If you don't feel offended, may I take liberty to ask you, 'Do you think she has become ineligible to be your wife, because she has lost all her beauty. Or, are you worried that she may be vegetable for life and can't be physically and mentally fit for an active married life? Or that she has been physically violated and acquired a stigma?

It's also a how the man's mind is wired and thinks, at least in India'!
She was progressively harsh with him.

'Oh no. I would be a barbarian, if I thought of Li'll'y in those
lines. You know me. I would love Li'll'y for what she is'.

'Then please prove your love; prove that you are a Real Man.
Li'll'y once told me that you were one and was very proud of you.
Please prove yourself that you are a REAL MAN!

There were no options. No arguments. He agreed to walk his
talk.

While she had posed similar questions to Kool's Mother, she
wept and said, 'If some tragedy like this struck my own Lakshmi,
would I disown her now? It was my daughter then and it is my
daughter now. Now that the question has been raised, I will prove
what I just said. I will command my son to marry it. If he doesn't
oblige, I will disown him as a son and never again look at his face!
It's a promise on the head of my beloved son'!

Joy had thus hastened the decision of Kool and Mother, the
only two, whose decision counted.

Even Cheng after a long argument with Joy felt comforted, if
not convinced. He was overwhelmed by the love and responsibility
that Joy had for Li. He had eventually recognized that Joy was right
and that her future lay with her adopted family and friends.

'What was the alternate'? Cheng questioned himself.

'A long life of loneliness in a Chinese hospital, without any
friends or family to visit her', he shivered at the thought.

However, he wasn't sure if Li would have agreed to this
wedding with Kula and if she ever thought of him other than as a
friend; as a lover, as his wife! Was he pushing Li into a wedlock that
she wouldn't have wished or approved?

Joy then had showed him a couple of selected passages from
her whatsapp conversation with Li'll'y, while Kool was on the run,
assisted by her.

Li'll'y had messaged, 'Kool did lose a real opportunity here. He
did not take me, though I offered myself to him, unconditionally,
without any commitments. I offered myself to him, the only man I
was waiting for all these years. Just this once would have been
enough for me, for all my life'... 'I was not fortunate for anything

more than his touch. I hope you will permit me this memory forever. Don't plead with me to take this feel of him away from me. I would lose more than I ever did and ever would. That's beside the point. What matters is that Kool proved he was more than hu-Man. He gave me lessons in Love and Trust, under that shower that I will never forget, ever. I hope I will never ever again betray my sister's trust'. While Joy showed this passage to Cheng, she was careful to censor the reference to 'Kool hugging Li'll'y's naked body', as she felt it would be insensitive.

Cheng was convinced that Li had been in love with Kula earlier, only to concede in favour of Joy and so his last doubts had been cleared before he agreed to the wedding. If there were any complications due to their nationalities and citizenship, he would resolve them with the help of Lt. Gen. Ping and Shastry.

When Joy spoke to her parents, they protested. But Joy was so determined and Kool was too dumb for words that they had to eventually concede, but not before they extracted a promise from Joy that she would marry a person of choice of the family soon and would not waste herself as a spinster or a saint in an ashram; something that she had considered while she laid out her plan for Kool and Li'll'y's wedding.

After the wedding, Kool assured Cheng, 'You have seen the power of Love and Family. Li'll'y will get well soon. She will play at the next Games, and to win her Gold'.

Epilogue

Some time that October, at Chennai, India, almost a year after the Games at Shanghai, he opened his morning newspaper, 'The Hindu' and read the following news;

"A senior Chinese official has credited President Xi Jinping with thwarting a coup, shedding new light on the arrest of six so-called "Tigers" under a national anti-corruption campaign.

Liu Shiyu, the Chairman of the China Securities Regulatory Commission, said on Thursday China's imprisoned XXXXXXXXXXXXXX and XXXXXXXXXXXXXXXXX, who is also behind bars, had plotted to "usurp the party and seize power." Mr XXXXXXXXXXXXXX had stepped down in 20XX and has since been jailed for corruption.

"…Their crimes of corruption as well as usurping the party and seizing power were scary. The Party Central Committee with comrade Xi as the core saved the party, the Army and the country, and, in a global scope, also saved socialism," Hong Kong-based The Standard newspaper quoted him as saying…"

He just smiled a knowing smile…

***

While she was seated on a wheelchair beside the groom, while the elaborate wedding ceremonies and rites were being performed, there was a burst of a string of firecrackers outside the marriage hall. She, who was staring into the oblivion unaffected by the ritual mantras and the yagna fire, seemed to listen carefully, all focused. Her eyes gleamed for those moments, belying her normally expressionless face.

She could accurately count a total of 107 firecrackers though they burst like rapid fire, aided either by the bizarre, singular, subconscious mission she either acquired during the abuse at the bunker or by the extraordinary ability she trained herself to discern the sight and sound of the TT ball in flight.

She was waiting, nay, praying for the last two of them, as though her living would not have served a purpose, without the ones that were missing. It took several minutes before the next… 'Bang'…; the no. 108!

Something told her that she had her revenge; for each of those horror nights that she was violated at the bunker that were marked by burns from the cigarette butts, one for each of the abuse; all except the first of the violation; the only one that wasn't marked by a burn. She was pleased, yet looked dismayed that the last, rather, the first of the 109 didn't happen. For her the first was as imperative as the rest of the 108 put together. She determined in her passive mind that was otherwise quite blank that she would make the first of the 109 happen, even if it takes her a lifetime and even if it consumes all her life energies – her bizarre, singular, subconscious mission…

***

On the same morning as a wedding in a small town in faraway India, and minutes before the three knots, a firing squad was lined up, somewhere in China, to execute one single person, codenamed 'Target No. 2'. Unusual for such executions, a Senior Prosecutor oversaw the preparations himself. Again, unusual for such executions, he personally handed over a loaded magazine to each of the several members of the squad with an instruction to empty the magazine on the Target, without any missing him.

He watched the rapid-fire execution, from close. He found that only one of the bullets missed the mark and hit the wall behind the Target, who was by then slumped in front of him full of riddles. So 107 found the Target. He walked up to the bullet riddled body lying on the ground in a pool of blood, took out his handgun and shot him once, 'This is the last of the personal return gifts from your victim; the number 108; without which neither her life nor mission will be fulfilled'.

Unfortunately, he wouldn't know of the first of the horror nights that wasn't marked by a cigarette burn that needed to be paid back; so he didn't reserve a bullet against it.

***

Just then the Nadhaswaram and Kettimelam (a traditional music band on auspicious days) reverberated through the hall and her marriage with Kool was solemnized as he tied the Mangalsutra in three knots around her neck. She smiled and turned to Kool and smiled that twinkling smile at him.

The families showered blessings on them using the turmeric mixed rice and flowers over the young couple, with tears flowing down their cheeks.

She had left India the last time with the feeling that 'One Life is Not Enough' to savour the pleasures of family life in India. Now she has come back again from Shanghai to Chennai, an Other Life in every way, to delight in the love of the family… Her own family!

Acknowledgements

This book is a product of two years of research and information collection. It also involved about four years (with some overlap) writing; several iterations of writing, feedback, learnings, development editing, improvement and re-writing! I should say that there were several professional writers, amateur writers, experienced editors, friends, relatives and members from reading clubs, who had done beta-reading of the novel and offered valuable feedback at various stages. It helped me to improve the storytelling substantially before it could be presented for publication.

I am overwhelmed by the kind of and volume of feedback from readers from across the world. I would like to personally acknowledge and thank a few of the noteworthy readers, whose contribution and encouragement has been immense in development of this book and to take the plunge; to publish!

***

I felt like sharing what some of the readers had to say in their own words!

V. Balasubramaniam (India – my English teacher, who taught me to 'appreciate' literature and before whom I bow, offering my first respects!) wrote: 'Ravi, I am seeing you evolve as an excellent writer. Best wishes'!

Micheline Brodeur (USA - Professional Editor) wrote: Ravi, I very much enjoyed reading your manuscript. The opening setting (table tennis)… is an interesting one… it is a love story, I also took it as a coming-of-age tale, and the evolution of the main characters within that context is a nice way to handle it.

You have a picturesque way of describing a scene that brings it to life for the reader. Some scenes that come to mind include Kula's mental table tennis play, the visitors to Kula's home after he wins the school tournament, and the Chinese boy's "attack" on Jay.

Chandrakala Balsubramaniam (India – House wife and a voracious reader) wrote: Ravi… The characters both in India and China display a variety of characterization. Lee, Cheng, Li'll'y, Ping of Death, all were portrayed well. The Gordian knot and the political climate there all described well... And the language and the flow of words fantastic! As for the novel is concerned it travels fast.. and you have almost make it equal to a visual.

Rachel Blackbirdsong (USA - Professional Editor) wrote: ...I must say that you've certainly packed a great deal of story into your work.

Nithyanadan (India – Businessman) wrote: Ravi... The plots both in India and in China have been wonderfully developed... Kula's brilliance in tracking the flight of the ball in slow motion, is imagination at its best (or is it real?)! Characterization of Kula, Li'll'y and Joy have been so well portrayed, which would make any reader to connect with themselves... have nicely brought out the customs and traditions of the Indian culture!

Sharon Lindenburger (USA - Professional Editor) wrote: Ravi ...you have the makings of an excellent and intriguing story... On a more whimsical note, I think your story also has movie potential.

Indumathi Prabhakar (India - Software Engineer) wrote: Very Interesting plot... realistic characters and situations makes you feel like Ur a part of the audience in the stadium of the nail biting matches and makes you curious to find out what's next...

Brooks Kohler (USA – Professional Beta Reader) wrote: Hi, Ravi... What I like about your story is it's a journey. I find readers tend to like them too. The story reads smoothly... It's not really a genre, but I see it as a journey or possibly even a coming of age story...

Bodhisatya Pal (India – Student and Beta Reader) wrote: Overall I find brilliant, gripping, catchy which creates a flow of excitement in the readers mind. I feel the 'What will be happen next' matters.

Prakash (USA – Software Consultant) wrote: Hi Ravi... Well-paced, well described, paints a good visual of locale and the characters... I do like the cast of characters... As a reader, I can emote with the characters well. I did feel the depth of the conversations between the characters. Pretty cool.

Sugandhi (My dear wife) writes: Ravi... This book has been written in a beautiful language, characterization has been portrayed so well...

especially the mind conflicts of Kula, Jay and Li'll'y.

...The Book 1 sets up the plot, the characters, the romance, the Table Tennis rivalry, the Politics, the treachery. The Book 2 moves really so fast, so thrilling – I couldn't stop reading...

Description of scenes and actions is excellent and realistic; visual like movie and gave me goosebumps... the chapter, 'Biting the Bullet' was too real! Wow! I felt that I was travelling on bus along with Kula and when it crashed, watched shreds of glass flying all around in slow motion, exactly like Kula saw it... There are plenty of scenes like that and I can keep writing whole day.

Saundar Narayan (London – Management) wrote: Ravi... Your book has all the makings of a great story, namely, a rise against the odds, love, jealously, sport and international intrigue. A good read.

***

I thank one and all!

My special thanks to Ravikumar Rajagopalan and Glen Caroll, (iptechs.co), who had designed and developed a beautiful contextual cover for the book.

I also thank Amazon for giving authors a platform to publish the books.

About me and my Work

I, Ravi Krish (short for Ravichandran Krishnaswamy) was born in India, near Chennai. I'm a Mechanical Engineer and MBA by education. I am happily married and my family includes my wife, my daughter, son-in-law and my grandson!

I have lived in Singapore and the USA and have traveled to several countries on business and as a professional. I consider myself fortunate to have had the opportunity to engage with the wonderful minds of people, wherever I had lived and traveled. I have tried to give shape to some of the interesting minds as my characters and bring them to life with my works.

A book lover myself, I'm passionate about the whole spectrum of science and applications of science that touches our day to day lives. My writing would carry a wee bit of Science and Logic, whatever genre it falls under.

***

'An other Tale of Two Cities – In the Dragon's Lair' – Book I and Book II, was written in empathy with and is dedicated to Laishram Sarita Devi, the Indian woman boxer, who refused to accept the bronze medal at the Podium ceremony at the Incheon Asian Games – 2014, as a protest against biased umpiring and was banned for One Year, and the likes of her.

The Vehicle that takes us through this journey is sports –Table Tennis to be specific. I'm sure the trials and tribulations of the heroic trio in Kula (Kool), Jay (Joy) and Li Ling (Li'll'y) would be felt and celebrated by all the readers as they fight for their Gold.

***

Having taken a title 'An Other Tale of Two Cities – In the Dragon's Lair', I feel I have taken an onerous responsibility of having to rise up to the original 'Tale of Two Cities' by the legendary Charles Dickens.

There are several similarities between the original 'Tale' and 'An Other Tale'.

Both are tales of triangular love and of supreme sacrifice, intertwining the lives, loves and times of the paired cities during the respective periods.

This modern 'An Other Tale' is a startling Adventure set in the back drop of the most turbulent times in China, since the coup attempted by the Gang of Four in the 1970s, just as the Dickens' 'Tale' was set in the times of the French Revolution. Though the news of the latest coup attempt in China was largely buried behind the iron curtain, when it did trickle out, the fact was acknowledged by a senior Chinese Official, and reported by the Hong Kong based Standard Newspaper on 19th October 2017, later to be echoed by 'The Hindu' (reproduced verbatim in the Epilogue of the book).

'An Other Tale' is also an interesting comparison of the contrasting cultures, societies, family ethos, value systems, politics, progress and personalities of the two Modern cities - Chennai and Shanghai.

Enthusiasts of the original Dickens 'Tale' would find that some of the chapter titles have resonance in 'An Other Tale – In the Dragon's Lair' - The Night Shadows, Recalled to Life and The Gorgon's Head - share the titles with the original 'Tale'.

The similarities end there. Everything else about 'An Other Tale' is refreshingly different!

The stories have been set in different Times, the Plots are different, the personalities are different; their experiences and the classes they represent are different. The morals and integrity of the characters are different, while they reflect the times they live in. The story telling styles are different... to spot a few differences.

Fact, Fiction and Fantasy

As any novel should be, An Other Tale of Two Cities – In the Dragon's Lair, is a blend of fact, fiction and fantasy in the right proportions and logically enmeshed.

Fact: Coup Attempt in China

One of the many storylines of the book portrays an internecine power struggle between a top politburo member and the President leading to an impeachment attempt on the President (a virtual coup attempt, considering Chinese politics). This fictitious plot was developed based on research on the political affairs of China at that time and had parallels with the real events in China.

The various factual events of significance; virtual run up to the coup attempt that were reported by three reputed newspapers, 'Nikkei Asian Review', 'The Standard' and 'The Hindu', have been chronicled (verbatim) or indirectly referred to in various chapters of the 'An Other Tale of Two Cities – In the Dragon's Lair'.

The Government of China admitted to the coup attempt, through an official press release by a Chinese Government official to the Hong Kong-based The Standard newspaper and was published on 19th Oct 2017.

The storyline had exposed the run up to the coup attempt right through the book that was written over three years, as the events were unfolding in China, long before the official admission.

Readers could also experience and enjoy the interesting titbits of current affairs, news from the recent past, anecdotes from history and mythology as they embark on the journey in the company of the heroic trio of Kula, Jay and Li Ling.

Fiction:
Life touches on all aspects of life and isn't bounded by genre. This book is an exciting journey of life, a modern Literary Romance and Culture Classic among other storylines; you will enjoy it!

This is my maiden published venture into writing. Expect more to come!

You can reach me at ravi.krish.author@gmail.com